Hearts
We
Lost

A Novel

By Umm Zakiyyah

Hearts We Lost

A Novel
By Umm Zakiyyah

ISBN 10: 0-9707667-5-0
ISBN 13: 978-0970766755

Library of Congress Control Number:
2011902174

Order information available online at
www.muslimfiction.com

Verses from Qur'an taken from Saheeh International, Darussalam, and
Yusuf Ali translations.
Published by Al-Walaa Publications
Suitland, Maryland USA
Printed in the USA

Acknowledgements

Acknowledgments, I think, are the most difficult to write. There are so many to whom an author is indebted at the completion of a work that to thank them all would be a book in itself. Nevertheless, I am grateful to all of those whose time, effort, honesty, support, and prayers assisted me in seeing this work to completion.

As always, I am most indebted to my Creator, Who gifted me with the pen. I am also indebted to my parents, Muhammad and Fareedah Siddeeq, who always made me believe in my talents, and in myself. They are the ones who inspired the mantra that I recited through adolescence and adulthood whenever I confronted a daunting task: *If the task before you is so difficult that there is only one person in the world who can complete it, why can't it be you?*

I too, as always, am indebted to my husband for ever being that "single believer" who felt I could do it, even if I thought no one could. I imagine that there would be no Umm Zakiyyah had Allah not gifted me with such a strong support in my life. I too must thank our daughter, Fareedah, whom we named after my own mother, and who, remarkably, reflected her grandmother's insight and ever-present support as she read and edited the original manuscript.

I also thank all the members of the Volunteer Reviewers Team, who dedicated their time, effort, and heart to this project. I wouldn't have gotten this far without you.

May Allah reward and bless you all.

And, as before, I send my warmest thanks and heartfelt appreciation to all those who have remembered me in their *du'aa* — their private supplications to the One who holds with Him all good. I know, in the end, it is you to whom I am most indebted.

Author's Note

Readers often ask about the poems I use in so many of my books, and the answer is they are mine. Sometimes they are poems inspired and penned from my own life's reflections and experiences. Other times, they are written for a particular story. The poems sprinkled throughout this book are of both types.

"O Mujahid, Shall I Tell You?" is a poem I wrote while saddened about the innocent children suffering in the world. "The Lesson" I wrote years ago as a part of a poetry contest online. "On *Tawheed*: A Life It Touched" I wrote while reflecting on my own spiritual development, but it has been revised and adjusted for this story. A revised excerpt of it readers will recognize from Tamika's song in *Footsteps*; however, the prose-poetry piece that appears here closely reflects the original version in full. All of the aforementioned poems have been previously published as individual pieces in various secular and Islamic publications. The other poems that appear in this work were written for this story in particular.

The story *Hearts We Lost* deals in part with the enigmatic world of dreams, and the dreams shared in the story have been taken, at least in part, from real dreams, and from my Islamic study of dreams. However, the events in the story are fiction; and, as I am not a scholar, they are not meant to represent any definitive information on this subject.

Hearts We Lost also broaches the topic of healing based on medical, non-traditional, and spiritual approaches. The information discussed within comes from my research on the methods and from real stories I came across during my studies. However, again, the events shared in the story are fictional and have been merely inspired by that research; they do not represent any definitive information in the fields. As such, the reader is encouraged to engage in in-depth study should any of the topics spark his or her interest.

Dedication

For the reviver,
who sacrifices the world and all that is in it,
to taste the sweetness of faith.

*"Islam began as something strange,
and it will return as something strange,
so give glad tidings to the strangers."*
—Prophet Muhammad, peace be upon him (Muslim)

Prologue

If I were to look back at my life and pinpoint a single event, a single moment that set everything moving in a different direction, it would have to be the first time I saw my wife in a dream. Naturally, I didn't know this would prove a pivotal event, and if I'm honest, except for its strange timing—it was the week Hasna and I became officially engaged—I forgot about it.

Until I saw it again.

There's something about things that keep happening, that keep coming back to you. Like a continuous tugging at the lapel of your jacket, at a certain moment, you're going to turn around and see who's there, and what they want from you.

I cannot say how many times since then I've seen the dream, not because it has been too many to count, but because I never thought of it as relating to a particular number. But after seeing the dream a third time, which was about a year after the first, I knew this was not a random occurrence. It was some sort of sign.

I'm not one to place too much value in dreams, but I think intuitively we all know that, beyond their inherent enigma, dreams at times do have some definite meaning in reality.

I too know, however, that there are people who claim second sight, telepathy, and the power of dream interpretation. I am not one of them. I am as I always have been, simply a man.

I relate this initial dream as significant only because there was an even more significant moment, years later, when I knew this was no ordinary vision.

This was the moment I saw the dream unfolding before me—in real life.

Part I

> *"This world in comparison to the Hereafter is as if one of you were to put his finger in the ocean. Consider how much you would have when you pulled it out."*
> —Prophet Muhammad, peace be upon him (Muslim)

One

"Do you love him?"

Sommer folded the paper she had used for note-taking then folded it a second time. A dark arched eyebrow was raised as she pinched the twice-folded white paper between her thumb and forefinger before running them along the crease. She reached for her Louis Vuitton handbag that sat on the floor next to her and pulled it onto her lap without looking at Yasmin. She primly opened the large bag, ignoring the shocked expression on her friend's face, and she dropped the folded paper inside before lifting the purse and letting it drop back to its place on the marble-tiled floor of the Jeddah beach house her husband's family owned.

Folding her arms over her chest until her diamond ring sparkled under the chandelier's light above their heads, Sommer narrowed her dark eyes as she regarded Yasmin. Her expression demanded a response.

Yasmin looked away, unable to conceal the stiffening of her jaw. She felt her face grow warm, and she hated Sommer right then. It had been a bad idea to come. If her parents had known that it was Sommer that she was visiting, they would not approve. But Yasmin had omitted that detail after securing her parents' permission to visit "a friend" after she and her parents returned to their Jeddah hotel suite after performing 'Umrah.

The look in her father's eyes had been disapproving, but Yasmin sensed that he wasn't inclined to refuse. Her mother had looked only worried. But Yasmin was twenty-three years old, and her parents were trying not to treat her like a teenager anymore. Besides, she had already proven herself trustworthy, at least following her last year in high school when her and Sommer's friendship ended abruptly.

Yasmin herself never expected to speak to Sommer again. And she hadn't. But right then she didn't know where else to turn.

"Does it matter?" Yasmin's voice was curt, and she feared that she was overacting.

But Sommer looked pleased that she had annoyed her friend. A mischievous, knowing grin spread across Sommer's powder-pale face, the light olive skin beneath peaking out only where her make-up met her ears and hairline.

In high school, this same grin had given Yasmin so much confidence in having the "popular girl" by her side. Now it only made her stomach churn in dread. Sommer was enjoying this, Yasmin realized right then. She shouldn't have come.

"Of course it matters."

The music that had been playing in the back room grew louder until Yasmin could feel it thumping in rhythm to her own discomfort. She was still covered in her black, over-the-head *abaya*, but she had removed her face veil and gloves. But she kept them within reach on the card table that separated her from Sommer. Yasmin had always felt uneasy around Sommer's brother Aziz. But because he had been popular in the boys' section of the private school that she and Sommer had attended in Riyadh, she never showed discomfort in front of her friend, especially after Sommer had told her that he thought she had the most beautiful eyes he'd ever seen.

Aziz's blaring music made Yasmin shift in her chair. She wished she had chosen to take a nap after returning from Makkah. If she had, she'd be having dinner with her parents right then instead of subjecting herself to this.

Why was it that a simple beat from a song stirred up so much emotion in one's heart? The soft rhythm reached deep and brought to surface so much, confirming for Yasmin, inescapably, how much of a fool she had been.

"What?" Sommer grimaced as she regarded Yasmin. The contempt that Yasmin had always sensed her friend held for her during high school became apparent in that expression. "You think you're just going to *use* some guy to repair your image and it's not supposed to matter to him?" She sniffed her disgust.

"I'm not using him," Yasmin snapped, but she caught the insincerity in her tone though she had never thought of her motives in that way.

Sommer was silent, and an eyebrow went up again.

Yasmin's gaze fell to her hands, and the sight of the deep brown olive skin reminded her of that day during their first year in secondary school when Sommer discovered that the Arab boy she liked was talking to a girl from the American school.

"*Life's so unfair,*" Sommer had blurted as she opened the bag of Doritos Yasmin had bought for them to share. They were sitting outside on break, leaning against a wall near a pair of glass doors. "*Your skin looks like crap, and* you *get the blue eyes.*"

"Is he a real American?"

Yasmin gathered her eyebrows and regarded her friend in genuine confusion. "What?"

"Is he a *real* American, or just some F-O-B toting the blue passport?"

It was then that Yasmin realized that Sommer had assumed that the man she wanted to marry shared their ethnic background, though only Yasmin's mother was Pakistani. Her father was Yemeni-Saudi. Even that had been a source of tension between the friends, as only Yasmin held a Saudi passport.

Though both she and Sommer had always wanted an American one.

"He's a real American," Yasmin said coolly. She didn't want to reveal more than she needed to. But if she were to get the help she had come for, she couldn't hold back too much.

An hour earlier, when Yasmin had arrived and explained her dilemma, Sommer had asked details only about the girl whom the "American" had been engaged to marry, and very little about the man himself. Yasmin had found that odd, especially as Sommer took out a pen and wrote furiously on a piece of paper as she spoke. Yasmin had imagined that Sommer could somehow help her get in touch with the man's family — without her own family knowing, of course — so he could reconsider her for marriage and contact her father. Sommer and her family had several close friends and family in the States, some of them having resided in the country for generations — hence their status as "real" Americans.

In school, Sommer was often critical of classmates who were "FOB's" — immigrants who, "fresh off the boat," had stayed in America only long enough to get the blue passport. Thereafter, they swiftly returned to their countries or to Saudi Arabia, where "American" was always neatly printed on formal paperwork like report cards and class rosters posted in the school's halls. Yasmin had always felt that Sommer's detesting the "fake" Americans was a bit much, but, then again, she herself had disliked them no less.

But that had been in another time, another lifetime, it seemed. Yasmin no longer cared about things like that. She would never have imagined that Sommer, after two years of marriage—to a very wealthy Pakistani businessman in Jeddah—and a son, would still nurse so much envy in her heart for people who had that which she felt more deserving of. Half the people she envied could never dream of living the lavish life she now took for granted, Yasmin reflected.

"Where does his family live? In America or Pakistan?" There was a tone of skepticism in Sommer's question.

"He's American," Yasmin said again, this time feeling for the first time since she arrived that evening that she had the upper hand. It didn't escape her that Sommer had omitted the mention of Yemen or Saudi Arabia in her inquiry. It was like being in high school all over again, when she was treated by Sommer and other classmates as if she had no right to her Arab blood. But, then again, maybe most of them never knew about her paternal side since her mother worked at the school and was known as "Yasmin's mom."

"He's Black American." She glanced at the clock as she added this detail.

Oh.

Yasmin could almost taste Sommer's shock, and defeat. In high school, this had been their dream, to marry a Black American. Of course then, their images had been immature ones, like that of the late rapper 2-Pac or the actor Will Smith, borrowed from their fascination with American music, television, and movies.

When Yasmin met Sommer's gaze a second later, she detected a twinge of envy as her friend's eyes grew grave. Sommer wrinkled her nose in disapproval, but it was too late, years late actually, as Yasmin had already gotten a glimpse of her friend's heart.

"But it could never happen," Sommer had brooded one day staring at the ceiling as she lay on the bed in Yasmin's room, hands clasped behind her head. The sound of a 2-Pac CD played with the volume turned low because they both knew Yasmin's parents would never approve of rap music in their house, of any music in fact.

"You never know," Yasmin had said from where she played in Sommer's hair as she sat with her legs crossed and folded in front of her at the head of the bed, her back against the headboard. A smile lingered on her face as she imagined the impossible. *"You never know..."*

Sommer's face was twisted in such marked disapproval that Yasmin sensed she was about to retract her agreement to help Yasmin speak to his family. Sommer opened her mouth to say something, but then shrugged.

"I'll help you," she said finally, her manner cold once again. She spoke as if assisting Yasmin was a tremendous favor and inconvenience. "But I don't agree with what you're doing. It's wrong."

Yasmin was unsure if her friend was referring to Yasmin's alleged crime of "using" the man or that of marrying an indigenous American. Yasmin doubted the disapproval was due to her parents not knowing, but she felt guilty nonetheless.

"I just want a chance to talk," Yasmin said more for herself than for Sommer. She couldn't shake the feeling that what she was doing was wrong, terribly wrong. She should have talked to her father about this. Perhaps he would be willing to contact the young man about reconsidering.

But the problem was that she wanted to talk to the young man herself, and she doubted her father would approve. Her father had lived in America for many years while completing his doctorate degree, and he had admitted on more than one occasion that the American Muslims were more pragmatic about matters like this. But he was still Arab at heart. He could never allow his daughter to speak to a man until at least the written marriage contract was complete, even if he were present while they spoke.

But Americans didn't approach marriage like that. They at least needed to talk to the person they wanted to marry. Chaperoned discussions were fine, and even expected among the more religious ones, but never would they agree to marry someone after only a *showfa*—looking at the girl without her veil— even if the "wedding" would be held an entire year after the written contract had been signed. It didn't give Americans any consolation that they could talk freely during that year, for that defeated the entire purpose of talking. They were already married by then.

"I don't like owing anybody." Sommer's voice had risen, and Yasmin could tell that Sommer herself was growing annoyed at Aziz's music that was now playing even louder.

Aziz was in the back room with friends of his brother-in-law's younger brother, and Yasmin heard them thrashing about although she couldn't imagine what they were doing. But she thought she smelled hashish.

"You don't owe me anything," Yasmin said, raising her own voice so her friend could hear her over the music. "It's just a favor I'm asking because—"

"No," Sommer interrupted, shaking her head, leaning to the side to reach for her bag again. "I owe you." The words were spoken humbly, as if in submission to something she had wrestled with for years. But there was an edge of bitterness in her tone. Her eyes were distant and regretful as she pulled the bag onto her lap again. But her dark eyes still held that sullen look that made Yasmin worry that she had made a mistake in asking Sommer's assistance.

Yasmin felt that sickness in the pit of her stomach again.

"But I've always hated that." Sommer contorted her face as she rummaged through the bag, her gaze on whatever she was looking for. And it was almost through gritted teeth that she spoke her next words, withdrawing the folded paper again and a pen thereafter.

"I never understood why you'd done something so *stupid* in the first place."

It was then that Yasmin was reminded of her own motivations for calling Sommer earlier that evening. Yasmin knew, even if she had been unable to admit it to herself at the time, that Sommer *did* owe her. Contacting some family and friends in Washington, D.C. was the least Sommer could do to make up for being the cause of Yasmin's inability to get married.

They had graduated from high school more than six years ago, and Yasmin had been the only one still held back by the past. Even her newfound religiousness hadn't allowed her to outlive the "image" Sommer imagined Yasmin wished to repair.

And Yasmin was in fact hoping to repair her image through this marriage. Love had never crossed her mind.

"But you should know," Sommer said as she unfolded the paper and smoothed it down on the card table in front of them, "that Americans don't take this issue of love lightly. If someone wants to marry them—" She paused as she lifted her gaze to meet Yasmin's, her face twisted in disapproval. "*Especially* an Arab girl," she said, acknowledging Yasmin's paternal blood for the first time. The acknowledgement made Yasmin uncomfortably aware that this meant that Sommer was being honest, and painfully so. "They think it's because the girl actually cares for them."

Yasmin looked away.

"Not because she's lost all hope in marrying her own."

Sharif dreamt of his father as he leaned the back of his head against the seat that, even reclined, gave the feeling of being closed in. Behind his lids, his father was as he remembered him, a man whose leather brown skin and dark eyes were symbols of one worthy of veneration, even when words did not pass his lips. Sharif saw his mother next to his father, her thin fingers gently touching the back of his father's hand, her other hand outstretched, index finger pointing to Asma. Sharif's sister had bent her stubby legs and watched with a toddler's amazement as her diaper, drooping heavy from a long night's sleep, moved on its own accord and swung like a pendulum, needing only the rhythmic, gentle urging of her upper body. Sharif saw himself then, only momentarily amused, unable to offer more than that because he was showing his father his seventh grade Spanish exam. The red ink strokes of the score "92" and the teachers hurried, barely legible "Good Job!" was more interesting, more pressing to him at that moment. Wali, a young boy at the time, sat with exaggerated disinterest, oblivious to his surroundings as he played Pac Man, the only video game their father allowed at the time.

Sharif opened his eyes only briefly, long enough to see that the seatbelt sign was still turned off. He could not bring himself to look at his watch. Already there was at his temples a throbbing threatening release if Sharif were to burden it with knowledge of more waiting. He shut his eyes and felt exhausted sleeplessness overtake him, even as he hadn't slept more than an hour.

The sound of a woman's voice prompted his turning his head in the direction of the sound. She was scolding her young son for spilling his drink on the stow tray and soiling his clothes. It took a moment for Sharif to register that she was speaking in Arabic because he understood every word.

He became aware of his staring only after meeting the gaze of the girl in the aisle seat, next to the boy. She regarded Sharif suspiciously, a sly grin on her face, and it took a moment before he turned his head. Perhaps he had turned too quickly, because a second later he found himself staring too forcefully out the window to his left, trying to erase the image of the girl's large eyes decorated by mascara—or was is kohl?—that had become mysteriously beautiful in that brief moment. The image disturbed him, and a full minute passed before he understood the reason for his unrest.

The young woman, before Sharif had drifted to sleep, had been wearing a *jilbaab*. The voluminous black garment had been draped from the top of her head and fell over her feet. Her face too had been concealed with a matching veil, and her eyes had been covered with a sheer screen and her hands with gloves matching the soft black fabric of her outer-garment.

Now, the authentic caramel brown of her Arab skin was palpable, reminding him of the two things he had hoped to forget for at least another three hours. He was no longer in Riyadh, and he was a man. At that moment, he didn't know which was more troubling.

Day glowed outside the small window. Translucent clouds faded into the sky's powder blue that exuded a luminance that strained the eyes even as the sun itself was not visible. Sharif willed himself to imbibe the beauty of this magnificent view, even as the scene had become suffocating in its monotonous singularity

16

during the long flight. He turned his head slightly and rested it on the stiffly reclined seat, inadvertently glancing in the direction of the girl.

In that brief moment, she caught his gaze and smiled so imperceptibly that its message lacked ambiguity. It was a smile of triumph, of familiarity — a gesture that Sharif had often, in the years before leaving for Saudi Arabia, returned equally imperceptibly, followed by a lowered gaze that only faintly allayed his fears of succumbing to human weakness.

Out of politeness, or masculine inclination — Sharif didn't know which — he smiled back. He caught himself, though a second too late, and turned his attention back to the darkened seatbelt sign welded to the ceiling of the cabin.

"Are you American?"

He heard her voice, a soft, resonant tone free of both Arab accent and Islamic hesitation, and he recognized the unrestrained kindness that marked an inappropriateness that had, most probably, been incensed the moment she removed the traditional garb to reveal a fitting "Go Terps!" T-shirt and equally fitting jeans.

Sharif nodded but refused to look in her direction. "Yes."

"I am too. I go to U-MD College Park."

He found the information intriguing despite himself. His home was thirty minutes from the school.

"What about you?"

"I graduated from Howard," he said, surprising himself by the ease with which he spoke. "But after that, I left to study in Riyadh." Despite his inclination otherwise, he shut his eyes, feigning exhaustion.

"So you're from D.C.?"

Sharif, even in the self-imposed darkness of his closed eyelids, was impressed and could almost see the look of recognition on her face. By circumstance or volition, Sharif didn't know which, but most Muslim immigrants he had met were unfamiliar with the historically Black university based in the nation's capital.

"Yes."

"I am too."

Sharif didn't know what to say in response but felt the growing discomfort of his silence. He had to temper his instinct to

17

converse more, to find out more about her. The temptation alone disturbed him and he felt a nostalgic longing for the mundane spiritual atmosphere of women in black *jilbaab* and men in white *thobe*, a singularity of appearance that he had taken for granted while living in a Muslim society.   Initially, the tranquil atmosphere had been a welcome refuge from the fast-paced, social lifestyle to which he was accustomed, but it soon became so commonplace that it evoked neither solace nor strain as his studies consumed him and the strange city became merely home.

The girl filled the silence, and Sharif became both relieved and disturbed at the sound of her voice that temporarily distracted him from the throbbing in his head. He hated himself for wanting her to be quiet, and he hated himself for not wanting her to stop — a selfish desire that would protect him from participating but allow him to benefit from the conversation nonetheless.

Sharif's desire to respond was so insistent that he had to turn his head to the direction of the window to discourage himself. It was rude, he knew, but he was growing more irritated by the second. When would this flight be over?

He loathed long flights and wished he could show his mother this moment. He wanted her to feel what he was feeling. Then, perhaps, she could understand why in the six years he had lived across the Atlantic, he had come home only twice, and why, even then, he had stayed only two weeks. He had, instead, opted to spend his vacations in Cairo, where he would study Arabic and Qur'an, both of which required his mastery if he were to graduate with his degree in Islamic jurisprudence, although both were already part of the program at his university in Riyadh.

"Whose bag is this?"   The school supervisor held up the weather-beaten designer backpack as she stood in front of the section D twelfth grade class, flanked by both her assistant and the girls' section vice principal.

The sloppy ink pen scribble of $S + K$ in exaggerated cursive was legible even over the "LV" company logo printed on every part of the leather of the student's bag. Everyone knew whose bag it was, but in typical student solidarity, even if they were far from being friends outside class, they stuck together. Besides, these "bag searches" were nothing short of mafia-type encroaching in the students' view. What business was it to the school what students carried in their book bags? It wasn't like they were carrying narcotics. *Gosh.*

Ms. Javeria stood in front of the room with her arms crossed, looking dutifully upset. The random "bag search" that was whispered among students to happen that day actually ended up being an entire school search instead. Lockers were checked, *behind* lockers were checked, on-top-of-lockers were checked, and even the mobile-phone hideout next to the school's canteen had been searched.

The students were livid. They had begun to realize that the school likely deliberately leaked the fact that there would be an "unannounced random bag search" that day. It felt like a set-up. Not even one bag had been searched, at least not the ones in students' possession.

This was a travesty of justice. What kind of school deliberately whispered lies in students' earshot as some sort of psychological ambush to catch them unaware?

There was an entire mobile sweep that day, too. Every few minutes, the intercom interrupted classes, asking, on average, about three students to report to the vice principal's office, where their mobile phones had already been confiscated. Students only had to sit tight while their parents were called about the presence of the mobile phone, as well as any "suspicious" messages or pictures found on them.

Sommer had been amongst the first of the mobile-phone transgressors called out of class earlier that day, and she had returned — two class periods later — during Ms. Javeria's Islamic Studies class. And Sommer was, in her words, "pissed off" because they had taken not only her mobile phone this time, but her SIM card too.

"Only your mother come get it," Sommer mocked the assistant supervisor's accent and poor English as she recounted the story in

19

barely restrained whispers to the students who sat near her. The laughter that exploded thereafter had annoyed Ms. Javeria, who had been writing on the board proofs from the Qur'an about respecting authority and telling the truth—a topic that, interestingly, was not covered in their course text. The students suspected that this too was part of the school's ploy to root out "contraband" being brought to school. Of course, very few students had enough presence of mind to care about what the teacher was saying, especially since they were quite sure she would slip into her lesson some diatribe about not bringing movie DVDs, music CDs, and mobile phones to school.

"Sommer!" Ms. Javeria's voice stunned the class to silence. She didn't often raise her voice. But apparently, the sudden laughter had irritated her thoroughly. "Enough."

Inadvertently, Yasmin glanced at Sommer apologetically. Sommer too had looked in Yasmin's direction after the teacher's outburst. The friends were seated far from each other, as they both knew that Islamic Studies was not a class they could play in. But Sommer met Yasmin's apologetic expression with a glare, her nostrils flaring in that moment.

Yasmin looked away, her face hot in humiliation, especially since other students had mirrored Sommer's accusing look. Yasmin absolutely hated her mother right then.

It was bad enough that Yasmin had to endure this class every single week, and now this sudden outburst directed at Sommer, and on a day that the students were already upset?

Yasmin was utterly ashamed that her mother took this class so seriously. She often wanted to disappear when her mother's eyes filled with tears as she recited Qur'an or talked about the blessings of *emaan*. What made matters worse was that Ms. Javeria was actually well-respected at the school and was, to even some popular girls, a favored teacher. Despite the subject having had a reputation for being the easiest at the school, many students started taking Islamic Studies seriously after Yasmin's mother took the job during Yasmin's third year in high school, after the students had gone for nearly three weeks with no teacher.

Everything had changed after that. The break for *Dhuhr* prayer toward the end of the day, which had been just another snack and gossip break for most students, began to be taken seriously by most students. Girls who had never prayed began to pray and even started talking about encouraging their parents and friends to pray. Even girls who didn't wear hijab started contemplating the importance of it. Everywhere Yasmin turned, there were whispers of how nice, sweet, and "inspirational" Ms. Javeria was.

And she despised it.

She resented being "Ms. Javeria's daughter." Yasmin didn't wear hijab, and she absolutely refused to put the head cover on, even when her mother insisted that she cover properly. But Yasmin was defiant. *Nope, you can't force me.* That was her mantra. Then her mother's eyes would grow sad, and as she pulled the covers over herself at night, Yasmin would feel bad, the image of her mother's deep sadness coming back to her. She'd always said that her mother cared too much about what people thought. But in those quiet moments, Yasmin knew that her mother simply cared "too much" for her soul. That's when Yasmin started to care herself.

But she couldn't reduce herself to being a "hijabi," at least not at school. She'd lose all her friends. The marginal popularity she had earned was *because* she wasn't religious. That she was bold enough to openly defy her mother, when so many other students felt ashamed to, made Yasmin all the more praiseworthy to Sommer and her friends.

"*Whose* bag is this?"

The supervisor stepped toward the students and narrowed her eyes as she scanned the class, the bag still suspended in the air. Ms. Javeria shook her head from where she stood near the board, a dry eraser marker still in her hand, in the gesture expressing her deep disapproval for her students being so obstinate.

The bag was Sommer's. Everyone knew that. The answer to the supervisor's question was literally written on the bag itself. *S + K — Sommer and Khalid.* The two had been an item for nearly a year now, and Sommer was now the envy of the senior class because she had secured for herself the boy known as the most popular, cutest, and smartest. That he was half-American only incensed the girls' envy. There was even a rumor that he was telling his friends he wanted to marry her.

But, of course, teachers and supervisors, true to their job, were stupid and oblivious. So stupid, in fact, that they actually imagined that their raised voices and stern gazes would make the students stoop so low as to betray a friend.

But that was unthinkable.

Sommer exhaled loudly from where she sat defiantly with her arms folded over her chest. Her expression was stoic and grave, as she stared right at the supervisor, apparently not carrying if she was discovered.

But her friends knew she did care. Having her mobile phone confiscated was one thing. But having to take ownership for the bag was another thing entirely.

Sommer had always planned for the worst with her mobile, as even Khalid's name had been saved under a female's so that neither the school nor her parents would suspect anything, even if they did come across the number stored in the list of recent calls and texts in her phone. It was a joke among her friends that Sommer wasn't "straight" because her real love was "Kholood," Khalid's female name in her address book.

The pictures Sommer had stored on the phone were merely of her and her friends — yes, at school — but the shots were obviously not random ones of uncovered teachers or hijabi girls. She would get in trouble if the mobile was found, she already knew, but not much. Her parents, as they came to retrieve the SIM card, would just grumble at how ridiculous the school's rules were, her father in the car waiting in the parking lot, her mother cursing at the principal in the Saudi Arabic she knew so well after having lived in the Kingdom all her life.

Sommer's parents hated the no-mobile rule, [for selfish reasons of course (they felt Sommer should always be a phone call or text away, even in Biology class)]. But that would work in her favor, even if caught — as she had been today. And they wouldn't think twice about this Kholood always texting to say "she" wanted to meet up at the mall. Except for Yasmin, Sommer's parents had no idea who her friends were, even if they were right in front of their faces.

But the bag was another thing entirely. Especially today. Sommer hadn't learned of the possibility of a bag search until she'd heard the rumor whispered among even the "good" students.

Oh crap.

Khalid had, upon her request, brought her some books and magazines from America that past summer, and she couldn't get caught dead with them, even if from "Kholood." She had brought them to school to show off in front of her friends. But she hadn't expected a bag search. *Stupid girl*, she cursed herself. *Always expect the unexpected.*

Sommer and her friends had been carefully situated behind a corner of the school during morning break when she heard the rumors of a bag search. That's when they frantically stuffed the contraband — and these really *were* illicit items (even by American schools' standards) — back into the bag and sought a hiding place outside. They decided against the mobile-phone hideout, not because they feared discovery by teachers, but because they feared discovery by students. This wasn't something Sommer even wanted other students to see. She could trust only her closest friends with this one.

That's why she had deliberately brought the material on the day that she knew Yasmin had some silly quiz to make up during break. She didn't want to chance having the "daughter of Ms. Too-Good" around although Yasmin considered Sommer her best friend. Somehow though Sommer sensed that Yasmin wasn't too far from following in her mother's footsteps. Yasmin's insistence on praying the five prayers (even if she never prayed at school) was proof enough that Yasmin was a *mutawwa'* at heart and that her friendship with Sommer's crowd was for selfish reasons. And that was a source of constant irritation to Sommer.

"Look," the supervisor was saying as she looked right at Sommer, her eyes resting on her so long that Yasmin could almost taste her friend's panic, though Sommer's cold eyes and folded arms revealed nothing as they met the supervisor's unblinking, "we already have a pretty good idea whose bag this is. That's why we came to this class."

Yasmin exhaled in relief when the supervisor turned to look at someone else, one of Sommer's friends, but at least not Sommer herself. Yasmin hated the way the school administration thought so badly of Sommer, always assuming the worst, even though having a bad reputation wasn't something that they could actually punish Sommer for, no matter how much they wanted to.

Yasmin suspected that they had found Sommer's mobile phone in that bag, and they probably even discovered that the texts from "Kholood" were a bit awkward to say the least. That would get them to researching and investigating, and Yasmin feared that it was only a matter of putting two and two together before they realized the truth. That would mean Khalid would be in trouble too.

"I'm going to ask you for the last time," the supervisor warned the girls. "Whose—"

"We take all you names, all you!" The assistant supervisor took a notebook from a nearby desk and opened it furiously. The student sitting at the desk opened her mouth in shock, indignant. It was her Islamic Studies copybook.

"Hey, that's my—"

"No talk! No talk!"

There was muffled laughter as her speech reminded them of Sommer's earlier mocking, and Sommer herself couldn't resist a mischievous grin toying at one side of her mouth.

"It's okay," the supervisor said turning to the assistant. "I'll just—"

"No, I tired of games playing. *Shoof. Maa 'adree...*" She started to shout at them in Arabic. *Look, I don't know what you think you're up to, but—*

"It's mine."

The sound of a chair screeching slightly as the student stood up to take responsibility interrupted the assistant midsentence. She looked up from the notebook, her hand still trembling from her unfinished tirade.

"*'Aysh?*" *What?* The assistant supervisor looked confused.

Yasmin raised her voice. "It's my bag."

The supervisor and the assistant exchanged glances, and the exchange made Yasmin painfully aware of what she had just done. She was only slightly cognizant of the shocked expressions on the students' faces, and that of the teacher.

Yasmin inadvertently glanced in Sommer's direction, and the look on her best friend's face sent her heart racing. She had never seen that look before, at least not directed at her.

Sommer looked horrified.

The reaction confused Yasmin, and she felt her palms sweat as she reached for the books on her desk in preparation to be dismissed. Or maybe it was out of desperation that she had reached for her books. She needed to reach for something. She felt so lonely right then, so isolated.

Yasmin shivered as she held her Islamic Studies books and copybook close to her chest. She was unable to shake the feeling that things were going terribly wrong, and that she was utterly incapable of doing anything to set them right.

"This bag for you?" The assistant pointed to the bag, as if Yasmin didn't know what bag was being discussed. It was the *only* one being discussed.

"Yes."

Yasmin's mother looked as if she couldn't decide between the shock that she felt right then and the hurt she nursed in her heart. Her mouth was slightly open, as if she wanted to speak, and her folded arms loosened in front of her, as if she wanted to reach out and stop this from happening. But Yasmin thought she detected a trace of fear in her mother's eyes. But what scared her most was her mother's uncertainty. Yasmin wasn't used to her mother looking uncertain, at least not at school. It was similar to the look Javeria often gave Yasmin after they'd had an argument about hijab. She would look...defeated, as if resigned to a fate she had no control over. With hijab, her mother's fear and uncertainty had been in knowing she could do very little to save Yasmin from what her daughter probably could never understand.

But, of course, Yasmin's mother knew it wasn't her bag. Javeria didn't even buy designer bags for herself, let alone for her daughter. So what did it matter to her if Yasmin covered for her friend? Was this going to be another lecture tonight to go along with the why-you-should-cover-yourself one?

"*Yalla,*" the assistant said. *Let's go.* She indicated with a motion of her hand that Yasmin was to follow the administration out the room.

The vice principal nodded her approval to the supervisor, who turned to Yasmin as she was already making her way around the desks. Yasmin was feeling a bit proud of herself for having had the strength to do this, even if she was a bit nervous about actually getting in trouble.

The supervisor turned to Yasmin's mother, her expression concealed from Yasmin who saw only the back of her head. In that moment, Yasmin felt her chest tighten as her mother merely stared back at the supervisor, a trace of defiance in her mother's eyes. Or maybe Yasmin had misinterpreted her mother's reaction.

But Yasmin couldn't shake the feeling of unease as she left her mother standing alone in front of the class to continue the lesson about respecting authority and telling the truth.

The chime of the seatbelt sign woke Sharif. The sound inspired both surprise and relief. He hadn't realized he had drifted to sleep. Instinctively, he glanced to where the Arab girl had been sitting and found her leafing through a magazine, the boy and his mother asleep next to her. Before the girl had opportunity to realize he was awake, Sharif rested his gaze on the window, reflecting on how difficult it would be for him, now that he was back in America—for good.

A knot formed in his chest, and his mind groped for other options. Perhaps he could return to Saudi Arabia as an English teacher. A lot of the brothers he knew did that. Or maybe he might even find a post teaching Islamic studies.

But he knew that, even as his restless mind resisted the obvious, he was not a teacher. He had not, even during his obtaining an undergraduate degree in both biology and education, aspired for a future in the classroom. He didn't even have any experience in the field, not counting his course requirements and his weak attempts at Arabic tutoring he had done in the homes of some American expatriates living in Riyadh. He had majored in biology because it was something that he loved, and he had majored in education because it was something that his father had loved.

The mere thought of standing before a class of restless, disinterested students inspired anxiety. But even if the restless, disinterested faces could be replaced by eager, inquisitive

26

students, hungry to learn, Sharif doubted he would experience a change of heart. In fact, he imagined that the latter would make him even more uneasy.

How then was he to survive as an imam in America?

Sighing, Sharif returned his gaze to the glowing seatbelt sign as his head began to throb—again.

It wasn't his idea to become the leader of the small Muslim community where he had spent much of his childhood, but right then he felt the weight of obligation upon him.

Despite his prior restlessness to escape the suffocating confines of the plane's cabin, as the flight made its final descent upon the shores of America, Sharif was overcome by dread.

Sharif exhaled as he exited the plane, barely able to hear his footfalls walking the portable corridor as the bustle of hurried feet and wheeled baggage rushed past him. Seconds later, with his single carry-on bag strapped over one shoulder, he entered John F. Kennedy International Airport. He had a two-hour layover before he would reach his final destination, but it was refreshing, at least partly, to be this close to home.

As he took his place in the line for American citizens, Sharif was struck suddenly by apprehension. He was native to this country, but the presence of security officers, sniffing dogs, and indurate kiosks made him acutely aware of how foreign his homeland had become since he had last visited in the summer of 2000—four years ago. Now, after the infamous terrorist attacks in September of 2001, his religious affiliation made him both a stranger and suspect at once, although his particular crime eluded him.

Perhaps it was not merely the desire for further study of Arabic and Qur'an that had halted Sharif's visits home. There was, too, the subconscious anguish at being viewed as a security threat, even as in all the twenty years he had lived in America before accepting the scholarship to study overseas, he had never seen the inside of a jail.

Now he prayed that he never would.

"Sharif! Sharif!" a voice called from the throngs of people waiting outside baggage claim at Washington Dulles Airport. His mother had told him they would be unable to meet him at the gate as they had when he had last visited, but after twenty minutes of fruitless searching, Sharif had begun to wonder if his family had made it to the airport at all.

Sharif strained his eyes to locate the sound of the voice.

A waving hand and a white-covered head was his first clue. The white cloth moved through the crowd until it revealed a young woman whose almond brown skin glowed with excitement as she finally located him.

"*As-salaamu-alaikum!*" she greeted with a grin she was unable to contain.

Before Sharif could determine who she was, the young woman shrilled in excitement and threw her arms around him in an embrace.

"Asma?" he said in surprise, gently pulling her away to get a better look.

She nodded eagerly, still unable to keep from grinning and obviously proud of herself for having grown so much. When Sharif had last seen her, she was only ten years old, but now she could pass for eighteen.

"Asma?" he said again, an uncertain grin now forming on his face. As his mind registered recognition, his eyes squinted in disbelief. Although he was just over six-feet, she stood inches taller than his shoulders though his memory of his sister was of her being barely taller than his waist.

"How old are you now, what, *seventeen*?"

"Look, Mom, he has a beard!" Asma was too excited to register his question.

It had been rhetorical anyway. Sharif knew that she would turn fifteen in November. The month of her birth had left him with memories too indelible to permit his losing count of her age, and the eleven years and three months that separated it from his own.

Still grinning uncontrollably, Asma motioned to her mother to come see Sharif. "And an accent!"

He had wanted to tease Asma about the *khimaar* she was wearing, the head cover indicating that she was now a young woman. But the taunt was halted as he realized the reason for her last exclamation. He didn't have a beard last time they had seen him.

It was then that he realized that his family had gone through some changes themselves.

In the small Muslim community over which Sharif was now to be imam, no Muslim man wore the traditional Islamic beard — and no Muslim woman wore traditional Islamic garb.

"Islam is in the heart," Sharif's father would often say. *"We don't need to prove to the world who we are. Allah already knows that better than we do."*

Why then was Asma wearing hijab?

Nadirah grinned at her son, tears glistening in her eyes.

Sharif's thoughts were interrupted by the look on his mother's face as their eyes met. Feeling his own eyes moisten, he looked away. She looked older than he remembered. Her braids were threaded with more gray than black, and he wondered if the extended distance between mother and son had taken a toll on her.

Nadirah embraced Sharif, and the familiar scent of her perfume reminded him of home. He struggled to keep his composure. How had he lasted so long away from his family?

"As-salaamu-alaikum," he said, his love for his mother aching inside. It had been too long.

Nadirah held her son for several seconds before letting go.

"As-salaamu-alaikum," a deep voice greeted a second later.

Sharif looked up and found a young man standing a couple of feet behind his mother. "Wali?"

It was difficult to recognize his younger brother beneath the carefully sculpted goatee and towering height. Sharif imagined that Wali had to be at least six-foot-two now, and his strong build was noticeable even beneath the large polo shirt and baggy jeans. Sharif suddenly felt insignificant in his role as the eldest.

Wali grinned and nodded, and even that motion suggested a cool self-sufficiency that had most likely developed in Sharif's absence. One hand tucked lazily in a back pocket of his jeans, Wali extended the other to greet his older brother, a safe alternative to displaying open affection.

"You better give your brother a hug," Nadirah playfully scolded Wali. But both Sharif and Wali knew that she was not joking. Their parents had not raised them to put on faces for the world.

Groaning, Wali smiled uncomfortably and stingily hugged Sharif, patting his older brother playfully on the back, as he normally did whenever an embrace was unavoidable.

"Get these bags into the car," Nadirah said to Wali. "Your brother's had a long flight."

Without argument or hesitation, Wali pushed the small trolley overloaded with baggage to the car parked several feet from the curb.

A security guard spoke sternly to Wali as he effortlessly lifted the bags into the trunk.

Nadirah had started to say something when she noticed Wali's contorted face as he responded to the officer.

"Let me get in the car," Nadirah said with a sigh, turning and walking toward where Wali unloaded the trolley. "I drove around this place at least six times, and they can't give me five minutes to greet my son."

Sharif followed his mother until she stood next to the driver's door watching Wali. Sharif decided to help his brother arrange the bags in the trunk. The task was making Wali visibly aggravated, most likely because the security guard still stood next to him with his arms crossed authoritatively as if expecting their family to break a law that forbade excessive trunk luggage.

Nadirah wore a smirk as Wali pushed the trolley back to the airport's baggage claim entrance and Sharif forcefully closed the trunk that needed more effort due to the amount of bags he had. Sharif was expecting a tease before his mother spoke; he figured she couldn't resist joking that he wasn't as strong as he used to be.

"Oh, don't be rude and just take off before greeting *everyone*," his mother teased.

It took several seconds before Sharif registered his mother's joke, and realized he did not understand it.

His face must have displayed confusion because his mother laughed. An uncertain grin formed on Sharif's face, and he was about to ask what the joke was when his mother took the hand of someone who stood next to her and said, "You can't forget the most important person."

"*As-salaamu-alaikum.*"

Sharif recognized the face and voice at once. Hasna greeted him with a hesitant smile, a shyness that was so unlike her that, for a moment, Sharif doubted that it was his fiancée standing before him.

As Sharif's gaze fell upon the woman, reality engulfed him before it even occurred to him that he should avert his gaze. His heart was a storm of emotions. Her presence made him forget that he had travelled at all, or that he had ever wanted to.

Or perhaps it was merely that he had not allowed himself to remember.

There was at that moment, in the dimming light of that early August afternoon, an air of distant familiarity, and Sharif found himself momentarily taken by what he had sought refuge from.

Airport passengers rushed past, their luggage dragging noisily behind them. Families and friends embraced as others squealed in excitement upon seeing each other. And cars double parked as drivers impatiently beeped horns.

Yet, it was the familiar scent of Hasna's perfume — the scent he liked most — that distracted him, eclipsing any possibility of registering his surroundings.

There was an attractive newness about her, Sharif noticed. Her hair was now cut low and dyed amber, only a shade darker than the milky bronze tone of her skin. Blue eyeliner accented her hazel eyes that regarded him with a reservation that suggested an unfamiliar strangeness about her. Shiny white pearls dangled from her ears and the 14-karat gold S for "Sharif" adorned the necklace that glistened from her bare neck. The silk white blouse that was neatly tucked in her navy blue slacks reminded Sharif of more than he would have liked.

Sharif lowered his gaze, and it was then that the discomfort paralyzed him.

What could he say? He had known that he would eventually have to face the issues he had been avoiding for so long, but he had not expected to face them so soon.

"Get moving! You're holding up traffic."

It was the security officer again, and this time Sharif obeyed. He got moving. He walked around the car to the passenger side and climbed in as everyone else followed suit. There was a lingering sensation that he had broken some unwritten rule, and it wasn't until his mother had started the car and music wafted through the car's speakers that he realized his error.

He had not returned Hasna's greeting, nor did he embrace her. And he knew that, given their past—and planned future—the latter was the greater offense.

"Now, when you go over there, Sharif," his mother had told him before he left to Riyadh, *"don't let those people make you forget who you are."*

But that's exactly what had happened. He could no longer remember who he had been in the first place.

Sharif had first heard of Yasmin through Hisham, a close friend of one of his instructors who had heard about him and invited him over for dinner nearly two years after Sharif began studying at the Islamic university. Eager to meet a Muslim brother from the region, especially the friend of a favored professor, Sharif accepted the invitation, and the many more that followed.

For months, Sharif spent his free time in the home of his professor's friend, and at times, in the home of the professor himself. Sharif had liked Hisham from the moment his professor introduced them. Despite their vast age difference and their backgrounds being worlds apart—Sharif an African-American and Hisham a Saudi of both Yemeni and Saudi descent—Sharif and Hisham related to one another as if they had known each other their entire lives. Amazingly, Hisham, like Sharif, had been born in Washington, D.C., where Hisham spent his early childhood, but Hisham had returned to Saudi Arabia just weeks after he began middle school. Hisham would return to the States many years later to complete his PhD at Howard University while his wife and children remained in Saudi Arabia.

Sharif had been completely oblivious when Hisham asked if he wanted to get married. Sharif had laughed good-naturedly and thought momentarily about Hasna but could not bring himself to mention her. His conversations with Hasna had become shorter, and he called her less. She herself did not seem enthusiastic to keep in touch. At that point, Sharif had begun to believe that what he had always feared would happen had indeed come to pass. *She found someone else.* But he had no proof for this suspicion. It was likely only his crippling insecurity that had led him to this conclusion.

"One day..." he had told Hisham, sighing jokingly. He then said more seriously, though a smile still lingered on his face, "I hope to. Just make *du'aa* for me, sheikh."

"I want you to meet my daughter." There had not been even a hint of humor in Hisham's eyes or tone as he spoke, but he was smiling as he said these words.

It had taken Sharif some time to register what the brother had said. "Your daughter?"

"Yes."

Sharif stared at Hisham, an uncomfortable smile tugging at one corner of his mouth. He was unsure if he had understood Hisham correctly. Sharif looked away, unsure how to respond.

A brief silence followed, revealing that Hisham was in fact speaking in earnest, and Sharif's first reactions were anxiety and insecurity.

Hisham had no idea that Sharif was not the promising, confident young man his professor imagined him to be. Sharif had been merely enjoying the comfort of anonymity. He was relaxed in the foreign land, relieved to be unburdened by image or impressions. Perhaps, his newfound confidence and charisma mirrored who he was at heart, but he doubted it.

Sharif had not intended to mislead anyone. Despite the flattery that he couldn't hope to contain or deny, Sharif had been raised to be honest, to not wear masks for the public, and certainly not for people who meant well for him, and their children.

Sharif had started to respond, prepared to divulge the truth. But he realized that there were no words for what he needed to convey. How could he find words to confess his imperfections when they were but varied and obscure?

"You don't have to answer now," Hisham had said, relieving Sharif of the burden of incriminating himself. "I want you to meet her first. Then we can talk."

A week later, against Sharif's inclinations otherwise, Sharif had sat in the living room of Hisham's home sipping tea when Hisham walked in with a young woman covered in full hijab. The ebony fabric flowed like a single sheet and concealed only partially a shyness that was apparent in her mannerisms, even as he could not see her eyes or hands.

Hisham and Sharif talked for some time before Hisham said something to his daughter, and Sharif saw the black fabric move hesitantly in a nod.

A second later she left the room, and Sharif continued talking to the brother, although his heart hammered in his chest as he feared that the meeting was over. That she hadn't even bothered to lift her veil indicated that she didn't like Sharif. She hadn't even allowed him the *showfa* that was customary in Arab culture.

The next hour had been strained for Sharif and he wished he hadn't agreed to come. But even as he thought this, he knew he wouldn't have refused. That would have been a severe insult in Arab culture, especially when a man's daughter was involved.

Then Hisham's mobile phone rang and the brother stood and told Sharif to come with him.

Sharif followed Hisham down a hall to a room, where they entered to find a young woman sitting and wearing a powder blue garment and matching *khimaar* that was pinned carefully about her head and accented the color of her eyes and the smooth brown skin of her face.

There was no conversation aside from their mutual exchange of the Islamic greeting, although her reply was more a hushed whisper than a distinct response in kind.

Although it was not the answer that was in his heart at the time of the *showfa* — as Sharif had no inclination one way or the other — Sharif had, the following day, told Hisham that he could not marry his daughter. Sharif said that his family had expected him to marry the daughter of a close friend upon his return.

It was the truth, but Sharif could not sleep after his refusal. He had no idea if he'd done the right thing. But he wasn't sure if it was his concern for Hisham's hurt feelings and Arab pride that made him doubt himself, or if Sharif himself wished he hadn't been so hasty in turning down the proposal.

Yasmin wasn't unattractive, but that wasn't a sensible reason to marry someone. Of course, seeing the young woman had made Sharif curious about her, and he felt inclined to get to know her better. But of course, that wasn't possible. No matter how kind Hisham had been since they met, Sharif couldn't forget that

Hisham was Arab. And to ask for more than what Hisham offered in the *showfa* was not something Sharif could do. It had already been a tremendous sacrifice on Hisham's part to offer his daughter at all, especially to a foreigner.

Perhaps that was where Sharif's anxieties lay. It was flattering, no doubt, to be considered worthy of marrying the daughter of someone as respectable as Hisham. But, ever his father's son, Sharif couldn't deny that he was offended that it was assumed that he wouldn't—or couldn't—refuse such an offer.

Naturally, Sharif's relationship with Hisham was awkward after that, although the brother was always cordial to him whenever they met, which in itself was rare since Hisham did not work at the university. And their meetings were even rarer after the *showfa*. Sharif was never invited to dinner again.

That night, Sharif's heart was heavy as he lay awake reflecting on the weighty tasks before him—his official fulfillment of the imam post next week, and his marriage to Hasna in December.

He tried to picture himself standing before a congregation.

The image was hazy, barely discernable beyond the thick fog that was clouding his perception. There was, too, the familiar knotting in his chest, a knotting that had, of late, become a noose tightening around his heart.

As a child, Sharif had been drawn to small things—toys, the sound of his father's car turning into the driveway, his mother's laughter. What was it about adulthood that complicated the trivial and dulled, almost completely, the greatest pleasures of childhood? His toys, once the center of his life, were now coated in layers of dust like antiques from a life past, and there was, in his dismal present reality, no cause to anticipate his father's arrival, or his mother's laughter.

Perhaps that was what had inspired—or compelled—Sharif to leave. He wanted to make up for what his family had lost during his ungratefulness in youth. He couldn't take back the past, but he could, at least, atone for what he had done, even if sins past were, by nature, irrevocable.

His father had been a man of dreams, a man of words, and a man of action. Dawud didn't merely imagine a different reality, a better existence. He talked about it as if it were real—and did something to make it happen. He was not one to look back and lament. He was one to look forward and hope, and believe.

That was it though, Sharif reflected. How had these traits missed him, his father's first son, his father's firstborn? Sharif was a dreamer, yes, but no more. He had no words or action, except his half-hearted efforts to follow in the fading footprints his father had left for him. But each time, Sharif fell short. And now he was left with a burden too weighty to bear and too personal to release.

The only choice that had been Sharif's own was his decision to marry Hasna. But now even that decision felt as if it were slipping from his hands.

Sharif did not want to lose Hasna, but his insecurity was self-destructive. He was pushing her away. He had often asked her what she saw in him, and each time she would laugh and say, "You. That's what I see in you. And I like what I see."

Then she'd sigh and say, "You don't give yourself credit."
Credit for what?

It was Hasna who had been the valedictorian of their senior class, homecoming queen for two years in a row, and runner-up for prom queen when he, her date, had not even been nominated as a possible choice. He was known as quiet, shy, and "cool" — in a literal, insignificant way — but that was it. He didn't have confidence to be much else. Out of school, he loved football and basketball, and played quite well, but in school, he didn't even have enough courage to attend tryouts.

It was a psychological barrier, Sharif knew. But how then does one remove such an obstacle? Knowing was half the battle, he'd heard. But for him, knowing was merely the laying before him the determination of whether there was a need for battle in the first place.

What if he believed that the obstacle he'd put up really belonged there? He wasn't fooling anyone, not even himself. He wasn't varsity material, nor was he the "girls' pick." So why pretend? Why entice himself toward an existence that could never be reality, an existence that he did not even want to be reality?

Sharif had, of late, found comfort in only one thing: being himself. Even if that was, by necessity, tempered by his desire to live up to the expectations of his father. But Sharif couldn't be

36

himself in the limelight, whether on a school's basketball court or before a congregation of Muslims. It was an excruciatingly difficult task, he imagined, to always subject oneself to the scrutiny of others, and measure oneself with a yardstick that constantly changed in both length and proportion—in a game that always changed rules.

Hasna was his contradiction of self, his one, single leap at perfection, or at least at having perfection in his corner. Having her for himself reassured him that he could have what everyone else coveted, without ever entering their playing field, or sacrificing his sense of self.

Then again, Hasna was not his trophy. She was not his triumph against all odds. She had been his childhood friend. In that companionship alone lay his reasons for winning her affection. He had, at moments, pretended that it had been otherwise, that there was something about him that made him stand out among his peers, and thus earn for himself a place in her heart. But the truth was that his and Hasna's bond had been born of their parents' friendship. And it had been cultivated in the long hours he and she spent in his kitchen cooking meals and in the living room listening to their fathers debate politics or reminisce on their youth in the church and their young adulthood in the Nation of Islam.

Oddly, neither Sharif nor Hasna had valued their time spent together while young. They had resented it. It was not a loathing for each other that inspired such contrary emotions. But theirs had been a forced companionship. Under any other circumstance, they would have, perhaps, even enjoyed their joint solitude. But they did not resent each other so much as they merely resented the solitary reason they found themselves staring into the sullen face of each other at least once each week.

Babysitting.

While Nadirah and Mona lounged on the balcony overlooking the backyard of Sharif's family home, and while Dawud and Karim pored over tattered yearbooks and photo albums on the soft carpet of the living room, Sharif and Hasna were the appointed keepers, not only of the dinner simmering on the stove and the dessert baking in the oven, but of Sharif's younger siblings, Wali and Asma, and of Hasna's baby sister Iman.

The task was not so much difficult as it was frustrating. Why were *they* babysitting their parents' children? Why were *they* cooking the meals?

The most challenging part of the task was juggling three things at once: finding a topic of conversation to pass time, preventing the food from overcooking, and, most aggravating, keeping Asma and Iman from falling down the stairs—and Wali from shoving them.

One of Sharif's most vivid memories of his time with Hasna was when Asma and Iman had fallen asleep and Sharif and Hasna sat lazily in their chairs facing the oven, watching the timer on the stove and waiting for it to sound. The voices of their fathers had drifted into the kitchen, and Sharif overheard his father speak humorously about something one of the ministers of the Nation of Islam had said.

Although he, like Hasna, was only thirteen years old at the time, he understood the humor in the statement, and a small grin crept on the side of his mouth. Then he chuckled. He heard Hasna groan next to him, and he glanced in her direction to find her rolling her eyes. Before he could ask for an explanation, she spoke.

"I wish they would find something original to talk about."

Sharif creased his forehead. He didn't know how to form the question that had developed in his mind, so for a moment, he just stared at Hasna.

"I mean," she said, rolling her eyes again, "it's not like they did anything significant. They were just a bunch of stupid guys wearing dumb suits and saying stupid things."

Sharif frowned. "You don't think your history is significant?"

She glared at him, and at that moment Sharif noticed how attractive she was. His heart began to pound, but he held her gaze, disappointment in his eyes although his defensiveness had been tempered by his sudden awareness of her beauty.

Hasna wrinkled her nose. "It's not *my* history. It's theirs."

"Come on, Hasna." He was suddenly conscious of his lanky, muscle-less form that was poorly hidden beneath his flimsy black Michael Jackson T-shirt and faded blue jeans that were wearing at the right knee. He smiled to offset what he was about to say. He wanted her to know he wasn't upset with her, although this calculated self-awareness was new to him, and distracting in the discomfort it was causing. "They fought for our rights to be respected as human beings."

She sucked her teeth. "Fighting for people because they have the same skin color? That's stupid." She exhaled audibly, as if bored all of a sudden, her gaze falling on the stove again.

"Anyway," she said, "it's not even Islamic."

He felt himself growing agitated, and he momentarily forgot he was trying to impress her. "You think it's un-Islamic to stand up for the rights of your people?"

She met his gaze with her eyes narrowed, and Sharif felt as if she were stabbing him with her grimace. Hasna's nose flared, and he wondered what he had said to make her so upset.

"*Whose* people?"

The question was a dare, as if his last comment had been an affront.

"*Your* people." He felt the defensiveness swelling in his chest. Who did she think she was talking to him as if he were a child?

"Those," Hasna said with her lip upturned and her head nodded toward the living room where their fathers' voices rose in laughter, "are *not* my people."

Sharif grew silent, and his disapproval must have shown on his face. He drew his eyebrows together. "What?"

"*My* mother," Hasna said as if she held a status several grades higher than Sharif and his siblings, "is not from this country."

Distracted by her claim, Sharif was unable to properly address the outrage he had felt at her insinuation. He started to say something in retort but was reminded of Hasna's mother Mona, his mother's good friend.

Hasna was right. Mona was not American. She was Pakistani.

Sharif was so accustomed to Mona's presence and her natural completion to the familial atmosphere that he often forgot that she had a background wholly different from him and his parents, and even from her own husband and children. Mona's pale olive skin and hazel eyes were a sharp contrast to the brown skin and ebony eyes of Sharif's family.

"Most of the time, people just think I'm Asian anyway," Hasna added, and Sharif sensed this was a point of pride for her.

Hasna's last comment had been unsettling, but he didn't understand this feeling.

"People can hardly believe Iman is my sister." Hasna paused, glancing momentarily in the direction of the stairs that led to the room where her sister and Asma were sleeping. "*She's* Black. Not me."

There was an awkward silence as Sharif registered the implications of her last statement. "But isn't she partly Pakistani too?"

Hasna shrugged. "Technically, yes. But not to us."

For a moment, Sharif could only stare, this time seeing Hasna as more bizarre than beautiful. He had no idea what she had meant by "us."

"My mother can only bring me when she visits her family. They won't let her bring Iman."

There was a strained silence between them.

"Why not?"

Hasna wrinkled her forehead and studied Sharif as if seeing him for the first time. Apparently, he should have already known the answer to his question. "Do you think they want *everybody* to know who our father is?"

It was a rhetorical question. But Sharif was confounded. Sister Mona's family didn't know Brother Karim? Why would it matter if they did?

Sharif had heard these sentiments expressed concerning interracial relations among Americans, but he had never heard of them amongst people of color themselves, and certainly not amongst Muslims.

She shrugged. "Anyway, it's better this way. For now, they just think our father's American."

Sharif creased his forehead. "He is."

At that, Hasna looked at him with a smirk growing on her face, too humored to correct his misunderstanding.

"Um…" she said, a grin still playing at one side of her mouth, "not really."

It took several minutes of tormented confusion for Sharif to understand. When he finally did grasp Hasna's meaning, he was deeply wounded. He felt more acutely his imperfections, imperfections that now went far beyond his attire.

The heat of the kitchen warmed his face and he found himself staring at the timer again, this time less conscious of its descending numerals than of his descending value, in Hasna's eyes and his own.

At that moment, he had wondered at Iman, whom his mother often doted on. Nadirah would squeeze the child's cheeks, cooing, *"Aw, you little cinnamon cake. So cute, so cute."* Sharif had thought little of his mother's constant praises of the child. All children were cute, weren't they? But now he wondered if the attention was a charity of sorts, to make up for what Iman would be denied later in life, in her own family—because of her father's skin color, and hers. A tone that they shared with Sharif.

For a moment, Sharif doubted that Hasna was telling the truth. He couldn't imagine Sister Mona speaking like this.

"Did your mother tell you that?" It was open skepticism, the only thing he could think to use in Brother Karim's defense, and his own.

She laughed and rolled her eyes, shaking her head a moment later at Sharif's naïveté. "Of course not."

He started to ask who had then, but something told him to hold his tongue. He had a lingering feeling that he had happened upon something so private, something so unflattering in its authenticity, that not even Hasna herself, let alone Sharif, should be privy to it.

Presently, Sharif watched with distant emotion as the fading headlights of a passing car created a distorted spotlight that moved and stretched across the ceiling of his dark room, stealing its presence through the sheer curtains that hung on the window opposite his bed.

What would he say to Hasna tomorrow? To Brother Karim? They had invited him to lunch and planned to discuss the upcoming wedding over the meal.

At the thought, Sharif felt suffocated. Could he really go through with the marriage?

Did he even want to?

The last question disturbed him.

Often he had doubted that he was worthy of someone like Hasna, and he wondered if he even had the ability to make her

41

happy. Before he had even left the States, there was little he could offer his fiancée. Even though he had obtained his undergraduate degree, he had no idea what he would, or could, do with it. At the time, Hasna had completed her degree in political science from American University, and her heart was set on becoming a lawyer.

After receiving his acceptance letter to study in Riyadh, Sharif had, in childlike innocence, asked Hasna if they could marry before he left, and if she would accompany him overseas.

"I can't live in a country like that." Her face was contorted as she shook her head, having not even given his inquiry a moment's consideration.

His heart was crushed. He had been restless with sleeplessness for three full nights before he had mustered enough courage to even present the idea to her. He had imagined the trip would not be so overwhelming if he could have his wife with him. But even if she wouldn't be able to accompany him, he had figured, at least she would be thrilled to finally be married and "really together," something for which she had said she was growing hopelessly impatient.

"If you want to go *there*," she spoke as if the mere mention of the Kingdom's name was loathsome, "you'll just have to wait for me. There's nothing for me there."

In the weeks he spent preparing for the trip, Sharif had grown pensive. Her last words would not leave his mind, or heart.

There's nothing for me there.

Not even *me*?

Two

"The Golden Age of *Islam*?" Sharif remembered the professor saying as the man furrowed his brows and studied the student briefly.

The three of them had been sitting in a small restaurant in Madinah months after Sharif had arrived in Riyadh. It had been his first trip to the Blessed City, where they had traveled after performing 'Umrah.

Sharif was accompanied by Dr. Mashal, a professor of English at a private university in Riyadh who was also a friend of one of the professors at the Islamic university, and Earl, a burly, freckled red-head first-year student at the Islamic university who was originally from Kentucky, where he had accepted Islam when he was fifteen.

Earl had made a comment challenging what he saw as a "Saudi version of Islam." It was a friendly debate, but Sharif could tell that Earl, like Sharif himself, was skeptical of what he saw as a longing for the past when Muslims should be looking toward modernization.

Sharif had remained quiet although Earl's sentiments had mirrored his own at the time, but the comment made Sharif wonder about Earl's motivations for studying in the Kingdom. Sharif himself had agreed to study in Riyadh only because it would give him the necessary Arabic language and Islamic history background needed for his imam position. Even his mother had been apprehensive because she feared that Sharif would be influenced by the very version of Islam that his classmate was challenging.

"If we have to be locked into the Islam of the past," Sharif's father had said once, *"what are we striving for in the present? To live in the past?"* His father had laughed, shaking his head. *"Then what about the Golden Age of Islam in history? Was that not the height of Islamic progress? And why can't we have that again, in our own time?"*

"Is that your proof of how Islam may evolve and improve?" Dr. Mashal took a sip of coffee from the small white glass cup that bore no handles, as was the traditional way to drink Saudi coffee, his eyes resting on Earl.

"It's one of them," Earl said after a thoughtful pause.

The professor lowered the small cup and nodded as if reflecting on the youth's response. There was a brief silence as he took another sip of coffee before setting it next to a plate of dates. When he spoke, his voice was reserved and gentle but held authority and wisdom that mirrored his age.

"When we speak of the earliest Muslims as being the best generation, son," he said, his thick, graying eyebrows gathering momentarily, "we too speak of a Golden Age of Islam."

The sound of the restaurant door opening as a customer left filled the quiet of his pause.

"But we speak of the gold in their hearts," Dr. Mashal said. "Not in their lifestyle, worldly accomplishments, or geographical borders."

He took another sip of coffee before he spoke again.

"This is the Islam we wish to emulate. Whatever evolution or improvement we can make upon other than that is fine, and even commendable."

He paused again before adding, "But you can never improve upon their spirituality or understanding of the Islamic faith itself. This is what makes them superior to us of later generations. Our greatest hope lies in coming close to mirroring those *hearts*. But we will never mirror them in truth, at least not as a generation.

"No Golden Age in history can contend with the gold that lay in their breasts, son. And don't let anyone, no matter how knowledgeable or studied, tell you any differently.

"If they do," he added, "they do not understand Islam."

Sharif lay awake pondering this conversation of years ago. He felt himself begin to drift to sleep as his exhaustion after the long trip began to take its toll. His last thoughts before his eyelids grew heavy were of his mother warning him to stay true to himself, and of having, perhaps, lost Hasna in being unable to heed his mother's advice.

Hasna sat staring distantly through the windshield as the night's darkness closed around her, making her solitude more acute. Her car was parked in front of the dimly lit coffee house, its frosted windows hiding from view whoever had stopped in although Hasna could make out the faint silhouettes of customers who sat near the glass.

"I'm gonna make you love me," the Supremes wailed soulfully from the car's speakers. "Oh yes I will. Yes I will..." the singer insisted with a confidence that was a sharp contrast to the anxiety that was tightening in Hasna's chest.

Before today, Hasna had told herself that the distance she was feeling from Sharif was due to their physical separation, not due to any change of feelings on his part, or hers. Granted, his occasional e-mails and half-hearted phone conversations had disintegrated into two-line messages and two-minute calls once a month, but whenever Hasna complained, Sharif had said that he had a lot on him at the university. And because Hasna did not want to believe any differently, she had accepted his excuse and resigned herself to patience until they could be together when he returned.

Hasna never liked the idea of his leaving in the first place. But her father, and the rest of the community it seemed, had been delighted at the opportunity. She understood their excitement, and their rationale even. But that didn't mean she shared their sentiments. To her, it wasn't necessary for Sharif to go abroad to "qualify" as an imam. Yes, he was young, and it was true that the growing Muslim community in the area was becoming increasingly competitive and multiethnic. Now, very few masjids were headed by imams who were not fluent in Arabic or had not completed at least some official Islamic studies overseas. So it made sense that the former imam would suggest that Sharif acquire the Arabic language and an Islamic studies degree.

It was selfish of her, Hasna knew, to want anything different for Sharif. But she was angry with Imam Rashad for arranging the trip. From the beginning, she had had a gut feeling that something would go wrong. But because she didn't entirely understand this intuition, she had remained silent. It was all she could do to keep from complaining. She and Sharif had waited long enough. Why would the community impose another six years on them, and from so far away?

"I love you," Hasna had said to him the last time they talked weeks before he returned to the States. It was how she normally ended their conversations.

"You too" was his customary response. But it had always been like that, even when they were college freshmen, at the beginning of their relationship.

But this time, there had been a long pause, as if he were unsure whether to say anything at all. The silence was so complete that Hasna had momentarily thought the line was disconnected.

"You too," he said finally, and Hasna heard him clear his throat a moment before he made some excuse to get off the phone.

It hadn't always been like that.

The two words stayed in Hasna's mind, forming a painful place for themselves there. She let the words repeat themselves and she studied them each time, as if in them lay some clue as to where Sharif's heart now lay, or perhaps where it had lain all along.

Was it possible that his hesitation in uttering the three words that had come so naturally to her was due to doubt of his feelings and not to the shyness that Hasna had always attributed to him?

His natural reserve had been the ever-present excuse that Hasna offered herself for his lack of affection and open interest in her.

The sudden humming vibration of a car's engine halting next to her vehicle distracted Hasna from her thoughts. She exhaled in relief. Her best friend had finally arrived.

Hasna had hated to disturb her friend, especially so late at night, but this was not something she could discuss on the phone, at least not in her house. She had wanted more than anything to move into her own apartment, but her parents convinced her to remain at home until the wedding.

"It's better," her mother had said, as if that explained everything. But Hasna wanted her own space—*needed* her own space, especially now that she was getting married.

The law firm she worked for didn't offer her an enormous salary, but the annual forty thousand dollars she earned was only slightly less than what her father brought home from the college he worked for.

Having her own apartment tonight would have helped tremendously. She needed the confines of her own space to sort out her feelings and seek advice from the only person she felt she could trust with the fragility of her heart. With her own apartment, her friend would not have had to meet her at a coffee shop, and they both would have the privacy they needed to help her navigate this new problem.

Or perhaps it wasn't privacy that made Hasna insist on meeting at the late night shop that doubled as a bar for light drinkers. The request was likely equally due to shame. It would be utterly humiliating to have her parents or, worse, Iman overhear what Hasna feared would reveal the crumbling of a relationship that had been set in motion before Hasna or Sharif understood any complexities of the heart. Iman was only fourteen and was unlikely to comprehend the significance of the information even if she happened upon it, but Hasna was not willing to take the risk. Her little sister was turning into an annoying "Daddy's girl" and Hasna didn't want to give the child any tattle-tell details to help her draw closer to their father.

"Hey stranger!" Hasna heard the muffled voice through the driver's side window where her friend had suddenly appeared after tapping on the glass.

Betraying her true feelings, Hasna grinned and turned off the ignition, halting the music abruptly. Still beaming, she opened the door and climbed out the car. Immediately, she was pulled into a friendly embrace.

In the warmth of Vernon's arms, Hasna felt her throat close. The kind gesture was a stinging reminder that Sharif had denied her even this. For a full minute she laid her head against her friend's broad chest and let herself imagine that it was Sharif holding her.

"Oh, Tweetie," Hasna heard Vernon's deep voice above her head. "It'll be all right."

She loved when he called her Tweetie. It was a nickname he had given her while they were in law school together. He had said that her yellow skin and hazel eyes made him think of the cartoon character Tweetie Bird. Initially, the name had been a joke between them, but it soon became a term of endearment that stuck.

"Let's go inside."

Hasna started to respond but hesitated. She was saddened when Vernon loosened his embrace to lead her to the restaurant. Until that moment, she didn't realize how much she needed the physical comfort of a friend.

Vernon closed Hasna's car door that had been still hanging open, and he took the keys from her before pressing the button to lock the car. He put an arm around her and pulled her close to him and guided her to the entrance.

The dark maroon vertical blinds covering the glass door danced gently when Vernon pulled the handle. He stepped back, releasing Hasna momentarily to let her inside before him. Instantly, Hasna relaxed in the intoxicating sound of Marvin Gaye singing "Mercy Mercy Me."

Minutes later, Hasna sat across from her best friend at a private booth, the back of Hasna's chair creating a wooden wall between her and the next booth. With her back to the entrance, Hasna could see Vernon's imposing form outlined by the doors that read "Employees Only." It was an ideal location. No one was in the adjoining booth.

"So how's Kenya?" Hasna reached for the menu that lay on the table in front of her, unable to shake the awkward feeling that was overcoming her. Hasna had always thought fondly of Vernon's personable, former-marine fiancée, but tonight was the first time Hasna envied her.

Like Vernon, Kenya was eye-catching. Due to her years in the military and exercise regiment she maintained afterward, Kenya sported an attractive muscular form that accented the rich brown skin tone that she shared with her boyfriend. Hershey was Kenya's nickname, and Hasna never felt the need to ask why Vernon had chosen the name. Hasna understood its aptness when she first met the woman months after her and Vernon's friendship developed in law school. Kenya really was the color of milk chocolate, and her smooth complexion made the name all the more fitting.

But they were an odd couple, Hasna couldn't help thinking. Vernon's six-foot bulky, former college-linebacker build and shiny bald head made for an intimidating frame next to Kenya's five-foot slender-yet-thick physique that was made all the more exotic by her mass of henna-dyed locks that hung to the middle of her back.

"She's good," Vernon said as he casually skimmed his own menu. "She says to tell you hello." He chuckled. "And to not let Sharif stress you too much."

"She knows you're meeting me here?"

Vernon met Hasna's gaze with his brows furrowed, a grin teasing one corner of his mouth. "Why? Are you thinking of dumping your lousy fiancé and replacing him with a real man?"

Hasna laughed beside herself. "Yeah right. And how will Kenya feel about that?"

"I didn't say anything about me," he teased. "I just asked if you were replacing him with a real man."

Hasna shrugged, a bit surprised by the sudden warmth in her cheeks. "Well, honestly, you're the only real man I know."

Although Hasna chuckled at her last comment, Vernon's expression changed to concern. He was quiet as he studied Hasna.

"Tweetie," he said, waiting for her to meet his gaze. "What's going on?"

Hasna drew in a deep breath. She couldn't look at him for too long, not without getting distracted.

Where should she begin? At the beginning of her and Sharif's relationship, when she should have seen the fault lines? Or when he left America to—

"Good evening," a perky voice interrupted her thoughts. Hasna turned to see a smiling, thin redhead with a hair bun held in place by two pencils, one which the woman removed in preparation to write. "My name is Bobbi, and how can I make this evening special for you two?"

"We'll take two Cappuccino Ice Houses with extra whipped cream," Vernon said, saving Hasna the need to respond. "And house fries topped with cheese and peppers."

Bobbi scribbled something on her pad. "Is there anything else you'd like?"

"No, thank you."

"Tonight we do have a house special with—"

"Thank you," Vernon said with a polite smile that told Bobbi what they really wanted. "That'll be all."

"Right," she said, flashing a smile. "You two have a good night."

"What happened?" Vernon asked once the server had disappeared back-first into the swinging doors of the kitchen behind his seat.

Hasna sighed thoughtfully. "I guess it's not what happened so much as what did *not* happen."

Vernon smiled. "Speak English, Tweetie. I'm a lawyer, but that doesn't mean I understand two languages."

She laughed. "I'm sorry. I guess what I'm saying is..."

It took twenty minutes for Hasna to recount Sharif's coldness at the airport earlier and their distant relationship prior to that.

Vernon was quiet and Hasna waited as he folded their menus and stacked them on the edge of the small table just as the server returned, perkier, with a large tray displaying their order.

"Two Cappuccino Ice Houses," she sang out, each glass making a thudding sound as she placed one before each of them. "Two orders of home fries..."

The aroma of the freshly fried potato wedges topped with melted cheese and jalapeño peppers teased Hasna's nostrils, reminding her that she hadn't eaten all day. She eyed the chocolate shavings atop the whipped cream adorning the cappuccino shakes, and she had to restrain herself from reaching for her glass right then.

"And..." Bobbi said as she artfully placed the napkin-wrapped silverware in front of them "...privacy." She shot Vernon another smile before winking at him and disappearing a second later.

"Tell me something," he said once Bobbi rounded into the kitchen again, this time carrying an empty serving tray. "Do you love him?"

The question took Hasna off-guard, and she forgot about the grumbling in her stomach. She felt her friend's resolute stare, but she focused on the utensils she was unrolling and setting before her.

"Summertime," a talented karaoke singer crooned from the restaurant's small platform that had suddenly become a stage, "and the living is easy..."

"Yes," Hasna said softly, feeling her heart pound at the confession. She still could not look Vernon in the eye. She felt so weak and pathetic with her heart laid so bare although it made no sense for her to feel so humiliated. Wasn't it only natural for a woman to love her fiancé? And Hasna had known Sharif before she had known herself. He was so much a part of her that she could barely recall anything in her own life that didn't include him in some way. But Hasna knew that it wasn't the truth of her words that disturbed her, but the answer to the question that she knew was coming next.

"Does he love you?"

Hasna shook the white cloth napkin and laid it across her lap before reaching for the iced drink and removing the paper from the edge of the straw. She took a sip, then another, before responding as honestly as she could.

"I don't know."

She was surprised at the even confidence in her tone, as if she were not expecting to break down any moment. She even met Vernon's gaze and did not blink as his eyes reflected kindness, empathy, and concern.

"Is this seat taken?" Vernon had asked on the day they had first met. It was Hasna's first day as a law school student and already she had felt isolated and alone in the lecture hall. Apparently, everyone else had known each other in undergrad. Hasna didn't want to believe there was something inherently flawed about her that inspired other students to keep their distance.

"No," she had muttered, a bit uncertain at the sudden kindness in such a cold, unfriendly atmosphere.

"You mind if I sit here?"

"No," she said again, this time noticing just how handsome he was. And just like that, he was all smiles, as if it were the most natural thing in the world to befriend an outcast. He took a seat next to her and had never left her side since.

But that was a lifetime ago, it seemed—before Hasna had known her life would wind up so hectic and confused.

Even with Vernon's constant companionship, Hasna had often wondered if she'd made the right decision choosing law school over her heart. It tore at her that she wasn't by Sharif's side when he needed her most. She could only imagine the anxiety and stress he was experiencing in a foreign country, and it only aggravated her own anxiety to know that his experiences were worsened by feelings of loneliness and abandonment.

Before Sharif had asked Hasna to join him overseas, he had never asked anything of her. And Hasna knew Sharif well enough to know that he had stressed compulsively before even posing the question.

Then why had she refused him without forethought or consideration?

It was true that she had no desire to live in such a restrictive environment as she imagined Saudi Arabia to be. She could not erase from her mind the sullen images of women weighed down by dull black sheets that hid even their faces from view. She imagined the women to be scurrying along the marketplaces quickly for fear of being struck violently by religious police. That these people claimed Islam made the image even more repulsive. She had never even covered her own hair except to pray, and she had no desire to restrict herself beyond that. How could Sharif imagine that she would be willing to live in such a rigid culture — ever?

Naturally, over the years, her thoughts had matured to realize that her image of the Kingdom was obscure, if not exaggerated and stereotypical. In law school, she was surprised when a professor spoke fondly of his years spent as a youth in Jeddah, where he graduated from high school and had formed many friendships, even amongst Saudis. And the professor was Gnostic. When she had approached him after class one day and asked about his experience in the Kingdom, he had laughed when she shared her own impression.

"No," he had said, shaking his head, still chuckling at her words. "It's not like that at all."

He added, "My wife and I hope to return there one day. We think it's a much better environment for our children."

The warmth of Vernon's fingers nestling hers brought her back to the present.

"Hasna?"

At the sound of Vernon's deep voice saying her name, Hasna focused her attention back to her best friend.

"Let me tell you something," he said, "honestly."

She drew her eyebrows together curiously, but before she could say anything, he spoke.

"I love you."

The words were so matter-of-fact, so honest, that her heart fluttered until she felt the warmth of her friend's affection permeate every part of her. Even if for only this moment, Hasna wished she was Kenya. Then she could be honest with him too.

She dropped her gaze shyly, unaccustomed to such open flattery.

"To me," he went on, squeezing her hands in his, "you're more than a friend. You're like a sister to me." He paused and waited for Hasna to look at him again. "Or a wife."

Hasna's eyes widened slightly. She didn't know how to respond. She parted her lips, but Vernon spoke instead.

"This is honestly how I feel. After Kenya, you're the closest person to my heart."

For reasons Hasna was not able to admit, the words *After Kenya* disappointed her deeply. But she wasn't ready to face the reason for this deep hurt.

"It's something I tell Kenya all the time. I'm just sorry I never told you."

"Why are you sorry?"

Now Vernon averted his eyes, but he tightened his grip on Hasna's hands. "Because I didn't want to come between you and Sharif."

"But how could you come between us when you have Kenya?"

He shook his head. "With me and Kenya, it's different. I tell her everything, and she tells me everything. From our past experiences, we understand how complex love is. Just because you love someone and want to spend the rest of your life with them doesn't mean you'll never have feelings for someone else."

"Here we are, the two of us together," the restaurants speakers now played the mellow tune as if mocking Hasna and Vernon, "taking this crazy chance to be all alone. We both know that we should not be together…"

Instinctively, they let go of each other's hands and sipped their shakes in silence.

"Kenya doesn't get jealous?" Hasna chuckled, unsure what was more awkward, the conversation or the song "Secret Lovers" playing in the background.

"Of course she gets jealous. And I get jealous too. Just like I have you, Kenya has close male friends who she needs to talk things through with."

Absentmindedly, Hasna nodded, now toying with a potato wedge between her thumb and forefinger, twisting the cheese around it in a spiral. She pondered the weightiness of his words as she lifted the warm piece to her month. She savored its seasoning as she admired the beauty of Vernon's and Kenya's open honesty — and trust. Yet, here she was, at almost ten thirty at night and neither her family nor her fiancé knew where she was, and likely had no idea she had gone anywhere in the first place.

"I envy you," she said finally. "I wish I could have what you and Kenya have."

"And I envy what you and Sharif have."

Hasna laughed. "And exactly what is there to envy?"

"He has you," Vernon said as he pulled his plate of home fries closer to him. "And a day doesn't go by that I don't wish it were me instead."

Three

Minutes before Sharif's plane had made its final descent to the Dulles airport, Sharif was looking out the small window next to his seat gazing distantly at the miniature winding roads, houses, and greenery. Ant-sized cars moved steadily along the roads, reminding Sharif of the toy cars he once played with when he was a boy.

"You'll ruin him," Nadirah would often complain.

Sharif's father would chuckle, give his wife a quick peck on the cheek, and say, "You're just a worrier."

His father took him everywhere. "This is my son," his dad would say in a way that made Sharif feel so proud that he found it difficult to keep from smiling. Whenever his mother would complain of how his father spoiled him, Sharif's father would give him a "man-to-man" talk about women and how to deal with them.

"Your mom," his father would explain, shaking his head as he drove. "She's just worried about you. That's how all women are, but you'll learn that soon enough." All the while, his father's eyes remained on the road, occasionally glancing at his son to make sure Sharif understood. "You just gotta let 'em worry." His father would smile. "But don't let it get you worrying." A laugh. "Your mom, you see, she worries about everything, but you just look out for her and love her for it. That's all you can do."

Each time that Sharif and his father went out, Sharif wanted a new toy car, and whenever he had the money, Sharif's father would get one for him. If his father was ever short of money, he would tell his son, "Don't worry, I'll get that one for you soon enough." And surely, as he said, he would buy the car, even if Sharif himself had forgotten about it. Sharif's collection of cars grew so huge that he had a special toy box for his cars alone. Often, Sharif would ask for a car simply because he knew he could get it though there were times that he did not care either way.

However complacent Sharif was about actually purchasing a particular car, his cars were his treasure nonetheless.

But they were also his source of getting in trouble with his mother.

At home, he played with his cars all day, and when his father returned home from work, they would play with the cars together, sometimes until dinnertime, which often upset Sharif's mother.

Although Sharif preferred the "Go-car-go" game with his dad — it was so much fun watching the cars skid off the hardwood floors and up against the walls and hearing them crash back down — he knew how to enjoy his cars alone too.

As loud and boisterous as his voice would allow, Sharif would roar through the halls, running the wheels of the small cars up and down the walls. His mother's protests only encouraged him, because he knew that after she yelled at him three times, his father would come to his aid.

"Let him be, Nadirah." His father would wave his hand, a half smile on his face as he gently squeezed his wife's shoulder to calm her. "He's a boy."

Sharif pretended that he did not hear, roaring more loudly as his father reasoned with his mother. "Vrooooom!"

"Yes, he's a boy, Dawud, but these are my walls."

If it were not the walls that she was complaining about, it was the dining room table, the kitchen sink (where Sharif gave his cars a "car wash"), the hardwood floors, or the plant soil (Sharif's favorite: After a nice "car wash" it was always neat to see how the dirt from the plant pots stuck to his cars. It made them look real rough, just how Sharif liked them).

"I'm so tired of you saying that," his mother had complained once. Sharif still remembered how her voice rose that day.

"Nadirah," his dad reasoned, chuckling between his words, "he *is* a boy."

"He's eight years old, Dawud. He's *not* a boy."

Another chuckle. "Nadirah —"

"No, Dawud, this is *not* funny."

The rectangle glow from the slightly open door disappeared as the door shut.

"Vrooooom!" Crash. *Go-car-go*. Craaaash!

"I'm so tired of you being so, so, so...careless." His mother's voice was shaking, Sharif could tell, even though it was muffled somewhat by the closed door. He could see moving shadows beneath the door.

Carwash. The idea came to him suddenly as he grabbed a handful of cars and hurried downstairs to the kitchen, dropping some on the stairs along the way. Sharif's heart was pounding wildly as he turned on the faucet full blast until the clear water appeared white as it made a rhythmic pounding against the metal sink.

Sharif fumbled through the cabinet under the sink in search of the dishwashing liquid.

"...so spoiled that we can't even..." His mother's voice wafted through the vent.

Ah, there it is, behind the box of trash bags.

"Why do you..."

He placed the stopper in the drain and squeezed the bottle until the entire bottom of the sink was covered in the blue liquid. As the white suds grew into small mountains, Sharif dropped his cars into the water and moved them about, splashing the water with them.

Footsteps.

Sharif's heart pounded. Was he in trouble? He quickly turned off the water, removed the stopper, and shook the suds from his hands as the footfalls approached. Why, he did not know, but he ran under the kitchen table, hoping his parents had not heard the screeching sound of the chair legs, which would reveal his hiding place.

Two pairs of legs passed the kitchen doorway.

"Nadirah," his father pleaded. There were no signs of laughter in his voice.

Slowly, Sharif moved forward and peered from behind a chair into the living room where his parents were.

His father was holding his mother's arm. "Please."

She yanked her arm free of his grip and grabbed her keys from the coffee table. "Dawud, just leave me alone." His mother was crying.

Crying?

But why?

Sharif's heart sank as the realization hit him.

His cars.

"Nadirah, just sit down and we can talk."

"I'm tired of talking, Dawud. You don't listen anyway." She sniffled. "All you do is laugh, and it's not funny." Her voice was high-pitched and whiny. "I'm trying to raise this boy to appreciate things and be grateful, and all you do is just give him whatever he wants. I'm tired of it."

"Nadirah," his father reasoned in a low tone, conscious that his son was likely in earshot, "let's just sit down and talk about this."

"Why, Dawud?" She turned and glared at her husband, her eyes gleaming with tears. "So you can just laugh at me? Or are you going to—"

"*Sharif*," Dawud said in a loud whisper, reminding his wife that their son could likely overhear. The sound of his name sent Sharif's heart pounding, and he drew back a bit.

"—sit here and tell me the same old story. That you hardly knew your father and you want to be a good father to him? That you want show him the love you never got? Or that we can't let being poor stop us from getting our son nice things? Well, wake up, David," she said, reverting to his English name, as she often did when she was upset. "Wake up! We don't *have* money to blow on some stupid toy cars that sit in that boy's room like he's Richy Rich. Good lord, Dave, he doesn't even have a proper bed! But no, no, he's got *cars*! Is that supposed to help us pay the car note, the mortgage, or all those silly bills you never bother to open because Sharif wants another car?"

"Now, that's not fair."

"Oh it's fair, it's fair."

"You know just as well as I do that buying those ninety-nine-cent cars don't put a hole in our budget."

"After you buy a million of 'em, it does!"

"Nadirah, please."

She started toward the door.

"Where do you think you're going?"

"I don't care."

"But I do."

"I don't!"

He held out his hand. "Give me the keys."

The keys jingled as she pushed them far into her pant pocket and slipped on her shoes.

"Give me the keys," he told her, raising his voice.

She opened the door, left, and shut it behind her. Dawud quickly opened the door and rushed to catch his wife. A moment later Sharif heard the car start and pull away.

Silence.

Sharif sat motionless under the table and stared without blinking at the front door that remained ajar. He cautiously swallowed as a lump developed in his throat. How long he sat there, he had no idea, but it felt like years.

Had his parents left for good?

Panic engulfed him.

Blinking, he swallowed again, and he slowly emerged from under the table.

I'll give the cars back, he made a promise to himself. *I won't play Go-car-go ever again.*

Mom!

Sharif walked slowly to the front door and stood at the screen door. Somewhere a dog barked. Sharif felt his eyes moisten but made no effort to "be a man." He could barely lift his arms out of weakness. In helpless surrender, Sharif leaned his head against the cold screen and felt the tears well and slip down his cheeks. Seconds later, his shoulders shook, and he heard a whimper escape his throat. The sound was awkward and familiar, and it was all he could to do withstand the aching in his heart.

But it hurt *so* much.

Sharif wiped the tears away with the back of his hand. He would be strong. He would be strong.

He had already made his mommy mad with his cars; he could at least make his daddy proud by behaving like a man.

His small shoulders shook under the heaviness in his chest. He fought the tears that demanded release. But they resisted.

Sharif's sobs became so horrible that it was difficult to imagine that the sounds were actually coming from him.

Outside the sun was setting. Soon it would be dark. Already, he could hear the crickets chirping, and he saw an occasional glow of lightning bugs in his un-mown yard. Usually, he and his father would run through the dandelions after the blinking lights, and catch them and let them tickle their palms and fingers until they flew away—or until Sharif's mother reminded them to mow the lawn before it got too late.

In the distance, a silhouette approached.

Mom?

As it came closer, Sharif became more hopeful. Then he realized that his parents had driven—not walked. Quickly, he closed the door.

Inside, he collapsed on the living room couch and cried even more. He had really messed up this time, worse than when he wrote really big on his homework paper to make his teacher think he wrote a lot of pages. A lot worse.

Outside, the screen door opened.

Sharif sat up. Why was somebody at the door? He tiptoed to the front window and parted the curtains slightly and peered out. There was no car in the driveway.

Before he could rush to the door and lock it, the door opened. His jaw trembled. He was uncertain how he should handle the intruder. In panic, he thought to run, but before he could, the person spoke.

"*As-salaamu-alaikum.*" His father was too engulfed in his own thoughts to notice his son's frightened expression at his greeting.

Sharif forced a smile to mask the fear that hammered in his chest.

He noticed the stains of sweat on his father's shirt, and the musty scent of outside filled the small living room. It was then that Sharif knew what his father had been doing.

"Where is she?" Sharif's heart pounded until he felt the throbbing in his throat.

Dawud smiled and rubbed Sharif's head, but the gesture seemed to exhaust Sharif's father. "Don't worry, son. She's fine."

"But where is she?"

It seemed like years before his father said anything.

When Dawud finally spoke, he gave Sharif the most memorable "man-to-man" talk that they would have.

That night Sharif learned about the serious condition his mother was suffering, a condition that required the combined patience of not only Sharif's father, but of Sharif too. This condition, his father explained, caused his mother (and all women afflicted with it) to behave erratically.

Doctors called the ailment "pregnancy."

Naturally, Sharif was terrified for his mother. He had heard of this affliction but had no idea what it was and what it did. Sharif's father assured him that, however strange and scary it all was, it was nothing to worry about. He told Sharif that his mother would return that night, apologize—after she had had enough of her mother—say she loved them both, and everything would be normal again.

Sharif was not convinced.

But sure enough, late that night, she did return, apologize, and tell them that she loved them. But for some reason, things never felt normal again. And having a baby boy arrive four months later did not make it any easier.

And Sharif would always regard Wali suspiciously, wondering how "the condition" had affected his little brother.

May Allah give you children just like you. These were the words that played over in Mona's mind just before she had gone to bed next to her sleeping husband the night before.

It was after one o'clock in the morning when she had stood in her night robe waiting in the living room, having halted her pacing at the sound of keys turning in the door. She crossed her arms over her chest and forced herself to remain calm, even as anger and relief gripped her at once. In the last hour, she had imagined that something terrible had happened to her daughter. She hated to disturb Nadirah so late at night, but she really needed to know if Hasna was with Sharif. Even when Nadirah told her that her son was alone and asleep in his room, Mona could not relax until she spoke to Sharif directly.

Her heart sank when Sharif had come to the phone groggy. No, he hadn't spoken to Hasna since he had seen her at the airport. Was everything okay, he wondered? Yes, yes. She's just gone to the store or something, Mona had said before getting off the phone.

But she hadn't been able to sleep after the call. She didn't think it wise to wake her husband and alert him. He would probably think she was overreacting, or, worse, begin worrying too.

This one she had to battle alone. At least until she was absolutely sure that something *was* wrong.

She had given in and considered waking her husband to have him call the police when she heard what she thought was a car turning into the driveway. But she continued pacing the living room, mind racing frantically, wondering what she'd do if it weren't Hasna's car.

Then she heard keys turning in the door.

"Where have you been?" Mona exploded, startling Hasna as she tried to slip unnoticed into the house.

When Hasna's eyes met her mother's, Hasna rolled her eyes. "Mom, please. I'm not in the mood. It's really late."

"Yes, I can see that. That's precisely my point."

"I know what time it is." Hasna kicked off her shoes and adjusted her purse on her shoulder.

"I'm your mother." Mona stepped closer to her daughter and pointed a finger at her, trying not to raise her voice louder than she already had. But seconds later she heard movement, and Iman, in her long cotton night gown, appeared at the top of the stairs with a look of sleepiness and worry on her face.

"Mommy?"

"Everything's okay, sweetie. You can go back to bed."

At that moment, Iman noticed her sister fully dressed and tossing her shoes on the rack. Iman seemed fully awake suddenly. "You're just getting home?"

Mona could tell the question was due more to shock than any desire to interrogate Hasna, but Mona cringed, knowing that Hasna would take offense.

"Iman, mind your business and go to bed like your mommy said."

The words were said sarcastically, and Mona didn't appreciate the way the remark had insulted her too. "Don't talk to your sister like that."

Hasna groaned and rolled her eyes as she passed her mother and started up the steps, the sweet scent of perfume lingering behind her.

Iman was still staring at her sister in confusion when Hasna pushed Iman out of her way, momentarily throwing Iman off balance. Iman had to catch herself by holding onto the banister to regain her posture.

"Hey! What was that for? I didn't do anything to you."

Ignoring her sister, Hasna disappeared down the hall and seconds later her room door slammed shut, its angry rattling echoing in the otherwise still house.

Iman looked to her mother, a question mark and hurt on her face as she was still recovering from her sister's brusque manner.

"Everything's okay, Iman." Mona wiped a hand over her face as she exhaled, relieved that Hasna was at least alive and well. "Your sister has a lot on her mind right now."

Currently, Mona stood peering out the kitchen window into the backyard, the morning's dishes piled in front of her. It was true that Hasna had a lot on her mind, she reflected, but it was not true that everything was okay.

The words of Mona's father spoken more than two decades ago assured Mona of that.

May Allah give you children just like you.

Simple words, really, Mona reflected as she now hugged herself in front of the window. She rubbed her arms as if the motion would somehow soothe her, and protect her from the fear of the prophecy unveiling itself in her life today.

Words, spat at a wayward daughter in a moment of anger, perhaps forgotten in the father's memory, yet— Mona thought of her daughter Hasna.

Mona lifted a plate from the sink and turned the stainless steel knob, and water rushed from the faucet in that motion. She felt tightness in her chest as she held the floral-trimmed glass plate beneath the clear-white stream, the hardened food loosening its grip on the dish in that moment.

Mona thought of her own flippant attitude as a teen, her complete disregard for what she saw as an overbearing, overprotective father, and her insistence on dating the American though it broke all cultural expectations and rules.

Even in the insobriety of rebellion against her family's "backward, FOB tradition," her father's angry prayer had been more terrifying to Mona than if he had cursed her outright.

And it terrified her even more today.

What if Allah answered that single supplication of an exasperated father calling out to his Lord? — even if he was a man who loved his prestige, his distinguished upper-class blood, and his six-figure income more than he loved his Lord or his religion.

The du'aa of the parent is answered.

Mona reached for the faucet's knob again, turning it, and the rush of water stopped suddenly. She started to stack the dishes on the counter next to the sink, the clinking a distant sound as the tightness in her chest squeezed her heart.

Was there any exception to this rule? *Could* there be any exception to words spoken by Prophet Muhammad himself?

"Sallallaahu'alayhi wa sallam , sallallaahu'alayhi wa sallam..."

As she opened the dishwasher, she whispered this supplication over and over again. It was something her mother would do whenever she was distressed, and right then it calmed Mona's anxiety. But not entirely.

The supplication asking for peace and blessings for Allah's Messenger made Mona wonder if she would be granted peace and blessings in her own life. Or if she deserved either.

She felt the familiar moisture welling in her eyes as her throat closed, her gaze on the dishes she was lining up neatly in the dishwasher.

"There are exceptions to this rule," an imam had told her once.

But right then Mona couldn't remember what those exceptions were. She remembered only leaving the masjid that day feeling hopeful and optimistic, only to, years later, return to feeling hopeless and despondent.

Mona remembered the sense of self-satisfaction she had felt, at least briefly, as she imagined that the prayer would not be answered because her father had been in the wrong at the time. He had no right to utter something like that to his daughter.

But that was before Mona understood that she herself had been wrong. And even if her father *had* been in the wrong, *Why worry about a prayer that promised nothing other than her future offspring mirroring her same innocence?*

At the time of her father's words, Mona was nineteen years old, a college sophomore and less religious than even her father at the time. At least he considered himself a Muslim, even if his lifestyle reflected only marginally that belief. But Mona did not use the word Muslim in connection to herself at the time, and she loathed hearing Pakistani friends and family remind her of Islam.

If it weren't for her having to identify herself with some ethnicity, she would not even have told others she was Pakistani originally. But it was a fact that she could not escape because of the constant inquiry, "But where are you from *originally?*"

Her aunts had said she was suffering from an "identity crisis," but Mona had felt that she was simply suffering.

This was more than two decades before September eleventh, but even at that time, Muslims, especially from "Eastern" countries, did not have an impeccable reputation in the American media. Honor killings, wife beatings, and women draped in all-black were the images that Islam evoked then. And Mona had been determined to escape every stereotype. She would not allow any impediment—even her own religion and family—to stand in her way of being a reputable doctor and a full American.

And she never did become a doctor. In fact, she never even made it to medical school. And although her blue passport suggested that she was fully American, she knew from her repeated painful experiences, especially after September eleventh, that her Western nationality too had eluded her.

She worried that Hasna was suffering from similar tragic dreams. But it was only Islam that Hasna was trying to escape, even as she wished to hold onto her Muslim identity.

"Are you a *scholar?*" Asma grinned at Sharif from where she sat across from him at the dining room table Sunday morning, a forkful of eggs poised midair as she eagerly awaited his answer. She looked younger than she had the day before at the airport when the white cloth framed her face. Her hair was now uncovered to reveal four frizzy braids, each bound by a pair of red-marble pony tail holders.

Sharif chuckled self-consciously and shook his head, reaching for the bowl of fruit salad that was in front of his brother before serving himself a heap. "No, not quite."

"Be he is an imam." Nadirah couldn't keep from smiling at her son from where she sat at an angle to him.

"Well…" He wasn't quite sure he was comfortable with that title either.

"Imam Sharif!" Asma chimed.

"Asma," Nadirah said, pointing her fork at her daughter, "don't talk with your mouth full."

Asma brought a hand to her mouth in embarrassment and giggled. After chewing her food and swallowing, she grinned at her brother again, waiting for him to meet her gaze. But he continued eating, ignoring her — on purpose, she knew.

"Imam Sharif!" she sang again.

"Asma," Wali grunted, "why don't you just shut up?"

"Wali." Nadirah narrowed her eyes in a warning.

"Sorry," he muttered. "But she is irritating."

"What are you so sour about?" Asma said.

"You." Wali glared at his sister.

"Wali, Asma," Nadirah said, "this is a *family* meal."

"So…" Sharif said, hoping to lighten the atmosphere, "what grade are you in now?" He was looking at Wali.

An amused smirk tugged at Wali's lips as he looked at his brother before squeezing syrup over his pancakes. "Grade?"

Sharif creased his forehead in concern. "Aren't you in school?"

"Wali graduated in June," Nadirah said.

His eyebrows rose. "Really?"

"Yeah, man. Where you been?" Wali shook his head, still smirking as he cut his pancakes with his fork.

Sharif really had been gone too long.

"What's your plan then?" he asked.

"What plan?"

"For a major. What do you want to study?"

"I wanted to do my own thing, but—"

"But you need an education first," Nadirah interjected.

"—Mom won't let me."

"Well," Sharif said, "a degree is important these days."

"But a business is more important."

"What business do you have in mind?"

"Real estate."

Sharif tried to picture Wali's smiling headshot in a real estate magazine. *Trust Wali Benjamin with your Real Estate needs.* No, Sharif couldn't picture it.

He wondered if Wali knew what the business would require of him.

"For starters," Nadirah said, "we're looking at a community college. That's our compromise. I hope after two years he'll be inspired to transfer to a university."

"Or be free to do what I want."

"What about you, Asma?" Sharif thought it wise to change the subject. "What grade are you in now?"

Asma glanced uncertainly at their mother. "I'm homeschooled."

"Really?" He looked at Nadirah.

"Well," Nadirah said, frowning at Asma, "this may be her last year."

"I thought you worked," he said to his mother.

"I do."

Sharif furrowed his brows. "Then how —"

"I'm not homeschooling her," Nadirah said, disappointment in her tone. "Mona is."

At the mention of his future mother-in-law, Sharif grew quiet momentarily. "Well, it's certainly better than public school."

"That's what I thought too." Nadirah shook her head regretfully, eyeing Asma.

Asma now sat with an elbow on the table and her head propped with a fist against her cheek. She was stabbing at her pancakes absentmindedly.

Apparently, Sharif had broached a sensitive subject. He didn't know what to say.

"But, Mom," Asma whined, "I'm almost finished."

"You certainly are."

Asma sighed and leaned back in her chair, folding her arms across her chest in frustration. But she didn't respond to her mother. This small show of defiance was already crossing the line.

Wali chuckled. "Asma's turning into a fundamentalist."

"Shut up, Wali," Asma snapped.

"You are." His eyes twinkled mischievously as he turned to Sharif, grinning. "We think she may be joining Al-Qaeda."

Sharif's eyebrows rose although he knew his brother was being facetious.

Asma's nose flared as she glared at her brother. "And *you're* turning into a *thug*."

Wali laughed. "Why, because I listen to rap music?"

A sly smile crept on his face. "You know, I think I'm going to buy you the latest Nas album. I think it'll change your mind about rap."

He slapped the palm of his hand against his forehead suddenly. "Oh, Asma. I'm sorry. How could I forget?" He looked regretful just then. "Music is *haraam*." He sang out the last word and wiggled his fingers at her as he said it.

Unable to stand it any longer, Asma pushed her chair back, the legs screeching against the wooden floor a second before she stormed out of the dining room, leaving her breakfast nearly untouched on the table. Sharif could hear her hurried steps as she retreated to her room.

Wali was still laughing to himself after they heard Asma's door slam.

"Wali," Nadirah said quietly, "that really wasn't necessary."

He threw up his hands in mock innocence. "Hey, it's not my fault she's joined Al-Qaeda."

"Enough." Nadirah's voice was raised authoritatively. "And I don't like you mentioning terrorists in connection to your sister, even if you're just joking."

"Sorry," he mumbled. But he was still chuckling as he picked up his fork to finish eating.

Sharif ate in silence, uncomfortable in the tense atmosphere. Although he did not show it, Wali's comments stung. They reminded him of his own dilemma—and presented a perspective he hadn't considered.

What if the masjid community refused to accept him as imam, especially once they realized that his views on Islam were different from theirs? He never imagined they would equate practicing Islam openly with being part of some extremist group.

In Riyadh, Sharif was so busy with school that he had been only vaguely aware of the post-9-11 propaganda against Muslims in the media. At the university, he had no television, but he had access to the Internet, where he would only skim the headlines when he signed into his e-mail account. But even from the little he was able to read, he could tell that his home was becoming a suffocating political environment for Muslims.

Before he was due to travel back to America this summer, he had stressed over the increased security in the airport. He was relieved when the trip was finally over and he was "off the radar" of non-Muslim airport security who would view his stay in Saudi Arabia and trips to Egypt with suspicion.

He had never considered that Muslims would regard him with the same distrust.

"Imam Rashad called this morning." Nadirah smiled in an apparent effort to focus on something positive. "He sends his greetings and asked if you could give him a call whenever you're over jet lag."

Sharif smiled. "I don't know if my body will ever forgive me for that long flight."

"I can't imagine." She shook her head. "I remember when your father and I went to Hajj. On the plane, I was thinking the whole time how I'd never do this again in life."

They both laughed.

"I had the same feeling," Sharif said, still smiling. "I don't understand how people do it every year."

"I don't either." Nadirah glanced at the clock on the wall.

"Get some rest though," she said, standing and beginning to clear the table. "I have some errands to run before your appointment this afternoon."

He creased his forehead. "Appointment?"

"Lunch at Brother Karim's."

Oh.

"Hopefully, I won't be long, but if I'm not back with the car, Karim said he could pick you up."

"No problem," Sharif said, betraying his true feelings.

"Oh yeah," Nadirah said, remembering something just then. "If you can talk some sense into Asma, I'd really appreciate it.

Ever since she's been going to Mona's, I feel like I don't know her anymore."

"Okay." But Sharif doubted he could be of any help.

An hour later, Sharif tapped his knuckles on Asma's room door and waited for a response. Asma didn't answer. When he knocked again and still received no reply, he called her name aloud.

"It's Sharif," he added, hoping she wouldn't feel threatened by him.

Sharif was about to return to his room when he heard the door being unlocked. A second later the handle turned and the door opened slightly.

"What?" Asma peered out, and although he could see only a fraction of her face, it was obvious to Sharif that she was still deeply hurt by what had happened earlier.

"Can I come in?"

There was a slight pause, as if Asma wasn't sure she should trust him. But seconds later the door opened, and Sharif stepped inside and Asma closed the door behind him.

The first thing Sharif noticed about Asma's room was the Barney bedcover and sheet. The purple monster smiled at him from his sister's crumpled bedding. Another stuffed Barney, the size of a kid's teddy bear, was lying on its side next to the pillow at the head of Asma's bed. The room's walls were painted purple, and Sharif had to stifle a grin as he remembered Wali's taunt, imagining just then the caption under Asma's name in a newspaper. *Al-Qaeda Member Has One Final Wish: Don't Hurt Barney.*

Asma picked up the stuffed purple monster with a green belly and held it close to her as she sat down on the edge of her bed.

Sharif sat down on the mattress next to her, unable to keep from grinning.

"Barney?"

Despite her sour mood, she smiled, though Sharif detected a hint of embarrassment in that expression.

He decided to leave her childhood friend alone.

"What's going on at Sister Mona's?"

Her pleasant expression immediately faded. "Nothing."

"Nothing?"

"Nothing important."

"Mom doesn't seem to agree."

She shrugged. "So what else is new?"

He was quiet momentarily. "What do you mean?"

"She never agrees with anything I do. That's what I mean."

"Never? That's a strong word."

"Well, almost never."

"Like what?"

Asma hesitated, and Sharif sensed she was trying to decide what was safe to say. "Like the music they listen to."

"You mean the Nas album Wali was talking about?"

"He was being sarcastic."

"I know that, but I was wondering if that's what's bothering you."

"Everything Wali does bothers me. He does it on purpose. It's not even funny."

Sharif nodded thoughtfully. "That's true. People shouldn't make fun of other people's beliefs."

She wrinkled her nose. "It's not other people's beliefs. It's *our* beliefs. We're all Muslim."

He pondered her words. "Ideally, yes."

"It's not ideal. It's true. We are all Muslim."

"That's not what I meant." He glanced at the clock on the wall, and Barney smiled back at him, the monster's right leg raised and left arm outstretched in some jolly dance move. But this smiling Barney had on what looked like rectangular sunglasses.

It took a second before Sharif realized the glasses were the result of someone coloring over the eyes in black marker.

"I mean," he said, "we *should* have the same beliefs as Muslims. But that's not the case."

"But that's not right. It's the same religion."

"But there are many kinds of Muslims."

"In the Sunnah, there's only one."

Sharif was silent at her last words. He didn't know how to respond. She was right. It was at this moment that everything began to make sense. Her hijab, Wali's taunts, their mother's concerns.

"Is this something you learned from Sister Mona?"

71

"No."

Taken aback, Sharif looked at her. "Then where did you learn it?"

"From Sister Irum."

"Who?"

Now Asma turned to Sharif, a confused expression on her face. "You don't remember Sister Irum? Imam Rashad's wife."

Yes, Sharif did remember her.

"Do you remember *anyone* anymore?"

He smiled, a bit self-conscious. "I guess I just need a reminder, that's all."

"Well, you better hurry up and get some reminders," she said, a half smile on her face. "I don't think they'll be happy to have an imam who doesn't even remember who they are."

"Does Sister Irum have classes at the masjid or something?" Sharif didn't like the tone of Asma's teasing, but he decided to ignore it. Perhaps, he was being too sensitive, as her words held a double meaning that Sharif knew was unintentional.

"No, she comes to Sister Mona's to teach us."

"Who else is in the class?"

"It's just me and Iman."

Sharif nodded. "Why does Mom want to take you out of the class then?"

Asma sighed and bit her lip, hugging the stuffed animal closer to her. "Like Wali said, they think I'm turning into a terrorist or something."

Sharif laughed. "I don't think so."

"I'm serious."

He shook his head. "Like you said, Wali was being sarcastic."

"That doesn't mean he doesn't believe what he said."

"Come on, Asma. Al-Qaeda?"

"Well, maybe not that part. But still..."

"I think what you mean is Mom doesn't agree with what you're being taught."

"But all she's teaching is Islam."

"Maybe so, but that's not how Mom sees it."

Asma's face crumpled in frustration. "So it's better for me to be around people who say God died on a cross while I have some

72

thug boyfriend than to be with someone saying I shouldn't listen to music?"

She rolled her eyes. "Now I see what Sister Irum meant when she said nowadays you have to do *da'wah* to *Muslims*."

Sharif grew quiet, remembering something he had learned in Riyadh. He had never thought about his own transformation in that way, but Sister Irum was right. And Sharif was living proof.

By the end of his third year abroad, which was his first year in the official Islamic studies program following his lessons in the Arabic language itself, he felt like a new Muslim. It was as if he were accepting Islam for the first time. Even the basic lessons on the difference between *emaan* and *kufr* were completely new to him. How could he have gone his entire life as a Muslim without knowing belief from disbelief? How could he have gone so many years without knowing even the foundation of the faith he claimed? Or even the minimum requirement to enter Paradise?

And how could he have gone so long without realizing he didn't know?

"But you can't blame people for not knowing, Asma," he said, glancing at his little sister's worried expression just then. "There's so much you still have to learn yourself."

"And that's what I'm trying to do. But Mom won't let me. To her, it's better if I learn that no religion is true and that homosexuals were born that way."

"Asma, don't speak like that. If you're truly learning about the Sunnah, then you'll know that your mother deserves more respect than that."

Asma did not respond. She lowered her head until her chin rested on Barney's soft head, and she sat reflecting for some time.

When Sharif looked at her, he saw that tears brimmed her eyes. In that moment, he felt aching in his own heart as he thought of how much he loved his mother, and how much it would hurt her when she learned that he too had changed.

But he could see no way around the pain. He was a different person now, a better person, he hoped. And why shouldn't he better when he now understood Islam better?

Before Sharif's studies, Islam had been *his* religion. Now, after his studies, it was Allah's.

Intuitively, of course, Sharif had always known that. But practically, he had not.

Islam is in the heart, he would tell himself, echoing his father's words. *You don't need to prove to anyone who you are. Allah already knows.*

Sharif sat in silence for several minutes before he put an arm around his sister, pulling her close to him in that moment. It was an awkward role for him, comforting his sister. It was something their father would have done. But their father had died when Sharif was fifteen.

Seconds passed in silence, and he heard Asma sniffle as she cried quietly next to him. But he willed himself not to become emotional himself.

"How was it when Dad was alive?"

Asma voice was small, barely above a whisper, and for a second Sharif doubted she had asked the question. He glanced at her, and he saw her looking up at him, eyes glistening as she wiped away a tear with the back of her hand.

Sharif drew in a deep breath and lifted his gaze to the window as he rubbed his sister's arm. "It was nice." He was silent as he recalled the day he thought his parents had left him.

He chuckled. "I remember the day I found out Mom was pregnant with Wali."

Tears still in her eyes, Asma smiled, and he met her gaze smiling too, moisture now warming his own eyes, but he fought the emotional display.

"Really?"

Sharif laughed to himself, mostly to keep the tears from coming. "Yes." His voice was thoughtful, distant. He drew in a deep breath as he smiled again at his sister a moment before he shared with her his memory of that day.

Asma's eyes lit up, and the tears were gone from her eyes when he finished. She was sitting up now.

"Really?" With one foot folded under her, she turned toward her brother as she held Barney on her lap, a grin forming on her face.

Sharif laughed. "Yeah. I had no idea what was going on."

Asma laughed too, shaking her head. "I remember him, but not so well."

They were quiet momentarily, thoughtful.

"Well," Sharif said, exhaling the word, "you were only three when he died."

"Almost four."

"I'm sorry," he said, smiling. "Yes, you were almost four."

At the reminder, a smile still lingered on his face, but Sharif felt his chest knot in the anxiety that he imagined would forever be associated with that terrible day.

"Is it true that Dad was the imam before Imam Rashad?"

Sharif nodded reflectively, and his voice lowered as he looked beyond Asma. "Yes, he was."

"Is that why you're going to be the imam now?"

He creased his forehead and looked at his sister, a bit taken aback by the question. "I don't think so."

"Sister Irum said you're going to teach everyone about true Islam."

"What?"

Asma grinned. "She said that's why they wanted you to go and study."

He sighed. "Oh, Asma. I don't know..."

"But you studied Islam, right?" Her voice was giddy in excitement. "And you know Arabic now?"

"Yes..." Sharif nodded and started to say something to explain that it wasn't that simple, but his sister's voice interrupted his train of thought.

"So you *are* a scholar." Asma smiled, a triumphant grin spreading over her face.

Four

"Do you have any idea, *any* idea what was in that bag?"

Javeria spoke through gritted teeth, her anger more palpable than any other time that Yasmin could remember. She pointed a finger at her daughter, who stood stark still, still wearing her school uniform as she stood in the living room of their home minutes after they returned from school.

Javeria herself still wore her black *khimaar*, the fabric now loosening from around her head. Her *abaya* lay in a bundle on the couch feet from them, where she had thrown it minutes before. Javeria's chin quivered, and Yasmin swallowed. Yasmin lowered her gaze slightly, too shell-shocked from all that had occurred to feel offended at her mother's finger pointing in her face.

"You think you know so much. You think you know what friendship is. Now you'll see that this has nothing to do with me or your father and our so-called strict rules or how we take Islam too seriously."

Javeria was alternating between English and Arabic and Urdu, as if even her mind couldn't decide which language was best to convey her fury. But Yasmin said nothing. She understood every word, and each pierced her heart. Each language shift was like a fresh attack, and Yasmin would feel the pain anew. Yet pain knew no language, and thus her suffering erected no barriers against any one.

"I tried to tell you to stay away from that family. All of those girls, in fact. But no, you knew better. 'They're my friends, Mom' you always said. But today, now," Javeria huffed, turning her back abruptly, "you'll learn who your friends are. And *Wallaahi*," she said, turning to face her daughter again as she swore by Allah, something she almost never did. In fact, she had taught her students not to swear by Allah, as an oath in His name should be uttered only when there was some great, dire need.

Yasmin shuddered as she recalled the supervisor tossing the filthy books and magazines on the desk of her office in front of Yasmin before saying this very oath. "*Wallaahi*, I would have never expected this of *you*."

At the sight of pictures, Yasmin's eyes had widened. She was utterly stupefied at what was before her. It took a full minute for Yasmin to even register what she was seeing. She had never in her life seen anything like it. She hadn't even known such filthy pictures existed. They were...*revolting*.

"Now tell me," the supervisor had said, a wicked smile on her face that Yasmin sensed was a triumph of some kind. Yasmin had shivered, her jaw trembling in terror of what was unfolding. "Where did you get these books?"

Javeria's eyes shone with tears as she shook her head at her daughter, defeated, as her daughter stood speechless before her. Javeria's voice was more subdued when she spoke again.

"*Wallaahi*," she said again, and Yasmin's throat closed at her mother's hurt, "you'll see that, after Allah, you have not one friend in that school except your own mother."

This was the memory that Yasmin nursed as she unpacked her bags in the quiet of her room. Her family had returned to their Riyadh villa the night before, but Yasmin had been too exhausted to unpack then.

Yasmin chewed at her lower lip as she recalled the look in Sommer's eyes when her taxi had arrived to take her back to the hotel.

"I don't like owing anybody," Sommer had said again. And this time Yasmin sensed the bitter resentment in her friend's tone. The darkness in Sommer's eyes warned Yasmin to never ask anything of her friend again. Whatever manner that Sommer planned to assist Yasmin with Sharif, it was going to be beyond what Sommer herself felt she owed, and it would be such that, after this, Yasmin could never feel justified in even thinking of Sommer again.

And that's what Sommer had wanted all along, Yasmin reflected as she stood to carry her hotel-laundered clothes to her bed, setting the small pile on the comforter. She unfolded the garments and smoothed them out with the flat of her hand in preparation to hang them in the closet.

Yasmin knew that Sommer was still blaming her for having been the very reason Sommer herself had graduated with an almost impeccable reputation — while Yasmin had been expelled from school, months before she was due to graduate from high school. It wasn't the flawless reputation that disturbed Sommer, but that Yasmin's selfless act had cemented it for her. She resented Yasmin for that.

Yasmin had finished her senior year quietly as a new student in a small private school that had opened only a year before and was housed in a cramped villa. When she graduated, there were only four other students in the ceremony. And none of them had she befriended. By then, even they had learned of Yasmin's reason for expulsion, and their parents had warned them to stay away from her. One student had studied her with a look of distant alarm whenever she saw her, as if trying to place Yasmin's seemingly innocent appearance with what lurked in her heart.

Experiences such as these made Yasmin realize how isolated she had been from the majority of Saudi society while enrolled at the private school. She learned that the nonchalance with which most girls at her school talked about boys, dating, and American movies and music, while shunning the open practice of Islam, was an anomaly in most other schools in the Kingdom. Although other schools were by no means flawless in the moral realm, the occurrence of such open rebellion against religious morality was rare, and frowned upon.

This knowledge made Yasmin that much more aware of just how horrific her bad judgment had been—and how far-reaching.

It wasn't long before nearly everyone in Yasmin's family's association heard of Yasmin's transgression, and a more distorted, incriminating version besides. But none of her parents' friends or family abandoned them amidst the slanderous rumors, and for that Yasmin was grateful. But the daughters dutifully kept their distance, and the sons' names gradually disappeared from all talk and hints of marriage to Yasmin.

What hurt Yasmin most though was that most close family and friends knew that she was innocent, yet still she was shunned. *It is wrong, I know,* her father had said once. *But to so many in our culture, honor is more important than truth.*

"And the sad thing is," Javeria had said to Yasmin a month later, the day that Javeria herself resigned and left the school. She and Yasmin were standing on the roof of the family villa just outside the small storage room, and Javeria was holding a tattered cardboard box she had used to pack the last of her belongings from school and Yasmin was holding another. "None of this had anything to do with you."

Javeria looked tired that day, spent, Yasmin imagined, from having been unsuccessful in clearing her daughter's name. "They knew all along whose bag it was. We all did. Even the girl's notebooks and pencil case were in there."

Yasmin wanted to ask why then had she taken the blame. But she couldn't speak. She hadn't uttered a word to anyone since the day of the confession. She heard her voice only in muttered whispers whenever she prayed. Other than that, her voice was dry, and she couldn't find her voice when she wanted to say something. Like now.

But if she could speak, she wouldn't speak about Sommer's bag. She would ask her mother how she was doing. And she would say she was sorry. And that she loved her, a great deal.

But the words got stuck in her throat.

"Nadhaam, Nadhaam..." Javeria said, waving her hand dismissively, her face contorted as she imitated how the administration had responded to her. *School policy, school policy. We punish the one who confessed.*

"Oh, Yasmin," she sighed. "I couldn't say whose bag it was. So all I did was make excuses for you."

Javeria set the box down and glanced out at the houses with lights glowing from windows in the night. She sighed as she leaned forward to open the storage room door. She had to pull it forcefully because it often got stuck. She hefted the box and slid it into the small space and then reached for the one Yasmin was holding out to her.

"It was about me the whole time," Javeria said as she set the second box on top of the other. She pushed it further inside when the door wouldn't close on the first attempt. It took some effort before the door was finally closed, and there was the sound of wood scraping stone with that motion.

"None of them liked what I was accomplishing with the girls," Javeria said.

"Before all of this happened," she said, patting her hands free of dust on the pants of her *shawar kameez*, "I'd heard it whispered on many occasions that I was overstepping my bounds, that I had no business getting into the private lives of those girls."

Right then Yasmin remembered her mother's look of defiance when the supervisor had turned to look at Ms. Javeria after Yasmin claimed the bag as her own. Yasmin had been so immersed in the struggles of her social life that it had never occurred to her that her mother had struggles of her own at the school.

"They tried everything to get me to stop what I was doing." Javeria drew in a deep breath and exhaled, her gaze again on the villas in the landscape. "But it was mainly because parents were complaining." She laughed to herself, but Yasmin could tell her mother found no humor in what she was saying.

"To them, Islam was a subject to be studied, read from pages of a textbook, and shut up after class.

"When they hired me, they expected me to treat my work like a job, and nothing else. The Ministry required the school to teach Islamic studies, so they did it once a week to say they did."

She shook her head. "They never expected the new teacher to actually *teach*, or the students to actually learn."

She glanced at her daughter. "But real teaching goes beyond the classroom, *habeebati*."

Yasmin listened, realizing that her mother knew a lot, much more than Yasmin had given her credit for. It filled Yasmin with regret to realize she had taken her mother for granted when she could have been learning from her.

"In Pakistan," Javeria said with a look of reflection in her eyes, "I respected my teachers. I even stood up whenever they came in the room, even if I was at my parents' house and they visited. That's the status teachers had when I was a girl. I never thought of their lessons as something to be stuffed on a shelf somewhere or to be listened to only to get a high mark on my report card. They were like parents to me. And that's how my father and mother taught me to look at them.

"This new approach to school," she said, shaking her head, grimacing, "all business and show. I don't understand it, Yasmin. I don't. I couldn't have done what the school wanted from me even if I had known it before I took the job. It's just not in me to keep worrying about offending someone." Her eyes grew distant again.

"In Pakistan, my parents would never side with me against my teachers. If my teacher said something, I was to listen and obey, even if it wasn't something my parents themselves would tell me.

"And the funny thing is, I never saw it as a contradiction that my teachers and parents said different things sometimes. In a way, I guess my parents were teaching me about life. They knew they didn't have all the answers, so they saw no reason to shield me from those who might have answers to things they didn't. Or even a different way of seeing something they already felt they understood.

"But this new way of thinking." She frowned slightly. "I don't understand. They say they want progress. But as soon as children start moving in that direction, they do everything they can to stop it."

Yasmin considered that, puzzled at the thought.

Javeria squinted her eyes, and Yasmin saw sadness there.

"But it's like that everywhere now." Javeria sighed. "Even in America and the UK. Pakistan is even changing. I hardly recognize the country anymore."

Javeria drew in a deep breath and exhaled as she started for the door leading to the villa. "Just pray for our souls, *habeebati*. That's all we can do," she said as she pulled the roof door open, stepping inside the villa, Yasmin behind her.

"You know the Day of Judgment is near when Muslims start opposing Islam."

The first thing Hasna noticed about Sharif when he entered the living room of her home and greeted her father was the attractive glow on his face. She had been nursing her hurt feelings over how he had treated her at the airport the day before, but upon seeing him, she felt the resentment loosen in her chest. When she had first seen his beard, she was turned off. She never liked beards. They always made men look unkempt. But now, seeing it for a second time, the beard really suited Sharif. It made him look older, in a more mature, distinguished way.

For some reason he seemed taller too, but that was most likely due to the long robe he was wearing that extended a few inches above his ankles, which were covered in black dress socks. It was an outfit she associated with Arabs, but like the beard, this new dress was attractive on him. The robe was loose, but its soft white fabric fell against his chest and arms in a manner that revealed his thin, muscular stature that Hasna associated with professional basketball players.

In this moment, Hasna remembered why she wanted to marry him. She had to restrain herself from greeting him with a hug. Instead she stood in front of the large couch in the living room, hands in the pockets of her jean skirt, waiting to be noticed.

The night before, Vernon had suggested that Hasna give Sharif his space.

"He has a lot to weigh," Vernon had said. "Living in a foreign country changes you in ways that're hard for others to understand." And Vernon was not speaking in theory. He had lived abroad several years himself.

Sharif was still shaking Brother Karim's hand and laughing at something Karim had said when he noticed Hasna standing about ten feet from them. For a moment, their eyes met and this time the awkwardness from the day before was gone. Today, she looked more peaceful, more mature even, as if she understood better the direction their relationship needed to take given all Sharif had learned abroad. The inflated self-confidence she'd shown during their distant correspondence was gone, and he detected a reserved mellowness about her, hinting that she was open to growth, personally and spiritually.

"*As-salaamu'alaikum*," he greeted before he remembered that he should be lowering his gaze.

"*Wa'alaiku-mus-salaam*." There was a shy smile on her face when she replied, and Sharif couldn't help smiling in response. But their conversation was interrupted by Karim asking if they were ready to go.

Sharif had assumed the lunch would be hosted at Karim's house, but Sharif was relieved that he would not be forced to endure the meal at Hasna's home. He imagined it would be too suffocating an environment for him to ponder all that was before him if he was surrounded by scenes from their shared past.

"Are you ready for December?" Karim asked Sharif an hour later after exchanging small talk over the food that had just been served. The restaurant played soft Indian music in the background, and Sharif's eyes grazed the *halaal* symbol on the centerpiece advertisement, indicating that the meat served here adhered to Islamic requirements. But Sharif was disappointed to see the Budweiser logo featured next to it.

Sharif felt his face go warm as he stirred the mango lassi with his straw. He could not look Hasna or her father in the eye although they both sat across from him at the booth. It was a good thing that they had come to the restaurant in the early afternoon. There were only two other customers there, maximizing the confidentiality of the conversation. Perhaps Karim had arranged it like this intentionally.

"I don't know." Sharif lifted the glass and took a sip of the lassi, a moist imprint left on the wooden table. Still holding the glass, Sharif ran a finger along the curvature of the imprint. The truth was too difficult for him to divulge right then. Given the circumstances, he decided that it was wiser to be diplomatic.

Karim turned to his daughter. "What about you?"

Inadvertently, Sharif glanced in the direction of Hasna and found her looking at him uncertainly. "I've been waiting for ten years," she said. Her honesty pierced Sharif's heart, prompting him to look away. "I don't know if that means I'm ready for December, but if it doesn't," she shrugged, "I don't know how much longer I'm expected to wait to be sure."

Karim chuckled uncomfortably. "Well, she's right about that."

Offended at the implication, Sharif creased his forehead, unwilling to keep quiet on this subtle accusation. He set his glass down. "Actually, I wanted to cut several years off of that, but there was *nothing* for Hasna in Saudi." He met her eyes unblinking, in that gaze reminding her of how she had hurt him deeply. Or perhaps he was the one in need of the reminder. "Even after *I* was there for six years."

Hasna's cheeks colored, and her gaze dropped as she used her fork to toy with her food. "That's not what I meant."

"It's what you said."

"It's not the same thing."

"It was to me."

She started to speak but stopped herself, biting her lower lip instead. In the awkward silence, dishes rattled in the background, an odd complement to the strange music.

"I'm sorry," Hasna said quietly.

Sensing the sincerity in her apology, Sharif regretted his remark. But he stopped short of apologizing. He would not offer her more than his understanding, even if he refused to acknowledge it aloud. Until this moment, he hadn't admitted to himself how much her remark had hurt. It revealed to him more than he could have determined on his own, and he now wondered why he had imagined it could be any different. Hasna had always been like that. Her comfort came first. What came second or thereafter depended on the circumstance. It was the reason she had gone to law school in the first place.

"*I'd never be caught dead in somebody's classroom,*" she had said when he had shared that he was going to double major in biology and education.

"*Why not?*" he'd asked.

"*I need something that can guarantee that I can drive at least a Volvo for the rest of my life.*"

Karim cleared his throat, apparently feeling like an intruder. "Sharif."

Sharif looked up, in that moment fearing that his expression revealed what he was thinking.

"I talked to Rashad for some time this morning." Karim's eyes grew serious as he reached for a glass of water. "And he said I shouldn't be surprised if you have a change of heart."

He looked at Sharif now then took a sip of water before setting the glass back on the table. "What do you think?"

"Change of heart about what?"

"Everything. Your religion, your life." He paused then regarded Sharif as if unsure what to think. "Your marriage."

This was the moment that Sharif had dreaded for the entire duration of his final year in Riyadh. For days he was restless in anxiety, no longer able to push the moment out of his mind with the intention of facing it "later." Later had now come, and the weighty reality was before him. And there was no option except to face it, directly.

Hasna sat before him, as did her father. Sharif had to make a choice, and there were only two options. Neither of them included the plans he had made in childlike innocence before he had left the country. Even if he wanted to, he could never again be the Sharif he had been when he and Hasna made their marriage plans official. He could never again be the Sharif who had mustered enough courage after sacrificing several nights of sleep to ask a question that he now knew she had expected all along.

Will you be my companion on this journey?

But now it was time for him to ask of himself the same question he had asked of her.

Will you be her companion on this journey?

What could he say?

People thought they could plan life, Sharif had reflected before leaving Riyadh for good. And when things didn't go their way, they could just call it quits, even when they had, by their own hands, sent their life spinning in an entirely different direction.

Accountability wasn't a part of the equation.

All is fair in love and war, people often said. But as a Muslim, Sharif knew that wasn't true. Every affair was bound by rules, and love and war were ones with strictures most binding.

Then again, what of a person who grew dizzy at the sudden shift in motion, even if inspired by his own hands? Could he really be blamed if he wanted the world to grow still beneath his feet?

Did he owe anyone an explanation for a simple change of heart, even if it meant a drastic change in others' lives? Was there any explanation he could offer to make someone understand that his heart, like his life, was all he had that belonged wholly to him? Should he sacrifice it to save someone else? If he refused, would anyone understand his motives?

Would he understand them himself?

No, he could not force someone to see his point of view. It was impossible to make others understand what could be seen through only his own eyes, his own heart.

But should he at least try?

Sharif had so long pondered the words he would utter to explain his decision—the option he knew would most justly preserve the carefully carved future both he and Hasna had sculpted for themselves, even if his had come years late. He had even drafted the right words in his head and recited them to himself more than once, carefully selecting the ones he imagined would inflict the least amount of pain.

But he'd never stopped to realize whom he was trying to spare—Hasna or himself.

So on that Sunday afternoon, a day after his six-year study abroad, Sharif, without forethought or plan, chose the other option, betraying everything he had coached himself to say for the past year.

"I've changed, yes." Sharif heard the words as if coming from someone else, and inside there was a tugging, a soft voice, telling him that he could still choose the option that did not betray who he was today. "But that doesn't mean I've had a change of heart."

He had heard that compromise was inherent to marriage itself. But now, after hearing the words that sealed his fate in a way that he could only fathom, he feared that compromise was also an impediment if resorted to before the matrimony itself.

In his peripheral vision, he saw Hasna's shoulders relax. He thought he heard her sigh in relief, but he could not meet her gaze to read what he'd find there. Not being completely honest with himself was difficult enough. How then could he confirm that dishonesty by looking at the one who would suffer most from his poor choice?

Then again, he wasn't sure if it were actually he who would suffer most in the end.

It was an odd position for him, Sharif couldn't help noticing, to be the one on the other side, the one doing the favor instead of being on the receiving end.

Was it that he felt too insignificant to say no, too small to refuse? He had always understood what this relationship meant to Hasna—accepting his company was a favor bestowed when she had so many other more promising options; and she had, in their years together, made her superiority quite clear—but now, it was Sharif bestowing the favor, protecting her feelings while neglecting his own.

But he also understood the reason his refusal would be so hurtful to her at all.

To be turned down by someone of worth was painful, yes, but it could only be expected. But to be turned down by someone unworthy was devastating—and more agonizing than the hurt itself.

"No," Hasna had said flatly to Sharif's inquiry to determine if she was willing to consider wearing hijab after marriage.

That night, it was this one response that kept playing over in Sharif's mind, precluding any likelihood of sleep although his body was desperately in need of rest. He couldn't help noticing the uncanny parallels it held to the response he'd received when he'd asked Hasna to accompany him to Riyadh.

Perhaps it wasn't the way she had responded that troubled him most, Sharif considered. This matter-of-fact manner was a part of Hasna's character whenever she felt strongly about something and was unwilling to change. But he also knew that she was more stubborn in words than she was in heart. On more than one occasion, she had proven that she was amenable when given the space and opportunity to turn the matter over in her mind.

That very night, Hasna had shown flexibility when he asked about her willingness to study more about Islam. She openly admitted that she had a lot of growing to do. She also shared that she now prayed every day, although she was, admittedly, not as regular as she should be.

No, it wasn't her response itself that disturbed him, he concluded.

It was that he sincerely wanted his wife to wear hijab.

But earlier that day, it had seemed like such a small point to insist upon, and as he thought of it now, it was insignificant in light of Hasna's willingness to study more about Islam.

But this small point troubled him nonetheless.

Like Hasna, Sharif had been taught that hijab wasn't necessary and that it proved nothing about what was truly in someone's heart. His own mother did not wear the head cover, and he could think of no woman he admired more. Growing up with a role model as monumental as his mother had meant that, as a child, the hijab meant little to Sharif. He associated it with a foreign culture, a foreign people. And a foreign expression of faith.

"Hypocrites," his father would sometimes say of the women in head covers and men in large beards. *"They're obsessed with the façade of Islam, thinking they'll get to Heaven with pieces of cloth on their heads and hair growing out of their faces. They have no idea about the spirit of Islam. That is in the heart."*

But even as a child, this argument had troubled Sharif. It was years before he could properly articulate his source of confusion.

It was true that the seat of Islam was in the heart. No one could or would dispute that fact, Sharif reflected. But the argument implied that outward obedience to Allah was indicative of a diseased heart—and that outwardly disobeying Him purified the heart.

Hypocrisy itself was a matter of the heart, yet only Allah knew what lay in the breasts of men.

And if what was on the outside mattered not at all in comparison to what lay within—

Then on what basis did his family call Muslims hypocrites in the first place?

After all, it was only their *outward actions* that people could see.

Why not then say these people's Islam also lay in the hearts, and that we couldn't judge them? Even as there was some indication of their religion in what could be seen.

"I like her," his father would say whenever Hasna and her family would visit. *"I hope you two get married some day."*

"No," Hasna had said frankly earlier that day in response to Sharif's question about hijab, *"I'm not willing to wear it."*

Sharif blinked in the darkness of his room as the scene repeated itself in his mind. There was a heaviness in the pit of his stomach as he recalled his weakness in, if not calling off the wedding altogether, in at least delaying it to give himself more time. But, as it stood, the date was only four months away.

He felt a knotting in his head until it ached.

"I wouldn't be caught dead in something like that," Hasna had once said years ago when Sharif himself had been repulsed by hijab. *"It is so tacky."*

"Why do they feel the need to show off their Islam?" Sharif had replied in agreement.

"*I have no idea,*" Hasna said, disgust in her voice.

Sharif shut his eyes, willing himself to sleep. He was exhausted and needed the rest. He had no idea how long this jet lag would weigh on his limbs.

Islam means submission.

The words returned to him as he felt the grogginess of sleep. These simple words were ones he had spoken often in response to a classmate who asked about Islam.

And a Muslim is one who submits to Allah.

Like an epiphany, in that moment between sleep and wakefulness, Sharif realized his community's greatest flaw—and what his own had been as a youth.

If outward submission wasn't a direction expression of the faith in one's heart, why then did Allah call His religion *Islam* in the first place?

He could have simply called it *Emaan.*

The woman stood in the lobby of the masjid, and Sharif's father, the imam, sat in his office chair facing the area where she stood, his door open as he smiled proudly at his son. Light from the sun illuminated the entire expanse of the lobby, shining brightly through the windows, making the marbled tile glow. The sound of Qur'an being recited reverberated throughout the entire area and seemed to be coming from outside, its source somewhere above the bright sky. The Arabic verses were the last four of Al-Fajr: "O reassured soul, Return to your Lord, well-pleased and pleasing [to Him]. And enter among My servants, enter My Paradise."

Sharif approached the lobby, drawn by the phenomenal recitation, the likes of which he'd never heard before, his heart trembling at its remarkable beauty. The first thing he noticed upon entering was the light. It seemed to be coming from every direction, even as its source was the rays streaming through the glass windows. He halted his steps and raised his gaze to the ceiling, which at that moment became like the bright blue of the sky, even though he had not left the building. He stood, tears brimming his eyes, wondering who was reciting these inimitable words, certain that it could be no mortal. He wondered if the voice was that of his Creator but recalled a moment later that no human who was not endowed with prophethood could hear the Voice of Allah in this life.

Sharif continued listening, watching in amazement as the sky shook, a trembling that mirrored the rhythm in his chest as the sound grew in beauty and intensity. At that moment, Sharif was able to discern only that the amazing sound and vibration was like that of a chain being dragged over a rock.

That was when he heard the laughter, as if coming from that same heavenly source, but he realized the sound was in front of him. That was when he saw her. And the realization came to him in that moment, with no ambiguity or doubt. She was his wife. Immediately, his heart was filled with love and yearning so weighty that he felt as if his heart would burst.

Sharif walked toward her, seeing only the soft black fabric of the jilbaab, the cloth draping from the top of her head and falling over her feet. Her veil was lifted but she was not facing him, so he could not see her face. Her gloved hand held the palm of a young boy, whose skin glowed the same golden brown as his wife's, whose cheek he could barely make out as he neared her.

She was talking to someone he could not see. He walked faster, drawing closer, until he was but a step away. That was when she heard him and quickly dropped the veil over her face, glancing behind her, sensing that a strange man was approaching. But she did not see him although he was right before her at that moment. Sharif opened his mouth to speak so that she would know it was only her husband and —

Sharif woke in the stillness of his room, a spiritual tranquility filling his chest. He ached to be in the company of his wife and the beautiful recitation. Heart still trembling as he recovered from the dream, Sharif blinked in the darkness as he slowly registered the surroundings that were momentarily foreign to him. It took several seconds before he remembered that he was no longer in Riyadh.

And that he had just had the dream again.

He could not recall how many times he had seen it in the last seven years, but in each of those years, it had been at least twice. Whenever he would see the dream, he would wake with increased faith and dedication to stay firm upon his religion. The dream had inspired him when he was down and motivated him when he was discouraged. Due to the constant spiritual turmoil his Islamic studies incited, the dream had been much needed during those years.

The first time he saw the dream was a week after he proposed to Hasna, and the dream had confounded him. At the time, he, like Hasna, was a junior year in college and did not even know he would be studying abroad (That proposition would come from Imam Rashad months later). Sharif had just entered the field of his major and had worked out the details of how he would take a job teaching high school biology to take care of Hasna. He too had decided, after many sleepless nights, that he couldn't stand waiting any longer. If she said yes, they would marry no more than a week after they graduated from college.

Sharif and Hasna had known each other since childhood and had openly admitted their feelings for each other during high school. It had been difficult enough to remain patient as their parents actively encouraged the relationship but categorically discouraged the marriage. Their parents told them that they were too young to marry and that, should they ever decide to marry, it would have to wait until they finished their bachelor's degrees.

It was unfair, they both lamented, even though neither of them had vocalized to their parents a desire to marry. Still, they felt it was unfair to be robbed of the opportunity.

Presently, Sharif glanced at the clock. The red letters glowed 3:49, a small crimson dot next to the top of the nine, indicating that the time was early morning instead of afternoon.

Now fully conscious, Sharif sat up and recited the supplication for waking, tossing aside his blanket and swinging his bare feet to the carpeted floor of his room.

He fumbled for the light switch on the lamp next to his bed until the room was suddenly illuminated, and, instinctively, he blinked until his eyes adjusted to the sudden light. He then walked over to the piece of paper he had printed and tacked to the wall the day before. Sharif saddened at the reminder that he would have to depend on this single printed sheet instead of the sound of the muezzin. He ached to return to where multiple calls to prayer reverberated throughout the entire city five times each day.

Sharif ran his finger along the rows that denoted the names of the current month, day, and prayer, along with its corresponding numerical time.

How could he stand this, greeting his prayers day after day, week after week, and year after year, forced to depend on the sterility of a columned chart to announce this monumental act of worship? Was it even possible to grow accustomed to something as lifeless as this?

Growing up, he had never heard the *adhaan* except within the confines of a masjid or from a radio or television. But even then the masjid itself was less a house of worship than it was a community center, a social hall, or a club house where members congregated for the weekly potluck, lecture, or party. Otherwise, it was virtually empty. For many masjids, if they were open at all during the times for *Dhuhr* and *Asr* prayers, the *adhaan* was greeted with eerie silence, and if one happened upon a masjid at this time, he would fine a lone imam leading himself in *salaah*— unless the janitor happened to be there to join him.

In Riyadh, the masjid was a place of worship where the believers congregated at least five times each day—answering the call of the muezzin, even during the workday, as businesses closed for *salaah*. In the States, most masjids were ghostly silent during weekdays' standard work hours—if they were unlocked at all.

Prayer, then, was not an act of worship associated with the masjid. It was associated with a prayer chart hung on the walls of homes inhabited by those believers conscientious enough to have even this lone indicator of daily worship. It troubled Sharif that he had, like most Muslim Americans, rarely pondered this complacency with the absence of the public *adhaan*—the single symbol that the early Muslims used to determine if a particular region was occupied by Muslims at all.

"Allah knows our hearts," Muslims would say if the topic was broached, excusing themselves of yet another Islamic responsibility.

It was disheartening to Sharif that this constant absolution of accountability—usually attributed to inadequate circumstances beyond the Muslims' control—would continue even when the believers' souls were seized at death. Even then, Muslims who

92

were content in their meager conditions would recite the mantra of the weak Muslim that they had rehearsed in life, hoping to escape, even in this final moment, the accountability that Allah had informed them of in His Book.

> *Verily, as for those whom the angels take [in death] while they were wronging themselves, they ask them, 'In what [condition] were you?' They reply, 'We were weak and oppressed in the land.' They say, 'Was not the earth of Allah spacious enough for you to emigrate therein?' Such men will find their abode in Hell – what an evil destination.*
>
> *Except the weak ones among men, women, and children who cannot devise a plan, nor are they able to direct their way. These are they whom Allah is likely to forgive,*
> *And Allah is Oft-Pardoning, Oft-Forgiving.*

Today, Sharif pondered the fact that Allah indeed knows what lies in the hearts, and he wondered at those who sought this knowledge as consolation.

AUGUST 9, 2004. FAJR. 4:56.

After reading the chart, he glanced at the clock again. He had an hour before the first prayer.

Sharif rummaged through the suitcase that lay open, still unpacked, and found the thin white pants traditionally worn under the Saudi *thobe*. He quickly pulled them over his pajama shorts before leaving his room and heading down the hall to the bathroom.

Back in the room, his face and arms still wet from *wudhoo*, he removed from the footboard of his bed the white *thobe* he had worn to lunch the day before. He pulled it over himself in preparation for *Qiyaam*, the voluntary prayer that the Prophet prayed each night.

Before going to Saudi Arabia, Sharif had prayed *Qiyaam* only in the last ten nights of Ramadan and had no idea it could or should be prayed at any other time. He now knew that it was not only permissible to pray *Qiyaam* throughout the entire year, but it was strongly recommended.

Sharif faced the direction of Makkah and raised his hands as if in surrender, marking the beginning of prayer. He recited aloud the first chapter of the Qur'an, reflecting on the meaning of the

Arabic words that he had learned to recite in Arabic for the first time when he was already twenty years old and a first-year student in the Islamic university in Riyadh, although he had been a Muslim all his life.

The realization of this favor alone made his heart humble in gratefulness to his Creator. Sharif had grown up saying his prayers in English, having been told, as the members of his community always had been, "There's no need to Arabize Islam. Allah understands all languages. Pray in yours."

> *Show us the Straight Way, the way of those on whom You have bestowed Your Grace,*
> *Not the path of those who have earned Your Anger, nor the path of those who go astray.*

"*Hal ta'rifuhum...?*" The professor's question hung in the air like an offering, *Do you know who they are? These people Allah discusses in this single prayer that we recite at least seventeen times a day?*

The university students were quiet, unsure if they had within them the knowledge to respond, even as the teacher looked at each of them, one by one, occasionally repeating the question as his eyes met that of a student.

Sharif had creased his forehead that day, having never thought of the words beyond the literal meaning. When the instructor looked at him, Sharif decided against responding, realizing his ignorance right then. Even if Sharif understood the words literally, he didn't know what they meant practically. And that bothered him. He had been praying this prayer for more than ten years, yet he had never taken time to learn what he had been asking for all these years.

"*Al-yahood wan nasaara,*" a student called out. *The Jews and the Christians.*

"*Ayyuwa...*" *Correct,* the professor said, a smile of triumph on his olive face, which was framed by a graying beard. *But those who earned Allah's Grace?*

The Muslims, the student said.

Hmm...Who agrees?

Hands went up, some with confidence, some with reluctance. But all hands were in the air in the span of ten seconds.

No, they are not, he said.

"*Kayf, ya shayk?*" How can this be, Professor?

Are you all Muslim?

Yes.

Is your life that Straight Path that all believers are praying to follow as they recite this prayer?

Silence.

"*Man ta'rif?*" Who can answer?

No one responded.

Can you look at your life and how you have lived it and say that others should take that Path, that others should follow you to earn Allah's Favor?

"*Kallaa,*" the sheikh answered his own question. *No, for surety, you cannot.*

Then who? Who represents this path?

The Prophet, peace be upon him? a student asked tentatively.

Hmm...Who agrees?

Hands went up, but only midway, and cautiously this time. But not everyone raised their hands.

My brothers, is the pronoun in this verse singular or plural? Are we asking to follow the path of a single person or a group of people?

A group.

Then who is this group?

Silence.

They are the Prophet, peace be upon him, his Companions, and those who adhere to their way, the professor said.

This, he emphasized, *is the only path to Paradise.*

And who are those who earned Allah's Anger? the professor asked.

The Jews?

Anyone who has knowledge and does not act upon it, the professor corrected.

And who are those who have gone astray?

The Christians?

Anyone who follows misguidance while thinking he is doing right, he corrected again. *And it is only the path of those who act upon righteous knowledge that leads to Paradise.*

Until he studied the religion for himself, Sharif had been of those who had gone astray.

He could only pray that now, after having been endowed with basic knowledge of his religion, he would be among those who act upon the righteous knowledge that Allah had given him.

Five

"The Sheikh never taught any of these things. Why would the community want me to study in a university that would teach something he was opposed to?"

It was Monday evening and Sharif sat in the leather chair opposite the desk of the imam at the masjid that he was to officially head that coming Friday. Opposite him, in the desk chair, Imam Rashad clasped his hands, his peach-colored face framed by a large grey beard that Sharif could not recall Rashad having before Sharif left to study.

So much had changed, and perhaps these changes were positive, but Sharif wanted to understand this sudden and drastic shift in ideology, and theology. But, most importantly, he wanted to understand his place in it.

There would be opposition, Sharif imagined, and he feared being faced with community uncertainty and discord. He could barely stomach the idea of the imam position itself, let alone the obstacles that would come along with it.

"Believe it or not," Rashad said, "we didn't even consider that."

Sharif furrowed his brows. "But my fath—"

"You have to remember something, Sharif. At that time, Islam was new to all of us. We didn't establish this masjid based on any specific philosophy or *madh-hab*. Your father, Karim, and I were the only Muslims in this part of Maryland at the time, at least as far as we knew. We just thought it was a good idea to have a masjid." He smiled reflectively. "We didn't even know what we'd do once we had it."

Sharif leaned back in his chair, scratching the skin beneath his facial hair. "But my father always mentioned the Sheikh…"

"Yes, the Sheikh was instrumental in bringing us back to Islam, but—"

"I thought you were always Muslim."

"I was," Rashad said, his thick grey eyebrows drawing together, apparently taken aback by Sharif's comment. "In Pakistan, my parents and grandparents made sure I prayed and fasted and anything else required of me. But once I came to

America and got married…" There was a pause and Rashad drew in a deep breath and exhaled audibly, and his gaze fell to a pencil he was now using to write something on the large desk calendar that covered most of the desk. "Well, let's just say things changed. I thought I was Muslim. But looking back, I think I left Islam not too long after I left my country."

"How did you learn about the Sheikh?"

"Your father mostly."

"Really?"

"Your father met him by chance after Karim told your father about a masjid in D.C. that he passed sometimes. Your father was just going there to take his *shahaadah*. You must have been a baby at the time."

"But I thought he became Muslim before I was born."

"He told me that one of the reasons he and your mother became Muslim was that they wanted to raise their son properly."

Sharif creased his forehead, intrigued.

"I think what he was saying to you was that they raised you from childhood as a Muslim."

Yes. Those were the words his parents had used. Sharif also recalled his father saying that it was Karim and Mona who were responsible for sparking their interest in Islam.

"What I'm trying to say, Sharif, is that our association with the Sheikh was limited. Your father was impressed with him, and that was all. Dawud kept in touch with him and attended his lectures when he could and shared what he learned. But the Sheikh had already returned to Syria before we even purchased this property."

Rashad shook his head, laying the pencil down. "I doubt the Sheikh even remembers your father today."

"But what about the other Muslims here? They speak highly of him."

"They speak highly of him because your father did. No one knew him except through your father's lectures."

A thought came to Sharif. "But why not you or Brother Karim? Why was my father chosen as imam?"

"It wasn't really a choice so much as it was just expected. Your father had a natural charisma, and he loved learning. He was always reading some book, researching some issue, and

98

pondering how he could apply that information either practically in his own life, or by imparting it to his students in the school where he worked. He was a natural teacher, and he applied that same zeal to Islam. Karim and I never even considered taking this position."

Rashad laughed. "You see how short my Friday talks are as it is, and the people are still nodding off. Imagine if I'd been the one inviting people here when we were first starting out."

Sharif couldn't conceal the humor he found in the imam's statement. Rashad was one of those people whose voice itself was a soporific. Two minutes into anything he was saying and you could look around and find one of two things among the congregation, someone glancing at their wristwatch or someone's eyelids growing heavy, if you didn't find both.

"And I think that answers your next question," Rashad said good-naturedly.

"Not really..." Sharif searched for the right way to explain. "I don't have my father's gift of words. These things are not inherited."

"But you have your father's charisma." Rashad paused thoughtfully. "And more besides."

Sharif drew his eyebrows together. "What do you mean?"

"You have your father's natural way with words, but you have your mother's quiet dignity."

Sharif wanted to respond but was quieted by the comment regarding his mother. He did not think of her as quiet, though his natural love for her as his mother made her dignified in his eyes. He had never considered her image in the eyes of others.

Sharif tried to recall times when she was in public, and it was difficult to recount. She was not one who enjoyed going out much. Sharif's father did most of the grocery shopping, and she would prepare the meals and do the housework because she didn't work at that time. She solicited help from Sharif and Wali on occasion though it was clear that her standards and theirs were different, thus she was most content cooking and cleaning herself. But Sharif did recall the moments he had crossed a line in public and his mother had been there to witness it. She would say nothing to him and would continue, effortlessly it seemed, nodding during to a pleasant conversation she was having or listening attentively to her husband speaking at a Muslim event. Whenever her and Sharif's eyes would meet, however, Sharif would see in them a message so distinct that it would have been less agonizing to hear it aloud. Sharif would then be restless with anxiety as an hour turned to minutes and minutes to seconds, the countdown to when they would go home, where he was sure to be justly punished for what he had done.

But never did she raise her voice in public, and she was generally not sociable though she wasn't antisocial either. During events like Eid, Sharif would often find his mother helping the servers or cooks, or quietly knitting, Asma or Wali playing at her feet.

Quiet dignity. Yes, his mother had that. His father could inspire fiery motivation in any crowd, and his mother could evoke admiration and reverence with her presence alone.

But Sharif saw neither in himself.

"But I'm not a teacher."

"I didn't say you were."

Sharif grew quiet, more doubtful of himself then.

"But you are a leader."

Sharif's eyebrow rose and he started to disagree, but before he could say anything, Rashad spoke.

"In history," Rashad said, "the best leaders have never been those who covet position or imagine themselves worthy of that role. They were those who, when circumstances dictated, rose to the occasion, even though they felt others would do a better job."

"And why would he even ask you something like that?" Kenya wrinkled her nose from where she sat on the floor of her living room Monday night. The fingers of both of her hands were at work twisting the roots of her hair so that the new growth would lengthen the locks and allow her scalp to breathe. "You weren't wearing it when he asked to marry you. Why would he ask you to wear it now?"

"That's what I was thinking." Hasna too was sitting on the floor, both arms behind her as she leaned her weight into them as carpet cushioned the palms of her hands.

"Now wait a minute, ladies." Vernon sat on the couch, his fiancée inches from his legs as she sat with her back to him, Hasna opposite them. Before this moment, he had been engrossed in some ESPN program about the star rookies for the new football season, pretending to be too engrossed in the highlights to pay attention to them.

He pressed the mute button on the remote control, abruptly silencing the talking head, an indication that he was inviting himself into the conversation.

"I have to disagree."

Kenya turned to glance at her boyfriend and rolled her eyes playfully. "Why don't you mind your business and let us do our girl talk?"

"If it were girl talk, you wouldn't be doing it in my living room."

"*Our* living room," she corrected. "We share everything in here."

"Then that includes conversations."

Hasna laughed. "He has point there."

"You can't side with him," Kenya joked. "That would be sexist."

"It'd be sexist if I sided with you."

"No, that would be friendship. Siding with him is sexist."

"Because I sided with a *man*?"

"Case in point," Kenya said humorously. "Vernon is not a man. It's the first thing he confessed to me after he asked to marry me."

Vernon threw a pillow at Kenya, and they all laughed.

"Seriously," he said, laughter still in his voice.

"How can you disagree?" Kenya said, now turning her body to face him at an angle, resuming her hair grooming a second later. "You can't ask somebody to change for you."

"He's not asking her to change, Hershey. He's asking her to grow."

Eyes widening playfully, Hasna lifted the pillow that had fallen next to her and raised it, threatening to throw it back at Vernon. "Are you saying I'm *infantile*, Attorney Sheldon?"

"Come on, Hasna," he said. "You can't tell me you don't see where I'm coming from."

"I can see that you've insulted me."

"No, my love, I'm giving you a compliment. Just because he's asking you to grow doesn't mean you're the one in need of growing. It's a matter of perspective. He thinks you should grow because he sees your lifestyle as inferior to his. But we all know who's really superior."

Hasna tossed the pillow to him and he caught it. "Okay, you're all clear. Lying to a woman is the fastest way to her heart."

She narrowed her eyes playfully. "Now, tell me the truth. What are you trying to say?"

"Let's be honest for a second, Hasna." His voice grew serious though he retained a diplomatic tone. "You're Muslim and—"

Immediately, Hasna felt a pang of offense in her chest. She hated when Vernon pointed out her religion to her. But she could not fault him. One of the things she loved about her best friend was his honesty. Without it, he wouldn't be Vernon. Besides, he wasn't trying to hurt her; he was just making a point.

"—Sharif just graduated from a prestigious Islamic university, so you can't exp—"

"Uh, I think the term *prestigious* is a bit extraneous here," Hasna said. "It's arguable whether it was even Islamic."

"Now, you can't be serious," Vernon said, distracted from his argument momentarily. "We can't debate something as fundamental as that."

"Objection," Kenya said. "She's the Muslim here. She should know."

"Okay, fine. We'll call it a Muslim university."

Hasna shrugged. "Okay, I can deal with that."

"So after studying in this Muslim university, can you really expect him to come home unchanged and not want to apply what he learned to his own life?"

"His life. Her life," Kenya said. "Two different things."

"No they're not." Vernon looked at his fiancée and motioned a hand to the living room around them.

"Remember your small point at the beginning of this conversation?" he said. "That this house is *ours*?"

Kenya nodded, running her fingers through her locks to make sure they were not entangled. "Yes, I remember."

"But who bought this house?"

She smiled and shrugged in response.

"I did," he answered himself. "But now that we're a couple, it's ours. Therefore, anyth—"

"But physical property is different," Kenya said. "I have the right to believe whatever I want."

"And I have a right to share something with you if I think it'll benefit you in the long run. And you have the same right with me."

"But you have to respect another person's lifestyle." She pointed to Hasna. "Do you think it's fair for him to ask her to live in *purdah*? Come on, Vern, give me a break. We're Americans, not the Taliban. Why should she have to wrap herself in Afghani rags while he's walking around wearing what he wants?"

"He's not asking her to do that."

"I think he is."

"No, he's not. He's gauging how committed she is to the faith they both believe in."

"Islam is in the heart though," Hasna interjected.

Vernon waved a hand at her. "Hasna, please. You know that's not true."

Her face grew hot in offense. "It *is* true. I don't have to act holier than thou to prove to the world I'm Muslim. As long as I believe in my heart, who is anyone else to judge?"

"I'm not talking about judging. I'm talking about commitment."

"Vernon," Kenya said with a sigh, "get to the point please."

"All I'm saying is that religion is not just a set of beliefs. If it were, I'd still be Muslim myself."

"I don't believe you ever *were* Muslim," Kenya said, rolling her eyes. "Your parents maybe. But not you."

"You can think what you want, Hershey, but I know what I believed then, and I know what I believe now."

Hasna had started to interject, but at this confession, she grew quiet. It wasn't that the information was new to her. Days after she and Vernon had met, Vernon had happened to pass her on campus while they were both on their way to lunch. After exchanging small talk and realizing they were both planning to go eat, they agreed to have lunch together in one of the popular university eateries. It was over this meal that Vernon divulged that his parents had accepted Islam when he was five years old and that he had practiced the religion himself until he graduated from high school. But by then his parents were divorced, and his mother had returned to Christianity and his father to live as an American expatriate in Cairo, where the family had lived for the duration of Vernon's middle and early high school years.

Vernon's former Islamic affiliation was the one thing that had both surprised and impressed Hasna after first meeting her best friend. It was refreshing to talk to someone who understood and respected her faith without the pollution of stereotypes and misinformation. However, Vernon had told her that he was no longer a religious person. But if he were to choose a religion, he said, it would be Islam.

Other than that, Hasna had never drawn the story out of him. It had been enough consolation to know that he respected Islam at all, and he was the only classmate she had in law school who shared that much in common with her. This common ground was probably the most significant in inspiring their friendship to develop as deeply as it had. And the feeling was mutual. Vernon had said that even Kenya could not relate to his affinity for Islam.

Hasna was quiet now. Religion was a rare subject of conversation, especially in Kenya's presence. If Hasna were completely honest, she was particularly uncomfortable with the subject herself, especially around Vernon. When she was with her best friend, she liked to focus on what they had in common. It was liberating to be around someone with whom it really didn't matter what differences existed between them.

"Are you serious, Vern?" Kenya's expression showed intrigue, and a grin lingered on her face. "You really believed all that stuff?"

He frowned slightly, apparently offended by her subtle mockery. "Yes, I did. And I tried to live like a Muslim too."

"You never told me that."

"Yes I did. You just weren't listening." His tone was serious, and for a moment Hasna felt uncomfortable, unsure if she should be hearing this. "You always thought I was joking."

"Well, you *were* always laughing when you talked about Islam."

"That's because it was an uncomfortable subject for me. But my father is Muslim, Hershey. You think I should respect him any less because of that?"

"That's not what I meant. I'm just saying, you made it clear that you and you father were estranged as far as you were concerned, so I just as—"

"That had nothing to do with his religion."

"—sumed it was because you didn't want to be Muslim."

"Hershey, please. You know I've always said I respect people's right to believe what they want."

"But this is different, Vern. Every time that man calls here, I can feel his disappointment through the phone." She shook her head. "If you respect his beliefs, he certainly doesn't respect yours."

"And I don't expect him to."

Kenya laughed. "You are too forgiving, Vern. If I were you, I'd—"

"If you were me," he interrupted, "you'd know my father like I do and respect him for loving me the only way he knows how."

Kenya shook her head, smiling. "Honestly, Vernon. That's why I love you. You have such a big heart. I can see why you think Sharif is totally justified in forcing his beliefs on his fiancée. It's not about Sharif, it's about your father."

"And what if it is, Hershey? What's wrong with that?"

The sincerity in Vernon's eyes and expression made Hasna turn away, and her heart ached. But Hasna didn't understand this sudden discomfort. Part of her suspected it was embarrassment; she wasn't as passionate in her reverence for her parents, or Islam.

Hasna could sense that the remark had embarrassed Kenya. Hasna could feel it in the sudden silence that permeated the room.

The quiet was suffocating. Hasna herself wanted to say something, anything to break the stiff atmosphere. But she already felt like an intruder. Her speaking would only make that feeling more pronounced.

"I'm sorry, Vern," Kenya said finally. "I didn't know it meant that much to you."

"It's not that, Hershey," he said, apology in his soft tone. "All I'm trying to say is you can't assume someone's trying to force their beliefs on someone just because they want them to be a better person."

Kenya parted her lips to say something but decided against it. Instead she pulled her knees close to her and rested her chin on them, her attention on Vernon. There was a softness in her eyes and expression, showing a sincere desire to learn something she hadn't known before.

In that gesture, Hasna saw how much Kenya respected Vernon, and it was then that Hasna understood why it was Kenya, not Hasna herself, whom Vernon loved most.

And why Sharif was unable to show Hasna the love and affection she desired.

Humility. That was what Hasna lacked. Yet it was what Vernon and Kenya shared and what joined them in an unseverable bond.

But with Hasna and Sharif, there was no bond. Because the humility was one-sided.

Sharif could not show Hasna love and affection—because she didn't have eyes or heart to receive it.

It was then that Hasna understood a deeper significance to Vernon's words.

Hasna, please. You know that's not true.

Why had he been so sure of himself?

Because love itself was not "only in the heart." True love was, by definition, shown through a person's actions, and enjoyed and felt by all those in the person's life.

So it was with faith.

Six

"Iman!" Mona stood at the bottom of the carpeted steps leading to the girls' rooms. It was Tuesday morning and she had just returned from the store. After Mona had unloaded the car, paper bags of groceries lined the kitchen table and floor, and she was exhausted. She had been up most of the night talking to her sister on the phone and she wanted to rest. She was not in the mood to put the items away, and many things needed to be frozen or refrigerated.

"Mommy!"

Mona heard her son's voice before she saw his small figure running toward her. The third of her three children, Adam was her only boy. Before Mona discovered she was pregnant with him, she had given up on having more children. Iman was ten at the time, and Mona was showing signs of menopause. It was disheartening to be growing old after only two children. It wasn't that she wanted a house full of babies, but she and Karim had always hoped for at least one son and one daughter, regardless of the amount of children they would have.

She swept Adam into her arms and embraced his small body. It was amazing to see him running around like a big boy now. He was only three. It seemed like yesterday that he was struggling to stand on his own.

"Where's your sister?"

"Her tummy hurts."

Mona groaned. Iman was probably upstairs with headphones on, Qur'an playing in her ears, and she had probably already taken two extra-strength Midol. When it was Iman's time-of-the-month, it was everybody's. The whole house went down with her.

Today, cramps or not, Mona decided, Iman was going to put the groceries away.

Mona made her way up the steps and knocked on her daughter's door. "Iman? *Iman*?" Mona's patience was growing thin. Every day it was a new story with her, anything to get out of her chores, and in the last two days her "body weaknesses" had increased. Part of Mona wondered if this sudden onset of illness was due to stress. Iman was often distant and despondent after seeing any of Mona's family or their friends, even if only in passing at a mall or Islamic event.

When Mona's sister had called Sunday night to say that a friend of their family who owned a henna and hair salon was inviting Hasna and Iman to a henna party at the parlor, Mona was reluctant. Iman wasn't allowed around her family, and Mona's sister knew that. But it was a peace offering, Mona knew, as her sister didn't hold the same view as their parents.

"And they're offering free hair styling," her sister had said, her voice hopeful.

Mona had sighed, realizing perhaps it wasn't such a bad idea. Mona herself was still struggling with styling Iman's tightly-coiled curls, and Iman herself hadn't settled on the best way to tame her head of hair. Maybe it wasn't such a bad idea…

"I can pick them up," Saira added before Mona could protest.

In the end, only Iman went with Saira Monday evening, as Hasna said she had already agreed to meet up with a friend at that time. Knowing that Iman would go alone increased Mona's apprehension, but she didn't have the heart to turn down Saira's kind offer.

But when Iman returned late that night irritable and upset, Mona didn't have the heart to ask her what had happened.

Mona now grew worried that Iman was still not well.

She really wanted one of the girls to help her put away the food. But Hasna was at work, and Mona's legs were aching from shopping. It had been difficult enough to unload all the bags; she didn't have energy to put everything away.

Mona was about to invite herself into Iman's room when she saw the handle turn slowly and a head peer through the crack. "Iman, can you please put away the groceries?"

"Mom?"

As the door opened wider, it took a second for Mona to realize it that it was Hasna, not Iman, looking back at her.

"Hasna? What are you doing here? I thought you went to work."

"I wasn't feeling well."

Mona sighed. Like she thought, the whole house went down when Iman was sick. "Where's your sister?"

"She's in your room."

"*My* room?"

"She said I was making too much noise."

Mona sighed and started toward the stairs, where Adam was making his way up toward her. A second later she turned back to look at Hasna, a thought coming to her just then. "Why are *you* in Iman's room?"

"I was, um, looking for something."

It was then that Mona noticed the white cloth draped from Hasna's neck, reminding her of how some women wore the scarf in Pakistan. Mona recognized the fabric immediately. It was the *khimaar* Irum had bought for Iman a year ago, and she had bought an identical one for Asma.

For a second Mona and Hasna didn't speak, their eyes meeting in acknowledgement of what this meant. Hasna lowered her gaze. Clearly she hadn't intended to be caught, and that touched Mona more. She wanted to embrace her daughter, but she withheld. Hasna was an adult, twenty-six years old, and even before she had grown that much, she had a strong sense of independence, and pride. Hasna wanted to do things her own way, and in her own time.

This was supposed to be a private moment, Mona realized. Hasna hadn't expected her mother to discover she was trying on the head cover, a clear indication that Hasna's heart was changing, even if it was years late.

May Allah give you children just like you.

Yes, Hasna was like her mother. After years of glorified rebellion, Mona had finally submitted to what she had intuitively known all along — that in life there was nowhere to run, except to Allah Himself.

Without a word, Mona turned around and started her quiet retreat down the stairs to her room, only then allowing herself to break into a wide grin. She had to wait until her back was to Hasna before she could openly display on her face the depths of her pride. She didn't want to disrupt the delicacy of this moment. This one Hasna needed to handle alone.

"Mom?"

Mona was halfway down the steps when she turned to see her daughter now holding two fistfuls of the fabric that was still draped behind her neck. "Yes, Hasna?"

"Can you show me how to put this on?"

Yasmin's eyelids fluttered open until she was fully awake, the late afternoon sun a dull orange glow outside her window. She sat up, throwing the covers from her in that motion, realizing that the time for *Asr* was fading quickly. She had lain down for a nap after praying *Dhuhr*, expecting to sleep only an hour. Her heart felt heavy as she slipped her feet into her house shoes and made her way to the bathroom connected to her room.

Yasmin shuddered as she turned the metal handle of the bathroom, unable to console herself after the troubling dream she had just seen. She grew nauseated as she was reminded of her meeting with Sommer. It was a bad idea, a terrible idea to have asked her help.

What was Sharif doing right then? Yasmin wondered, her mind drifting to something pleasant. It was still morning where he lived, so he might be preparing for work. What was it that he did anyway? She couldn't remember. Their meeting had been brief, and, of course, they hadn't had the opportunity to speak to each other. But her father did mention something about Sharif being a… *an imam?*…or perhaps it was a teacher her father had said.

A *teacher*?

But how would they live?

Yasmin stopped herself.

Why was she assuming that Sharif wanted her at all? Why did it matter what his profession was? He had turned her down after only the *showfa*.

Yasmin turned on the faucet, feeling a headache coming on. She held her palm under the running water to gauge its warmth. She let the water rush between her fingers, feeling humiliated right then. What had she been thinking? She couldn't marry a *teacher*.

The mirror reflected a woman grimacing.

You could do better, the woman was saying to her. *You* have *to do better. Your reputation depends on it.*

In that moment, Yasmin saw Sommer's contempt for her in the blue eyes that glared back at her.

What? The eyes regarded her with disdain. *You think you're just going to use some guy to repair your image and it's not supposed to matter to him?*

Yasmin averted her gaze and quietly made *wudhoo* in the solitude of the bathroom, unable to ignore the sickness erupting in her stomach.

She doubted that marrying Sharif would repair her image even if he had wanted to marry her. She would be the laughing stock of her friends.

What friends?

Yasmin halted her *wudhoo,* her wet palms stilling as they wiped her face. A moment later she continued the motion, feeling tears stinging the back of her eyes.

Wallaahi, you'll see that, after Allah, you have not one friend in that school except your own mother.

When Yasmin lifted her gaze to her reflection, the woman looked sadder than she had moments before, the disdain gone from her eyes. For a moment, Yasmin felt sorry for the woman opposite her.

Wallaahi, the sad eyes said to her in a whisper, *you'll see that, after Allah, you have not one friend in this whole world.*

Except your own family.

And Sharif, if you let him.

In her room, Yasmin pulled the floral prayer garment over her as she thought of Sharif. Right then, she could not deny that she found him attractive, and it had little to do with him being American. She had long since outgrown her fascination with rappers like 2-Pac. Sharif's attractiveness was a spiritual one, and Yasmin felt that they could get along well together.

Yasmin had never expected him to say no to her father. She had spent her time wondering if she herself would say yes. Her indecisiveness toward marrying him had been the subject of the conversations she had with her parents leading up to the day of the *showfa.* It had been a difficult decision for her father to settle on Sharif as the right person for his daughter.

Yasmin tucked the cloth of the prayer garment's scarf under her chin, feeling her insignificance right then.

She had heard that American men viewed Arab women as rare beauties. Unlike most Arab men, she was told, Americans preferred women of color, especially those of deep brown olive complexion. Women of darker tones, especially from foreign lands, were seen as possessing an exotic beauty, and it was every American man's dream to have such a woman for himself.

Such was the "women talk" she had often heard whispered in circles of Arabs who mingled with Americans and their wives.

But now she doubted its authenticity.

Americans don't take this issue of love lightly...

Perhaps Sharif's reservations had nothing to do with her superficial traits. It was more likely that he had said no simply because he had no compelling reason to say yes. After all, who was she but a mysterious woman...beautiful perhaps...but mysterious and unfamiliar nonetheless.

Yasmin raised the back of her hands to her shoulders and recited the *takbir*, signifying the start of prayer. As she prayed, she had difficulty concentrating due to all that had been on her mind after her nap. Her heart scolded her for her arrogance, and she submitted to the reality that, regardless of whether or not Sharif would ever reconsider her, she had no cause to think herself better than he, even if he were merely a teacher.

"Here!"

Even as she recited *isti'aadhah*, seeking refuge in Allah from Satan as she tried to regain concentration, Yasmin could not forget the scene from the dream—the woman's dark eyes narrowing at her as she tossed a small box to Yasmin, clearly wanting to be rid of the sight of Yasmin on her doorstep.

The steps leading to the door of the woman's house were of weathered and broken stone, and Yasmin had left behind her the wide expanse of a lush green landscape to reach the uncomfortably narrow alley that led to the steps. Yasmin felt suffocated as the stone walls of the suddenly dark alley seemed to crush her as she frantically hurried to the steps, feeling desperate to get the box from the woman. The skin of her shoulder and arms was scraped as she moved forward in the narrow corridor, and she felt the stinging sensation of blood there.

The stone steps appeared at the end of the alley and descended into what looked like a murky pit. Yasmin halted her steps suddenly before descending, and her heart urged her to turn back. But she was reminded of the box, so she willed herself forward, drawing strength from her desire to have it in her possession.

The woman appeared at the doorway dressed in rags that barely covered her filthy skin. Repulsed, Yasmin withdrew from her, but only a step; after all, she had come for the box, and she would get it, even if it killed her.

"Here!"

Yasmin caught the box just as the woman slammed an iron door in her face, a door Yasmin had not noticed before.

The box was light in her hands, and this confused Yasmin, as she had thought the box would be…

Just then, there was a fluttering in the box, as if a large moth was struggling for release. The box itself began to tremble, and with each trembling it grew heavier. But Yasmin held on, the horrible shaking causing her scarf and shawl to slip from her, falling in a heap on the ground. The more she held on, the more her garments slipped from her, until both the weight of the box and her fear of exposure forced her to let go.

Upon releasing the box, Yasmin reached immediately for her garments, struggling to cover herself again. But she grew distracted as the box burst open and what looked like a black moth escaped and grew into a large, flat bird-like creature with two wide black wings and no body.

It flew away in the distance, and a moment later Yasmin was in a bedroom where a beautiful girl slept. In the dream, Yasmin knew the girl to be the one Sharif would marry, but Yasmin felt no jealousy at the sight of her, only raw terror. Frantically, Yasmin wondered how to help the girl, but the girl could not see her…as Yasmin was not even in the room herself. She saw the girl only because she, at that moment, was as if the girl herself, but Yasmin knew she was not.

Suddenly the black-winged creature descended upon the girl, and Yasmin felt as if it were herself in the bed right then. The creature wrapped itself about the girl, waking her in a fright. Desperately, the girl fought the dark wings, slapping and clawing at them to break herself free. But her desperation became despair as she realized the wings had become part of her skin, part of herself. But still she fought and fought…

Yasmin woke with a sick feeling in her stomach, and regret in her heart. Even as she finished prayer and sat quietly reciting the *adhkaar* on her prayer mat, she had that same eerie feeling that she had had in her heart upon waking—

That the dream was somehow connected to her visit with her former best friend.

"But why would you want to *live* there?"

Sharif sat in the living room of his home Tuesday afternoon, the phone to his ear, a feeling of *déjà vu* coming to him. He knew Hasna wouldn't be excited about the idea of living in the country Sharif had come to love more than his childhood home in America, but it was burdensome to hear the raw disappointment in her voice. It had been the simple sharing of his heart's desire, not the expression of a definite plan.

But her reaction reminded him of the same question that was often asked of him by Americans he had met in Riyadh. More than once he tried to articulate what he felt, thinking of his nearness to the Holy Cities, his being surrounded by believers, and his hearing the *adhaan* for every prayer. He tried to express what it meant to hear Allah's Words being recited from dozens of masjids at once, how it felt to experience the camaraderie of believers standing in closed ranks around the city, and the inspiration it evoked to walk the streets and give salaams to a passing stranger and know that he could respond in kind, because Islam was not only a religion and a way of life. It was a language itself.

A language of faith.

And it was spoken in Riyadh.

Often Sharif's explanation was met with blank stares, confused expressions, and even marked disgust, verbalized by degrading comments about Arab culture or about Arabs themselves.

It was then that Sharif was reminded of what he had already known.

There were some questions you simply could not answer, because there really was no way to explain. A person could not place his life in the palm of another and have the stranger examine it with the same eyes and heart of the one who had placed it there.

Understanding was not passed on with words, or with the indication of a perspective not considered before. Not even the faculties of hearing and sight aided one in comprehension.

Because understanding was transmitted through the heart.

Sharif started to respond to Hasna but stopped himself, remembering at that moment another lesson he had learned.

Often, people don't ask questions because they really want to understand. They ask to seek evidence to assure themselves they need not live like you.

"But you can be around Muslims in America," a brother had said once in response to Sharif.

Currently, however, Sharif was unsure how to respond. By agreeing to go forward with the marriage itself, Sharif had already sacrificed more than he could measure. He could not offer a compromise on something for which his heart itself did not offer such.

"Because I want to raise my children in an Islamic country."

There was a brief pause before Sharif heard Hasna grunt in response.

"Muslim country you mean?"

Sharif felt his jaw tighten at this disintegration of the conversation.

Hasna had called him to say that she had thought things over and that she might consider wearing the hijab one day.

It was good news, yes, and it should have been wonderful news. But there was the subtle hint that he read behind her words, a hint he caught only because he knew Hasna so well.

You can't make me; the decision is fully mine.

Sharif had no intention of forcing Hasna to do anything, but if she was to be his wife, did she imagine that a decision as serious as this rested in her mood alone? For the Muslim wife, there should never even be the question of force, as the husband would not be in a circumstance that required it. The wife would have already complied on her own, because that's what Muslims do when they learn of Allah's commands.

And if what Allah desired of her was worth only *considering*, should her mood allow, what of Sharif's own desires of her after they were husband and wife?

And now this? *Muslim* country?

It was becoming the cliché excuse for those who wished to make no efforts to live around Muslims, even within America itself. If it wasn't a *"No, it's a Muslim school, not an Islamic school"* comment, it was *"No, it's not Islam they're following, it's culture."*

"What do you mean?" Sharif asked, his calmness betraying his growing irritation with the conversation.

Hasna laughed. "Come on, Sharif. You know those people don't follow Islam, they follow culture."

"For example?" Sharif knew the tone of his voice revealed that he was less than pleased with the question, but he could not bring himself to care. It was disturbing that Muslims who viewed with disdain the prospect of living around other Muslims actually imagined that those who preferred Muslim societies had no idea that the current political and religious state of the Muslim world was less than perfect. He supposed it was just another absolution of responsibility: Oh, no, I can't live *there*. They don't practice Islam *fully*.

And you do? Sharif wanted to ask. But he held his tongue.

"You're kidding, right?" Hasna's tone was characteristic of those who looked down their noses at those from Muslim countries. "Please tell me they haven't brainwashed you into believing that the stuff they're doing there represents true Islam."

Sharif wasn't good at arguing, especially with Hasna, and he rarely took the bait. Her arrogance had always been pungent, but he had always chosen to overlook it and focus on her positive traits. But right then, he couldn't recall what they were.

"If what they're doing isn't Islam," he said, his confidence both shocking and pleasing him, as it was rare he got in a word edgewise with Hasna, let alone a confident one, "what should we call what you're doing, since it's much less than that?"

The silence was so complete that for a second he thought he had disconnected the line. "Hello?"

"I'm here."

Her tone was cold and distant, but Sharif was unmoved. At that moment, he couldn't care less how she felt. He just wanted to make sure that she had heard every word. He was tired of her self-righteousness and the way she talked to him as if she were doing him a favor by letting him hear even the sound of her voice.

At least the people she criticized had something to show for the Islam they claimed, he thought to himself. What about her? She rarely even prayed.

The line was silent again, but he refused to speak. If she wanted to talk, let her. He would say nothing until she herself gave him cause to speak, even if it meant having the phone hung up in his ear, a childish strategy she often resorted to when her feelings got hurt—even though she hurt his as a matter of course.

"Vernon told me this might happen."

Her words had come slowly and purposefully, and they settled over Sharif in the same deliberate way. He could taste their bitterness even as his mind was delayed in fully registering their meaning, and what they implied.

Mention another man. It was a hit below the belt. Apparently, Hasna had wanted to make Sharif taste every bit of the venom in her words, and suffer from every one.

And it worked.

She sighed and in that sound was a vicious taunting that told Sharif that she knew she had won—and that she was enjoying his subsequent suffering more than she had the triumph itself.

"I was just hoping he was wrong."

In that moment, Sharif felt his inadequacy. He had been a fool to ever imagine that he meant anything to Hasna at all. It was as if he, again, was an adolescent crumbling in his fragile self-esteem as he sat next to her in his kitchen, hoping she didn't notice his flimsy T-shirt or the hole tearing through his jeans at the knee—or if she did notice, that she would still accept his company, however meager it was, even if he could never have her for himself.

Vernon. The name itself left an unpleasant taste on Sharif's tongue. He remembered the name from an e-mail Hasna had written during his first year in Riyadh. Seeing a man's name in an e-mail from his fiancée was naturally troublesome to Sharif. He imagined it would disturb any man. But it hadn't been terribly significant at the time. It wasn't unusual for Muslims from his small community in Maryland to speak casually to the opposite sex. Sharif himself had done it as a matter of course when he had lived in the States.

A year after the initial e-mail, during his second year in Riyadh, Hasna mentioned Vernon again. This time Sharif had grown concerned. To casually talk to a male classmate was one thing, but to have a lasting friendship with one was another thing entirely.

Even in Sharif's circle of non-Muslims friends from high school and college, this had been a red flag. It simply was not in a man's nature to relax in the knowledge that his woman was cultivating a relationship with another man, no matter how platonic it appeared, or was claimed to be.

Hasna's bait hung in front of Sharif, and he felt the palms of his hands grow moist as he held the receiver to his ear.

Now what?

Hasna's unspoken question was unmistakable in its affront, and it was the ultimate in-your-face.

"Well..." Sharif said coolly.

His shattered ego was laid before him, hopes of its revival gone. But his utter helplessness was tearing at his pride. He had no idea what he would say—after all, what *could* he say to revive his dignity after suffering such a deadly blow? But he could not bow in the face of viciousness. As a mere human, he carried with him at least a grain of self-respect, and that alone demanded that he not give her cruelty the last word.

"I guess he's a smart man," he said finally.

Hasna laughed, a tinge of relief and triumph detectable in that sound, because their relationship was now back to where it was supposed to be—with Sharif beneath her and humbly so.

Sharif could tell she wasn't registering his true motives for the statement. Then again, neither was he.

"Yes," she agreed, confidence returning to her voice just then. "He knows a lot."

It was then Sharif remembered from an e-mail the mention of Vernon's fiancée. Kuwait? Katie? Keisha? No, it was a country's name...

Kenya. It came to him just then.

"He must," Sharif agreed, a smirk forming on his face. "Because he chose Kenya over you."

Change comes in stages, Sharif had heard. It wasn't something you could force. But it was something you could influence, for better or worse.

The hardest thing, though, about being an influence for change, was realizing it beforehand. Sharif hadn't asked to be a beacon for change, but the responsibility had been handed to him nonetheless.

"It's what your father would have wanted," his mother had said seven years before, the day after she, Karim, and Rashad revealed to him their plan for the community.

At the mention of his father, Sharif had grown quiet, that haranguing guilt eating at him again. He could not oppose an absent father, and most certainly not to the woman who was widowed by the loss. Nadirah was not trying to make her son feel guilty, Sharif knew, but the guilt crippled him nonetheless.

With the ghost of his father haunting him and his mother's corporeal presence a living testament to the loss, Sharif had silently consented to study abroad, even as he hadn't in his breast the slightest desire to board the plane.

Saudi Arabia was a country on a map, a word printed alongside the longitude-latitude grid that fenced the blues, greens, and browns of cartoon lands. It was a place his middle school social studies teacher had asked the class to picture with their eyes closed, as the students, restless and sweaty, sat in cramped desks, the air conditioner blowing out warm air from where it was wedged into the wall.

Saudi Arabia was a land of a strange language, of a foreign people, a world of National Geographic and Discovery Channel, and was separated from America by an ocean and a continent—and from Sharif Benjamin by immeasurable distances of the heart.

In private Sharif had sulked, lamenting the tremendous sacrifice that this trip would mean for him. He didn't care about the acceptance letter from Montgomery County Schools that was folded in his drawer, or the transcript that revealed that he had maintained a grade point average that earned him a place on the Dean's Merit List at his school. He wasn't worried about even the prospect of leaving his mother, brother, and sister alone after being their second caretaker after his father had died.

It was the prospect of losing Hasna that he grieved when he had sat alone in his room, nursing the anger and guilt that burned in his chest. The extended wait — *six more years* — was agonizing enough, but the prospect of losing her completely was even more agonizing to his fragile self.

Frantically, Sharif's mind had searched for other options, the first of which was that he wouldn't go. He was almost twenty years old, an adult. Couldn't he just say no?

But then he'd see the graying strands in his mother's hair, the wrinkles next to her eyes when she smiled, and the exhaustion on her face when she returned from work. And he'd remember her laughing with their father, or brushing her husband's cheek with a kiss, or her saying, with a roll of her eyes, *O Lord, not another car for Sharif.*

And then the protest would get stuck in his throat, replaced with the choking of his heart, and in silence he would retreat to his room. The implacable pain would continue to seize him until he thought his chest would burst. In anguish, Sharif would bite his fist to keep from making a sound when he whimpered, even when his eyes could offer no more tears.

No matter how much he had tried, he was utterly helpless in warding it off. There remained the haunting reminder that it was he, Sharif himself, who was responsible for his father's death.

Presently, Sharif sat quietly on the carpeted floor of his living room, having completed *Asr* prayer minutes before. The conversation with Hasna returned to him, this time in his heart instead of his mind. His cruelty gnawed at him, and his chin quivered in recognition that this was not his first sin of this kind.

It was a quiet heartlessness that defined him, Sharif realized at that moment. Not the quiet dignity that Rashad had imagined.

He wasn't being modest in saying he was not fit for the role as imam. He was being honest.

Sharif knew the darkness that lurked in his chest. Why should it be inflicted on anyone, let alone dozens of believers imagining that he would offer them guidance of some kind?

It was like playing part in a sick ruse for Sharif to accept the title *Imam* before his name, and then ask others to recite the lie on their tongue. It was better to back out now than to one day have the curtains pulled to reveal a charlatan in scholar's garb.

Sharif felt like the emperor is the story *The Emperor's New Clothes*. The people had stood in shock as the emperor paraded proudly before them, imagining himself to be sporting the most exquisite of garments, while he wore nothing but his underwear, oblivious to what was plain to everyone else.

Except in Sharif's version, the roles were reversed. It was the people's illusion, not the emperor's, that cloaked the emperor in royal garments, whereas Sharif himself knew all along what everyone else could not see.

"*Look.*" Sharif flinched at the memory, and it was as if his father stood before him right then. Dawud's thinning patience was detectable in the raised tone he was using with his oldest son. "*Just take out the garbage, and mop the floor.*"

"*Wali's old enough to clean up. Why can't he do it?*" Sharif rarely talked back to his father, but that night he had somehow gotten the nerve.

It had been a Wednesday, the night before Asma's birthday, and Dawud and Nadirah had planned a small party for the following evening. But the preparation needed to be done the night before because everyone except their mother had work and school the following day, which meant that there was no time for major cleaning before the guests arrived.

"*I didn't ask Wali. I asked you.*"

"*Wali's not a kid anymore.*"

"*Sharif!*" This final breaking of patience by his father was meant to stun Sharif into realizing his transgression.

But Sharif's voice grew louder than he had ever dared to speak to his father before. "*I'm tired of this. I can't stand this stupid house.*"

At this point, Sharif had expected a hand across his face, or at least an intimidating lecture, but Dawud showed no visible reaction to his son's outburst.

Sharif, in a show of defiance, angrily grabbed the overflowing garbage and yanked it from the plastic canister, not bothering to tie the black plastic ends. An empty can and orange peels fell to the floor in that motion. He then opened the back door and tossed the bag outside, not caring that its contents spilled onto the ground. After slamming the door shut, nearly shattering its glass window, Sharif pulled the mop from the kitchen closet and jabbed it into the pail of dirty water. He then slapped the mop across the kitchen floor, leaving streaks of soiled water on the white-marbled tiles, meanwhile mumbling complaints under his breath.

The entire time, Dawud stood in the doorway of the kitchen watching his son grumble and mutter protests just loud enough for him to hear, but Dawud himself did not utter a single word. Dawud's face was remarkably calmer than it had been moments before, and when Sharif had thrown the filthy mop back into the closet, not bothering to even close the door, Dawud had only looked at his son. There was a quiet resolve in Dawud's eye and it was as if he were seeing Sharif for the first time, this Sharif could feel under his father's gaze.

Dawud and Sharif looked at each other for a moment. Sharif's nose flared and he was breathing aloud. Dawud's lips were drawn together in disappointment, his expression calm.

"We'll speak in the morning," Dawud said after nearly a minute had passed.

Sharif saw his father turn and retreat to his room.

A second later, Sharif heard his father's door close. The soft sound underscored the solidity of his father's promise, and a change in the direction of a father-son relationship that had carved a friendship that would remain forever frozen in time.

That was the last time Sharif ever saw his father alive.

No one ever knew the exact cause of death. The official autopsy report listed heart failure. But Sharif's father had been a healthy man. He exercised regularly and ate only natural foods. He made all his food from scratch and kept himself abreast of natural remedies and herbs. Nadirah said that the report couldn't possibly be true.

For Sharif, however, it had taken several months to even accept the fact that his father was gone, and that he would never see him again. For those months, Sharif didn't think of the autopsy or what the doctors said.

He couldn't even admit that his father had died.

Daily, Sharif lived in denial as his heart ached for his father, and he tore his mind to pieces frantically searching for any evidence of there being some mistake.

Many nights he woke from sleep, heart racing because he thought he heard his father's car turning into the driveway or his key turning in the front door or him entering Sharif's room.

Sometimes Sharif would dream his father had really returned and was lightly punching him in the shoulder, saying playfully, *"Wanna play Go-car-go?"*

Yes, Daddy, Sharif would whisper to the darkness although he was in his last years of high school and hadn't played with his cars in years.

Presently, as he sat on the carpeted floor of his living room, there was that familiar emptiness, a hollowness that spread in his chest. Upstairs, the sound of the vacuum wheezed back and forth, a sign that Asma was finishing her chores.

In the solitude of the moment, Sharif felt the burning behind his lids. He bowed his head and bit his knuckles to suppress the whimper crawling in his throat.

"This is my son," his father would say with a pride that spread to his smiling eyes.

"Is there anything else you care about other than making that boy happy?" his mother would complain, playfully rolling her eyes.

"If he's happy, Nadirah," his father would reply, *"I'm happy."*

A soft sound escaped Sharif's throat as the sound of Asma's vacuuming faded upstairs.

Heart failure.

Yes. It was true.

Because Sharif had been his heart.

Part II

Seven

O Mujahid, shall I tell you of my brother,
Of my sister, my confidante, my friend?
Or shall I tell you of my father, my mother
My neighbor —
Or my sin?

We spend our days in laughter
And our nights in rest
Our prayers are but mumbled words
And movement of the limbs

Yet another home explodes
And tumbles to the ground
Ashes of dirt form clouds
Rising, floating, settling down
A young boy shades his eyes
The sun is blaring
He cannot see
He is looking for his mother
And at home, my mother is serving tea

I am on bed, reclining, relaxing
On my face is a smile forming
At one corner of my mouth
I do not hear the boy whimper
I do not hear the boy cry
I do not see his mother
I do not see her die

The phone rings
I answer
It is my confidante, my friend
She is telling me of a party
Tonight
Be there, she says
I laugh

Of course I will
Where else would I I be?

The boy's cry grows louder
Until it is a sob
Tears spill from his eyes
And slip, like rivers, down his cheeks
He has been robbed

Stolen
His heart is stolen
He is all alone
Daddy was stolen years ago
Now Mommy is gone

Somebody help me,
He cries
Somebody hear my plea
Abi, Ummi
Can you hear me?

Can you hear me?
My mother calls from downstairs
Hurry, I am serving tea
With a sigh, I toss aside my magazine
But not before saving my place
I want the jeans in the picture
The ones with the cuffs trimmed in lace
I'll die if I don't get them,
I think to myself
Abi'll say no, Mom'll say,
Buy 'em yourself

But I don't have enough money
I've nothing in my pockets

And the boy has nothing in his hand
Quietly, he kneels
Something is glistening in the sand
A ring

His mother's ring
From her wedding day
He holds it a moment more
His whimpers die until they're but soft whispers
Like dust clouds upon the shore

In the kitchen, I frown
My tea is cold
And it's not chai today
Peppermint, I think angrily, is getting old
I gulp the honey-sweetened liquid
And return to my bed

The boy stands
His legs are weak
I pick up my magazine
I find the picture I want
And grin
Soon they'll be mine
Soon, I think, but I don't know when

I am on bed, reclining, relaxing
On my face is a smile forming
At one corner of my mouth
I do not hear the boy whimper
I do not hear the boy cry
I do not see his mother
I do not see her die

The phone rings again
I answer
It is my confidante, my friend
She is telling me of the party
It's no longer tonight
Be there, tomorrow, she says
I sigh and shake my head
Where else would I I be?

For I spend my days in laughter
And my nights in rest

My prayers are but mumbled words
And movement of the limbs

Somebody help me,
The boy cries again
Somebody, anybody, hear my plea

Abi, Ummi
Can you hear me?

O Mujahid, shall I tell you of my brother,
Of my sister, my confidante, my friend?
Or shall I tell you of my father, my mother
My neighbor —
Or my sin?

Sharif stood in the kitchen of his home late Thursday night, the thin newsletter still in his hand.

He had been unable to sleep and had come downstairs hoping that food would satisfy his grumbling stomach even if it wouldn't satisfy his hunger for ideas for tomorrow's talk at *Jumu'ah*.

Sharif had thought nothing of the stack of junk mail on the table — credit card advertisments, department store magazines, and colorless newspapers. It had been out of sheer boredom and detached curiosity that he had picked up the newsletter that lay on top. He was planning to skim it as he ate a bowl of cereal with milk. *Brain food*, his father would have called it, this late night breakfast meal. And that's just what Sharif needed, some food for his brain.

Sharif couldn't even safely call his want for ideas *mental block*. He had no ideas that could be blocked in the first place. But he had been suffering from anxiety, mental and otherwise. And he knew of no one who could give him any idea what he should talk about from the *mimbar* the following day.

Sharif had been carrying the newsletter to the refrigerator when he read the title. *Islam's Call*. He frowned, his curiosity simmered by disappointment. He tossed the newsletter back on the pile.

Why did so many Muslim periodicals carry bland names? he wondered. It didn't help that the publication looked like it was produced from a cheap ink-jet printer with a dying cartridge instead of a decent printing house.

Sharif had started to skim through the junk-mail pile in favor of perusing a local drugstore's discounts on cough medicine and chewing gum when he saw the poem.

"O Mujahid, Shall I Tell You?"

Intrigued, Sharif reached for the newsletter again and began reading.

It wasn't until he had finished that he realized he hadn't eaten or sat down, nor had he remembered to.

The house was quiet except for the occasional creaking of a floorboard or the distant ringing in a vent, and it was in the quiet stillness of his home, the darkness of night surrounding him, that the inspiration suddenly came to him.

Carrying the paper to his room, Sharif skipped the stairs two at a time, suddenly inspired to write his first Friday *khutbah*.

Sharif had never stood before a congregation to deliver a talk, and he had spent the whole of Thursday—from *Fajr* to *'Ishaa*—drafting and redrafting his speech, taking a break to only pray, use the bathroom, or get something to eat. But nothing he wrote had satisfied what he wanted to convey.

Imam Rashad had offered to help, and for a moment Sharif had actually considered accepting the offer. But then he remembered his own agony as a victim of the imam's droning during Friday *khutbah*'s of years before, and Sharif changed his mind.

Yes, Sharif was desperate. But he wasn't that desperate. Even if he were, there were less extreme measures he could take.

In his room, Sharif turned on a lamp and sat in the chair in front of his desk. He quickly opened the half-filled notebook he had been using earlier and began to scribble down his ideas before they left him.

After filling three handwritten pages, he glanced at the newsletter that lay next to him on the desk.

Umm Sumayyah.

He wanted to give due credit when he quoted from the poem. But he doubted the author would even care about the oversight of an insignificant imam of a masjid as small and unknown as his.

To date, there were only fourteen families who frequented the masjid, and due to jobs, busy schedules, and Imam Rashad's impeccable reputation in holding a crowd's interest—for sleep—many of them attended *Jumu'ah* elsewhere if they could help it.

From that perspective, except for knowing the ethics of avoiding plagiarism, Sharif thought he would be doing the author a favor if he left her name out of his speech. She probably wouldn't want the connection.

Sorry, Umm Sumayyah, he apologized in his mind as he jotted her name down on his notebook. *Think of it as charity. If you've been to any of our Jumu'ah's in the last ten years, or have known anyone who has, you'll understand my predicament.*

Before going to bed, Sharif made *sajdah* for gratefulness, prostrating to Allah to thank Him for allowing him to come across the newsletter, which was most likely intended to be trashed or recycled. Wali had probably forgotten to sort the recyclables (again), but this time Sharif was grateful to his brother. Things didn't happen for no reason. Allah had a plan for even the loosening of a single leaf from a branch, or for allowing Wali to forget his chores.

And finding the newsletter had been the loosening of Sharif from a bind.

For the first time since he arrived in the States, Sharif felt good about his first day on the job. It was true that he did not belong in the imam position. But he also knew that, after spending six years in Riyadh for this expressed purpose and after hearing his mother say that this had been his father's dream, Sharif really didn't have much of a choice.

When Sharif glanced out the window of the imam office early Friday afternoon, he saw that the parking lot of the masjid was almost filled. It took a second for him to register what this meant, and when he did, his chest tightened in anxiety.

"I hope you don't mind," Imam Rashad had casually told Sharif on the phone the day before, after Sharif had turned down the imam's offer to assist him in writing the talk. "But we told a few people that we have a new young imam taking over the *khutbah* this week."

Sharif had said he didn't mind, and until now he had forgotten about the comment. He had imagined that the former imam was inviting some old friends who would be doing Rashad (and Sharif) a favor by stopping in to show their support. That way, Sharif wouldn't have his sister and brother as the only members of the congregation (besides Brother Rashad), smiling politely and pretending to be inspired while trying their best not to glance at their watches or nod off (though he imagined that Wali wouldn't mind stretching out right in front of him).

But this was far more than a "few", and they were not all old. They were of varying ages, races, and ethnicities.

Sharif willed himself not to look out the window again and instead sat at the imam's desk—which was now his—and held his forehead in his hand, his elbow propped on the desk as he made silent prayers to Allah that the task before him would be made easy.

Sharif didn't appreciate being put on the spot like this though. He suspected that a full-fledged advertising campaign had taken place, even if only by word of mouth. He wondered who else had been involved. He imagined today's crowd couldn't be the work of Imam Rashad alone.

His mother? Brother Karim? Sister Irum? Perhaps, all three had a hand in this.

Didn't they realize that Sharif had spoken only once before a crowd? And that was during a freshman speech course at Howard. But that crowd had been students who themselves had to face the same crowd when they delivered their own speech. In such an environment, there had been little room for judgment, especially since, except for the professor, they all were to be in the same uncomfortable position as Sharif had been when he spoke (if one could call reading quickly from a paper held in front of his face a speech at all).

However, today was entirely different. Sharif wouldn't be excused for stutters, or for his mind going blank, or for reading from his notes if he got too nervous to go through with this. And he wouldn't be given a chance to start over (as his kind professor had given him rather than allow him to fail).

Sharif didn't even have the margin of error on his side.

You couldn't stand before a group of Muslims and make blunders in information related to their souls and expect them to excuse you.

Sharif drew in a deep breath, continuing his *dhikr,* but it was difficult to keep from getting both overwhelmed and anxious. Sharif could only pray that in Rashad's passive mention of the "new young imam from Riyadh" to those "few" people, Rashad hadn't shared Sharif's so-called "way with words" or "quiet dignity."

At the reminder, the anxiety in his chest returned.

He couldn't do this, he feared, not now.

A second later, the *adhaan* sounded through the intercom of the masjid, announcing that the time for *Jumu'ah* had arrived.

"*Innalhamdalillaah. Nahmaduhu…*" Sharif began by reciting the *du'aa* that the Prophet customarily used to open his speeches. He was conscious that the Arabic, and corresponding translation, would be foreign to many community members, who usually began talks by simply seeking refuge in Allah.

"Verily, all praise is due to Allah," Sharif said. "We praise Him and seek His help and ask His forgiveness. And we seek refuge in Allah from the corruption of our souls and from the ill of our deeds. He whom Allah guides, there is none who can misguide him. And He whom Allah leaves astray, there is no one who can guide him. And I bear witness that nothing has the right to be worshipped except Allah alone, Who has no partner, and I bear witness that Muhammad, peace be upon him, is His servant and Messenger."

Sharif took a deep breath and let his gaze fall to his notes that lay on the podium before him, the drumming in his chest having slowed after the opening *du'aa.* But he was acutely aware of more than fifty men, women, and children hanging on to his every word.

The crowd was not enormous, and was in fact much smaller than Sharif had feared, but it didn't escape Sharif that almost every face in the prayer area was that of someone he did not know. He recognized the attire of the men and women from Pakistan, and the features of those from Egypt, Somalia, and Ethiopia. Among them, too, were Americans, whom Sharif had recognized at once. And, of course, there were those from areas he could not determine.

The women sat behind the rows of men, and, except for those for whom the masjid was home, they were all covered in Islamic attire, the color and style varying based on ethnicity, Islamic inclination, and preference. Sharif was taken aback when he saw that several women were wearing the traditional black *jilbaab* that he associated with Saudi Arabia, but he was pleased. The sight warmed him and made him feel for a small moment that he was back in Riyadh.

"I begin this *khutbah* by saying words that were inspired by the those of Abu Bakr, may Allah be pleased with him, after he accepted his role as caliph of the Muslims, although I know my task before you is much humbler. And I apologize in advance for my faulty speech, as I know these words are probably not the most appropriate for a *Jumu'ah khutbah*. But I spent the entire day yesterday and several hours into the night trying to find the right words to share with you today. But because of a single fact that I fear will become more or less apparent to you, if not today then someday shortly thereafter, I had extreme difficulty in fulfilling this task. And that is because I am not qualified to be standing here at all."

Sharif took another breath and rearranged his notes although they were already situated before him. The ruffling of the papers distracted him as the sound was carried through the microphone, setting Sharif's heart pounding again and making him painfully aware of the expecting crowd.

Faltering, Sharif wiped beads of sweat from his forehead and felt his hands tremble as he realized the honesty of his last words. Self-conscious that his nervousness was betraying him, Sharif went on to share the words he had adapted from the speech of Abu Bakr in hopes of making them suited for today's talk.

"As most of you know, I have been chosen as the Imam of this community although I am not the best among you, nor am I the most knowledgeable in this task. So, I ask each of you, if I ever fall into error, please correct me and show me the right path. If I do what is right, based on the Book of Allah and the Sunnah of His Messenger, peace be upon him, I ask your support and assistance, because I cannot do this alone.

"Truth and righteousness are a trust, and falsehood and impiety are a breach of that trust, so I ask Allah to guide me, and you, to Truth and righteousness, and away from falsehood and from any deeds that are displeasing to Him..."

Completing the first part of his speech, Sharif recited some verses from the Qur'anic chapter *Qaaf*, as it was a *soorah* the Prophet sometimes recited during *Jumu'ah*.

In the second part of the *khutbah*, Sharif recited the verses that he felt most apt in addressing those members of the congregation who had been taught that the essence of Islamic faith rested in the heart alone.

Do men think that they'll be left alone on saying, "We believe" and that they will not be tested? We did test those before them, and Allah will certainly make known those who are truthful from those who are lying.

When Sharif glanced at the crowd, he was moved to see that many of them had tears in their eyes. He himself was reflecting on the meaning of the Arabic words before he conveyed them in English, and their powerful meaning gripped him, as he wondered which group he would be assigned during the final trials of life.

"And who of us truly believes?" he asked rhetorically, his tone conveying a sincerity that suggested he didn't know if he himself was included amongst the truthful believers. "And who of us is lying?"

Tears filling his own eyes, he recited, his voice rising with the beauty of the Words of Allah,

*Behold, in the creation of the heavens and the earth and the alternation of night and day —
These are indeed Signs for men of understanding —
Those who celebrate the praises of Allah,
Standing, sitting, and lying on their sides.*

And contemplate the [wonders of] creation
In the heavens and the earth, [praying]
"Our Lord! You did not create this aimlessly.
Glory to You! Give us salvation from the penalty of the Fire."

"...Our Lord, we have heard the call of one calling to faith [saying],
'Believe in your Lord,' and we have believed.
Our Lord! Forgive us our sins,
Blot out from us our iniquities
And cause us to die in the company of the righteous."

In closing, Sharif said, tears still in his eyes, "These are the characteristics of the righteous, those who do not merely say, 'I believe' and then expect an eternal reward after they die.

"They are those who testify openly that, 'Yes, I believe, and I dedicate my heart, my words, my actions, and my entire life to you, O Allah."

Sharif looked out at the crowd, eyes squinted. "But shall I tell you the characteristics of those who will lose in the Hereafter, people like me and you, who—as Muslims suffer around the world, or even next door—relax in the comfort of their lives worrying about the latest fashion or television show?"

He paused. "I think these people are best described in a poem by the author Umm Sumayyah titled, 'O Mujahid, Shall I Tell You?'..."

After leading the prayer, Sharif had planned to retire to his office, but he was swarmed with handshakes and warm embraces. The brothers asked about the university where Sharif had studied, how long had he lived in D.C., and if he knew so-and-so. Some of the older brothers surprised Sharif by asking if he was married. Brother Karim also came up to greet him, a proud smile on his face as he drew Sharif into a hug. Imam Rashad too came to greet him.

"Now," Rashad joked, patting Sharif playfully on the back, "the brothers don't have to bring pillows and blankets to *Jumu'ah* anymore."

After they recovered from friendly laughter, Rashad asked Sharif if it were okay if he entered the office to take out some of his belongings and make a few phone calls.

Sharif chuckled in response and said, "To me, it's still yours."

By the time Sharif left the prayer area, most of the congregation had gone home.

In the lobby, Sharif smiled at the scene of Muslims chatting amongst themselves, the sun's rays spilling through the glass windows and reflecting light on the marbled tiles beneath where they stood. Sharif heard laughter amidst the conversation, the sound soothing Sharif and reminding him that he had just completed his first *Jumu'ah* as an imam.

He had stressed so much over the talk that it was difficult to believe that it was actually over. There had been a few blunders, he reflected a moment before he decided to find Wali and Asma, but Allah had pulled him through.

Feeling exhausted from the long night and the morning's stress, Sharif glanced at his watch. He had borrowed their mother's car and had to pick her up after work. He still had two hours before that time, but he wanted to go home and rest.

As he passed the imam's office, he saw Imam Rashad sitting behind the desk jotting down some notes on a sheet of paper. When their eyes met, Rashad greeted Sharif with a heartwarming smile, in that single gesture letting Sharif know how proud he was of him. Sharif saw in Rashad's eyes that he felt that they had made the right decision when they asked him to take the position as imam.

Sharif was moved, at that moment immediately reminded of his father and how he had once sat behind that same desk. Right then Sharif wondered what his father would think of him now, and if he would have made him proud.

He hoped so.

Sharif heard Asma's voice, and he walked toward the other end of the lobby where he saw some sisters chatting amongst themselves.

"I know!" a voice said, and he was certain that it was his sister.

Sharif saw Asma facing his direction talking to someone who was wearing the black *jilbaab* that he had seen some women wearing earlier. The woman's gloved hand was holding that of a young boy, who tugged at her hand before glancing in the direction Sharif.

Distracted, Sharif halted his steps and stared at the boy. The child's smooth brown features held a distant familiarity that Sharif could not place. He had seen the boy somewhere, Sharif was certain, but where…?

"Asma," Sharif said, his eyes lingering on the boy for a few seconds.

Sharif glanced at his watch from where he stood a comfortable distance from his sister and the woman, remembering his tight schedule just then.

Asma continued chatting with the veiled woman, apparently having not heard him. The woman then laughed at something she had said.

Sharif wanted to get his sister's attention, but he didn't want to come too much closer because he could see that the woman's veil was lifted, most likely because she was facing the hall that led to the women's entrance to the prayer area.

"Asma," he said taking a step closer so that his sister could hear him, cautious not to approach from an angle from which he would see the woman's face.

At the sound of Sharif's voice, the woman stopped laughing. Glancing behind her, she pulled the veil over her face, suddenly aware that a man was approaching. In that moment, Sharif was able to make out the brown of her cheek that matched the smooth complexion of her son.

It was then that Asma noticed her brother, her face immediately reflecting an apology as her eyes widened slightly, realizing that she hadn't registered the passing time.

"Asma, we have to go," he said as she looked at him.

"I know. I'm sorry. I forgot you were waiting."

Asma quickly greeted the sister with a cheek-to-cheek hug, saying that she would call her later, and playfully rubbed the head of the boy before joining Sharif.

"I have to get some things from the imam's office," he said. "But you can go on to the car." He handed her the keys.

"And if you can find Wali," he added, "that would help."

"He left already."

Sharif creased his forehead. "How? I have the car."

"He said he was going somewhere with a brother."

Sharif shrugged. "Okay, as long as Mom doesn't mind."

On the drive home, Sharif noticed that Asma was unusually quiet. She stared distantly out the window, clearly disturbed by something, a marked contrast to the playful attitude she had had during the conversation with the veiled woman.

"Where did you find that poem?" she asked, glancing at Sharif for the first time, her eyes reflective.

He met her curious gaze before turning his attention back to the road. "You mean the 'O Mujahid' one?"

"Yeah."

"I found it on a pile of old newspapers in the kitchen last night."

Asma creased her forehead as she studied her brother curiously, as if seeing him for the first time. "Really?"

"Yes." Sharif laughed. "You'd be surprised the treasures you can find when Wali doesn't sort the recyclables like he's supposed to."

Asma rolled her eyes, a grin lingering on her face. "When does he ever do anything he's supposed to do?"

Sharif chuckled uncomfortably, realizing their conversation was bordering on backbiting Wali. It also reminded Sharif himself of his own flaws the night he spoke to his father for the last time.

"Well..." Sharif sighed thoughtfully, feeling an awkward kinship to his brother's struggles. "Wali's a man now. He has a lot to do, so we shouldn't give him a hard time."

"What does he have to do?" Asma laughed. "Sleep all day?"

"Asma, don't say that."

"I'm serious. That's all he does."

She shook her head, grinning. "I bet when he wakes up, he actually thinks he cleaned the whole house."

"I don't think that's true."

Asma laughed again. "Like Mom always says, *He's living in a dream world.*"

"She didn't mean that, Asma," Sharif said, although he imagined that Asma was probably correct in her summation. "She meant that he's still trying to figure out what he wants to do with his life."

"And I'm sure he's getting all the answers in his dreams."

Sharif started to respond in disagreement—

But his sister's last words jogged a memory.

...in his dreams.

The boy.

In his dream.

That's where Sharif had seen him.

Sharif pressed the breaks so quickly that the car jerked him and his sister forward. The car screeched to a halt, and their backs slammed against the leather seats with the sudden stop.

He had nearly run the red light as the realization came to him.

"Sha-*rif*," Asma said, her voice raised. Her eyes were scolding as she glared at him.

But Sharif barely registered her reaction.

The imam sat in his office facing the area...smiling proudly as he thought of Sharif...

Imam Rashad.

Light from the sun illuminated the lobby, making the marbled tile glow...

The sun's rays shining through the lobby's glass windows that afternoon.

Sharif heard laughter, as if coming from a heavenly source, but he realized the sound was in front of him...

The woman's laughter he had heard.

Sharif walked toward her, seeing only the soft black fabric of the jilbaab... Her veil was lifted but she was not facing him. She was talking to someone... He drew closer until he was but a step away. That was when she heard him and quickly dropped the veil over her face, glancing behind her, sensing that a strange man was approaching ...Her gloved hand held the palm of a young boy whose skin glowed the same golden brown...whose cheek he could barely make out as he neared...

The woman Asma had been speaking to.

Sharif's heart raced, the pounding now a discomfort in his chest. He felt the palms of his hands grow moist as they gripped the steering wheel, the traffic light a dim red glow in the bright afternoon sun.

Asma.

He glanced at his sister, whose face was contorted, still recovering from the sudden stop.

"Sharif, you should be careful," she said, annoyed. "You're driving like Wali."

Sharif said nothing as the light turned green and he carefully lifted his foot from the break and gently pressed the gas pedal, the car moving forward smoothly this time.

When he pulled the car into the driveway of their home, Sharif was still silent, his mind a flood of thoughts. It was difficult to think clearly.

Who was the woman? Was she divorced? Was the boy her son?

In the house, Asma walked into the kitchen, and Sharif followed, realizing that the answers to these questions lay with his little sister.

As Asma rummaged through the newspapers and sales papers that still lay on the table from last night, Sharif opened the refrigerator and surveyed its contents although he could not even think of eating right then.

"Where'd you put that newsletter?" she asked. "I was looking for it all day yesterday."

"Who was that woman you were talking to?" Sharif asked, his voice calm, his mind only vaguely registering that she had been asking him something else. Sharif detected a slight quiver in his speech, but he was pleased by the natural tone in his voice.

With one hand, he removed the carton of milk from the top shelf and closed the refrigerator with the other. He then reached for a box of cereal that was on top of the freezer, setting the box and milk on the counter while he found a glass bowl and a spoon for himself.

"What?"

After pouring the cereal and milk, he held the bowl and turned to see Asma looking at him, the question still on her face. He leaned against the counter casually and repeated himself before lifting a spoonful of cereal to his mouth.

"That woman. The one with a son. Who is she?"

Asma wrinkled her nose, distracted from her own inquiry as she registered his. "A woman?"

"Yes, Asma," Sharif said, a slight edge in his voice. "You were talking to a woman when I was looking for you."

"No I wasn't."

Sharif groaned.

But a moment later, his frustration was halted as he wondered if he had imagined the whole scene...

Was that possible?

But how...?

He creased his forehead. "You weren't talking to someone when I came to get you?"

Asma blinked, her face still contorted. In the few seconds that it took her to process her brother's question, Sharif doubted his sanity.

But he was certain that he had seen a veiled woman when he had—

"You mean right before we left?"

"Yes," he said, growing slightly aggravated with all the questions. "She was wearing a black *abaya*. She had a little boy with her."

For a moment, Asma just stared at Sharif.

"You mean *Iman*?"

Sharif laughed. "No. I'm talking about just now, Asma. Right before we left the mas—"

"I know," she said, still staring at Sharif, a question on her face. But this time Sharif sensed that it was not connected to what she had asked moments before.

"That was Iman," she said.

Asma studied her brother a second more. "Why?"

For a few seconds, Sharif just stared at Asma, his face registering the confusion he felt right then. "Iman? *Hasna's* sister?"

A hesitant grin creased one side of Asma's mouth, mild amusement in her eyes as she registered understanding of the source of Sharif's confusion.

"Yeah, I know," she chuckled a second later, shaking her head in agreement. "I was shocked too when I first saw her."

Sharif's heart pounded self-consciously. How did Asma know about the dream?

No, he stopped himself. That was impossible. She must be referring to something else. He hadn't mentioned the dream to anyone.

"Hasna says she looks like a ninja in all that black." There was laughter in Asma's voice as she shook her head again.

"*What?*" Sharif was agitated by the mention of Hasna, and by the comment that mocked the *jilbaab*. But his mind couldn't focus on that right then.

"Even Sister Mona thinks it's too much." Asma shrugged as she thought of something.

"I wouldn't wear it," she said. "But I don't think it's too much. If that's what she thinks she's supposed to wear, why should it bother anyone else?"

"But who was that boy then?"

"What boy?"

"Next to her."

"Adam."

Sharif blinked, hoping that nothing drastic had happened while he was gone.

Amused laughter was in Asma's expression as she drew her eyebrows together, placing a hand on her hip as she studied Sharif. "Don't tell me you forgot Adam *too* while you were gone."

Adam...

It was then that Sharif remembered the e-mail from his mother a few years back.

"Just writing to let you know Sister Mona had a healthy baby boy last night. They named him Adam."

...Oh.

Sharif didn't know what to say.

Asma's expression changed, distracted by a sudden thought. She glanced at the junk-mail pile on the kitchen table, her face appearing worried just then.

"Sharif, do you remember where you put that newsletter you found?"

"What newsletter?"

"The one with the poem in it."

"Yeah, it's uh..."

Where *was* it?

"I think it's on the desk upstairs in my room."

"Can I have it back if you're finished with it?"

Sharif carried his bowl of cereal to the table, his mind befuddled, unable to fully comprehend what he had just learned.

He sat down, his body feeling heavy in the wooden chair.

Iman?

No... That was impossible.

He must have misinterpreted the dream... Maybe it was his wife's sister he had seen...?

But no, he had been sure that the woman was his wife...

But how...?

"You can have it," Sharif said to Asma, distracted as he sought to understand what this all meant. "I don't need it anymore."

Asma started out the kitchen to retrieve the newsletter from his room, but she halted in the doorway.

A second later she turned to Sharif, an uncertain expression on her face. She waited for him to meet her gaze.

Sharif looked up, but his mind wasn't on Asma.

"Who told you about that poem?"

It took a second for Sharif to register her question although he was looking directly as his sister when she spoke.

"Nobody," he said, turning his attention back to his meal.

"Then why did you read from it today?"

He shrugged. "I just saw it in the newsletter and decided to."

He reached for a newspaper as he brought a spoonful of cereal to his mouth. He opened the first page, chewing the food as his eyes skimmed the headlines, his mind elsewhere.

"You didn't know whose it was?"

He paused his reading, slightly annoyed by Asma's constant questions. "No. I just saw it on the kitchen table."

He looked at her again, annoyance in his contorted expression as he regarded her. "What does it matter to you anyway?"

"Because that was just a sample. I didn't want anybody to see it yet."

Eyebrows drawn together, it took Sharif several seconds to understand what Asma was saying.

"*You* did that newsletter?"

"Yes," she said, defensive, apparently offended by his surprise.

"By yourself?"

"Well, it was Sister Irum's idea. But me and Iman collected the articles and everything."

"Wait a minute." He set down his spoon, giving his sister his full attention. "So that, uh, *Calling to Islam*—"

143

"*Islam's Call,*" she said.

"That's not *real*?"

Asma shrugged. "Not yet, but it will be *inshaaAllah.*"

She shrugged again, self-conscious just then. "That was just a sample. We wanted to show it to Imam Rashad and…well, to you, I guess, to see if we could use it for the masjid."

"But where did you find the articles?"

"We just asked people to write them," she said. "Sister Irum said that's better."

"So you *know* Umm Sumayyah?"

Asma creased her forehead. "Umm Sumayyah?"

"The one who wrote the poem."

Her face relaxed. "Oh yeah. I forgot about that," she said, chuckling with a wave of her hand. "That's just a pen name."

"A pen name?"

"Yeah." She smiled, obviously proud of herself. "You like it?"

For a second Sharif just stared at his sister, in that moment seeing her for the first time. So much had changed since he had left. He felt old right then, and completely disconnected from the community he was to lead—and from his own family.

He had known that Asma had grown into a young woman. But that poem…

He had no idea she could put words together like that. He was stunned. And impressed. He didn't know what to say.

"So Umm Sumayyah is a pen name for you?"

Asma blinked, her smile fading as her eyebrows drew together. She shook her head a second before saying, "Not for me. For Iman."

Eight

When Iman was three years old, Mona shaved off all of the child's hair. The obstinate curls would twist and turn into coils that took Mona over an hour to comb through, and the next day, they would do it all over again.

"I wook wike a boy!" Iman had complained, stomping her feet as Mona swept up the piles of hair.

"It's better than having no hair at all."

"I wook wike a boy..." Iman whined again, having just learned from the eyes of a child the basic difference between boys and girls: Girls have hair. Boys don't.

When Nadirah saw Iman, she laughed so hard that Mona thought her friend would double over. "Mona, haven't you ever heard of corn braids?"

"*Corn* braids? As in what we eat?"

"No, as in the braids that look like rows of corn."

At that moment, Mona noticed Nadirah's hairstyle. "Is that what you call it?"

"Yes, that or corn rows." Nadirah continued laughing, shaking her head.

"Let me teach you," Nadirah said a second later, offering for Mona to use her own daughter's hair for practice.

It took Mona a full week to get a single braid right, and that was with full-day sessions at Nadirah's house or Nadirah at hers. When Mona finished the solitary row in Asma's hair, Nadirah had joked to Mona, saying, "Now I'll call you Moneequa."

"What?"

"Never mind."

"I can't wait till Iman's old enough to do her own hair," Mona had said with a sigh after some time.

"Well, don't rush things," Nadirah told her. "Then she'll be old enough for problems you wouldn't have dreamed of right now."

This was the sentence that played over in Mona's mind as she sat next to Iman in the doctor's office Monday afternoon. Iman lay on the dull gray mattress of the patient bed, a paper gown drawn around her like a jacket, another paper gown laid across her lower body.

Iman's appointment had initially been with her pediatrician although Iman hadn't seen the doctor since her last check-up four years before. However, the doctor that now stood before Mona and her daughter was an obstetrician-gynecologist whom the pediatrician had called in after Mona explained that Iman's primary symptoms were an irregular monthly cycle and painful menstrual cramps.

It had taken some time for Mona to recover when the pediatrician had said, "I think you should speak to the OB-GYN."

"No," Mona had said, shaking her head, "not for me. For my daughter."

"Yes, I understand," Iman's doctor had said, "but my specialty is pediatrics, Ms. Khan. My patients are all children."

"But Iman is your patient. We've been coming to you since she was three months old."

"Yes, I know," the pediatrician said. "But now she's a teenager."

Mona blinked, slowly registering what the doctor was saying.

"With these symptoms," the pediatrician said, "she needs an OB-GYN. This is an adult issue."

It was then that Mona had the epiphany.

Iman stood next to her mother, one inch taller than Mona's five-foot-three height, and the black fabric of Iman's *khimaar* framed the delicate features of her face, the cloth falling like a curtain over the front of the black over-the-head outer garment that now sat on her shoulders, the matching face veil lying on the patient table. Iman was wearing the clothes of a Muslim woman who had reached the age of puberty — and more clothes besides.

Even though the garment obviously adhered to the Islamic requirements of looseness and modesty, it was obvious that the garb concealed not the body of a child, but that of a fully developed woman. As if seeing Iman only now after several years, Mona realized Iman could pass for eighteen, and Iman became a strange woman standing next to her where her daughter should have been.

Currently, the OB-GYN scribbled some notes on a paper as Iman still lay on the bed, knees slightly bent beneath the paper garment, her bare feet flat on the examination table.

"She'll need some iron supplements for the anemia, and we may need to—"

"Anemia?" Mona's voice was etched in concern.

"Iron deficiency," the doctor said, handing the prescription to Mona and standing with the motion. "That's what's most likely responsible for the headaches and fatigue."

Mona rubbed the top of Iman's head, the fabric of the scarf awkward beneath her touch. A concerned expression was on Mona's face.

"*She's just a hypochondriac,*" Hasna had said when Mona mentioned that she was thinking of taking Iman to see a doctor. "*They won't be able to diagnose that. But they can tell you nothing's wrong,*" she had joked, "*which is basically the same thing.*"

"You may also want to consider birth control pills to—"

"What?" Mona glared at the doctor. "My daughter is a *Muslim.*"

Even as she said it, Mona detected the break in her voice, the fault lines in her logic. For a moment, there was sharp silence in the room. The doctor's nose flared for a brief second, and the OB-GYN looked at her watch before slipping her hands into the oversized pockets of her white coat. Mona could tell from the doctor's expression that she had been offended by the comment, and disagreed with the implications, in their testifying to Iman's innocence and to the doctor's guilt.

Mona imagined the doctor repeating the conversation to a colleague later, mocking how indignant Mona had been at the suggestion.

I can't believe these people, Mona imagined the doctor saying, *living in such denial. As if religion ever makes any difference*—a laugh—*except in how bad you feel afterwards.*

"Ms. Khan, I understand your religious sensitivities, but the pills will be used to regulate her menstrual cycle, not to keep her from getting pregnant." The doctor glanced sideways at Iman. "Although that's an option she can consider if she should ever need them for that."

It was Mona's turn to get offended, but she decided to leave the discussion alone. However, she had caught the doctor's subtle message to Iman: *Ignore your mother, and take care of yourself. We both know what you might do when she's not around.*

"Isn't there some medicine we can use to do that?"

"This is the medicine we use."

"But it seems a bit—"

"I understand it's not the most ideal way to address the problem, but it's a proven method for normalizing the cycle."

"But is it really necessary?"

"That's up to you. An irregular cycle isn't harmful in itself. Many women have it throughout their lives with no apparent cause to be concerned. But occasionally, it's a symptom of something else."

"Like what?"

"Endometriosis is a strong possibility in cases like these. But for now, we can't say for sure."

The doctor reached for a small prescription pad and scribbled down something else. She then handed it to Mona.

"In case you change your mind."

Mona accepted the piece of paper with a nod, the scene evoking memories of Mona's own prenatal visits during her pregnancies with Hasna, Iman, and Adam...and her first visit to an obstetrician before she got married.

"So this could be something serious?" Mona's eyes were on Iman, who was absently studying the biological charts on the wall next to the bed.

"There's no evidence to suggest that at this time. Heavy cycles, back pain, fatigue, headaches..." The doctor shrugged. "These are all common in otherwise healthy women. They're also becoming increasingly common in young adults whose bodies are still adjusting to the hormonal and physiological changes of puberty."

Distracted, Mona wondered about those for whom the symptoms were in fact indicative of more serious problems.

"However, if the pain is persistent or unbearable for her —"

Mona thought immediately of how Iman described her abdominal pains.

" — then you should bring her in for further analysis."

"But how do you define unbearable?"

"If it keeps her from normal activities, or if she is unable to go to school for several days at a time, especially if the pain is not premenstrual or connected to her cycle."

Mona thought of how she had assumed Iman was menstruating the day she returned with the groceries. But Iman had not been, although she was due to start any day now, so it was possible that the pain was in fact premenstrual.

"But for this, we can prescribe some medicine to help with the pain."

"She takes extra strength Midol now. I'm not sure if she needs something stronger though."

"If the Midol alleviates the pain, there's no need for a prescription, but I can write one for her in case she needs something stronger."

On the ride home, Mona had turned on a lecture tape to keep her mind distracted. It wasn't her daughter's anemia diagnosis or the possible endometriosis that troubled her most. She herself had suffered from similar symptoms as a teenager and remained in relatively good health, the symptoms now having disappeared. Mona's diet adjustment and daily multivitamins had corrected the anemia, and after having children her cycles became regular and the pain of her menstrual cramps had lessened significantly.

What troubled Mona was the idea that she and Iman could actually share a doctor. The thought was unsettling. Mona had somehow accepted that Hasna was a woman now, but with Iman...it was different. She was her baby girl.

Was this the "mid-age crisis" that women her age suffered? The crisis of identity? A crisis due not to living in denial concerning their own age — but that of their children.

But Iman was still a child. She was only thirteen.

Or was she fourteen now?

Mona rubbed a hand over her face as she continued to grip the steering wheel with the other as she drove.

She *was* getting old. She couldn't even remember her own child's age.

Mona glanced at her daughter, but Iman was staring distantly out the passenger side window, her mind elsewhere. Mona wondered what her daughter was thinking right then.

Although that's an option she can consider if she should ever need them for that...

The words rushed over Mona, taking full meaning right then. Slowing to a stop behind a line of cars at a red light, the fear crept into Mona's chest. In that moment, she saw what a man would see when he saw her daughter, even as Iman's face was covered with the black face veil she now favored. Her dark eyes, accented by the thin slit in the veil, were large and outlined in thick eyelashes that seemed to roll back instead of curving upwards. Iman was a bit heavy for her age, but the extra weight was not off-putting; it actually added to her adult appearance.

Before this moment, Mona had never thought of Iman as physically attractive. Naturally, as a mother, Mona loved her daughter beyond the superficial, but it had always been Hasna who inspired Mona's admiration—and her family's. Hasna's fair skin and hazel eyes, the traits that Hasna had inherited from Mona herself, had always inspired awe in onlookers, Desi and American. Although Mona had been estranged from her family— after marrying without their knowledge or permission (a crime unforgivable in her culture)—it was Hasna who had been the peace-offering.

Twenty-six years ago, Mona had returned home for the first time in more than a year when she stood at the front door of her parents' suburban Baltimore home. Hasna was wrapped in a soft blanket and was sleeping in the crook of Mona's arm, only a month old at the time. Mona had timed the visit so that her father was at work and only her mother would be home. Her mother had always had a weakness for children, especially those still in diapers. Mona was hoping too that the baby's white skin and rosy cheeks would erase some of her parents' deepest concerns about her marriage to a Black man, the most pertinent being the possibility of Pakistani friends and family finding out. Hasna's innocuous appearance gave Mona's mother the cover she would need should the rumor ever reach that far.

Yes, she did marry an American, shame, shame, her mother could say. *But look at this beautiful baby. Her face is like* noor – *light!*

That was how Mona's own countenance had often been described as a child.

Most likely, there would be no need to lie, Mona had figured as she reached up to press the doorbell of her parents' home.

In Desi circles, like in circles of many cultures foreign to American soil, "American" was a synonym for "White." Such an intercultural marriage was frowned upon, it was true. But occasional exceptions, and even preferences, were made for White Americans, particularly for sons. And the culture allowed, albeit begrudgingly, the same exception for daughters from time to time.

It was unthinkable, however, to even *consider* – let alone openly discuss – the possibility of marrying an American of color, much less a *Black* one, even for a Pakistani male.

How much more contemptible would such an idea be for a daughter?

At the reminder, Mona felt the familiar fury return.

After twenty-seven years of marriage, the injustice of her culture unnerved her. Was every culture plagued with double and triple standards like this?

Her family had come to America seeking the "American dream." Like it had been for so many immigrants, the flawless image of equal opportunity, "justice for all," and love for all humanity was the song of their hearts. But the American hymn soon droned to become an off-key tune to a dying song, as their expectations became a mere heaviness of heart – and a cracking under the weight of faltering hope.

Often Mona's father had grown furious at the mistreatment of foreigners in the so-called land of opportunity.

"But this is *America*," he would fume, a distinct Indo-Pak accent detectable in those words.

Her father and mother had worked day and night to earn American degrees and American salaries – and American passports. They had imagined that these papers would guarantee their respect as fellow Americans, and would be a rites of passage to authenticity in this land of liberty.

Yet, time after time, they ran into the hard, cold brick wall of mistreatment, as their strange names, distant homeland, and olive skin (though fair, was not "fair" enough) robbed them of the opportunity to be viewed as equal to White Americans.

At times, Mona's parents appealed to the consciences of indigenous Americans by citing civil rights legislation. Her parents had even evaded job lay-offs and triumphed in run-ins at school and work based on this legislation.

It was ironic though, Mona reflected as she made her way home that afternoon with Iman in the passenger seat next to her, Iman still staring distantly out the window, that the legislation her family cited as a means to gaining respect as full Americans was in place only because of the sacrifices and selfless work of the very Americans Mona's family viewed with disdain.

However, as much as Mona herself would have been inclined, she could not cite her family's Islamic affiliation as a point hypocrisy in the colorism and racism they harbored amongst "dark" Desi's — and all Black Americans.

Islam had never been an integral part of her parents' lives in the first place.

Was it possible that Iman was suffering from all of this?

Mona glanced at her daughter, whose attention was still on the passing scenery and lampposts, and she felt her heart ache in the love and fear she felt for her baby girl.

Would Iman, like Mona, rebel against the injustice of her reality and seek solace in the company of a man she felt wouldn't judge her for who she was — or imagined herself to be?

No, Mona couldn't imagine Iman making the same mistakes she had. Iman was too spiritually conscious for that.

But what mistakes would Mona push her daughter to make?

"May Allah give you children just like you!"

And what if He did? With Hasna *and* Iman?

The thought terrified her.

There was nothing in Mona's past or present spiritual reality that made her deserving of someone as committed to Islam as Iman was. Was it possible then that Iman's commitment was not heartfelt, her half-heartedness like rifts shifting beneath the surface? Or perhaps this was a form of rebellion against an upbringing that had subtly taught Iman that she was unworthy.

The guilt gnawed at Mona and was unrelenting.

In that moment, she kept her eyes on the road. She was unable to look at Iman as a solitary memory returned, haranguing her…as did her father's curse.

It was a conversation that no mother should have had with her daughter. Iman was but four years old when Mona had told her…

Mona had spoken in the most diplomatic manner she could, as if diplomacy would lessen the grating reality to a child. Mona had no choice, she had convinced herself back then, but to explain to her youngest daughter why only Hasna could come with her to visit her family.

Naturally, Mona had explained it as something out of her control. She had presented it as if it were a cruel judgment her parents had laid down—an explanation that absolved Mona of both culpability in the crime and responsibility for its censure.

But even then, so many years ago, there had been an unspoken question that dangled between mother and daughter as she spoke convincingly, *too* convincingly, in the suffocating atmosphere of the room.

Yet, there it hung, that proverbial elephant in the room.

But why didn't you make your own ultimatum, then, Mommy? That you and Hasna would come only if I could come too –

Whether the family liked it or not.

It wasn't that Mona hadn't tried to navigate the rigid barrier.

She had once, when Iman was two years old, brought Iman with her on a visit, hoping the familial bond alone would inspire a desire for the child's company. After all, this was her mother's granddaughter.

But the racism was impenetrable.

"If you want to be a part of this family," Mona's mother had said upon seeing the unmistakable brown of Iman's skin, and the dark "Negro" eyes and tight curls crowning her head, *"she can never come here again."*

How had this knowledge wounded Iman?

What pain had it carved in the hollows of the child's heart? What agony had she suffered as a result?

And what agony did she carry with her still?

The painful conversation had never been mentioned after that harrowing summer afternoon.

But it haunted every space between mother and daughter since.

Even at the tender age of four, Iman's face had crumpled, revealing shock and hurt that the child could not contain as she registered an understanding that she shouldn't have had at so young. Yet, seconds later, there had been, even as tears glistened in the child's eyes, a quiet acceptance, and Iman's reaction was subdued as her jaw quivered in an incredible effort not to cry.

But there was too, Mona recalled, the barely discernable flash of resentment in the luminescent ebony of the young girl's eyes.

And that had terrified Mona. But just as quickly as Mona had seen it, it was gone, and Mona was left wondering if she had imagined the resentment she had seen moments before.

Iman's eyes had danced as the child looked away from her mother, in them tears shining, tears that Iman had successfully suppressed from letting loose. She had folded her arms in a pout, the gesture a loose reflection of the defiance Mona had detected seconds before.

But Iman avoided Mona's gaze, as if she were protecting Mona from what this would mean to her as the mother, instead of the other way around.

"It's okay, Mommy," Iman had said, her voice rising in a high-pitched, childlike tone. Her confident manner of speaking was a sharp contrast to Mona's apologetic manner of minutes before. Iman spoke with sincerity, as if there were no emotions attached at all. Iman breathed audibly, in that sound indicating that her words had taken so much from her, and she quickly wiped her eyes with a pudgy palm before any tears could fall. One arm was still folded across her chest, but it was slipping to her stomach as she spoke. "You can go without me." Her voice was almost cheerful, and this made Mona realize the irreversible pain she had inflicted, causing the child to lie to her mother—and herself. "I don't want to go anyway."

It was the moment that a line had been drawn between them, a line in the sand of their lives that gashed both of their hearts at once. And with each moment thereafter, it created a crater of distance that had become unsurpassable with time.

How then could Mona make up for the unspeakable disappointment that surely her daughter harbored in a mother's sins that bore an uncanny resemblance to those of Mona's own mother?

"But shall I tell you the characteristics of those who will lose in the Hereafter?"

Iman heard the voice of Sharif in her mind as she gazed distantly at the parked cars and familiar homes she and her mother passed as the car turned into their neighborhood.

"People like me and you..."

Tears had already filled Iman's eyes that Friday when she heard Sharif recite in a way that penetrated her heart. It was rare to sense so much sincerity and meaning from a recitation alone.

Before then, Iman had resigned herself to the fact that deep reflection would happen only in Sister Irum's class or in the privacy of her room when she listened to Qur'an CDs while she read in English along with the reciter.

"... who – as Muslims suffer around the world, or even next door – relax in the comfort of their lives worrying about the latest fashion or television show."

At the reminder, Iman had dropped her head from where she sat in the carpeted *musallaa*, ashamed of herself.

She was guilty. She had felt helpless as the new imam reminded her of her faults. Iman often complained to Asma how unfair her parents were, favoring Hasna in everything. But as Sharif called the congregation's attention to the suffering in the world, Iman realized her own sin.

Ungratefulness.

"I think these people are best described in a poem by the author Umm Sumayyah titled, 'O Mujahid, Shall I Tell You?'..."

Iman had been lost in self-reproach when she had heard these words. But it wasn't until she heard the familiar refrain that her heart caught in her throat.

O Mujahid, shall I tell you of my brother/Of my sister, my confidante, my friend?
Or shall I tell you of my father, my mother/My neighbor –/Or my sin?

If there had been even the slightest possibility of there being some remarkable coincidence in the pen name and title, that possibility was completely eliminated when she heard, reverberating throughout the *musallaa* of the masjid Friday afternoon, the very words she had penned in the privacy of her room and had shared with no one but her best friend.

The tears she had been fighting earlier still moistened her eyes, but the sheer shock and confusion she felt at hearing her words recited from the mouth of the new imam eclipsed any possibility of them spilling forth. For that brief moment, she had been simply...*stunned*.

She felt her heart drum in her chest as he continued the poem, an incessant pounding that created a pulsating in her ears.

How did this happen? she had thought. Did Asma give it to him? Was this some sort of surprise announcement that the masjid had accepted *Islam's Call* as their official newsletter? Why hadn't Asma told her?

Shouldn't Asma have *asked* first?

Then Iman realized something.

Asma had called the day before to ask if she had, by any chance, left the sample newsletter at Iman's house.

"I can't find it anywhere," Asma had said when Iman had told her that she didn't have it.

"We can just print it out again," Iman had said.

"I know, but still..." Asma had sighed. "I just don't like losing things like that. What if someone finds it?"

Iman had laughed. "And what would anybody do with it if they found it?"

Asma had grown silent momentarily. "All that work... I don't want anyone to take our idea."

The memory had returned to Iman as she sat in the prayer area that *Jumu'ah* afternoon, and she immediately looked at Sharif standing before the podium, his eyes intent, clearly moved by the words he was reading.

Sharif had found the newsletter, Iman realized just then, and he hadn't the slightest idea that it belonged to his little sister.

Iman's hands trembled, but Iman didn't know whether this was due to fear of being discovered or sudden flattery that she was unable to temper. Perhaps, it was both.

But it was at that moment that Iman had felt the most stabbing twinge of ungratefulness.

And, even in the quiet of the car as she sat next to her mother as they neared their home following the doctor's appointment, Iman was painfully aware that she still hadn't fully recovered from her sin.

Hasna doesn't deserve him, Iman had thought as she sat in the prayer area, flanked by believers with tears in their eyes, their hearts and minds on Allah and their souls.

Yet Iman's heart was aflame with both resentment and despondence, hating her sister at that moment more than she ever had before then.

He's too good for her.

The resentment Iman understood, as it was a familiar sentiment of her heart.

Daily, Iman lamented Hasna's innumerable favors that she herself had been denied. Initially, Hasna's budding relationship with their Pakistani family had been the sorest spot for Iman.

But now… Iman didn't want to think of it.

Her sudden aching despondency had been beyond her comprehension.

It wasn't until Iman heard the doctor discuss the possible treatments for her irregular cycle that she began to pinpoint the source of her deep disappointment.

Will I ever be able to have children? Iman had wondered when the doctor glanced at her, pity in her eyes.

It wasn't Iman's possible health problems that Iman feared would be an impediment to her dream of becoming a mother. It was her flagrant flaws that she had been ever aware of, as early as four years old.

She was overweight and unattractive.

Even Iman's mother did little to hide her discontentment with these painful facts.

And these two traits, Iman knew, were the reason her grandparents couldn't accept that she existed.

How then could Iman expect a man to desire her?

A family's love for you was natural, automatic even. If Iman's repugnancy was such that it could disrupt even natural feelings, what of affection that was cultivated only by choice?

As if reading her mind, the doctor had looked at Iman with pity, in that glance suggesting that it wasn't completely impossible for Iman to have a husband, and that Iman might even one day have to worry about regulating childbirth instead of her menstrual cycle.

It should have been consolation, a source of hope, that sympathetic glance. But it had made Iman's melancholy only more pronounced. Iman's mere need for such reassurance, and from a doctor who had only met her moments before, spoke volumes of Iman's distasteful appearance. Iman's future was bleak as far as relationships were concerned, Iman already knew, so she should have been grateful that the doctor had at least shown empathy.

The words from Sharif's Friday address had returned to Iman as she lay on the examination table listening to the doctor explain the normalcy of her abnormalities — another form of pity, Iman knew.

But in truth, this grim explanation was a mercy compared to what others were suffering in the world, Iman reflected as the doctor droned on about medicines and treatments.

Inadequacy was something Iman should simply accept as a meager trial of hers in this transient life. What of the suffering of those like the orphan boy she herself had so artfully written about in her poem?

Shall I tell you...of my sin?

For reasons she could not discern, Iman thought of Hasna and Sharif getting married as she sat in silence next to her mother as the car pulled into the driveway of their home. It was then that the despondence closed in on her until she felt her stomach wrench in agony and self-pity.

That Monday afternoon, the choking sadness and resentment became unbearable as the sharp pains stabbed at her sides, leaving her gasping for breath and inspiring her to retire to bed after following her mother inside the house.

Tears stung her eyes as she pulled the covers over her shoulders and chin, her face crumpling as she refused to cry. *It's okay, Iman,* she consoled herself, her voice, even in her mind's ear, sounding too high-pitched and childlike to be sincere. Quickly, Iman lifted a palm and wiped away the moisture gathering in her eyes, lest tears reveal to her own heart the depths of her pain. There was a piercing pain she felt just then, and a hand slipped down to massage the cloth over her stomach. Meanwhile, a cheerful voice reassured her in her mind, *I don't want to get married anyway.*

Nine

"Do you know anything about the interpretation of dreams?"

Sharif stood in Rashad's empty living room Monday afternoon. Cardboard boxes were stacked along its weathered white walls, and sunrays streamed through the bare windows, tiny dust particles floating in the light. Rashad had invited Sharif to view the property in hopes of selling the house to a fellow Muslim instead of back to the bank from whom it had been mortgaged.

The question had been casual, but the anxiety Sharif was nursing was dizzying. He had no idea whom he could consult without feeling tormented in discomfort and embarrassment. He had no intention of sharing the dream itself, but the subject itself was awkward. He could hardly believe he had broached it just now.

The world of dreams was one Sharif hadn't given much thought. He understood that dreams held significance in Islam when understood according to the guidelines of the Qur'an and Sunnah, but Sharif hadn't imagined he would ever need clarification of those guidelines himself.

Until Friday, the recurrent dream had been an enigma that remained in the realms of the unknown, a persistent question tugging at the back of his mind, in the quiet of his private thoughts. Sharif never imagined that the vision he had seen during slumber would intrude so completely upon his reality.

Rashad chuckled from where he pulled packaging tape across the flaps of a large cardboard box. "No, I'm afraid not," he said. "I can barely understand what's going on while I'm awake."

A hesitant smile creased a corner of Sharif's mouth, but his mind was elsewhere. He didn't know what to say.

"Why?" Rashad tore the packaging tape on the jagged metal of the tape dispenser. He then ran his palm across the top, smoothing out the air bubbles. "What's on your mind?"

Sharif shrugged. "I just wanted to learn more about the subject."

He walked over to where Rashad flattened the last part of the tape. Sharif then lifted the box and carried it to where the others were stacked, placing it on the floor in front of them.

"In Islam," he added.

Rashad regarded Sharif with his forehead creased. "Didn't you study dream interpretation in Riyadh?"

"We studied the basic Islamic principles..." Sharif's voice trailed.

Sharif felt the absurdity of the scenario. He was the religious expert in the community. How then could he respond to Rashad's question without betraying the true intentions behind his own? He couldn't admit that it was consolation he was seeking right then.

"But we didn't focus on the interpretation," Sharif said. "It's not considered an Islamic science."

The awkwardness of the moment permeated the space between them, and Sharif wondered if Rashad sensed that there was something more to Sharif's faulty explanation.

Rashad nodded thoughtfully, his eyes surveying the room to see if there was anything left to pack.

"To be honest," he said, "it's not something I place too much value in."

Rashad paused before glancing at Sharif again. "That's how we got ourselves into trouble in the first place."

Sharif creased his forehead. "What do you mean?"

"It all started with a dream," Rashad said, humor in his tone. "That's where the Sheikh took his teachings."

"Really?" The information was new to Sharif, and was troubling in more ways than he could admit.

Rashad studied Sharif for a moment. "You didn't know that?"

"No..."

"He said the Prophet, *sallallaahu'alayhi wasallam,* came to him and told him that he had reached the *yaqeen.*"

Sharif nodded. He had heard of this sort of misunderstanding of the Qur'anic instruction to worship Allah until you reach the *yaqeen* — the "certainty" — which referred to one's death.

Rashad shook his head, clearly disturbed at the memory. "And that he no longer had to busy himself with rituals and mundane worship."

161

Rashad sighed, his gaze toward the bare windows momentarily. "He had us following a *tazkiyah* program that only he and other *awliyaa'* had knowledge of."

"*Awliyaa'*?" Sharif repeated, taken aback. "The Sheikh considered himself a close friend of Allah?"

"Yes. That's how he had the authority to teach us how to purify ourselves through special *dhikr*."

"But *Islam* is our purification," Sharif said.

Rashad chuckled, shaking his head in agreement. "And it also has its own instructions for *dhikr*."

He lifted the roll of tape again and began to seal another box.

"The funny this is," Rashad said, coughing in laughter, "now it seems so simple, so clear." He shook his head, an amused expression on his face. "A Muslim purifies himself in the way the Prophet purified himself. And *dhikr* is part of that purification."

Sharif nodded, distracted by his own thoughts.

"It reminds me of something I read once," Sharif said seconds later. "*No one asks you to abandon the path of the Prophet, except that he replaces it with his own.*"

Rashad squinted, his eyes in reflection. He nodded a second later. "Now, *that* is very true. Very true."

They were quiet for some time as Rashad pulled tape over the flaps of another box, and Sharif situated the boxes along the walls.

"I'm not a scholar," Rashad said, prompting Sharif to glance in his direction. "But my rule of thumb is this. If I can't verify a dream with something I can point to in reality, then it should remain in the world of dreams."

The law offices of Wynmore and Associates sat unobtrusively in an office park in Bethesda, Maryland, surrounded by freshly mown grass and pines that sweetened the air as one ascended the flower-lined walkway leading to the polished oak wood double doors of the suites. A light glowed from one of the windows behind a cypress that stood as both guard and embellishment of the office where Hasna sat behind her desk as the sun set Monday evening. A stack of papers was before her, and a single sheet lay in her lap as a cup of coffee grew lukewarm on the desk before her.

Hasna read the lines of the page again before groaning and putting it back on the stack. She had fifty more pages to read and a report to type for Attorney Wynmore before she could go home, although her boss would be in the comfort of his while he read the e-mail attachment. But she could not concentrate.

"He must. Because he chose Kenya over you."

The words would not leave her, and like acid, they ate at her until the burning caused anger to rise in her chest. Hasna was furious with Sharif. The *audacity*. He had *no* right to trample on something so close to her heart.

But even as she grew livid, she detected the hypocrisy in her offense. It was, after all, her fiancé who had said these words. Shouldn't it be the mention of the one she intended to marry, and not the mention of Vernon, that inspired such rage? Especially at the suggestion that he had chosen someone more deserving of his affection.

What then was wrong with her? Where did her heart lay? Did she love Sharif?

Or was it Vernon she really loved?

Since the fateful conversation with Sharif, Hasna had so badly wanted to vent. Naturally, her first choice would have been her best friend. But each time she shaped her mouth to complain or felt the urge to pick up the phone, something stopped her. It was like the scene from the movie *My Best Friend's Wedding* when the main character was chasing her best friend, a male she secretly loved, but who was chasing his own beloved fiancée. "But who's chasing *you*?" another friend had asked her.

This was the question that dangled before Hasna, haranguing in its profundity.

Even if she were to get the sympathetic ear she desired in her fury with Sharif, there were at least three ironies in the sympathy alone. One, Vernon would listen in empathy then hang up and return to the companionship of the one he loved. Two, Hasna could get that empathy only if she confessed her feelings to the very one she was bitter in being unable to have.

But the third irony was the most heartbreaking. It was the truth of Sharif's statement that stung most. Vernon *did* choose

Kenya over Hasna, and what could Vernon possibly say in consolation that would not in itself underscore this painful truth?

Yet there was another aggravation to the whole scenario.

Hasna loved Sharif, too.

This was something Hasna had not thought much about in their years of engagement. Yes, such affection was to be expected between those engaged to be married. But theirs hadn't been a love she felt insecure in, or even grateful for.

After all, it had been Sharif who stood to gain the most from their relationship, in Hasna's view. Although she had never said it aloud, Hasna knew full well that she was his trophy and he her charity case, her evidence of a sympathetic heart. She had pitied Sharif while he adored her. It was the perfect scenario for the carefree future she had imagined for herself. *"Better to marry the man who adores you than the one you adore,"* she had often heard women say.

But now Hasna wondered at this was perverted logic. It offered women a guidepost to marry men they could control. Why was it so important to women that their lives be forever guided by their own hands, and not at all by the hands of the men who married them?

It was injured pride that had made Sharif's comment cut so deep, Hasna realized just then. She hadn't expected him to look down on her. She had always been the one who'd done that to him.

His words were like a hard, cold slap in the face, and they incited an indignant rage that she could not hope to mollify.

Yet they made her respect and desire him more.

Hasna wondered at this sudden streak of humility and admiration for her childhood friend. He had left his home and made a man of himself, while she had remained in hers and become a fool.

Chasing the prestige of law school and passing the Bar, Hasna really imagined she would be invaluable to the world of men. But the two men she desired most had hearts turned elsewhere. Vernon to a woman who held only an associate's degree and a light resume in the military, and Sharif to a religious ideology that Hasna viewed with disdain, an ideology that caused her worth to shrink in his eyes.

At the thought, Hasna reached for the cup of coffee on her desk and took a sip of the lukewarm liquid, hoping to calm the fury that was returning right then.

Sharif was a religious fanatic, Hasna thought angrily. To him, Islam was just one big show for the world. Cloak yourself in burlap rags and grow a beard like an scruffy bum, and your way to Paradise is paved, golden gates and all. No heart, no feelings. Just image. That was all it took.

Hasna, please. You know that's not true.

Vernon's words returned to her, stabbing her in the heart and exposing her inadequacy for what it was. It was only her hurt pride that her angry thoughts had reflected, not a true summation of what she believed.

Hasna held the coffee mug inches from her lips, her hand cradling the cold ceramic as she shook the cup, her eyes peering thoughtfully into the darkened liquid that reflected a contorted version of her face.

Tears filled her eyes as reality slowly enveloped her, and she accepted the truth for what it was. Vernon didn't love her because she wasn't Kenya, and Sharif didn't love her because she refused to be the best of herself.

In this weak moment, Hasna felt her chest tighten as her heart accepted the truth of the conjured spirituality that she had cloaked herself in for so many years.

Not weighed down by visible religious commitment, Hasna was able to uphold the image she coveted, the only image that had mattered to her. Like the voluminous cloth of believing women and the full beard of believing men, her sacrilegious image merely reflected values that she held dear in her heart, even if she, like they, hadn't yet reached the depths of what that image conveyed.

No, it wasn't those cloaked in loose cloth or wearing large beards who thought the path to Paradise was paved based on image alone. It was those who did not even make an effort who held that illusion.

Yes, amongst the veiled women and bearded men, there were certainly pretenders masquerading as faithful, but these were not the Sharifs of the world. They were not even the masses of

Muslims, whose overt faith was simply a painful reminder to the true pretenders of their own spiritual weakness.

Hasna sighed, setting the mug on her desk as she submitted to her grim reality. She was more concerned with mirroring the Western status quo than with mirroring affiliation to any faith.

Hers was the ultimate saving face. Scorn those who have more guts than you. Hasna saw it at work day after day.

How had she missed in herself this obvious hypocrisy?

Even in the political science books Hasna had read for law school, it was always the *doers* who were held up as icons and martyrs. Meanwhile, the "silent believers" would forever stain the pages of history as the quiet cowards they were—saying and doing nothing that would upset their comfortable lives. Even when it was the right thing to do.

But those Muslims aren't perfect, Hasna defended herself bitterly. *They do so much—*

Hasna stopped herself.

Allah wasn't asking for perfection. He was asking for effort.

Forget everyone else. Where is your effort?

Hasna let her gaze fall to the piles of folders and papers atop her desk, the disarray an eerie reflection of her life right then. Yet this is what she had worked so long and hard for, she thought sullenly, this "glorified disarray" that allowed her to put *Attorney* before her name and nothing behind it.

Yes, there were those Muslim women who had worked hard for the attorney title and had pure intentions and a firm purpose. They saw beyond a metal name plaque affixed to an office door, and even beyond the form-fitting business suits and Prada heels that bore only the façade of a woman of talent and success.

The façade Hasna had coveted for so long.

Sharif could not love her, Hasna concluded sadly as she leaned forward, her elbows now resting on her cluttered desk. Because he was embarking upon true faith. And until Hasna loved herself, and her religion, enough to do the same, she would be forever chasing the likes of Vernon. Those who belonged to someone else.

And who had long since given up claiming a faith that held no connection to the reality of their lives.

Or hearts.

"Where will you go after you move?"

After praying *Maghrib* with Rashad in the masjid, Sharif had returned with the former imam to the house to load the moving truck and take a final tour of the house. He and Rashad now stood outside on the brick terrace that framed a small pool that glistened under the porch light, appearing abandoned amidst the un-mown lawn lining the fading bricks.

"To Pakistan."

Sharif gathered his eyebrows. "You're leaving the country?"

Rashad's olive skin glowed under the dim light, and his deep reflection created folds of skin next to his eyes as he gazed at the fenced yard. "There's nothing for me here."

The words hung in the space between them, reminding Sharif of Hasna's same sentiment spoken years before. But Hasna had been talking about Saudi Arabia, and Rashad was talking about America, their home.

"I know it will be a sacrifice." Rashad spoke as if speaking to himself. "But it's what we think is best." He paused before adding quietly, "Considering everything that we've already lost."

Sharif looked away, Rashad's last statement acknowledging what had remained unsaid between them since Sharif's return.

The question had often formed in Sharif's mind, but the reminder of what he had read in his mother's e-mail and in the attached link made his throat close, silencing what he could find no words to express.

"It was Jafar's idea," Rashad said with a sigh. "But it took some time for us to accept the idea of leaving him here."

Sharif's gaze fell to the pool, where he noticed some weeds and leaves floating on the water, moving gently with the night's soft wind. It was dark outside now, and light glowed from the windows of the house neighboring Rashad's from the back. Sharif heard the barking of a dog and the engine of a car stalling as it pulled into the driveway of a home nearby.

His thoughts wandered to Hasna, and he wondered if he would talk to her again. Part of him hoped he would not, but another part of him, his heart, hoped that he would. He wondered what either reality would mean for their future or if their silent impasse meant their future was unspeakable too.

"We wanted to wait for an appeal…" Rashad's voice seemed distant in the night. Sharif heard Rashad take a deep breath and exhale. "But that request was overruled."

Sharif tried to imagine his childhood friend behind bars, but it was a difficult image to muster, and even more difficult to sustain.

His last memory of Jafar was of arms raised high above his head, revealing a sweat-stained shirt as he blocked one of Sharif's shots as they played one-on-one on the pavement of the basketball court down the street from the masjid. Jafar had teased Sharif for having a weak jump shot, and emboldened by the insult, Sharif had shoved past his friend in a dribble to deliver a solid dunk in Jafar's face.

"Ooo…" came the howls of neighborhood kids watching the game.

Then Jafar had embraced Sharif, smacking him playfully on the back before saying, "Good game."

Sharif heard dry laughter next to him and glanced at Rashad, but Jafar's father was still lost in thought. "The boy wasn't even *praying*." Confusion contorted Rashad's face. "I doubt he even knew what jihad meant."

There was thoughtful silence and Sharif felt crushed in the unrequited hopes of a father imploring America to give the best life to his son.

"What did they say was his crime?" Sharif's voice sounded strained, and he felt awkward speaking the question aloud.

Rashad coughed in laughter, but Sharif could taste the raw disappointment in that sound. "Horseback riding and archery."

Amused at the absurdity of the charge, Sharif laughed too, though his humor was subdued by frustration burning in his chest. "When did that become a crime?"

"*Minority Report*," Rashad said.

Sharif gathered his eyebrows and looked at Rashad. "What?"

"The movie. Punish the criminal before they commit a crime. It keeps the world safe." Rashad grunted. "Just in case."

"A trial of intentions," Sharif said dryly, remembering the film just then. He hadn't imagined that it was a foreboding to the lives of American Muslims.

Sharif shook his head. "And who knows anyone's intentions anyway?"

Rashad huffed, bitterness in that sound. "The only people's intentions *we* know are the ones putting the innocent on trial."

Silence lingered as they both reflected on what was said.

"It's funny," Rashad sad suddenly, laughter in his voice. "I never thought much about it before."

Sharif looked at Rashad, whose hands now rested in the pockets of his dress pants.

"I used to always say 'I can be fully American and fully Muslim at the same time.'" He laughed, shaking his head, but pain still glistened in his eyes. "It really upset me that Muslims would actually disagree with me."

Sharif creased his forehead, searching for Rashad's meaning.

"Now I know that it wasn't my argument they had a problem with," Rashad said, eyes squinting as he seemed lost in thought. "It was the illogic they took issue with."

He looked at Sharif, distant amusement in his eyes. "If it were true, there would be no need to argue, would there?"

Ten

"[Western] military power was used to conquer bodies, media power to conquer souls."
—Khalid Baig, *Slippery Stone*

In the darkness of dawn Tuesday morning, Sharif returned home after praying *Fajr* in the masjid. He hoped to nap briefly before returning to the masjid to organize his office and write down his official plans for the direction of the community. But his optimism was tempered by the conversation of the night before. Sharif was distracted by thoughts of Jafar living out the rest of his life in a jail cell, his family a thousand miles across the ocean.

With three life sentences and no possibility of parole, Jafar's future was bleak, and it tore at Sharif to know that at only twenty-four years old Jafar was tasting the dead end of life. But it was admiration Sharif felt for his friend when he thought of the self-sacrifice Jafar was suffering by encouraging his family to relocate back home, although they had before then imagined that home would forever be suburban Maryland or at least on the shores of America.

Rashad and his wife were American citizens, as were Jafar and their other children, and they had expected to taste the fruits of what that meant.

And they had.

Though it was not the fruit they expected to find on the tree.

Fully American and fully Muslim, they were.

Or was this an oxymoron in the eyes of those who had sealed Jafar's fate, even as he had no crime on his record before being caged like a criminal for the rest of his life?

If it were true, there would be no need to argue, would there?

Sharif had lain awake Monday night weighing Rashad's ponderous statement and turning it over in his mind. Initially he did not understand Rashad's point, but as Sharif had driven home with a sliver of light breaking the horizon that Tuesday morning, Sharif understood.

There was a fundamental difference between an American nationality and an American ideology.

By definition, a nationality was compatible with any lifestyle, religion, or walk of life. After all, what was a nationality but an indication of the piece of land to which a person held a passport? But an ideology, could not be fully compatible with any lifestyle, religion, or walk of life—if that system held an ideology of its own.

Would a person argue that one could be fully human and fully Christian at the same time? The argument itself was quizzical, as one's humanity was simply a reality of creation and indicated nothing about one's ideals, spirituality, or outlook on life.

But a religion, like an ideology, went beyond the realm of a mere life form and geographical location. It offered dictates and guidance through which the life forms lived—and where they lived.

What then did it mean to be American at all?

It was a question Sharif had never considered.

Did "American" mean that one of fifty states was home? Or that a person held certain principles to be true?

It was true that the ideologies of human equality, justice for all, and equal opportunity were principles that were at the heart of Islam. But it was also true that the ideologies of the ultimate authority of the people over that of the Creator and the separation of religion and government were completely foreign to Islam. That made the American ideology and the Islamic religion incompatible on at least those two points.

However, it was true that most Muslims were more than willing to cast aside these fundamental beliefs in favor of a comfortable American life, or at least reduce these obvious incompatibilities to theory alone.

Thus, the imprisonment of Jafar and thousands of other innocent Muslims raised an even weightier question than that of Islamic ideology itself.

Was there in the very core of American principles an unequivocal intolerance for Muslims themselves—even as American ideology heralded freedom of thought and religion to all? Even if conflict in belief system was cited as justification for the imprisonment of Muslims in the "land of justice and equality," what then could explain the sentence handed down to Jafar, who at the time held no Islamic ideology at all?

"If they gain dominance over you, they would behave to you as enemies and extend their hands and their tongues against you…and they long for you to disbelieve."

"Here you are loving them, but they do not love you…"

The words of the Qur'an stunned Sharif in their veracity, an undeniable summation of the reality in which Western Muslims daily lived. Often Sharif had read these verses, but he had thought little of their meaning, his mind trained to reinterpret the meaning of any verse in favor of his American life — and ideals.

Sharif's heart was in agony for those like Rashad, whose love had moved them to give up citizenship in their own homes, imagining that the sacrifice would somehow gain for them and their families an honor and prestige that only America could bestow.

"Is it honor they seek among them? Nay, all honor is with Allah."

Fully American and fully Muslim?

Sharif turned the question over in his mind as he pulled into the driveway of his home just as the sun peaked over the horizon Tuesday morning.

It was possible, Sharif conceded.

But not until Americans themselves re-embraced the American concept that ideologies themselves were malleable.

"Sharif?" Nadirah called from the kitchen upon hearing the front door open.

"Yes, Mom, it's me."

"Did you eat?"

Nadirah returned the cover to the pot after adding butter to the grits. She turned to see her son standing in the doorway to the kitchen, a look of exhaustion in his eyes. He wore a lightweight black jacket over a long sleeve checkered shirt and baggy dress pants. She was pleased that he wasn't wearing the Arab garb he had favored since he returned from abroad. She had told Sharif that she didn't think it was wise to dress so conspicuously foreign given the current political climate that viewed Muslims with suspicion for the slightest offense.

"It doesn't matter what I do," he had said, shrugging, and Nadirah didn't like his defeatist tone. "If I'm Muslim, I'm guilty before there's even a crime to commit."

"But you don't have to be a sitting duck."

He had sighed before saying dryly, "I wonder what advice we could give to a Black man with the same luck."

Currently, Nadirah brushed his forehead with a kiss.

"I'm not hungry," he said.

"You should eat anyway." She walked over to the cabinets and removed a plate and silverware. "Sit down."

In the corner of her eye, Nadirah saw Sharif shrug off his jacket and hang it on the back of a chair before walking to the sink to rinse his hands. There was an awkward silence after the sound of running water ceased and he walked over to the table and sat down. She saw him rub a hand over his face, his eyes lost in thought a moment later as he chewed at his lower lip.

"Did Brother Rashad tell you about the house?" Nadirah glanced behind her as she dipped a large serving spoon into the grits and let the heap slip furtively onto the plate in soft lumps.

Sharif looked distracted momentarily before he responded. "Yes, ma'am, he did."

"What do you think?"

He shrugged as Nadirah placed eggs and turkey bacon on the side of his plate, her back to him. "It's nice, but I don't have the funds to buy something like that."

Nadirah carried the plate to the table and placed it before him before returning to the stove to prepare her own. "I don't think that will be an issue."

"It will be for me."

"He didn't tell you that he wanted to put it in the masjid's name?"

Sharif furrowed his brows as Nadirah carried her plate to the table. "No. He just said he wanted to sell it to me."

She shook her head as she sat down across from him. "He said that because he wants you and Hasna to use it as a family home."

At the mention of Hasna, Sharif averted his gaze and lifted a forkful of eggs and grits to his mouth. For a second Nadirah watched him in silence, her concern from the last two days returning.

"Sharif?"

He paused eating and looked at her, his eyebrows raised in innocence. "Yes, ma'am?"

"What's going on with you and Hasna?"

Nadirah had been indecisive about bringing up the sensitive topic. Before Sharif had returned from Saudi Arabia, it was all Mona and Hasna talked about with Nadirah. But after his return, the topic was brought up only on the day before the lunch Sharif had with Hasna and her father.

Concerned about all the preparations necessary for the December wedding, Nadirah had called Mona Friday night to ask if she needed any help. Mona had grown silent in response and said that Hasna hadn't mentioned anything about it to her. It was an awkward moment. Nadirah decided to leave the issue alone. She told Mona to call her once Hasna gave her the details. But in her heart Nadirah knew she would receive no call.

"Nothing," Sharif said simply.

Nadirah watched as he continued to eat in silence, thinly veiling the anxiety that his reply was supposed to conceal.

Nadirah didn't know what to say. She knew there were some issues there, but how could she address them? She didn't want to pry, and she didn't want to make him uncomfortable. Then again, it was possible that he was simply being honest. Perhaps nothing was going on. And that was likely the problem.

"Did you get a chance to talk to Asma about school?" Nadirah decided it was safest to change the subject for now.

"Yes, ma'am."

"Did you encourage her to reenroll in school?"

Sharif shook his head. "I didn't know you wanted that for her."

"Sharif," Nadirah said, laughter in her tone. "That's why I asked you to speak to her. I'm not pleased with what she's learning at Mona's."

He creased his forehead. "I thought it was Sister Irum's class that was the problem."

Nadirah nodded. "Yes, that too."

"Something happened with Sister Mona too?"

Nadirah drew in a deep breath, her eyes resting on the patio behind Sharif. The sun was starting to rise and a faint yellow glow peered from behind the trees.

"Sharif," she said, exhaling as she gathered her thoughts. "Yes, it's Irum's class that I'm most concerned about, but it's not only that."

"But Sister Irum is leaving in a couple of weeks."

Nadirah drew her eyebrows together. "Where is she going?"

Sharif regarded his mother, and Nadirah grew uncomfortable under his gaze. Was there something she should know?

"You didn't know they're going back to Pakistan?"

"They're leaving the country?" This was the first Nadirah heard of the subject.

"Yes, ma'am. That's why Brother Rashad is selling the house. I thought you knew."

She shook her head. "I thought they were just moving to a new neighborhood."

Sharif seemed disappointed for some reason, but he didn't say anything. Instead he continued to eat in silence, his eyes growing distant again.

"Well," Nadirah said, "that's good. I think that's better for everyone."

Sharif stopped eating and stared at his mother as if seeing her for the first time. "How is that good?"

"Sharif, sweetheart, they're going through a lot right now. With Jafar's arrest, I think going back home will be better for them."

"Yes, but not for us. We need them here."

Nadirah regarded her son, disapproval on her face. "For what?"

"What *don't* we need them for?"

"If you're worried about the imam position, I'm sure you can handle that alone."

"It's not only that. They're really important to the community. And even for Jafar. He needs a lot of support. I don't know how we can replace his family when they —"

"Replace his family?" Nadirah glared at her son, hoping he wasn't saying what she thought he was. "What do you mean?"

Sharif was distracted momentarily. "We'll have to see if there's anything we can do to help him. Maybe we can even visit him, taking turns."

Nadirah blinked, indignant. "You will *not* get involved with that boy."

Sharif looked shell-shocked. His eyes widened as he stared at his mother. For a second he didn't speak.

"But Mom..." His voice trailed as he regarded her, as if unsure what to say. "We have to."

"No we don't, Sharif. That's not our problem. That boy got involved in some things he had no business in. As sad as it is, that's what happens when you start believing Islam is a bunch of rituals. The entire spirit of Islam is lost, and the next thing you know, you're open to any sort of foolishness."

For a few seconds, Sharif just stared at his mother in disbelief, and Nadirah grew concerned.

"Sharif, you *do* know what he did, right?"

Sharif blinked. "I didn't know he did anything."

"He was involved in some terrorist plot, he and a few other boys who call themselves Muslims."

"*He* said that?"

Nadirah laughed, amused by her son's naiveté. "Of course not. But it was all over the news. They even quoted him saying 'This country is going down.'"

Nadirah shuddered at the memory, shaking her head in disgust.

Sharif set his fork down, still blinking. "Mom, but how can you be sure that's even true? What if he didn't even say it?"

"But why would they make up something like that, Sharif? Do you really think they'll give someone three life sentences if he didn't commit a single crime?"

"Yes, I do."

Nadirah's jaw dropped, and for a moment she couldn't speak. "Sharif," she said, now blinking in disbelief herself. "Things don't work like that."

He folded his arms. "In this country it does."

"Now," Nadirah leveled with him, hoping to tap into Sharif's intelligence and good sense, "I know this country doesn't have the best history in the justice department. But I don't think they'll just make up things like that."

"So it's *Jafar* who's lying?"

Nadirah could hardly believe she was even having this conversation. "Did you speak to Jafar yourself? Did he tell you he was innocent?"

The questions were rhetorical, but for a moment she feared that her son had in fact spoken to his friend.

"No, but I spoke to his father."

"That's not the same thing."

"Well, he pled not guilty. Isn't that the same as saying he's innocent?"

"No, it's not. Criminals plead guilty every day, and they know they're guilty."

"You're saying Jafar's a *criminal*?"

"No, I'm not, Sharif. I'm just saying just because someone pleads not guilty doesn't mean they're innocent. Besides, I'm—"

"But you asked if I spoke to Jafar, and I'm saying he pled innocent."

"Innocent of what though? Innocent of saying those words or innocent of being a terrorist?"

Sharif creased his forehead, a question on his face.

"Sharif, what I'm trying to tell you is that Jafar said some things he shouldn't have. I'm sure he didn't imagine it could be understood as a crime, but it was. To Jafar, he was just saying what he thought. But as Americans, we think it's very serious."

"That's assuming he said it in the first place."

"It was a *quote*, Sharif."

"What if it was a quote? I can imagine a thousand scenarios where someone could say the same thing and not mean a bit of harm."

Nadirah shook her head, disturbed. "How?"

"In a game, for one. My friends and I used to say things like that all the time when we played Cowboys and Indians. Even when we played basketball, we'd say things like that."

"That was for *games*, Sharif. This was in reference to an entire nation."

"During archery and horseback riding?" Sharif shook his head in disbelief. "Those are sports, Mom." He laughed. "If he meant it for real, why were his enemies his own friends who were playing archery too? It makes more sense to say that in front of some government building if that's what he meant."

"But Sharif, you can't —"

"What happened to his seventy excuses? He's still a Muslim."

At the reminder of the hadith that her husband favored, Nadirah grew quiet. In that moment, she began to see Sharif's point of view, even if only marginally.

"Is this what *I* can expect?"

The question confused Nadirah, and she looked at her son with a confused expression on her face. "What do you mean?"

"If I'm ever wrongly accused," Sharif said, "are you going to say I must have done something?" He regarded his mother, his eyes gleaming in sincerity and pain. "Or are you going to go on the fact that I'm your son, and I'm Muslim?"

Nadirah didn't know what to say.

"Mom, shouldn't that mean more than what a newspaper says? They don't even *know* me." Sharif's nose flared. "And they don't know Jafar. But we do, Mom, and you know he would never say something like that unless it was in fun."

"But how do we know that?" she said quietly.

"How do we know anything, Mom?" He sighed. "Some things you just have to take on faith."

"But this is not a simple matter."

Sharif looked at his mother, and in that moment Nadirah felt her heart ache, a sudden guilt gnawing at her.

"But, Mom," he said, and in that sound, Nadirah felt her throat go dry as she realized how blessed she was to have her son safe with her at home and not in a jail cell, or buried beneath the ground. "What *is*?"

There are people who walk the earth without sin, and when they err, as all humans do, Allah says, "I have forgiven him for the sins of his past, the sins of this moment, and any sins he may do in the future. For he has asked Me for forgiveness, calling out My Name, and I have responded to his supplication by calling out his, saying, So-and-so, I have forgiven you."

These were the words Karim reflected on Tuesday evening after returning from work. The words were ones Karim had heard mentioned in a speech, or perhaps a book, he couldn't recall. But he knew they were the reflections of someone who had put into words the reason his heart was attached so completely to the scholars of Islam, as this is how he imagined their affair with Allah to be.

At that moment, the words returned to Karim, and he thought of Sharif.

Karim had always noticed there was something different about Dawud's son. Even as a child, Sharif was quiet where others were talkative, guarded where others were insistent, and doubtful where others were certain. It was obvious that Sharif never felt comfortable in crowds and would never be found before people in any authoritative way. The limelight was not something that he could relax in, even as his traits in private could easily earn him that prominence.

There were times that Karim would stand at a distance and watch Sharif play basketball in the neighborhood court near the masjid. Whenever Karim would see Sharif pump his arm after making a basket, Karim would smile. It was a side of Sharif one rarely saw unless they were blessed to witness private moments like these that Sharif assumed were shared only by him and his friend Jafar and a few young boys from the neighborhood.

The first time Karim had mentioned his desire for Sharif to be part of his family was when Sharif was only ten years old. At the time, Mona had laughed saying that it was a bit early to think of things like that for Hasna.

But it wasn't long before Mona herself had to admit that Sharif would be ideal for their daughter. This observation was partly the reason that Karim and Mona had encouraged Sharif and Hasna to spend so much time together during visits. Babysitting and watching the meal were only covers for a deeper intention, one that was shared by Sharif's parents themselves.

Joking, Karim would say for many years to Sharif, "You're going to be my son-in-law one day."

In keeping with his humble nature, Sharif would grin uncomfortably and avoid Karim's gaze, but he never said anything in response.

Karim had been young once, so he knew that Sharif didn't mind the idea. It was insecurity that kept him from thinking it possible for him to win Hasna's affection, and it was insecurity that kept Sharif from initiating it himself.

"You think he's having second thoughts?" Mona asked presently from where she sat on the edge of their bed, hands folded in her lap and her forehead creased in concern.

Karim drew in a deep breath and exhaled. "Yes."

Mona grew quiet momentarily. "Do you know why?"

"I think we all do."

Mona's gaze fell to her hands, but she didn't say anything. In that gesture, Karim knew that she understood what he meant.

"At this point," Karim said with a sigh, "it's up to Hasna. There's not much we can do."

Mona looked at him. "But how is it up to Hasna? I think it's up to Sharif. He's the one having doubts."

"Love," Karim said using his wife's pet name, "Sharif is having doubts because of Hasna. We both know that."

"Then why did he ask to marry her at all? This is how she's always been."

He was silent momentarily. "Perhaps. But I think he's just realizing what's been obvious to everyone else all along."

Mona frowned, offended. "Hasna tries hard. She does the best she can."

"I didn't say she didn't."

"But you're making it sound like this is all her fault."

"That's not what I meant, Love. I'm just saying she has some things she has to change if she wants this to work."

"And what about Sharif? He has to change too."

Karim smiled, thoughtful, humored by his wife's assertion. "What does he need to change?"

"I'm not saying I see anything wrong with him. I'm just saying no one's perfect."

"I know he's not perfect, Love, but it's obvious that he's much more mature."

"Why? Because he studied overseas? That's not a fair measurement."

"Mona, you know that's not what I mean. He's always been more focused. It's just that after studying, things are becoming clearer to him, and now he knows what he wants in a wife."

"Hasna's willing to cover. She even asked me to teach her how to wrap the scarf."

Karim shook his head. "This isn't about hijab, Love. This is about his future. Nadirah still doesn't wear hijab, but she's much more focused than Hasna."

"Nadirah is a grown woman, Karim. You can't compare her with Hasna."

"I realize that. I was only saying this isn't about hijab."

"To me, Hasna *is* focused," Mona said, and Karim detected a mother's stubbornness in her tone. "Maybe not in the same way Sharif is, but she's focused."

"Mona," Karim said, his eyes resting on the wildlife painting above their bed, "let's be honest here. A focused woman doesn't sneak out of her house to meet a man she has no business talking to, while she's engaged to someone else."

Mona's eyes widened as she met her husband's gaze, clearly shocked that Karim knew about that night.

"Yes, Mona, I know about it. I heard her leave."

For a second, she didn't know what to say. "Why didn't you say anything?"

"What good would it do? It wasn't going to bring her back home."

Mona's gaze fell to her hands again, and she toyed with her wedding band. "But how do you know she met a man? It could have been a woman."

"I tried to convince myself of that too," Karim said. "But I think it's that friend of hers from law school."

Mona was quiet, and Karim could tell from his wife's expression that she was thinking the same thing.

"At first I let it go," he said. "I figured it was innocent enough. I myself talk to females at work all the time." He shook his head. "But this is different."

They were silent for some time.

"This isn't friendship," Karim said. "It's infatuation."

"But he's engaged too," Mona said quietly, hurt in her eyes, but she would not look at her husband.

"Yes, I know." Karim sighed.

"She told me they want her to be the best man at the wedding in May."

He gathered his eyebrows. "You mean a *bridesmaid*?"

Mona shook her head, still avoiding her husband's gaze. "No, the best man. It's supposed to be a joke because she's his best friend."

"She *told* you that?"

"Yes."

"But…"

"She wanted to know what I thought about a dress she wanted to have made."

"So the best man is wearing a dress," Karim said dryly, but inside he was furious with his daughter.

"Well, it's not a normal dress." Mona chuckled, but Karim could tell it was due to embarrassment. "It's like the business suit women wear to work, except it's black and the top looks like the tuxedo best men usually wear."

Karim stared at his wife, disbelieving.

Mona laughed again. "I know. That's what I was thinking. But to be honest, it actually looks quite feminine."

"Mona."

"Karim, come on, you know I don't agree. I'm just letting you know she won't be cross dressing or anything like that."

Karim rolled his eyes to the ceiling, but he couldn't calm the fury that was building in his chest. "What did you tell her?"

Mona was silent momentarily. "I told her it wasn't my style."

Karim didn't know what to say, he was so angry with Hasna. How could she have stooped *that* low? Even if she saw no problem with the joke, what about the image of her family? Didn't that matter to her?

"Couldn't you have thought of something else to say?" Karim said.

"I was thinking the same thing." Mona shook her head, clearly regretful. "But at the time, I was so surprised, I couldn't even think."

Karim looked at his wife, his eyes narrowed. "You still think she's focused?"

Mona rubbed her face in exhaustion. "I like to believe she is."

Karim shook his head, jaw clenched. "Yes, Mona, I do too. But we have a nice young man to worry about. You think it's fair to throw him into something like this?"

Stunned, Mona glared at her husband. "Wait a minute, Karim. I don't think it's fair to suggest she shouldn't get married because of this. You have to remember that this is a different generation. This type of thing is normal for them."

"That doesn't make it right."

"I don't think it's right either, Karim, but we have to look at it from her point of view."

"What would that be?"

"That it's just a joke between friends."

"But this isn't something to joke with."

"To her, it's just a unique dress. If she thought something was wrong with it, she wouldn't have asked what I thought."

"What if that's *why* she asked what you thought?"

Mona blinked, distracted, clearly having not considered the possibility. "I don't think so."

"Why not?" Karim challenged. "To me, that's more sensible. I'd hate to think she asked because she didn't have *any* idea it was wrong."

"But why does it even matter at all? This isn't our problem. This is between Hasna and Sharif. Let him decide what he wants to do about it."

"How will he if he doesn't even know?"

Mona narrowed her eyes and folded her arms. "Please tell me you don't plan to share this with him."

"If he's going to make a decision, I think he should know what's at stake."

"You make it sound like marrying our daughter is a punishment."

"Well, maybe it is."

Mona's jaw dropped. "How can you say that? She's a human being. Everybody makes mistakes."

"This is not a mistake, Mona. This is a character flaw." He paused before adding, "A serious one."

Mona bit her lower lip as she shook her head, clearing disagreeing with her husband. "What about us, Karim? Were our mistakes character flaws too?"

Karim started to speak but grew quiet as his wife's meaning slowly registered. But he didn't want to think of their past right then. Though it haunted every moment they spent together.

For most couples their wedding day inspired reminiscent sighs as they recalled the joyous day. But for Karim and Mona, it was something they tried to forget. With the typical mindset of Americans above the age of eighteen, Karim and Mona had married simply because they wanted to. He hadn't consulted her father or family, and she hadn't either. It was ignorance that inspired the decision, but it wasn't out of spite. They didn't mean to disrespect or hurt anyone. They honestly had no idea that anyone else should be involved. Mona had said that her "culture" required the family to know, but she, like Karim, had no idea that this aspect of Desi culture was really a part of Islam—and that without the father's permission, there was no marriage at all.

But given their predicament, the knowledge wouldn't have changed their resolve to get married. But it would have put a tremendous burden on them at that time. The marriage was more an act of desperation than it had been evidence of infatuation or love.

Two weeks before the sudden decision, Mona had visited a doctor after feeling nauseated and weak. She had thought little of the fact that her cycle hadn't come because it was often irregular. But when she went for an appointment, she did a routine urine test after which an OB-GYN was called in. That's when she learned she was two months pregnant, and when she told Karim, marriage was the only way he could think to right their wrong.

Ironically, less than four weeks after they eloped, Mona miscarried. But what was done was done. And there was no way to turn back the clock and erase the past. But by then, neither of them wanted to.

It wasn't until Mona was pregnant with Iman, their second child, that they both realized that their ignorance held with it a greater crime: They were living in an illegitimate relationship because the marriage had not met Islamic standards of matrimony. The news sent them into a frenzy of stress.

What *now*?

They talked to an imam in D.C., who told them they would have to separate and seek permission from her father. When Mona explained to him her family situation, the imam himself intervened, contacting Mona's father on her behalf.

"Tell her she can do whatever she wants" was the message her father gave to the imam when he had called. *"Because she's not a part of this family anymore."*

Naturally, the imam didn't know what to make of this angry statement and Mona and Karim remained separated for almost three months. Then the imam discovered that Mona's father didn't pray or fast. And the imam was unsuccessful in contacting any of her uncles, and her grandparents lived in Pakistan.

That was when the imam accepted the role as her guardian, albeit reluctantly, and performed the ceremony himself.

"But that was different," Karim said, his tone revealing that he himself was not convinced.

"It was worse." Mona's arms were folded as she spoke, her voice tight in pain and regret, but Karim could not look at her. "A hundred times worse."

Karim's chest tightened as the doubt about the legitimacy of their marriage returned, but he could not voice these doubts to his wife.

But he imagined that she too carried the same uncertainty in her heart.

"Let's let Sharif and Hasna decide if this is a character flaw," Karim said finally.

"How? Are we going to start uncovering people's sins?"

He sighed. He couldn't argue with his wife.

"No," he said finally, exhaustion in that word. "We'll just let them make the decision based on the ones that have already been exposed."

Eleven

"It is well known amongst those who live in non-Muslim lands the numerous harms of that. Among these are the abandonment of fundamentals of the religion; scorn of those who follow its precepts; indulgence in sin, even by those who intend to fear Allah; illicit relationships between men and women; and displeasure with what Allah loves and pleasure with what He dislikes."
—Scholarly Discourse on the Importance of *Hijrah*

Tuesday night Hasna again sat alone in the law office where she worked, the light in her office glowing conspicuously in the otherwise empty suite. Tonight she had put on a music CD to calm herself as she read. She hadn't finished her reading from the night before, and she needed the soothing voice of Mariah Carey to keep her mind clear.

Naturally, her boss was upset with her, but there was little Hasna could do to stay focused. Part of her was starting to wonder if she wanted to be a lawyer at all. Although Hasna enjoyed her work, doubt had been distressing her for the last two days. It wasn't the profession she doubted. It was the lifestyle that came along with it. It didn't have to be that way, Hasna knew, but she couldn't imagine coming to work covered in a scarf and excusing herself from meetings or court cases to pray every time the sun changed position. As a Muslim, she knew it was the right thing to do, but practically, she felt it was a bit excessive. It was difficult to imagine that her five minutes of mumbled prayers and half-hearted bowing would make any major difference in the world, or in her life even.

But, most significantly, Hasna couldn't imagine giving up her close friendship with Vernon. Being around him was what inspired her to come to work each day. What was so wrong about that? Aside from their flirtatious joking and licentious conversations, Hasna and Vernon's relationship remained platonic.

But Hasna couldn't deny that it was becoming more difficult to quell the desire for something more.

Initially, thoughts of a romantic relationship had merely lingered in her subconscious, and she thought of it only as a hypothetical. When Sharif had said to her on the phone two years before that it was impossible for a man and woman to remain friends without at least their hearts desiring physical companionship, Hasna was offended.

In response, she had remarked sarcastically that his ideas about Islam were becoming more fanatical by the day. She had laughed after she said it, but he had not. Instead, he had grown quiet, making Hasna self-conscious and acutely aware of the inappropriateness of the joke. He then made some excuse to get off the phone and return to his studies.

This was the conversation that came to Hasna's mind as she listened to the soft sounds of Mariah singing "Hero" while she read. At that moment, Hasna wondered if she should give up her friendship with Vernon.

She thought of how Vernon listened intently while she spoke and how he was honest with her, even when it hurt. She thought of how he, out of everyone she worked with, was the only one who didn't judge her harshly for her Islam. She thought too of how Vernon's laughter spread over his face until it reached his eyes, and how her heart fluttered when he embraced her...and of his strong physique that his work shirts did little to veil.

No, even if Hasna wanted to, she couldn't let their relationship go.

And she didn't want to.

It was like the words to a song she had heard on the radio some years ago, *"If loving you is wrong, I don't wanna be right."*

Perhaps it was these enticing lyrics that had made Hasna lightheaded as she woke this morning, thoughts of Vernon swimming in her mind. Cloudy remnants of a dream she vaguely remembered of him had made her dizzy as she dressed for work, inspiring her to select the outfit she was still wearing as she sat alone in the office that night.

Hasna had changed three times before she decided on what she would wear to work, and her hands trembled in excited anticipation as she slipped on her final choice, unable to believe she was actually putting it on.

Hasna knew her mother and father wouldn't approve of the short turquoise skirt that revealed a hint of her thighs and the silk pearl blouse that dipped several inches below her throat although it was standard business attire for Hasna's friends. It was an outfit Hasna had bought from the mall months ago, but she had hung it in her closet never imagining she'd ever have the nerve to put it on. But when Hasna had looked at herself in the full length mirror that morning, she was so taken by how appealing she looked in the chic suit that she couldn't take her eyes off her reflection. She had put on the matching high heels, telling herself she wouldn't actually wear them to work, having thought they would be too much. But when she saw how they accented the muscles of her legs, she knew she didn't have the heart to take them off.

In case her parents were downstairs to see her leave, Hasna had pulled on a long, loose skirt over the one that was sure to draw disapproving glances and remarks from her parents. Hasna's heart had raced all the way to her waiting car in the driveway, where it took her a full twenty minutes to calm down after she pulled off and drove to work. But by the time she pulled in front of the office suites, her nervousness was replaced by a bolstered self-confidence, her only anxiety being her concern that perhaps Vernon for some reason would not come to work today. She quickly slipped off the elastic-band skirt and tossed it in the back seat before touching up her makeup using the rearview mirror. A minute later she walked briskly up the walkway to work, fully conscious of the desirous gazes of men and jealous stares of women who weren't accustomed to seeing her dressed provocatively.

Hasna's heart pounded uncontrollably when she saw from the window Vernon's car pull into the suite parking lot minutes after hers. When he walked in the building, she had made it a point to pass him in the hall.

"*Hasna?*" Vernon said when he saw her, unable to tear his eyes from her.

Hasna had laughed, pretending to be casual although she was secretly hoping he appreciated every inch of her appearance, even the sparkling gold of the necklace that once held the pendant S for Sharif.

"You like it?" She grinned bashfully. "I thought I would try something different today."

He blinked repeatedly, clearly still recovering from the sight. "You should warn people before you do something like this." He shook his head, a grin lingering on his face. "How do you expect us to concentrate today?"

Currently, the guilt for these transgressions created an uncomfortable knotting in her chest, but in the solitude of the office suite, a smile formed on her face as she felt triumph for having tormented Vernon like she had. A part of her felt disgusted with herself for these thoughts, but there was a stronger flame of longing for Vernon in her heart.

Despite the illicit reason for dressing as she had, Hasna intended to keep the sensuous outfits coming each day. She knew full well the effect this would have on her best friend—after all, he was a male, and what male wasn't weak? But Hasna didn't plan for anything to come of her teasing except the fun she often heard her single friends brag about in working with married men. And she planned to have the same harmless fun with Vernon at work.

Hasna had lived her life as a Muslim, sticking strictly to the rules of chastity, never imagining that she would be reduced to such base desires of the heart that she nursed right then. Hasna was by no means the example of the perfect Muslim, but there were certain lines she hadn't dared to cross, though there were moments with Sharif during high school that she had come close.

At the thought of Sharif, Hasna felt the familiar anxiety return to her. She was intimidated by him, she realized right then. And she hated him for that. She never expected his Islamic studies to turn him into someone she loathed and desired in ways she couldn't temper or comprehend. It would make more sense if it were one or the other—abhorrence or desire—but these conflicting emotions she could not understand. She wished the matter was simple, then she could either pursue the relationship or leave it behind her and move on to something else.

Maybe her sudden streak of playing dress-up in the halls of work was less about punishing Vernon than it was about punishing Sharif.

At the thought, Hasna felt suddenly ashamed of herself. A sickness came over her, and she wondered at her life. What was she doing with herself? Certainly, this "harmless" game she was playing had no winners, at least not in the Islamic sense.

This was pathetic, Hasna thought with a groan. Her parents didn't raise her like this. Why then had she been so excited to break the rules? Was she suffering from low self-esteem after all these years? Or was she grieving the loss of Sharif and trying to prove to herself she was valuable to someone, even if it wasn't to him?

She could have any man she wanted, Hasna thought to herself, her pride returning just as suddenly as it had gone. She shouldn't waste her time grieving over someone as selfish as Sharif. All he wanted to do was shape her into a mindless housewife so she could be locked up at home with no life except pitter-pattering about the house serving him.

Hasna, please. You know that's not true.

The words stripped the indignant tirade from her mind and replaced it with sour guilt, the fermentation of the sins she carried in her heart making her stomach churn.

Hasna wanted Sharif back, that was all. And all she had to do was pick up the phone and ask him to accept her, and forgive her for taking him for granted for so long.

Hasna lifted her eyes to the phone that was but an arm's reach away, the dead weight of worthlessness and transgression making her heart heavy and sick. She needed Sharif, she realized, because with him she could come to know the better part of herself. Maybe she would even wear the Islamic garb she had loathed for so many years. Maybe she would even leave America and live in Riyadh as he had dreamed. Maybe she would actually be a good Muslim and no longer live in the concocted farce she had imagined as faith.

What then was stopping her from just calling Sharif and saying she was sorry and asking for forgiveness?

Does he love you?

Vernon's question hung before her, evoking the image of the sincere concern for her that was reflected in her friend's eyes as he had sat opposite her that night at the coffee house. She recalled the affection she had felt when Vernon embraced her after having been robbed of that simple gesture from the one who asked her to spend the rest of her life with him.

This is honestly how I feel. After Kenya, you're the closest person to my heart.

She thought of how these simple words made her face grow warm, and how her heart had danced in flattery at his confession.

Could Hasna give that up? A friendship with someone whom she felt she had known her entire life?

The question hung in the quiet of the office until she realized with candid certainty that, yes, she could give it up, if only for the sake of her soul.

But she wouldn't. And that's where her problems lay.

These thoughts lingered in Hasna's mind as she heard a soft knock at the office door. In the background, Mariah Carey and Boyz II Men sang a melody about lost loved ones, and Hasna's heart grieved the loss of Vernon and Sharif at once.

Startled by the sound, Hasna turned to see the door opening, her heart beating wildly in fear, suddenly becoming self-conscious in her outfit as she imagined her father coming to find her there.

"Anybody home?" a voice asked.

When Vernon stepped inside, a wide grin on his face, Hasna could not keep from grinning herself, she was so pleased to see her best friend standing only feet from her. Vernon's large form filled the doorway a moment before he approached her, the scent of his cologne tickling her nostrils and momentarily intoxicating her with its sweetness.

"Hey," she said, noticing the soft crispness of the silk cream of his shirt and rich black of his dress pants — an outfit he hadn't had on earlier that day. "What are you doing here?"

He lifted an unopened bottle of sparkling apple juice. "I thought you could use a break."

"I thought you went home."

"I did."

Still grinning, she stared at him, her body still turned awkwardly in the chair so that she faced him. "Why'd you come back?"

"Kenya's in a bad mood." He shrugged. "And I didn't want to be there."

"What's up with her?"

"Cold feet I guess."

"What do you mean? She's having second thoughts about May?" The question was intended as a joke, but Hasna detected a trace of hope in her tone.

"Could be."

Vernon glanced at the open window then back at Hasna. "Let's go for a drive."

"Now?" Hasna laughed. "I have work to do."

"So you're turning me down for Attorney Wynmore?" He frowned playfully.

"Okay, you win." She stood, stacking the papers with the motion, conscious of the outfit that she knew was complimenting her form well.

"Where to?" she asked, a curious smile on her face.

He wore a smirk as he put an arm around her shoulders and steered her to the door. "It'll be a surprise. Besides, with what you did to me today coming in here like that, I don't care where we go. I can't stop thinking of you."

Her eyes widened in flattery and she started to say something, but he brought his index finger to his lips.

"Shhh…," he said. Their eyes met as he shushed her, and Hasna's heart pounded wildly again. "Don't spoil the mood."

Thirty minutes later they sat on a picnic blanket in a quiet park that overlooked lush scenery, a small pond a few yards away.

"Where are we?" Hasna asked, looking up at the starry night.

"We are…" Vernon said as he set a clear plastic cup in front of her and opened the sparkling juice, "spending quality time together."

Hasna giggled. "As best friends." She reached for the cup and held it while he poured her drink.

"As you like." He winked as he poured himself a cup.

"What's that supposed to mean?" She held the cup in front of her, unable to keep from smiling at him.

"It means you decide where we go from here."

Hasna felt her heart drum more forcefully. She lowered her gaze, afraid to look him in the eye. "What about Kenya?"

"Is that my first hint?"

"Hint about what?"

"What you want with this relationship."

Hasna's cheeks flushed. "I don't know."

"Well, you need to speak up. You already know where my heart lies."

"Yeah," she said dryly, now pulling at some grass next to the blanket with her free hand. "You already told me that."

"What did I say?"

Hasna shrugged. "That after Kenya, I'm your best friend."

Vernon laughed out loud, throwing his head back slightly.

Hasna creased her forehead, a grin lingering on her face. "What's so funny?"

He continued laughing, recovering a second later.

"What?" Hasna said, now laughing herself.

"I guess it's a woman thing, huh?" He was shaking his head now, still chuckling.

"What did I say?"

"Nothing."

"Come on, Vernon. That's not fair."

"I'm not joking. You said nothing, nothing at all."

"What's so funny about that?"

"Because I was hoping for a little more."

She gathered her eyebrows. "A little more of what?"

For a second he just looked at her. "More than nothing."

Hasna started to speak but when she saw him gazing at her, she looked away. She let her gaze fall to the pond in the distance, its water glistening in the moonlight.

"I do too." Her voice was almost a whisper, her heart in her throat, and her hands trembled at the confession, her face warm with embarrassment. A second later she felt the strength of his hand on her chin before he turned her face to his.

As crickets chirping softly in the night and water rippled in the distance, Vernon looked at her and she lifted her eyes to his before he spoke, his eyes telling her she could have what her heart desired all along. "Then why didn't you say something before?"

193

Sharif woke in the night, a sick sensation in his stomach. In the darkness of the room, verses of the second chapter of Qur'an wafted from the small stereo opposite his bed, giving the still night a tranquil atmosphere. As his mind registered the familiar surroundings, thoughts of Hasna swam in his mind. His chest tightened in distress at the reminder. For some reason he felt as if he had just spoken to her although he knew this wasn't possible. The last time they had spoken was when he had insulted her by mentioning Vernon's choosing Kenya over her. At the reminder, Sharif felt ashamed of himself, the weight of his sin making his heart heavy in his chest.

Before going to bed, he had put on a CD to listen to *Al-Baqarah* while he rested. He needed the soothing words of Allah to clear his mind and to relax his body that was becoming tense from stomach pains. He knew the sick feeling was most likely due to stress, and the Words of Allah being recited in the night had quelled the pain significantly.

After praying *'Ishaa* at the masjid earlier that night, Sharif had sat on the carpet of the *musallaa* regretting the role he had played in inspiring the current standstill in his relationship with Hasna. He was being unfair, he realized then. How could he expect things to be different between him and Hasna when things were simply as he had left them when he went to study in Riyadh? Hasna wasn't being wayward. She was just being herself. Like Sharif himself had been before he experienced life in a Muslim land, Hasna was merely a victim of her circumstances. Hasna needed only patience and time to see the error of her ways. It wasn't fair for Sharif to act as if he had known Islam his entire life, when he had had only rudimentary knowledge of the religion before his studies.

With doubts about his stalled relationship with Hasna weighing on him, he had stood alone in the otherwise empty prayer area and prayed *Istikhaarah*, the prayer the Prophet customarily prayed when making a decision on something that was not specifically enjoined or recommended in Islam.

After leaving the masjid, Sharif had felt he should go ahead and marry Hasna. He conceded that he was being unfairly judgmental. He and she had come from the same background, and it was only his studies abroad that inspired a different point of view. Yes, his perspective on life was more spiritually astute now, but that clarification could be the guidance he used with Hasna in their home.

Besides, who else was he supposed to marry?

As he drove home, Sharif was reminded of his repetitive dream of the veiled women, and for a moment he wondered if it were a true vision, some miraculous sign from Allah. As he considered this, he felt a headache pulsating at his temples as he recalled that Iman was the woman in the dream. Was it possible that something as bizarre as marrying his little sister's best friend could actually mean something for him in reality?

To be honest, it's not something I place too much value in. That's how we got ourselves into trouble in the first place.

The reminder of Rashad's statement halted Sharif's straying thoughts of Iman. Could these words have been a sign from Allah too? A warning to keep him focused in case he put too much value in the dream?

But weren't dreams worth *something* in Islam?

The implication of the question hung in the quiet of the car, the engine a soft murmur as he drove. Sharif listened to his silent thoughts, the endless possibilities floating in his mind. Night surrounded him as he reflected, whispers of cars passing a rhythmic background to his thoughts.

If I can't verify a dream with something I can point to in reality, then it should remain in the world of dreams.

These were the words that had halted Sharif's thoughts that night, inspiring his conclusion that the dream should remain in the enigmatic world from which it had come.

Sharif silently scorned himself for imagining otherwise. What was he thinking anyway? Yes, Iman was physically a woman, but she was in all other respects still a child. How could he even imagine that the vision was blessed? Certainly, something that farfetched must have come from his subconscious, or from Satan himself.

But what about the Prophet's marriage to Ayesha?

This gave Sharif pause.

Iman was certainly older than Ayesha had been. But that marriage had been divinely inspired, Sharif reminded himself.

And what if this one were too?

Sharif put on a Qur'an CD to drown out his confusing thoughts as he steered the car into the neighborhood of his home.

It was Hasna he would marry, he decided. If the dream meant anything at all in reality, it was that Hasna could be like her younger sister had appeared in the dream.

Nothing else seemed plausible to Sharif, at least not in a manner that he felt comfortable voicing to someone else, much less to Brother Karim. Sharif couldn't imagine his mouth forming the words he could say to Iman's father to make him understand what Sharif had seen in his sleep.

This certainly was not something he should put any value in.

But that night, after Sharif had finally drifted to sleep, he had a disturbing dream. He was certain that it was from his subconscious because so much of it was what he had been thinking about during the day. Yet as he blinked in the darkness, the thought of marrying Hasna made him feel sick, the image of her in the dream returning to him in the solitude of his room.

Hasna was scantily dressed, the worn fabric barely covering what a bikini would, while Sharif himself wore a flowing shirt that extended past his knees. He was standing in the living room of his home preparing to pray when the ground to his left suddenly opened to reveal Hasna laughing loudly at something from the bottom of the stairs. Physically, she was more beautiful than he had ever seen her in life, but in the dream Sharif's heart recoiled in disgust as he saw her there. Her laughter echoed, bouncing off the walls of the basement where he heard from next to her the laughter of a man. Sharif knew immediately it was Vernon. At the realization, it wasn't jealousy that gripped Sharif, but fear – fear for his own soul.

Suddenly, Sharif felt an urgency to pray. Heart aching in agony over his childhood friend, and over the fragility of his own spiritual state, Sharif lifted his hands to signal the start of prayer, tears filling his eyes as he thought of how easy it was to lose one's way.

As he recited from the Qur'an, he noticed a woman standing to his right – Iman, he knew, without turning his head to see. He recognized the flowing fabric of the jilbaab, but this time her veil remained lifted although he could not see her face as he prayed.

Fanatics! Hasna had yelled, her voice the curdling roar of a beast that was only partially mortal. Bursts of ferocious laughter from Hasna's friend followed the outburst, making Sharif tremble in fear and recite louder in prayer. Meanwhile, his wife was undisturbed by the commotion as she prayed calmly listening to the soothing sound of Qur'an escaping his throat.

Currently, Sharif looked at the time, his body sickened by the image of Hasna in the dream. At the thought of his former resolve to marry her, Sharif felt the bitter bile of nausea rising in his throat. And, as he had in the dream when he had heard Hasna's repulsive laughter, Sharif felt a sudden urgency to pray.

"Hasna. Hasna. *Hasna.*"

Hasna heard her name as if from a distance, her body shaking with the sound. She felt the pressure of someone's hand squeezing her shoulder in an urgency that jolted her awake.

Hasna blinked until she saw the bluish silver of the dark sky sweeping the landscape of her entire vision, and she was momentarily entranced by the remarkable beauty of what she beheld. She heard the distant sound of birds chirping and the soft splashes of water, and she felt the coldness of the ground beneath the thin blanket on which she lay. She wondered if she was recovering from a dream. She glanced about her, expecting her eyes to adjust to reveal the familiar surroundings of her room, but instead she was met with the strained expression of a man she vaguely recognized who was shaking her awake.

"Tweetie?"

At the sound of her nickname, Hasna's heart raced in sudden recognition of reality. She sat up quickly and saw in Vernon's eyes that he too had just awakened from sleep.

"You awake?" he said, the concern piercing her heart in dread.

"Yeah, what time is it?" Her voice was groggy and concealed the panic she felt right then.

"Girl, you don't want to know." He rolled over and thrust himself to his feet.

As if she herself didn't need to do the same thing, Hasna watched in bemusement as Vernon frantically gathered his things and picked up their trash from hours before.

"It's five thirty in the morning." Vernon's face contorted in apparent disgust with himself.

"*What?*" Hasna bolted from her place, and she hurriedly gathered her belongings beside her friend.

In the dim light of dawn, Hasna could see the glistening of spider webs in the trees and a hint of the dirt color of the pond, the natural scene less appealing than it had been the night before. A bug tickled the bareness of her leg, and repulsed, she stomped her foot until it fell on its back by her foot. Its legs moved as if taunting her with its insistence at life, and the sight made her grow sick at the reminder of what had transpired in the darkness of night.

Next to her, Vernon scolded himself, his expression revealing uncontainable frustration a second before he carried the blanket in a heap under his arm as he walked briskly to the car. It did not escape Hasna that there was not even the slightest reminiscence in his eyes.

"Tweetie, you gotta hurry up." Now standing at the car and facing her, Vernon's face revealed impatient agitation, and his eyes bore an aggravation that Hasna never before associated with him.

After slipping on her shoes, Hasna walked quickly toward him, her ankles twisting uncomfortably as the heels of her shoes dug into the soft ground with each step. Vernon opened the trunk and tossed the blanket inside as Hasna reached the car and let herself in. She tapped the back of her foot against the side of the car to release some of the dirt. Sighing, Hasna dropped her purse at her feet and shut the door.

Vernon muttered curse words the entire ride back to their office, where Hasna's car was still parked. Minutes into the drive, he banged his fist on the steering wheel, infuriated with himself. Startled, Hasna blinked from where she sat in the passenger seat next to him, her elbow propped at the base of the window as she held her forehead in her hand. A second later, she turned her attention to what was beyond the cold glass next to her.

Hasna concentrated on the passing scenery to keep from thinking about what must be going on at her house right then, and about her growing agitation with Vernon next to her acting as if she had ruined his life.

Hasna's stomach grew sick as she realized that she had left her cell phone on her desk at work, having forgotten completely about it when Vernon interrupted her reading the night before. Hasna didn't always carry it with her, and she sometimes purposefully turned it off, as she had the night she met Vernon at the coffee house and had come home late. But the day before, she had left the phone on and told her parents she would be at the office catching up on the details of a case that her boss needed her to review.

Vernon cursed again as they pulled into the parking area in front of their office, the first hints of daybreak illuminating Hasna's lone car in the otherwise vacant lot.

Vernon didn't look at Hasna as he halted his car in the space next to Hasna's and waited for her to get out. Hasna reached for the purse at her feet, the humming engine urging her to get out and go home.

Thin rays of the morning sun reached inside the window next to her and blinded her vision momentarily. She reached for the handle of the car door and held it, her heart racing until she felt the pounding in her head. Her arm brushed the car door next to her, a barrier between her time spent with Vernon and the world in which she was now compelled to live. She didn't want to open the door. She didn't want to cross that threshold into the unknown and traverse the rocky paths of the distorted future that awaited her there. She wanted to stay where she was, in the intoxicating cooling warmth of Vernon's car at the break of day, and the even more inebriating comfort of being this close to him a moment more.

Hasna's tongue went dry as her heart begged her to stay where she was, hoping that Vernon would tell her they could hold on to this moment, for now and forever, and they could leave the cruel strictures of this world behind. She wanted the night back and a thousand nights more, when she wouldn't have to wake up at all.

It didn't have to be like this, Hasna's heart cried. They could make the magic last for years to come and escape inconspicuously from the troubles that lay ahead. Maybe they could drive a hundred hours into the horizon right then and now. They didn't need Sharif or Kenya or the complications they would bring. They could make a life for themselves, just Vernon and Hasna living in tender seclusion. They didn't need anything more th—

"*Hasna.*" Vernon's voice interrupted her thoughts abrasively, and she flinched at the sound.

She turned to him and saw that his eyes were fiery red and his jaw was clenched. But the longing of moments before made her imagine that she could make things better for him. Hasna parted her lips, a question of hope on her tongue…

"I have to *go*," he said, now glaring at her, erasing in that gesture all her hopes of moments before.

Her face grew hot in offense, and she wrinkled her nose at his tone. "Vernon, you're not the only one in a bind here."

"Hasna, please, not now. I have to get home."

"I do too."

"Then get *out.*" His eyes widened in emphasis, his words a command that threatened an outburst more callous and grating than the one already unveiled. It was obvious that he was not in the mood for talking, or for reminiscing on a future he'd likely dismiss as a fantasy that couldn't be real.

"You don't have to yell."

"Hasna." He was gritting his teeth now. "I have to get home *now.*"

"Why? So Kenya won't know the truth?" Hasna folded her arms, her hurt feelings inciting a defiance that made her obstinate despite the irrationality of what she had imagined for their relationship. She met his gaze evenly, refusing to move.

Vernon exhaled through his nose as he tucked his lower lip to calm his anger. "Look, Hasna. Get out the car and we can talk later."

"I want to talk now."

"We'll talk later."

"Why not now? I don't think another five minutes will make any difference. We're already screwed."

"Hasna." Vernon's voice was calmer than it had been seconds ago, but Hasna could tell he was no less aggravated than he had been then. "I'm sorry if this seems a bit rude," he said drawing in a deep breath and exhaling as if gathering the patience he needed to gently urge her to leave. "But get the *hell* out my car before I shove you."

Hasna's jaw dropped in shock, but Vernon held his glare unblinking, letting her know he was not joking in the least.

"*Now*."

Infuriated, Hasna rammed her weight against the door as she opened it. She climbed out noisily and her purse banged against the window as her furor escaped in grunts. She slammed the car door as hard as she could, unleashing all her anger in that motion while glaring cruelly at Vernon the entire time.

But by then Vernon's eyes were looking behind him as he backed out the parking space, his calm not the least bit disturbed by her dramatic display. A second later he positioned the car and turned his head as he pulled the car forward, the sound of the engine fading as he sped out the parking lot and turned onto the road. The car blinked in the rays of morning as the early light illuminated the car until it disappeared out of sight. Vernon had not even glanced in Hasna's direction — neither for consolation nor to see if Hasna got safely into her car.

Arms folded in protest at his vicious affront, Hasna stood alone in the parking lot next to her waiting car, and she heaved breaths of fiery offense. But the only sound that greeted her was that of birds chirping and flapping their wings in preparation for flight. She lifted her gaze momentarily in their direction as they moved forward in search of food, reminding her of the start of a new day in a world that submitted to a flawless schedule in the alternation of night and day.

She dropped her gaze to the pavement at her feet, still recovering from the brusque treatment of moments before, and she reached into her purse to remove her keys, the jingling a taunting reminder of her parents at home. Her body heavy with sin and unrequited desires of a broken heart, Hasna turned to her car and pushed the key into the lock.

Then why didn't you say something before?

Vernon's voice from the night before was a baritone whisper in the soft breeze of morning that even then made her legs weak. Her eyes filled with tears at the memory as her heart burned with bitterness and desire, and she wished she could turn back the hours of day and rewrite her life from the moment she woke with dizzying fantasies swimming in her mind.

The calling of birds chimed in the sky above as Hasna fell forward in shame, her torso against the car and a bent arm on the car's roof above the driver's door. Her shoulders shook in pitiful grief as she rested her face in the crook of her elbow and sobbed. The tears wet the sleeve of her silk blouse and seemed to come from the pit of her stomach, the pain was so deep.

Behind her in the distance, the sun rose higher in the horizon, its rays glowing arms reaching out to embrace the world. The morning light illuminated the chic suit that was now soiled from the cold ground that was Hasna's night bed. Above, the heavens spread in an enormous canopy and shielded the sulking woman and her abandoned car as the woman ailed an aching heart about to burst.

The pens had been lifted and the ink had dried, and even the birds taking flight for their morning meal could not erase the solidity of what their slumber had delivered in nights past. For they were but one magnificent creation of many, whose present reality, like that of past and future, was penned in a Tablet written more than 50,000 years before.

The record sat preserved and undisturbed as those on the earth beneath hurried to work or overslept. Or argued or made amends. Or laughed at what amused them or cried at what cut deep. Yet, even as they grieved for what was never meant to reach them or they longed for that which was out of their hands, their actions were merely a fulfillment of every stroke on the Tablet. Their very breaths counted down flawlessly to the Hour written therein. And those who traversed a single path beneath would see the recompense of every solitary deed.

Twelve

"I see what you do not see and I hear what you do not hear. Heaven has moaned and it has a right to moan. By Him in Whose hand my soul is, there is not a space of even four fingers width in which there is not an angel who prostrates his forehead before Allah.
I swear by Allah that if you knew what I know, you would laugh little and weep much, and you would not take delight in women but you would go out to an open space and call on Allah for help, [and say] 'I wish I were a tree that could be cut down and cease to exist.'"
—Prophet Muhammad (peace be upon him)
(Bukhari)

On the verge of laughter, Wali cupped a hand over his mouth, lifting his other to point at Sharif as Nadirah related how Sharif had taken a bath in the toilet when he was four years old.

It was Wednesday morning, and Nadirah sat with her three children around the kitchen table, having finished eating breakfast minutes before. Sharif had returned from the masjid after praying *Fajr* to find the kitchen table set with pancakes, beef sausage, turkey bacon, and eggs.

"What's the occasion?" he had asked as he took a seat across from Wali. Nadirah had said that she just wanted to spend quality time with her family before going to work that morning.

"The *toilet*, man?" Wali chuckled, shaking his head.

Sharif wore a grin as he remembered the day he had decided he could take his own bath.

"He always wanted to do things himself." Nadirah smiled as she shook her head. "He even unrolled an entire roll of tissue and placed it next to him."

"For what?" Asma grinned as her eyes lit up in amusement.

"To dry himself."

Wali burst out laughing. "And you want to give *me* advice?"

Sharif himself chuckled, remembering.

"And when I found him," Nadirah said, nodding her head toward Sharif as she grinned, "he had tissue pieces stuck all over him after drying off."

The table roared with laughter, and Sharif wore a smile as he listened to his mother talk.

"And I caught him just as he was dipping his toothbrush in the water to brush his teeth."

"No way!" Wali shook his head. "Man, I can make money off stories like these. I can't wait till everybody learns the truth about Imam Sharif."

"Well, if you're going to write the tabloids," Nadirah said jokingly, "you may as well tell them about the time he tried to fix dessert for me and your father and topped our strawberry shortcakes with shaving cream."

A smile lingered on Sharif's face before he spoke. "What was I supposed to do? I was just learning to read." He chuckled. "And the bottle did say *cream*. You can't blame me for that one."

"Maybe you should have read the word before it," Asma suggested, teasing.

"I did," Sharif said. "I just thought it said *saving*. And that's what I was doing." He smiled. "I was saving cream. I made sure I put the rest of it in the refrigerator."

They all laughed.

"Did I tell you all about the time he was trying to dirty his beloved cars in my plant soil outside?"

"Come on, Mom," Sharif said good-naturedly. "Why are you picking on me? Asma and Wali did silly things growing up too."

"No, ma'am." Beaming, Asma leaned forward, resting her elbows on the table. "You didn't."

"Well, this one's short," Nadirah said to Sharif, apologizing in her tone. She then turned to her daughter, humor in her expression.

"Well, this day he went outside and accidentally dipped them in what the neighbor's dog left for us."

Asma and Wali laughed.

"Needless to say, he wasn't pleased with the results."

"And remember when me and Iman got into that food fight?" Asma said to her mother.

At the mention of Iman, Sharif grew uncomfortable and picked up his fork and reached for a cold pancake although he had already eaten his full.

"Oh yeah." Nadirah's eyes lit up. "I remember that."

A thought came to Nadirah a second later, a smile on her face as she looked at her daughter. "But that wasn't funny, Asma. I was really upset with you for using my spaghetti sauce to smear in each other's hair."

"But I only remember throwing a meatball."

At that, Nadirah laughed, and Sharif couldn't suppress a smile as he too recalled how Asma had intended to smack her friend with one last strike, but the meatball landed on Nadirah's forehead instead.

"I didn't appreciate that by the way," Nadirah said, recovering from laughter.

She glanced at the clock on the wall and stood, lifting her plate with the motion. "It's been nice," she said with a smile, "but I have to get to work."

Asma and Sharif followed suit. They helped Nadirah clear the table by stacking dishes and carrying them to the sink. Nadirah scraped the leftover food into storage containers and placed them on the table, working in silence for several minutes as she sealed each.

After the breakfast dishes were stacked on the counter next to the sink, Asma rinsed them before placing them into the dishwasher, the water from the plates dripping through the wire racks. Nadirah opened the refrigerator and arranged the sealed containers on shelves, shifting some vegetables and condiments to make room for the leftovers. She then rinsed her hands at the sink, looking at the clock again.

"Hey Sharif." Wali still sat at the table toying with a half-eaten pancake drenched in syrup on his plate, the only dish left on the table.

Sharif glanced at his younger brother from where he closed the kitchen closet after removing the broom in preparation to sweep the floor.

"What's going on with Hasna, man?"

Sharif halted his sweeping motion and regarded Wali with his forehead creased. It was unlike his younger brother to ask about Sharif's personal life. "Why?"

Wali shrugged, his gaze falling to the food he was stabbing absently with a fork. "I saw her yesterday."

Sharif resumed sweeping the floor, unsure how to respond. He worked in silence for several seconds before speaking. "Where?"

"I guess it's where she works." Wali lifted a shoulder in a shrug. "I went with my business partner to look at some property in Bethesda."

Sharif nodded as he cleaned, feeling uncomfortable with the conversation. From the corner of his eye, he saw his mother standing in the doorway of the kitchen. She had started to leave to get ready for work, but she turned back around when Wali mentioned Hasna.

"I almost didn't recognize her." A half smile creased one side of Wali's mouth, and Sharif could tell that Wali was troubled by something.

"Why wouldn't you recognize her?" Asma laughed, glancing back at him from over her shoulder as she dropped a handful of silverware into its plastic compartment in the dishwasher. "You've known her your whole life."

Wali chuckled uncomfortably. "Well, you wouldn't have recognized her either."

Sharif saw his mother step back into the kitchen, her arms folded, brows furrowed in concern. But Sharif could tell that his mother was more concerned with the appropriateness of Wali's statements than with what he was saying about Hasna.

"Why wouldn't she have recognized her?" Nadirah's tone rose authoritatively, making it clear that she preferred an end to the conversation more than she did a response to her inquiry.

Wali cut the pancake with a side of his fork, his gaze still there, his contorted expression conveying more than a verbal response would have. He was silent, and his attitude conveyed defiance of his mother, but Sharif sensed there was something deeper to his display.

"Wali." Nadirah raised her voice in a dare, taking a step toward her youngest son. "I asked you a question." She shook her head with her eyes narrowed, challenging him. "What are you trying to say?"

"Nothing," he muttered, clearly bothered by the negative attention.

"Then don't bring this topic up again unless you have something to say."

"I do have something to say," he said, obviously offended, glancing sideways at his mother. "But you're acting like I'm lying or something."

"I didn't say that, Wali, and you know it."

"You didn't have to."

"Well, I'm sorry if I made it seem like that. I just don't think it's fair to insinuate things without proof."

"I'm not insinuating." Groaning, he rolled his eyes and shook his head. "I'm just trying to help my brother."

Sharif cringed, concealing his feelings of embarrassment as he quietly continued cleaning the floor. He thought of the dream he had had the night before, and he dreaded what Wali would say. He glanced at his younger brother and saw sincerity in Wali's expression.

Asma busied herself loading the dishwasher, the clanking of dishes making it clear she was not a part of the conversation.

Finally, Sharif stopped sweeping, his curiosity and concern piqued, as was his discomfort. He folded his arms, the broomstick standing in the crook of one arm. "What happened?"

Wali shrugged, stealing a glance at his mother. He was silent for several seconds, and Sharif feared his brother would not respond. "She just looked..." Wali's face contorted again. "...like a whore."

"Wali!" Nadirah's voice was sharp, and even Asma turned to look at her mother, startled.

"I'm serious," Wali said defensively, his voice rising.

"I don't want to hear any more of this. Whatever you thought you saw —"

"I *know* what I saw." Wali met his mother's eyes evenly.

"Maybe it wasn't Hasna," Nadirah said.

"It was Hasna, all right."

"But Wali, you can't —"

"Mom, I'm telling the truth." Wali banged his fork down, and the table shook. "You can think what you want. But I just don't think Sharif should waste his time with—"

"You can't judge someone for how they dress, Wali." Nadirah's tone was calmer, but Sharif detected uncertainty, as if she were trying to convince herself more than she was her son.

"Should I not judge her for having some guy hugging all on her too?" Wali was looking directly at his mother when he spoke.

The kitchen grew quiet. Even Asma couldn't keep from staring at Wali, her eyes widened, a dripping glass suspended in her hand as she looked over her shoulder at him.

Sharif felt the discomfort of the night before return, and his stomach knotted. His nose flared as he drew in a deep breath and shook his head. The news was deeply disturbing, but for some reason Sharif was not as surprised as he should have been.

Vernon. The name left him with a sick feeling. That's who was hugging Hasna, her "best friend."

"We're just *friends*," Hasna had said defensively on the phone a couple years before.

And Sharif had had no doubt that she was telling the truth. But he also knew what "just friends" meant in American society—a license to play with fire while feigning complete innocence at the same time.

Unsure what to do in the awkward silence, Sharif resumed sweeping the floor although the floor was now clean.

There was the sudden sound of screeching on the tiled floor, and Sharif looked up to see Wali pushing himself out of his chair.

"Think what you want." Wali's expression displayed anger and frustration.

Sulking, he walked toward the kitchen door, his face still twisted in offense. As he passed his mother, he said, "And she was acting like a whore too."

Iman was vacuuming the carpet of the living room, creating soft patterned rows that she followed in parallel lines, when her work was interrupted by the sound of the front door opening.

Her father had left for work less than an hour ago, and her mother was downstairs in bed after having been awake most of the night nursing anxiety about Hasna. Iman's mother had fallen asleep on the couch and was awakened by her husband when he entered the living room for *Fajr* prayer, Iman trailing behind him, Adam still asleep downstairs, as he still was right then.

The night before, Iman had followed her mother's repeated calls to Hasna's cell phone with calls of her own, imagining that Hasna would pick up eventually. However, the phone had rung repeatedly in her ear until she hung up, defeated. She had dragged herself to bed, the beginning of nightmares forming in her mind as she thought of what might have happened to her sister. Before going to bed, Iman had asked her father what they would do if Hasna didn't come home, and he had sighed before saying, "Pray for her, sweetheart. That's all you can do."

The response was logical enough, after all, praying was all they *could* do in such a circumstance. But it was his tone that had confounded Iman. She knew her father did not know where Hasna was, as no one did, but his response suggested that he had an idea. After *Fajr* he had used the same tone when he told Mona to go upstairs and get some rest.

Currently, Hasna appeared in the doorway, and Iman's eyes widened in pleasant surprise. Iman smiled as she turned off the vacuum, and she started to greet her sister when she noticed Hasna's appearance. Hasna's eyes were cast down, and she wore a dingy silk shirt and a long wrinkled skirt that appeared too clean for some reason. Hasna's eyes were slightly red and swollen, ghostly shadows around them.

Hasna showed no visible reaction when she saw Iman standing several feet from her except to offer a barely perceptible nod of recognition.

"Iman!"

It was their mother calling from downstairs.

"Iman!"

Before Iman could respond, Iman heard footfalls approaching quickly and Mona appeared at the top of the steps, pulling her robe closed with her hands. "I thought I heard the—"

At that moment, Mona's eyes met those of Hasna, who offered the same emotionless greeting she had to Iman moments before.

Mona's eyes registered shock, but a second later her forehead creased in bewilderment as she took in Hasna's appearance.

Iman expected her mother to ask where Hasna had been, but Mona simply stared. Hasna slipped off her high heel shoes, dirt stains soiling the turquoise that matched nothing else she wore. Hasna drew in a deep breath and folded her arms, but Iman sensed the gesture was more out of exhaustion than preparation for a fight.

Mona held Hasna's gaze for several seconds, the look of concern never leaving her face. Mona then walked over to her oldest daughter and cradled her in an embrace without saying a word. Moments later, Iman heard sniffles, and she thought it was her mother who was crying, but she was taken aback to see Hasna's shoulders quivering in her mother's arms.

"It's okay, baby," Mona said, her own eyes brimming with tears as she rubbed Hasna's back. "It's okay."

Perplexed, Iman watched as her mother guided Hasna out the living room, her arm nestling Hasna close to her, as if shielding Hasna from harm.

Moved by the emotional display, Iman blinked back tears of her own, a lump developing in her throat, though she saw no reason to cry.

Slowly, Mona retreated up the stairs, Hasna leaning into her, shoulders continuing to tremble beneath her mother's embrace. Mona guided Hasna with each step until they reached the top of the stairs. In the hall, Mona walked with Hasna until they stood before Hasna's room, where Mona turned the handle with her free hand.

A second later Mona disappeared from Iman's view as she walked with Hasna through the door that closed quietly behind them, leaving Iman with the melancholy of the scene settling at the back of her throat.

In the quiet of the living room, Iman sensed the irrevocable nature of the moment and detected a slight shift in the world beneath her feet. She felt it in the silence of the room. The vacuum stood next to her, and the patterned rows lined the carpeted room only halfway. Yet the divide between that which she had completed and that which had been disrupted seemed to represent the fault line of the moment, her house chores now a worry of days past. The somber reality created a looming cloud portending quiet rain that would slowly build to a torrential storm soaking a thousand tomorrows to no end.

In that moment Iman felt the triviality of her prior frustrations with her sister, and the weighty magnitude of her sin of ungratefulness to her parents. Her mother and father now carried a weighty burden that weakened even Iman.

Iman stood still in the half-vacuumed living room wishing she could soothe the pain her sister nursed right then. Iman wanted to erase the faulty prints that had led Hasna down this path, even as Iman had no idea the nature, or weight, of Hasna's offense.

But there were some transgressions that were too heartrending to mollify, and too errant to set right.

These are the sins, Iman recalled her father saying once, *that are punishments in themselves.*

Thirteen

"Among the people who came before you was a man who killed ninety-nine people. He asked who was the most knowledgeable man in the world, and he was directed to a monk. He went to him and said that he had killed ninety-nine people and was repentance possible for him? The monk said, 'No,' so he killed him, making it a hundred.
Then he again asked who was the most knowledgeable man on earth and was directed to a man of knowledge. He said that he had killed a hundred people, so was repentance possible for him? The man said, 'Yes, who can come between you and repentance?
Go to such-and-such land, where there are some people worshipping Allah Almighty. Worship Allah with them and do not return to your own country. It is an evil place.' So he went and then, when he was half way there, he died. The angels of mercy and angels of punishment started to argue about him. The angels of mercy said, 'He came in repentance, turning with his heart to Allah Almighty.' The angels of punishment said, 'He has not done a single good deed.' An angel came in a human form and they appointed him arbitrator between them. He said, 'Measure the distance between the two lands and whichever one he is nearer to, that is the one he belongs to.' Allah then commanded the earth to stretch itself until the man was nearer to the land to which he was going, so the angels of mercy claimed his soul, [and he was thus forgiven for his sins and entered Paradise]."
— Prophet Muhammad (peace be upon him)
(Adapted and compiled from reports collected by Muslim)

Hasna remained home from work for an entire week, having called in sick claiming to have come down with the flu. She spent most of the time in hibernation, locked in her room. She rarely mustered the energy to speak to anyone in the house, and even when she did speak, it was little more than the mumbled Islamic greetings accompanied by a terse nod. She had gone back to the office only once, to pick up her phone, and it had been late in the evening when she was sure Vernon would not be there.

She kept the phone on the night stand next to her bed and checked for messages at least twice every hour, telling herself that she was waiting for her boss to call. But deep inside she knew it was Vernon's call she was anticipating.

But it never came.

For the first three days, Hasna expected the call and was fuming in upset, ready to curse out Vernon and tell him to never call again. She was certain her absence at work would make him worried enough to at least send a text message of concern. But by the fourth day after hearing nothing from him, her infuriation turned to anxiety, insecurity laced in an obsessive longing that made her restless at night. There were moments she picked up the phone, hand trembling as she scrolled down to his name. But before she pressed the call button, the self-doubt gripped her.

She scorned herself for making him angry that morning in the car. She scolded herself for drifting to sleep and not being mindful that he lived with Kenya and was thus pressed for time. She considered that perhaps she was not beautiful to him anymore.

But mostly she cried. Hasna never imagined that a soul could hold so much pain, and that heartbreak actually hurt. Her chest ached for hours on end, and there was nothing she could do to pacify her agony except to imagine seeing Vernon again.

Whenever she heard her family praying downstairs, the guilt would gnaw at her, reminding her of her sins. At the sound of Qur'an being played from Iman's room, Hasna tasted the stench of her depraved state and realized there was no hope for her. She wondered what Hell would be like, certain that there was a chained column there reserved just for her. She wondered if it were possible to bear the torment with patience.

Hasna thought of Vernon, and she understood for the first time why he had voluntarily left Islam in favor of his own life. It was easier to live in denial, and Hasna hated that everything around her was a bitter reminder of her decadence.

In her mind, Hasna separated the world of Islam from her own reality. She imagined that she didn't deserve to be Muslim, and that the religion was better off without her. It would be better for everyone, she told herself, if she left spirituality alone.

Hearing her father recite Qur'an was the most difficult for Hasna because it reminded her that she should be standing behind him in prayer. To drown out the recitation, Hasna plugged iPod earphones into her ears, preferring to sulk in self-pity as she listened to singers moan soulfully about broken hearts and lost loves. Hearing the music fill her ears, Hasna felt as if the whole room were enveloped by the songs, and her heart lifted in hope as she imbibed the stories of lovers reunited and forbidden romances rekindled.

For hours Hasna drowned herself in the sonnets of those speaking through enticing melodies. She would carry the iPod to the bathroom so that she could remain connected even there. When her battery ran low, she put the iPod on its speaker base and let the sounds permeate the room. She swayed her body to the enrapturing lyrics, studying her movements in the mirror, her esteem bolstered as she beheld her beautiful reflection gliding with her. At those moments, she felt a certainty in her heart. Vernon would call. Vernon would beg her to forgive him. Vernon would renew his love. How couldn't he when he recalled how breathtaking she was?

But a week passed and she received not even a text message or e-mail from him.

"Sharif, the phone's for you."

Asma stood in the doorway to her brother's room, sleepiness in her eyes Thursday afternoon as she rubbed her lower arms that were exposed by the Barney T-shirt she was wearing. A week had passed since Wali had relayed how he had seen Hasna dressed at work, and over and over Sharif replayed in his mind what his brother had said, his heart wrenching in fury and jealousy.

Sharif had heard the phone ring as he sat in front of the computer checking his e-mail, but he did not move to answer it. He didn't want to acknowledge his subconscious desire to speak to Hasna. He often found himself wondering about her, what she was doing at that moment, his concern intensifying in the absence of news.

Oddly, his desire to speak to her had increased after hearing Wali's negative report. There were moments that Sharif was inclined to call Hasna, but his greater intuition compelled him to leave the situation alone. Yet he couldn't deny that he cared for her still, and perhaps always would, even if her spiritual degeneration made it impossible to rectify their relationship in any meaningful way. He had grown up with Hasna, and as such, she was like family to him. The affection that had been nurtured between them was something he could not remove from his heart even if he wanted to.

Sharif picked up the phone next to him and offered the salaams, and he was greeted with the reply of a man speaking in Arabic to him.

"Sharif? Haadha 'Abdullah min Sa'udiyyah."

Sheikh Abdullah, Sharif recognized the voice immediately. He was the professor who had introduced him to Hisham, the Yemeni-Saudi who had offered his daughter in marriage to Sharif.

"Yaa, sheikh. Kayfa haal? Kayfa awlaad?..."

It felt good to speak in Arabic again. The conversation reminded Sharif of his time in Riyadh, and he began to feel homesick for the Muslim land.

Sharif asked about the sheikh's health and family, and the sheikh asked about his. Abdullah asked how Sharif was adjusting to America, and Sharif told him, honestly, he wished he could return to Saudi Arabia. Abdullah told him he could arrange a visa for him if he liked, and he could find Sharif a teaching post or a position translating for the university.

The proposition was tempting, but Sharif felt obligated to fulfill his role as imam. He told this to the sheikh, and Abdullah said he understood but that if Sharif changed his mind, give him a call and he'd be happy to assist.

"Gulee, Sharif, anta muzawwaj wa laa lissa?" *Tell me, Sharif, are you married yet, or no?*

Sharif laughed, the question obviously meant as a friendly tease. *"Laa, sheikh, laysa ba'ad..."* Sharif said. *No, sheikh, not yet.* Sharif laughed before joking, *And I have no idea if I ever will be.*

What about the nice young woman Hisham told me that your family arranged for you?

It didn't work out, but I'm still hopeful something will.

Tell, me Sharif honestly, as we're brothers, was this the only reason you refused my friend?

Sharif knew the sheikh was referring to the marriage to Yasmin. Sharif felt awkward as he thought of his prior anxiety and self-doubt, and his indecision about Hasna. He wondered if he should share this with his teacher.

No.

So you were displeased?

The sheikh's frankness was unexpected, but Sharif liked it nonetheless. It was better than skirting around the issue.

"Laysa ka dhaalik…" Sharif said. *No, it wasn't like that. I was very pleased.*

Sharif hesitated before mentioning that he had also seen a recurrent dream that was confusing him.

"Wallaah? 'Aysh al-ahlaam? Mumkin, tugulee?" Really? What dream? Can you tell me?

Sharif wanted to explain further but realized it was difficult without giving some background.

It's a long story…

It's okay, I have time.

Where should Sharif begin? Or should he begin at all?

Sharif thought of what Wali had said about Hasna, and what had happened with Iman in the lobby of the masjid. Should he share this with the sheikh?

Sharif definitely needed another perspective, and Rashad's reaction had left him even more perplexed.

Perhaps Sheikh Abdullah had studied the subject of dreams in depth. The sheikh had spent years under the tutelage of some of the most notable scholars in Saudi Arabia, who were also respected worldwide.

Perhaps the phone call itself was from Allah, an indication that he should ask the sheikh's opinion. How often was it that a person had the privilege of speaking personally to a person of knowledge, who had studied in depth the traditions of the Prophet?

It was an opportunity Sharif should not let pass, he decided.

Sharif then shared with the sheikh everything that had led up to the very conversation they were having right then.

Fourteen

*"There is a group of Allah's angels who move about the streets
searching for people who mention Allah.
When they find a gathering of dhikr, they call out to each other,
'Here is what you are looking for.' They then cover that group with
their wings right up to the sky. When these angels return to the heavens,
their Lord asks them, although He knows the answer, 'What were My
servants saying?' They say, 'They were describing Your holiness and
greatness, and were busy praising You.' Allah then asks, 'Have they
seen Me?' The angels reply, 'By Allah, they have not seen You.' Allah
says, 'What would they have done if they could see Me?' The angels
reply, 'They would then be even more active in their worship,
glorification, and praise.' Then Allah asks, 'What did they want from
Me?' The angels reply, 'They asked You for Paradise.' Allah says,
'Have they seen it?' They answer, 'No, by You, they have not seen it.'
Allah says, 'What would they have done if they had seen it?' The angels
answer, 'Had they seen it, they would desire it more eagerly and would
work harder to earn it.' Then Allah asks, 'From what did they want Me
to protect them?' The angels answer, 'They wanted to be protected from
Hell.' Allah says, 'Have they seen it?' They answer, 'No, by You, they
have not seen it.' Allah says, 'What would they have done if they had
seen it?' The angels answer, 'Had they seen it, they would have feared it
and run from it even more.'
Then Allah says, 'Be My witnesses, I have forgiven them.'
One of the angels then says, 'But among them was a person who is
not one of them. He had simply come for something he needed. Allah
says, 'I have forgiven him too because he happened to sit with them.
Anyone who sits with such people will not be disappointed.'"*
— Prophet Muhammad (peace be upon him)
(Bukhari)

Friday night Sharif sat in the *musallaa* of the masjid, having
recited the opening *du'aa* to begin his first class. There were
about twenty people present, most of them women and no one he
recognized other than his sister Asma and four others, three

sisters and one brother with whom he had had minimal acquaintance before he left to study.

After much thought and having prayed *Istikhaarah*, Sharif had settled on the topic "Foundations of Islam," planning to focus on the basic tenets of the Islamic faith. He had given a lot of thought to the best way to approach the misunderstandings that were common in his small Muslim community. Although finding the correct approach was a daunting task, Sharif decided that the challenge should not be too difficult given that all errors in Islam, minute and detrimental, were rooted in a singular common mistake among Muslims — not understanding and practicing Islam as the Companions had under the tutelage of the Prophet.

In theory, most Muslims accepted the high status of Companions like Abu Bakr As-Siddeeq and 'Umar Ibn Al-Khattaab and 'Uthmaan Ibn Affaan, but it was the practical application of this acceptance that was missing in their lives, even amongst those who were most vocal in claiming allegiance to this single correct path, Sharif had reflected.

As the Prophet prophesized would happen, a great portion of the ummah were eager to imitate the Jews and Christians, whom they loved and admired more than the Prophet and his Companions themselves. This love was most evident in Muslims' willingness to shed the most visible hallmarks of Islam, the traditional beard for men, the required hijab for women, and even the congregational prayer in the masjid. The priorities of modern Muslims, in both Muslim and Western lands, followed the general rule that Islam should be practiced only insomuch as it did not conflict with the established culture of non-Muslims.

However, the dilemma before Sharif was even greater than this. He had to address not only the prioritizing of worldly matters over the religion, but the more serious problem of the removal of religious mandates altogether. In addition to the belief that Islam was in the heart, there was also the prevalent belief that the Qur'anic guidance for dress and behavior and even narrations of generations past, particularly regarding prophetic miracles, were merely symbolic parables with little or no meaning whatsoever in reality.

It was the ideal conclusion for someone wishing to blend into the society with which he was already part while enjoying the forbidden fruits of what that membership would bring.

It was also the natural result of a person who recognized the veracity of Allah's religion but was not prepared to act upon what that recognition required of him.

As Sharif had seen in himself, the Muslims subscribing to this ideology were not consciously trivializing Allah's laws. It was simply a matter of human psychology, social psychology actually.

As social psychologists had documented for decades, the psychological pulls of conformity were so compelling that any person repeatedly exposed to something began to accept it as normal, if not preferable, even if he intuitively he knew it to be morally wrong or illogical. After acceptance came implementation and admiration — and ultimately scorn of that which was previously recognized as moral and correct.

For Muslims, the natural psychological reaction to such dissonance had simply translated into spiritual jargon (and religious laxity) that absolved them of accountability in adhering to what was enjoined and narrated in Allah's Book and the authentic prophetic reports.

"I want to start tonight by discussing the famous story of Adam and Eve," Sharif said from where he sat on the carpeted floor facing his students, conscious that even this story was interpreted figuratively by most Muslims in his community.

But the existence of something symbolically does not negate its existence in reality.

This was the epiphany that Sharif himself had had, relieving him of this spiritual misunderstanding.

You have to crawl before you can walk.

Still water runs deep.

An empty barrel makes the most noise.

These were the adages that had come to Sharif's mind following the sudden realization.

When reciting these truths, people usually spoke figuratively — to share a profound lesson about life, and the spiritual symbolism the Creator placed all around, in humans' tangible reality.

This was what made the figurative lessons so profound.

Sharif considered sharing these points to his class, in relation to the story of Adam and Eve.

"This story is significant to the foundations of Islam," Sharif said, "because of two subjects I want to address tonight. One, the meaning of Islam itself. And two, that which contradicts its meaning."

At that moment, Sharif decided against the tangent. It was something he could address later, *inshaaAllaah*.

"If we look at this story," he continued, "we find that our father Adam, peace be upon him, was favored by Allah and lived in the Garden, as did his wife Eve, or *Hawa*, as we refer to her in Arabic. As we know, they were living peacefully and were free to live and eat as they wished, and were given but one instruction. *To not approach a single tree.*" He paused, hoping to emphasize this point.

"Imagine, here we have a man and woman given all the delights a heart can desire, in a Garden granted to them by the Creator, the Generous. What more could they want?"

Sharif glanced at the Qur'an that sat before him on a small wooden stand. "Let me read to you from the story as it was told by Allah in the Qur'an…"

And "O Adam, dwell you and your wife, in the Garden and eat from wherever you will,
but do not approach this tree, lest you be among the wrongdoers."
But Satan whispered to them to make apparent that which was concealed from them of their private parts. He said, "Your Lord did not forbid you this tree except that you become angels or become of the immortal." And he swore [by Allah] to them, "Indeed I am to you from among the sincere advisors." So he made them fall, through deception. And when they tasted of the tree, their private parts became apparent to them, and they began to fasten together over themselves from the leaves of the Garden. And their Lord called to them, "Did I not forbid you from that tree and tell you that Satan is to you a clear enemy?" They said, "Our Lord, we have wronged ourselves, and if You do not forgive us, we will surely be among the losers."

After translating the Arabic recitation, Sharif asked, "What strategy did Satan use to convince Adam and Hawa to approach the only tree that was forbidden to them?"

Sharif squinted his eyes as he looked at the small crowd. "What did he say to our parents to make them fall into sin?"

A brother leaned forward, and a sister looked down at the carpet as if deep thought.

"He told them, *No, this doesn't mean what you think it means. It means this.*" Sharif motioned with his hands, indicating an opposite position. "But all along Satan knew that he was lying.

"But let's think on this for a second," Sharif said. "Here you have Allah, the Creator, the Provider, the Sustainer, the Owner of all pleasures seen and unseen, telling our parents that they can live and eat as they wish. But He says to them to not approach this *one* tree or else they'll fall into harm."

He paused, reflecting. "How then is it possible that someone could come between that and make them forget something as clear and powerful as an instruction from Allah himself?

"Do you think they forgot that Allah is their Lord?"

Sharif regarded the brothers and sisters before him. "Or did they merely forget *themselves*?"

There was a thoughtful pause before Sharif shook his head finally. "It's difficult for us to imagine this mistake. Because it was all so clear, so *obvious*." He shook his head again.

"This is what I used to think when I heard this story as a child. I mean, it was so *clear* that they should stay away from the tree."

He paused.

"Except when it's the tree of our *own* lives."

A brother nodded thoughtfully, and a sister drew her eyebrows together, lost in self-reproach.

"But let's look at the words of Satan for a second," Sharif said. "He didn't say, 'Hey, eat from that tree.'"

Some brothers and sisters chuckled quietly or appeared amused.

"He said that it was actually *good* for them if they did."

Sharif smiled while looking out at the students.

"And who did Satan claim to be when he told them?" Sharif paused, a smile lingering on his face before replying, "Their *sincere* adviser."

Sharif glanced at his notes before raising his head.

"So Satan inspired the first sin by following a simple tactic." Sharif was silent momentarily. "What was this tactic?"

A brother looked as if he were inclined to raise his hand and respond, but decided against it.

"He changed the meaning of something already defined by Allah." Sharif let the students reflect on his words before repeating this point.

"He changed the meaning of something already defined by Allah." Sharif raised his voice and emphasized every word.

"And this, brothers and sisters," Sharif said, "is the same trick that we are falling for today."

Sharif saw some of the students begin to nod in agreement.

"In the name of modernism, moderation, or just in the name of our own lives. At home. At work. At school. *Every*where. We are allowing 'sincere advisers,' non-Muslims *and* Muslims, to come to us every single day and *re*define something that has already been clearly defined by Allah."

Yasmin watched, utterly helpless, as the girl's desperation became despair as she realized the wings had become part of her skin, part of herself. But still the girl fought and fought…

Suddenly Yasmin was back in her own bedroom, and a small white box sat upon her bed. In that moment, she knew it was the one she had been seeking when she had gone to see the woman. Yet, the box that she needed had been here, on her bed, the entire time…

"Maa 'adree ta'weel al-ahlaam, habeebati…" I cannot tell you what these dreams mean, my love. I don't have enough knowledge.

Yasmin sat opposite *'Ustaadhah* Anood on a cushion of a floor couch that lined the walls of the Qur'an teacher's sitting room. Plates of dates and a stainless steel pitcher of Saudi coffee sat on a glass table in front of them, small glass cups next to it on a serving tray.

With her large dark eyes deep in thought, Anood reminded Yasmin of Sharif momentarily. Anood and Sharif shared the same deep brown skin tone, and spiritual beauty on their countenance.

But Anood's face and eyes were those of an Arab, and Sharif's were those of an American.

Yasmin had come to her teacher for advice, having been distressed about the dream after seeing it a second time, this time with the dream ending in her own bedroom. Yasmin hadn't wanted to share with Anood what had occurred between her and Sommer, but she had. She somehow felt it was relevant. The Arab blood in her made her reluctant to share with anyone details from her personal life, but Yasmin was distressed and confused. She needed to talk to someone, and Teacher Anood was the only person she felt she could trust.

"Laakin anti darasti ma' al-'ulamaa." But you studied with the scholars.

"Ayuwa, darastu ma'hum. Laakin..." Yes, I studied with them, but dream interpretation is not an Islamic science they teach, my love. In many ways, dream interpretation is more a gift or skill than it is a definite science. Yes, there are definitely foundational principles in dream interpretation, but this is all I'm familiar with.

They were quiet for some time.

But you should not think too much of these dreams, Anood told Yasmin. *Dreams are not meant to distract us from real life. And they hold no definite place in Islamic law. They cannot tell us right from wrong, or guide us in any acts of worship.*

But there are some that are from Allah, Yasmin said. *Aren't we supposed to pay attention to these?*

Yes, but that's only if we can be sure they're from Allah. How can you ever be sure of that?

Yasmin was quiet momentarily.

Seconds later, she heard Anood draw in a deep breath and exhale, her eyes growing deep in thought before she spoke.

But it is true that I have some experience with dream interpretation, Anood said. *My father used to have the skill, although even he did not interpret every dream someone shared with him.* Anood shook her head. *And today, the Muslims are having many. This is because we are close to the Day of Judgment.*

Yasmin studied the creases next to Anood's eyes as she spoke. Yasmin had heard of Anood's father. He had been a respected scholar in the Kingdom.

"Katheeru ta'weel il-ahlaam min 'ilm il-firaasah." Much of the interpretation of dreams comes from firaasah.

"Firaasah?"

It is the ability to determine much about a person from their countenance. In some countries, it is studied as a science. But like dream interpretation, it is more a gift or a skill.

I never heard of it.

Well, it is not talked about much these days. But 'Umar ibn Khattab, may Allah be pleased with him, had this skill. American scientists call it "intuition" and say that humans unconsciously use eye movements and hand and body gestures to give clues about what they are thinking and intending. Anood paused, taking a sip of her coffee. *But it is more than this.*

Did you study firaasah?

My father taught me what he knew. But, again, it is not an exact science. As is the case with dream interpretation, humans err in their explanations and understanding.

But is that a good reason not to try?

Anood clicked her tongue in disapproval. *This is not something to play with, my love. We don't go about guessing without knowledge. It is against Islam.*

Besides, Anood added, *there is also the fact that reality can be greatly affected by how we interpret a dream.*

Yasmin creased her forehead. *"Maa fahimt."* I don't understand.

"Shoof…" Look, if you really believe something means something, even if it doesn't, Allah may decree that things occur in the way you believe them to be.

Yasmin's eyes widened. *Really?*

"Tab'an." Of course.

I didn't know that.

"I am how My Servant expects Me to be," Anood quoted a famous Qudsi hadith.

Yasmin nodded, recalling the prophetic narration. *"Sah…"* That's true...

So be careful, habeebati.

Yasmin was silent for some time.

But I do think your dream has some meaning.

She looked at Anood suddenly. *You do?*

Anood looked away. *But I could be wrong…*

Tell me.

Anood drew in a deep breath. *I don't know the exact meaning of the dream, habeebati, but you should keep away from your friend.*

Yasmin grew quiet, reminded of her parents having told her the same thing.

I have no idea what she plans to do to help you, Anood said. *But my feeling is that she plans to harm you and the girl in some way.*

Yasmin's heart fell, and she dropped her gaze.

I can say nothing of a surety, habeebati. But this is my feeling. In many cases like these, people resort to sihr.

"Sihr?" She stared at Anood in disbelief. It had never crossed her mind that Sommer would seek the help of jinn. She had asked Sommer's help because of the *people* her friend knew in America. Yet... Yasmin didn't want to think of it.

Yasmin had studied the spirit world as part of her Islamic studies courses in high school, but the subject had always been a theory, and an eerie one.

As I said, I cannot speak for your friend. But, unfortunately, this sort of thing is common amongst people who do not practice Islam.

But why would she want to hurt us?

I didn't say she wants to hurt you. I said this is my feeling.

But still...

In any case, I think you know the answer to that better than I do.

In the weeks that followed the first class, Sharif continued conducting classes in the masjid. Amongst the Muslims in the area, word spread about the "power" of his lessons, and by the beginning of October, a few weeks before Ramadan, attendance had increased until there were more than seventy students in the class.

Sharif began to recognize more faces from his home community although most students were from communities he did not know. Some students attended only out of curiosity and would come to only one or two classes while others, eager to learn, were more frequent.

The sudden prominence of his classes made Sharif uncomfortable. But it indicated that Muslims were not as complacent about their religion as he had previously thought. More than anything, it seemed, Muslims were searching.

The spiritual impotence of the society had left Muslims hungry for guidance and direction. Many were in and out of one Muslim group or another, in search of that single truth that would feed their souls and inspire a momentous yet lasting change in their lives.

Some of Sharif's students were becoming torn between their prior ideologies and what they were learning in his classes. For most of them, it wasn't the veracity of Sharif's lessons that they doubted, but their ability to actually live up to what they were learning, particularly in the current political climate that discouraged any apparent Islam.

Naturally, it was easier to believe that the precept of moderation in Islam dictated the need to moderately practice the religion itself, as opposed to pointing to the fact that Islam itself was moderate. Sharif himself had felt similarly before studying.

The religion is easy, he would tell himself. *Don't put hardships on yourself. If you can't pray at work, pray at home. If it's hard to keep up all the prayers, don't burden yourself with these rituals. As long as you believe in your heart, that's the most important.*

In preparation for the month of Ramadan, Sharif decided to shift the focus of his classes to the Islamic concept of purification of the soul.

Tazkiyah, spiritual purification, was a vast concept that encompassed the entire religion, yet the seat of it rested in the driving force behind every act fulfilled and every word spoken—the heart.

Within this piece of flesh lay the single most significant indicator of the affair of every human being, whether Muslim or non-Muslim. The functions of this organ were vital to both physical and spiritual life.

Yet the spiritual reality of what lay within the breast was so complex that a person was not always aware of his own sincerity, or lack thereof. A mere turning of the heart in favor of people's approval instead of the Creator's was likened to minor *shirk*, the worshipping of other than Allah. This alteration of intentions was so inconspicuous that the Prophet had said that it was more hidden than a black ant crawling on a black rock on a moonless night.

Thus, this concept was in need of constant revisiting in the life of the Muslim, and Ramadan offered the most opportune time to address *tazkiyah* of the soul.

Sharif also wanted to address the topic because innovated *dhikr* circles were becoming increasingly common among American Muslims in the area. These gatherings, which were conducted in a manner unknown to the Muslims at the time of the Prophet, were often termed "*tazkiyah.*"

Most of the participants meant well, Sharif knew.

And so had he when he wasn't praying regularly.

But good intentions alone are ineffective in protecting a person from mistakes, he had read once.

Yet, they were very effective in ensuring that a person would likely never see the mistake in the first place.

How was Sharif to address this in a class? This task was more daunting than the lesson on the Adam and Eve story.

The popular "gatherings of *dhikr*" were ostensibly for the remembrance of Allah or for praise of the Prophet, but Sharif himself witnessed that the teachings of Allah and His Messenger were remembered less during these circles than those of the group's favored sheikh. The recited "*dhikr*" was not taken from specific hadith but was based on a dream of a revered sheikh or on his specialized "path" (drawn from his secret knowledge), as Rashad had shared with Sharif.

In one class in early October Sharif clarified that proper *tazkiyah*, which was the religion of Islam itself, was based on purifying the soul by practicing the religion—and engaging in *dhikr*—as had the Prophet and his Companions, the true *'awliyaa* of Allah.

Sharif had begun the class by reciting some verses from the Qur'an that specifically praised the believers who lived at the time of the Prophet.

If they believe as you believe, then they are rightly guided…

…

You are the best people produced [as an example] for mankind…

227

Sharif also recited Allah's stern warning to those who followed a path other than that of the Prophet and the believers who followed him.

Whoever cuts himself off from the Messenger after guidance has become clear to him and follows a path other than that of the believers, We shall leave him on the path that he has chosen and land him in Hell, what an evil destination.

"I don't like what you're teaching." Nadirah stood with her arms crossed in front of her as she leaned against the counter next to the sink as the food she was preparing for dinner simmered on the stove.

Asma was setting the kitchen table as she glanced at her mother, sadness in eyes. But she did not look at Sharif.

Sharif sighed, having expected this confrontation. He stood across from his mother holding the door of the refrigerator open, having been looking for condiments that they could use for dinner.

"But, Mom, I'm only teaching what I know is right."

"No, Sharif." Nadirah shook her head as if correcting a child. "It's what you were *taught* was right. There's a difference."

Sharif removed glasses of ketchup and French mustard and closed the refrigerator door. "Then how do we ever know what's right?"

"We don't."

He creased his forehead and started to speak.

"But we can certainly know what's wrong," she said before he could say anything.

In Nadirah's disapproving gaze, Sharif felt the burden of his mother's disappointment. Sharif didn't want to have this conversation, especially not in front of his little sister.

"If we can know what's wrong," Sharif said as he carried the glasses to the table, "then we can know what's right."

"Sharif," Nadirah said, drawing in a deep breath, as if unsure how to convey the weightiness of what was on her mind.

Sharif drew in a deep breath of his own. He glanced at Asma, but she was concentrating on aligning the silverware on the table.

"Our learning is more a process of elimination than it is a process of gaining knowledge," Nadirah said.

"Yes," she conceded, "there are things that we know. But those things don't change with time because they're basic. But the more complex parts of life are not fundamental. This is why we can never be sure what's right, but we can be sure what's wrong."

Sharif's back was to his mother momentarily as placed the two glass jars in the middle of the table. "But if we learn what's wrong, then we learn what's right too."

Nadirah sighed. "No, sweetheart. There are things we can never understand until we die. Religion is one of those things."

Sharif turned to his mother with his brows furrowed. "But religion isn't complex. Everybody knows that—"

"That's the problem, Sharif. You're convinced that everybody knows something that they don't. It's not even possible." She shook her head, her face twisted in disapproval.

"And how would you even know that?" Nadirah asked, her eyes narrowed as she regarded her son, her arms still folded in front of her. "What makes you think *you* know what everybody else knows?"

She shook her head. "This is what I'm trying to tell you. These people think they have a monopoly on Islam. But in reality, Allah is the only one who could claim that."

"I didn't mean it like that. I'm just saying that everybody recognizes that they have a Creator, but they don't nece—"

"But that's not true, Sharif. Everybody doesn't recognize that."

"But they do. It's just not always conscious."

Nadirah coughed in laughter, but disappointment was apparent on her face. "If it's not conscious, then it's not knowledge."

Sharif folded his own arms and lowered his gaze, hoping to temper his growing frustration. He didn't want to argue with his mother.

"You're teaching things that are debatable, and *wrong*." Her voice rose. "Yet you're acting like there's no other perspective even *allowed*."

Sharif felt the urge to respond, but he withheld, his gaze still averted to the floor.

"Islam is not a bunch of rigid rules of *do*'s and *don't*s. It's a religion of the *heart*. It's a religion of your *life*. It's a religion of your *soul*."

An awkward silence followed as Asma passed them to go to the sink. A second later the sound of water running filled the quiet between them as Asma rinsed a dish next to her mother.

"But, Mom," Sharif said quietly, looking at his mother just then, his arms still crossed, "what does that mean?"

It was a rhetorical question, but as soon as he had asked it, Sharif knew his mother had misunderstood him.

"It means that Islam is a private matter between a person and their Lord," Nadirah said.

Nadirah narrowed her eyes, and Sharif looked away. He wished he knew a tactful way to have this discussion. He hated to see his mother upset.

"And you have *no right* to disrupt that relationship."

Sharif sighed. "But how can learning about Islam disrupt a Muslim's relationship with Allah? It can only make it better."

"Yes, that's true. But only if you're learning about Islam and not some *Arab*'s interpretation of it."

Sharif winced.

He had grown up scorning Muslims of Arab descent, so the comment shouldn't have stung as much as it did. But tonight it cut deep. It felt like a personal attack.

Sharif remained silent, his thoughts straying to the raw hypocrisy of Americans' own discontentment with prejudice. It seemed a disease that no one escaped, Sharif reflected. Not even those who bore the African slave's dark skin and history of cruel mistreatment.

As a teen, Sharif had sustained an indelible scar on his own psyche following Hasna's snide remark about her father's skin color, a hue that reflected Sharif's own complexion. The combination of his youth and insecurity had left him vulnerable to the debilitating inferiority that had followed him to adulthood.

It was not Hasna who had hurt him, he realized just then as he stood opposite his mother in the kitchen that evening. It was the cruel reality in which she had lived that had cut him deep.

And Sharif had imagined himself and his family immune.

Yet the entire foundation of his community's Islamic creed was rooted in the scorning of Arabs, even as it was rooted in the teachings of an Arab himself. The Sheikh had become discontented with his own "Arabized Islam" and was thus inspired to found a religious ideology that freed him, and his followers, of the "ritualistic shackles of the East."

It was as if Islam was a contest of nations vying for a unique interpretation instead of an unalterable universal guide for people of all races, ethnicities, and lands.

They don't have some patent on Islam, he'd often hear elders say when he was growing up. *We can have our own fiqh.*

And why can't we have our own school of thought? someone else would say. *They have it.*

It wasn't a desire to embrace some newly uncovered truth that was responsible for the eagerness with which Sharif's small community of Americans accepted the teachings of the Sheikh, but a desire to distance themselves almost entirely from the Islam of Arabia.

Children born from the womb of Western media and moral laxity, the community members viewed "fanaticism" as less a term referring to truly fanatical acts like terrorism and oppression of women than a term referring to any outward commitment to Islam that even remotely resembled the Islam practiced in Arabia. Seeking their own "American expression of Islam," they viewed with distrust and scorn any traditions that had been passed down generation after generation in the foreign land.

Even if the tradition was from the Prophet himself.

Currently, Sharif started to respond, but the sound of the front door opening interrupted him. Distracted, Nadirah creased her forehead and left the kitchen to see who it was, disappointment still lingering on her face.

"Mmm," Sharif heard Wali say from the living room, his jovial tone a sharp contrast to the atmosphere of moments before. "What's that smell?"

"Dinner," Sharif heard his mother say evenly, the front door closing.

"Good," Wali said, now entering the kitchen, a grin on his face, rubbing his hands together. "Because I'm starving."

An amused expression developed on Sharif's face as he greeted his brother, but his thoughts were still on the argument with his mother.

But when he saw Nadirah smile proudly and start to serve the food, the urge to argue left him.

Sharif smiled himself, grateful to relax in the company of his family.

"I am too," he said in response to Wali, pulling out a chair for himself. "Let's eat."

Fifteen

The bright red bow was the first thing Hasna noticed when she entered her office early Monday morning in mid-October. The red ribbon bound the small box that was wrapped in iridescent gold paper and sat on her desk next to a stack of papers she had been reviewing the day before.

Vernon. It couldn't have come from anyone else. Hasna should have been excited to receive the gift, but it was more than a month late. A week after that fateful night spent in the park, Hasna had returned to work to witness the cold treatment by her former best friend. Vernon barely even looked at her when they passed in the halls, and when they were forced to be in each other's presence during meetings or when conveying work-related messages, Vernon spoke to her with the distant cordiality befitting two co-workers, not former best friends. It was as if he had not known her at all before that night—as if the night had not happened at all.

Hasna set her purse on the desk and lifted the small box that was lighter than she expected, although she didn't know she had expected anything at all. She tore the gold paper and tossed the wrapping into the trash bin next to her desk. Her heart started to pound as she held the white box in her hand, and she recalled her and Vernon's last moments together before the argument. She wondered if this was a peace offering between friends, or a request to rekindle what they hadn't had opportunity to savor.

Hands trembling, Hasna sat in the soft office chair, her eyes resting on the box in her palm. She wanted to lift the lid and satisfy her curiosity, but she also wanted to hang on to this moment, uninterrupted. Hasna was afraid that her shifting emotions would shatter the fragility of her hope for a relationship renewed.

But Hasna didn't want Vernon in her life. She had already begun to start her life anew. In the last two weeks, she had even begun to pray regularly, although she was still struggling to pray on time. Vernon's coldness had given her opportunity to reflect on her soul, and on the flicker of faith that was left in her heart. Stricken by the grief of regret, Hasna had been forced to face the rawness of her sin. The bitter sickness she felt in her stomach at the realization of her spiritual pollution was almost too much to bear.

Hasna's sin was one that she had not imagined a Muslim could commit, although she knew, in theory, that everyone was human and thus prone to sin. But now she felt a world apart from this former naiveté, and she wondered at Muslims like Sharif, who had been able to maintain a level of purity she could no longer fathom.

Was it possible to make it work with Sharif? Would he forgive her?

Would he have to know that she had sinned at all?

The longing Hasna had felt for Vernon had transformed into an agony she was suffering for having lost Sharif, and so completely. It would have been better to have separated for something more benign. But the concept of infidelity was not something she had considered, or even prepared herself for.

But she had fallen into it.

Never think you're above committing any sin, her father had said to her once. *It is the sin you never could imagine committing that you are most vulnerable to. Because you've offered yourself no protection against it.*

Only days before, in the solitude of her room, Hasna had brought herself to say the words she had been unable to utter since the burden of her sin overwhelmed her with recognition of accountability. Tears in her eyes, Hasna had raised her hands to Allah, chin quivering as she uttered, "O Allah, I have wronged my soul, so forgive me."

Simple words, they were. But it was as if a rock lay upon her tongue, choking her and obstructing her speech when she had begun to speak the phrase many a night before. When the words finally passed her lips, Hasna's body had trembled, and her nostrils grew moist as she felt her utter poverty before her Lord. Before this moment, she had wondered if it were possible for her to be forgiven at all. She felt so unclean, so pitifully filthy, it just didn't seem right that she should have even hope for a place so pure and flawless as Paradise. She felt it was selfish of her to even ask for pardon or mercy. Because she didn't deserve it.

"You're right," Mona had said to Hasna after Hasna had replied flippantly to Mona's urging Hasna to ask for forgiveness, even as the specifics of Hasna's sin had not passed between them. *"You don't deserve forgiveness."*

At the time, Hasna did not know whether to feel relieved or offended at these words.

"None of us do," her mother had added. *"That's what the goal in life is, in the end. To be granted the mercy and forgiveness that none of us deserve. And Allah gives only to those who ask."*

Currently, Hasna lifted the lid from the box.

Hasna blinked in surprise, and a hesitant smile creased one corner of her mouth as she set the box on her desk so she could remove the pendant. The pendant was gold with the yellow face of Tweetie Bird engraved in it.

She reached behind her neck to unfasten her gold chain. She then slid the pendant on the necklace and re-clasped it, smiling as she felt the coolness of the charm beneath her neck. Once the letter *S* had hung there; now she bore a symbol of her own.

Hasna was about to return the lid to the box when she noticed a piece of paper on the side of the box. It was rolled into a small scroll, and a thin red ribbon was tied on it, making her think of a miniature diploma.

She removed the paper roll and tugged the string loose. She then unrolled the scroll, finding slight difficulty due to its size.

"I'm sorry, Tweetie. I love you. We need to talk."

Hasna's heart fluttered in flattery and anticipation as she read Vernon's ink strokes that were smooth and deliberate, evidence of his taking time to write to her.

Smiling, she adjusted her purse on her shoulder and lifted her fingers to her throat to feel the smooth engraving of the bird. Still cradling the pendant with two fingers, she left her office to find Vernon.

"I'm thinking that we should also have a column about Islam," Iman said from where she sat next to Asma in Sharif's office at the masjid Monday morning. She handed the young imam the revised edition of the newsletter, reaching across the desk, her gloved fingers pinching the sides of the paper.

Sharif nodded as he accepted the paper, and Iman saw his eyes stop momentarily on the "O Mujahid" poem. She averted her gaze as she recalled the awkwardness of that first *Jumu'ah* prayer. Her heart pounded at the memory. She folded her hands on her lap hoping that he didn't notice her nervousness.

It had taken weeks for Asma to convince Iman to have this meeting, but Iman was still unsettled. Of course, Asma did not understand Iman's hesitation, having assumed that her friend simply did not want to go through with what they had planned. But it was much more than that.

Iman herself couldn't pinpoint exactly what was making her apprehensive, but she knew that she grew self-conscious every time she saw Sharif. She couldn't stomach the idea of talking to him directly. She had known him when she was a child, and he had even babysat her, so she shouldn't have felt so uncomfortable in his presence. But he was a man now, and he was the imam.

The way Sharif's beard framed the brown of his face made Iman's face go warm every time she saw him. Now he was sitting opposite her.

Iman wondered what he would think of the newsletter. She knew it wasn't perfect, but she had revised it more than five times. She had no idea how much better she could make it.

Her hands shook as she saw him lean forward slightly, reviewing the pages.

"I think it's necessary," Sharif said. His deep voice made her heart flutter more. She couldn't get used to the sound of it. She heard him speak every Friday afternoon during *Jumu'ah* and every Friday night for the classes, but for some reason his voice made her uncomfortable now as he spoke to her.

"What do you think of 'A Glimpse of *Emaan*?'" Asma said to her brother. "Iman thinks that's what we should call it."

Inadvertently, Iman glanced up and saw Sharif look at his sister with his brows furrowed, confusion in his eyes. He started to speak but seemed hesitant. Iman looked away. Why did Asma have to embarrass her? Iman hadn't asked Asma to share her idea. That could have waited.

"For the Islamic column or for the newsletter?" Sharif asked.

"For the column. We already named the paper."

He nodded. "I like the name... But a lot of people don't speak Arabic, so maybe we should call it 'A Glimpse of Faith.'"

"But everybody knows the word *emaan*."

"Yes, I know, but I think it's better if we say *faith* instead."

"The Arabic sounds better though."

"It's okay," Iman said, glancing at her friend. "It doesn't matter. I think he's right."

"What about using it for the title of the paper?" Sharif asked.

"But it's already called 'Islam's Call,'" Asma said, frowning.

"I was thinking..." Iman said, her voice cracking all of a sudden. She cleared her throat. "What if we made the title based on the masjid? You know, since it's going to be just listing events and classes."

Sharif glanced at the newsletter and nodded, considering the idea. "That's true. I didn't think of that."

"But the masjid is just called The Masjid Center." Asma contorted her face. "That's corny."

"We don't have to call it that," Sharif said. "But I think that...she's right. It won't make sense to have a fancy title for a paper that is focused mostly on community events. If we were using it for something else, then maybe we could —"

"Then why don't we use it for something else?" Asma shook her head. "I just don't think anyone's going to want to read about a bunch of events. We can make a separate section for that."

Sharif turned a page of the newsletter, and Iman took a deep breath, recalling the article she had written inside. "The Death of Islam," she had called it. But now she wondered if the title was too much.

For some time, Sharif seemed engrossed in what he was reading. A few minutes later, he glanced up, and Iman looked away, their gazes having met momentarily.

"Asma says you're Umm Sumayyah."

Iman felt her face go warm. It was a question although it was phrased as a statement. She nodded, her eyes on her gloved hands. "It's just a pen name," Iman said quietly.

There was an awkward silence.

"I like it," Sharif said. "I mean, for the articles," he said quickly. "I think it's good to be anonymous."

"That's what Sister Irum said," Asma interjected, agreeing. "She said that way people don't judge your writing based on you. They'll just judge what you wrote."

Sharif nodded. "She's right."

At the mention of Sister Irum, Sharif was reminded of his friend Jafar. Brother Rashad had returned to Pakistan, and Sharif thought about Jafar daily. He wondered how he was doing and if he was okay. Or if it were even possible to be okay in such a condition.

The guilt of having not even sent a letter of correspondence had begun to eat at Sharif. Shouldn't he visit him? Wasn't that the least he could do?

On impulse, Sharif had called the Department of Corrections and was told that visits to any correctional facility had to approved beforehand and that the inmate had to put the visitor's name on an approved visitation list.

Sharif had hung up feeling defeated. He had no idea it would be this complicated. He didn't even know what prison Jafar was in.

"Do you like it?" Asma asked, grinning, standing up slightly to see what he was reading.

It took a second for Sharif to realize that his sister was talking about the article "The Death of Islam" by Umm Sumayyah.

He didn't know what to say. Yes, he did like it. Very much. It was as if she took the words from Sharif himself and arranged them into a compelling essay. The article was discussing how Muslims were abandoning Islam in favor of "belief in the heart."

"...In the Qur'an, whenever Allah makes an exception to a condemned group," one line of the article read, "you never find the phrase 'except those who believe' unless the words 'and who do righteous deeds' follow it. Therefore, it's not possible to say that we can avoid blame by believing only..."

"*MaashaAllaah*. It's very interesting." Sharif decided it was best to be modest in his praise. He didn't want to make Iman as uncomfortable as she already was. Having lasted this long in the meeting had been difficult enough. He wondered how much longer he could sit here behaving like an imam when he was wondering if it were possible to be a husband.

He scorned himself for this thought. *She's only....what?...fourteen?*

But that dream...

Sharif had already suffered a couple of blunders in the last few minutes alone. His lack of enthusiasm for the title "A Glimpse of *Emaan*" had less to do with it being unpalatable than with it reminding him about the glimpse of Iman he had wanted in the dream. He couldn't imagine reading a column every month with the title and thinking about the young woman instead of his faith. And it wasn't necessary to confirm that she was Umm Sumayyah. He already knew from his sister that Iman was using the pseudonym in her writings.

It was difficult to imagine that Iman had actually written the articles and poetry. Her words were that of a mature, studied woman, not a fourteen-year-old child.

"*Laysat sagheerah.*" *She's not a child*, Sheikh Abdullah had told Sharif on the phone after he had shared with the sheikh his dilemma. *She is young, yes, but a child is a person who hasn't reached the age of puberty.*

But in this country, she's considered a child.

No, the sheikh disagreed, *she's considered a "minor." There's a difference. But, yes, socially, Americans think of her as a child, but technically, she is a young adult, even in America.*

"But what do you think we should do?"

The question startled Sharif momentarily, and it took a second for him to realize that it was his sister speaking, and she was referring to the newsletter.

"Should we use it for the masjid?" Asma added.

Sharif was quiet as he reviewed the last lines of Umm Sumayyah's article, still distracted by the maturity of her language and outlook. He wondered if she was a child prodigy. He had read about that.

Or maybe she was just mature for her age. Physically and mentally.

If I can't verify the dream with something I can point to in reality, then it should remain in the world of dreams.

Was Iman's maturity the sign "in reality" that Sharif had been looking for?

Talk to her father, the sheikh had said.

I can't do that, Sharif had said, self-conscious.

You don't have to propose. But you should talk to him. You say he's like a second father to you. You'll never know what the dream means until you see what he says about it.

"But how will we print it?" Iman asked. Sharif glanced in her direction, but she was looking at Asma.

"Can't the masjid print it?" Asma said.

Sharif took a deep breath and leaned back in his chair, exhaling. "That's the problem. We don't have the funds."

They were quiet momentarily. Asma held a look of deflated hope on her face.

"What if we do bake sales?" It was Asma's suggestion, and she was looking at her brother.

"But that won't be enough," Iman said.

"What about getting advertisers?" Sharif said. "That could cover the costs."

Iman nodded, and Asma glanced at her friend uncertainly.

"But where will we find them?" Asma said.

"We'd have to look for them ourselves," Sharif said.

"But how?"

"The phonebook is one place to start."

Asma frowned then folded her arms. "That will take too long. How will we publish the first issue by Ramadan?"

Sharif wrinkled his forehead. "You want the first issue out by Ramadan?"

"Why not?"

He was silent momentarily. "Asma, I don't know if we can do that…"

"Maybe we can focus on Muslim businesses," Iman suggested. "That way we don't have to go through the yellow pages."

Iman's eyes were attractively large, Sharif noticed just then despite the veil covering the rest of her face, and she had long eye lashes. He dropped his gaze to his desk, where he set the newsletter and picked up a pen. He scribbled something on the calendar.

"Okay, then let's shoot for Ramadan. It should start in about ten days or so." He wrote a note in the box for October twenty-third. "I don't know if we can have it published during the first week, but let's try to have the first issue ready by the second third of Ramadan."

"But how will we pay for it?" Asma said, concerned.

"Let me worry about that," he said, feeling confident all of a sudden. "Just see how much support we can get for Shawwal."

"So it's going to be monthly?"

"I don't think it can be weekly."

Asma nodded, and she and Iman looked at each other momentarily. Asma shrugged. "Okay."

"We can meet weekly though," Sharif said, unable to temper his own selfish anticipation for the meetings. "That way we can gauge how everything's going."

"What will we call it though?"

Oh. Sharif had already forgotten about that. He looked at his sister. "Between you and…uh…Umm Sumayyah, I think you can come up with something."

"Can't we just keep *Islam's Call*?"

Sharif shook his head. "We need something to represent what the newsletter is about."

"Can we please not use the name of the masjid though?"

"That's no problem."

"When should we have the name by?"

Sharif glanced at the clock on the wall although it was the calendar he should be looking at. "What about Friday? Maybe we can meet after *Jumu'ah*."

Asma looked at Iman, a question on her face.

"That's fine," Iman said softly.

"Okay, then *inshaaAllah* I'll see you Friday after *Jumu'ah* then."

"I'm sorry, Tweetie, I really am."

Hasna stood in front of Vernon's desk with her arms crossed, having just told him how hurt she was. Vernon sat leaning forward, his hands clasped, sincere regret in his eyes.

"I had Kenya to worry about."

"How is she?"

He took a deep breath and scratched his head as he leaned back in his chair. "Better."

"What did you tell her?"

He shook his head, his eyes lost in thought. "The truth."

Hasna's eyes widened, and she started to speak but found no words. Was it possible that their relationship was that open and honest? She felt a twinge of jealousy at the thought. "But…"

"Not everything, Tweetie, of course not."

Hasna exhaled and shook her head. She chuckled self-consciously. "I was about to say…"

"No, no, no." He laughed himself. "I just told her we went to a park to talk and you had a lot on your mind, and before we knew it, it was morning."

"And she *believed* you?" A grin formed on one side of Hasna's mouth.

"Well… She had a lot of questions, of course."

"And you answered every one?"

"Yes."

Hasna shook her head, unable to believe what he was saying. She admired him. He really had guts.

"What it boiled down to was the fact that it all made sense," he said with a shrug. "I told her I went to the store first." He glanced at Hasna, amusement in his eyes. "Which was true."

She laughed.

"And of course that took some time. I told her I didn't even meet you at the office until late."

"And the park.... How do you explain just running off like that?"

"I told her it was spur of the moment. I felt it gave us a quiet place to talk." He paused. "In public."

Hasna chuckled and shook her head, her arms still folded.

"Why are you laughing?" Vernon asked.

"Because I can't imagine..." She was still grinning.

"Well, May is still on, if that's what you're worried about."

At the news, Hasna felt defeated. She was hoping that the incident would alter at least that arrangement. She nodded. "That's good."

"You're still my best man, right?"

Just then Hasna recalled picking out the black-tuxedo dress. "As long as we're still best friends."

Vernon grew quiet, and he averted his gaze, making Hasna's heart pound. Was the pendant a goodbye gift? Was requesting this talk his way of parting on good terms?

"I don't know," he said. His deep voice was barely above a whisper. He looked at Hasna, and they held each other's gaze. "Is that even possible now?"

Hurt, Hasna bit her lower lip and looked down at her feet, which bore fashionable heels. "I don't see why not," she said.

"We made a mistake," she conceded. She drew in a deep breath and exhaled, shocked by her own honesty. "A stupid mistake," she added. She shrugged. "Life goes on. We don't have to give up everything because of it. It doesn't have to happen again."

Vernon sighed, shaking his head. "But Tweetie, it happened, and that means things will always be different between us. That won't change. Even if it doesn't happen again."

"But can't this just be something we learn from, Vernon? Why does everything have to end because of it? It just doesn't seem fair."

243

Vernon was silent, and she lifted her gaze to his and saw confusion on his face.

"I didn't say I wanted everything to end. I'm just saying—"

"But that's how it's been this past month. You barely spoke to me."

"But, Tweetie, I had a lot on my mind. I mean, what happened was..." He looked away. "...really confusing."

She dropped her head, recalling her own spiritual turmoil and how difficult it had been to simply utter the words asking for forgiveness. "I know. It was for me too."

"That's why I had to pull back. I just never did something like that before."

Hasna said nothing. He already knew she hadn't either. Her crime was greater than his. But they didn't mention this. It was understood.

"And I keep thinking of my father..."

Hasna creased her forehead, looking at Vernon. "Your father?"

"How he raised me."

She sensed he was broaching the topic of Islam, and she grew uncomfortable. She didn't want to discuss religion right then.

"I'm not religious anymore," Vernon said, his eyes squinted as his gaze grew distant. "But I know right from wrong. And what we did was wrong."

Hasna sighed. "Yes, I know. Don't remind me."

"But, Tweetie, it's not that easy. It'll always be with us."

"In our minds, yes, but—"

"In our hearts too." Vernon waited for her to meet his gaze.

"Don't you understand what this means?" he asked, a pained plea in his eyes.

She felt herself losing hope. She couldn't imagine losing Vernon as a friend. She shook her head. "No, I guess I don't." Her voice was a whisper, but her soft tone barely veiled her sore disappointment. She had hoped for more.

"Tweetie," he said.

She looked at him, feeling tears gather in her eyes.

"It means we have to make a choice," he said, shaking his head slightly. He still looked at her, apology in his eyes. "A really hard choice."

There was a long pause. Hasna didn't want to respond.

"Do you understand?"

"Yes," she said finally.

"Remember what I told you in the park?"

The question took her aback, and she looked at him, a question on her face. She started to say she didn't remember, but he spoke before she could.

"And I told you that it's up to you."

It means you decide where we go from here.

Reluctantly, she nodded, recalling his words.

"I don't want to come between you and your soul," he said. "I know how tormenting that is." He shook his head. "I care too much for you. Don't you realize that's what's been bothering me most?"

Hasna's eyes widened slightly. She didn't know what to say. No, she didn't realize that.

"Kenya I can handle," he said. "Couples break up and make up every day."

His eyes glistened. "But it's breaking you that I can't handle," he said. "Because how can you put someone's soul back together?"

Hasna was quiet, her gaze on the floor, her thoughts distant. She had no idea he cared for her this much...

"I avoided you because I didn't want to be responsible for that. Sometimes I wish Kenya was to me like Sharif will be to you."

His reference to the future made her self-conscious, and she thought of December. Was it possible that they could make up before then?

"What do you mean?" Her voice was a whisper. She didn't want to risk breaking down.

"I just wish my wife could help me spiritually." He drew in a deep breath. "But that's out of my control now."

"Maybe she will help you," Hasna offered, but she detected the noncommittal tone in her voice.

He shook his head. "No," he said, sighing. "I realize I can only get that through someone like you."

Hasna glanced at him, her brows furrowed.

"But you have Sharif," he said sadly. "And I know I can't offer you the same thing, so I just work with what I have."

245

She glanced at a certificate hanging on the wall before returning her gaze to her friend. "But Sharif and I are no longer engaged."

Vernon's eyes widened. Seconds passed as he registered what she had said, and she could see in his expression that he was blaming himself.

"And it had nothing to do with you…us, I mean."

"But…"

"Don't worry, Vernon. It's nothing you can do about it."

"Tweetie, I'm sorry to hear that."

She felt the tears filling her eyes, but she fought them. "I think it's for the best anyway."

They were quiet for some time.

"Well," he said as they heard someone approaching in the hall. "Like I said. It's up to you where we go from here. I don't want to ruin your life any more than I already have, so —"

"Vernon, don't say that."

"No, Tweetie, let me. It's true." He sighed. "If it were up to me, we could relive that —"

The door opened, and Vernon cleared his throat. "We'll talk later," he said softly, sitting up.

Hasna wiped her eyes and nodded as she made her way back to her office, smiling cordially to her boss as she passed him.

But inside she was grieving. She regretted having blamed Vernon for his coldness — when it was Hasna he had been hurting for, not himself.

Sixteen

"O Messenger of Allah, who are the people who are most severely tried?" He replied, "The people who are tested the most severely are the Prophets, then the righteous, then the next best and the next best, and a man will be tested in accordance with his level of faith; the stronger his faith, the more severe will be his test."
— Prophet Muhammad (peace be upon him)
(Sahih, adapted wording from Ahmad)

Through the glass in the correctional facility's visiting area, Sharif saw a young man in a pale, one-piece jumpsuit walking with the guidance of two uniformed officers. The man's hands were bound in chains, as were his feet, making movement difficult. An officer wearing a blank expression placed a hand on the man's back until the man sat down. The officer then lifted a heavy ring of keys as the inmate raised his hands until the shackles on his wrist were unlocked, giving him free movement of his hands. However, the officers stood behind him a few feet as the young man picked up the phone that was connected to Sharif's phone on his side of the glass.

"As-salaamu'alaikum." Jafar was the first to offer the greeting after Sharif lifted his receiver. Shadows of the young man Sharif had once known slowly revealed themselves beneath the beginnings of a beard, tired eyes, and a strained smile.

Sharif felt a pang of sadness as they looked at each other a moment before he replied in kind. It was one thing to read about his friend being imprisoned, and it was another thing entirely to sit opposite him and witness a glimpse of that life. Even the glimpse was unbearable.

Sharif felt unsettled sitting in the prison's area for no-contact visitation. The area's immaculate yet bland appearance was a taunting irony of what it really represented, to him and his friend.

His mother wouldn't approve if she knew where he was right then. But it was an early Monday afternoon in mid-November, and Sharif had dropped her off at work before beginning the forty-five-minute drive to the prison.

Through reading some archived articles on Jafar's case, Sharif discovered that an area masjid was active in rallying financial and spiritual support for the inmates whom the Muslims felt were wrongly accused in the post-9-11 Islamophobia that was plaguing the nation. He contacted the imam of the masjid and was invited to visit the Islamic center so that the Muslim leader could meet Sharif personally. The imam then promised to do what he could to have Sharif listed on Jafar's approved visitors list.

Once Sharif's application had passed successfully, Sharif had been gripped with trepidation. What if he would be viewed suspiciously for having contact with a convicted "terrorist"?

Sharif had read a transcript of the case that was available on the Internet and, like Brother Rashad had said, it was like reading the script of *Minority Report.*

"First of all," the judge had said in the transcript, "we want to make it clear that the defendant is not being tried on any crime. No crime was committed. This trial is to determine his intentions…"

The legal jargon made it difficult for Sharif to decipher exactly what his friend was accused of, but this beginning line of the case's transcript made one thing clear: Even those accusing Jafar of a crime knew that he was innocent. It was merely a question of whether or not he would have remained innocent had he not be incarcerated when he had.

But even that perspective was giving the justice system too much credit in Sharif's view. Ironically, although the case was ostensibly about Jafar's "intent to commit a crime," all of the evidence against him was based on his having "supported wittingly or unwittingly" the *ideology* that sparked the 9-11 attacks.

How could a person unwittingly support an *idea*? Moreover, how could he be jailed for it?

Among the "proofs" used against Jafar were a series of short e-mail exchanges between him and another Muslim, who was now free after accepting a plea bargain that included his "cooperating" to testify against people like Jafar himself.

In the transcript, the most incriminating e-mail was one in which Jafar reportedly had said, following a series of post-9-11 hate crimes in the area, "I hope no one bothers my family. I don't know what I'd do to them."

Was that the *most* they could come up with?

"So what brings you here after so many years?" Jafar wore a smirk on his face, but Sharif could see in his friend's eyes that the glass between them represented more than Sharif's inability to be near his friend physically. Their worlds were separated by a vast open space that put them forever on diverging paths that would likely never cross, literally or figuratively.

Sharif smiled uncomfortably, at that moment noticing the glow that emanated from Jafar's face despite the dark sadness in his eyes, veiling a tragedy of life itself.

"Well, it took me some time to catch up with you," Sharif said.

Jafar chuckled then pointed to the prison identification digits on the breast of his inmate uniform. "Well, my number's still the same. You should've given me a call."

Sharif chuckled in response. "Yeah, well, you know, I didn't have your number with me in Saudi Arabia."

Jafar's forehead creased as he adjusted the phone to his ear. "You were in Saudi Arabia?"

Sharif became self-conscious just then, noticing one of the officers glancing at him in disapproval. "I was studying there. I told you about it before I left."

Jafar squinted his eyes and was quiet for several seconds. "Oh yeah." His eyes held a distant recollection, as if remembering a world of centuries ago. "I forgot about that."

They were silent momentarily.

"And here I was thinking you abandoned your friend." Jafar grinned.

Sharif grinned too although he was uncomfortable with the joke because it touched so close to reality.

"Tell me, how is everyone?" Jafar said, his voice now serious.

"They're good, *alhamdulillaah*."

"My father told me you're the new imam now."

Sharif averted his eyes, a hesitant smile creasing one corner of his mouth. "Yeah, I guess I am."

"How were they?"

Sharif furrowed his brows. "Who?"

"My family. Before they left."

Sharif dropped his gaze. "They were fine."

"My father said you asked about me."

He nodded. "Yes, I did."

"I appreciate that, man."

The words touched Sharif in their sincerity. He hadn't thought anything of the inquiry except that he felt compelled to know what Rashad needed from him and the community after Rashad's family left. Now Sharif saw how significant a mere visit or inquiry was in Jafar's world, where human contact itself was rare, and genuine concern even more so. He recalled with detached melancholy the conversation he had had with his mother about Jafar.

That's not our problem. That boy got involved in some things he had no business in.

If someone who had known Jafar as a baby could say this about him, what of those who knew only what they had read in the papers?

The question came to Sharif suddenly, and the answer too.

At least strangers had cause to speculate, regardless of how unfounded their suspicions were. Certainly, everyone who was behind bars wasn't innocent. How could they be sure Jafar wasn't amongst them?

Sharif couldn't imagine the psychological and emotional turmoil Jafar was suffering under such conditions. It was like the words of Martin Luther King, Jr. that Sharif had read once. *In the end, we will remember not the words of our enemies, but the silence of our friends.*

Theoretically, the Muslims were all brothers, a single body that ached in unrest if pain was suffered by a single limb. Yet, in reality, most Muslims sought comfort in their own beds without even a thought or prayer for those like Jafar, who would never again see his bed until he was lowered beneath the ground.

The best of the Muslims were those who, in the confines of their homes, whispered a quiet sincere prayer for believers like

Jafar. But most held sentiments like those Sharif's own mother had expressed.

They must have done *something* to get themselves in trouble, was the Muslim sentiment of the day. *Otherwise, they wouldn't be there.*

"You still got that weak jump shot?"

Sharif's eyes met Jafar's, distracted from his thoughts at the sound of his friend's voice.

Jafar grinned.

"I don't know, man," Sharif said, grinning hesitantly himself. "I haven't played in a while."

"They don't play basketball over there?"

"They do, but you know... I was busy studying."

An awkward silence followed, and Sharif and Jafar held each other's gazes momentarily.

"How are you, man?" Sharif asked, his expression conveying deep concern. "I mean, really?"

Jafar averted his gaze and was quiet for some time. Finally, he drew in a deep breath before exhaling audibly.

"What do you think?" He met Sharif's gaze, his jaw clenched. Immediately, Sharif regretted the question. "This isn't exactly a five-star hotel."

"I'm sorry." Sharif realized the absurdity of the question, and the insensitivity. What did he expect Jafar to say?

Jafar shrugged and huffed, obviously upset with himself for his reaction. "There's no need to apologize." His voice was low, and his eyes, though still averted, held a recollection of suffering that cut Sharif deep. "It's what everybody asks." Jafar sighed again, his eyes glancing at the ceiling as he shook his head. "I guess I just get tired of the question."

Sharif didn't know what to say.

"The truth is, I really don't know how I'm doing. Each day is different. Some days I wish I didn't have to wake up." He glanced to the side self-consciously. "But giving up isn't an option. Even though sometimes I wish it was."

Sharif's chest tightened in anxiety.

A shadow of a smile formed on the side of Jafar's mouth as he met Sharif's gaze. "If you think about it, serving three life sentences isn't so bad. That's what I tell myself."

251

Sharif held his friend's gaze, unsure how to respond.

"I'm thinking, if I can just get through *one* life," Jafar said. "Then I won't have to even worry about the other two."

The friends were silent momentarily until Jafar broke into laughter, and Sharif, realizing the joke, laughed too. But he really felt like crying.

"Anyway," Jafar said, recovering with a chuckle until he held a reflective expression, "the way I see it, the whole world's a prison."

A smile lingered on Sharif's face as he listened, nodding.

"And I think it's all for the better anyway."

"*This world is a prison for the believer*," Sharif said, reciting the words of the prophetic hadith.

Jafar nodded. "Yeah, I think about that hadith a lot. And it's true." He shrugged. "Sometimes I wonder if I could survive if I ever got out of here."

Sharif's forehead creased, a question on his face.

Jafar chuckled, but it was clear that he was not humored. "Sometimes I even feel sorry for people like you."

Taken aback, Sharif's eyebrows rose. "Why?"

"Because if you think about it," Jafar said, "in here I'm forced to stay focused on my soul. There's nothing else to do." His eyes grew sad, and Sharif's throat closed.

O Allah, have mercy on him, Sharif prayed in his heart. *Give him patience, and take his soul as a believer.*

"So, in that sense, I'm free." Jafar paused, gathering his thoughts.

"But people like you," Jafar said, looking at Sharif, reflection deep in his eyes, "you're out there living your life, stressing over stupid things and feeling sorry for people like me."

Jafar shook his head. "When you're the ones doing life in a prison."

Sharif drove home, his heart heavy with emotion. The world around him seemed to have shifted. He passed people pumping gas, mothers pushing baby strollers, and cars filling the parking lots of shopping centers. It was the same routine everyday for most people. They lived oblivious to the world of people like Jafar who would live out their final days in the cold solitude of a jail cell.

Before visiting his friend himself, Sharif felt the urge to dismiss Jafar from his life, psychologically and practically. It was easier that way. One did not lament what didn't exist. He had even entertained the thoughts his mother had voiced — before she even voiced them.

What if Jafar did deserve punishment? What if it is a terrorist?

But these were the speculations of the spiritually weak, Sharif realized in self-reproach, who veiled cowardice in the cloak of self-justification. It was easier that way. Then Sharif could go to sleep in the warmth of his own house and shake his head at the "misguided," who were stupid enough to end up behind bars.

As if people chose their fate.

Meanwhile, Sharif could shout at rallies decrying injustice and spend his days fighting for the right to be considered a victim.

At the thought, Sharif felt the familiar exhaustion.

Visiting Jafar clarified for Sharif why he was so discontent. He no longer had energy for political banter. It seemed that it was the only struggle that existed at all amongst Muslims — the right to attain victim status.

Yet they ignored those who were really victims.

But it was an odd fight, Sharif reflected as he drove home. Didn't your need to fight itself suggest that you are already a victim? And if you spend your life fighting to be called a victim, what exactly is the prize you hope for in the end?

The opportunity to secure a proverbial noose around your neck?

But it wasn't the inferior category that troubled Sharif. Because it could certainly be a means to a greater end, as it had been for minorities in centuries past.

But too often the victim category felt like an ends in itself.

Sharif just couldn't see himself feeling triumph at being officially a second-class citizen when he had every right to be first-class.

It was disheartening that Muslims' efforts were spent rallying in front of stiff, indurate buildings, signing their names to endless petitions, and demanding apologies for injustices that an insipid

"*I'm sorry*" issued by a paid publicist could never correct, or even marginally address.

Was this life?

Scribbling a slogan in magic marker on a piece of cardboard glued to a wooden stick, and shouting at the top of your lungs?

Shouting to people who had ears to hear, but hearts that made them deaf.

Sharif sighed, calming himself.

Perhaps there *was* something to say for having over 100,000 signatures on an e-mail petition circulated about the world.

But then what?

Would I go to my grave and await an eternal reward in Paradise for having pressed "send"?

Or was there more our Lord demanded of someone who said, *I believe?*

That night after praying *'Ishaa* in the masjid, Sharif guided the car into the familiar neighborhood of Hasna's home. After returning to the masjid office after visiting Jafar, Sharif reflected on the recurrent dream he kept having about Iman. He had no idea what it meant, but he couldn't rest until he had clarity. He had prayed *Istikhaarah* before making the call to Karim earlier, having still been a bit shaky about the whole ordeal.

But people like you, you're out there living your life, stressing over stupid things…

Sharif had told Karim he wanted to discuss something important, and Karim agreed for Sharif to meet him at eight o'clock. Sharif felt a tinge of guilt for having not specified what was on his mind. He knew that Brother Karim was assuming that he would talk to him about Hasna, and it was possible that Karim was hoping that Sharif and Hasna could make amends.

Sharif had no idea how he would tell Brother Karim that that wasn't possible. Sharif had no idea what was going on in Hasna's life right then, but even if she had improved somewhat, he and she were different people with conflicting values and outlooks on life.

Sharif also thought of what the sheikh had pointed out to him on the phone. He was an imam now. He could not view the issue of marriage as he had in the past. The decision was definitely a personal one and subject to his preferences, it was true. But there was so much more to consider, Sheikh Abdullah reminded him. He was now an example for an entire community of believers.

Could Sharif feel comfortable in that role with an openly non-practicing wife by his side?

The question had confounded him. Sharif had not considered that perspective.

If you want to know the character of a man, Sharif had heard once, *look at his wife.*

Would Sharif feel comfortable with Hasna representing him, and so comprehensively?

Sharif knew the answer to that, and there was no need to rationalize.

He had no idea what the dream meant. Perhaps, it was pointing him to Iman in the literal sense, even if for years later when she was old enough to marry. Then again, it could be figurative and pointing him to what Iman represented, a righteous woman.

Either way, it was pointing him away from Hasna. That was clear.

Whatever Allah decreed from this point on, it was important that Hasna's father knew where Sharif stood. If sharing the dream only made Karim realize that it wasn't possible for Sharif to marry Hasna, then that was progress.

Sharif's chest knotted in dread in the silent darkness surrounding the car as he pulled into the driveway of Hasna's home.

Was he really going through with this?

Sharif's heart pounded and he made a silent *du'aa,* supplicating to Allah, asking Him to guide his words and make it easy for him.

It was the month of Ramadan, Sharif reminded himself. The Month of Mercy. If there were any right time to do this, it was now.

Taking a deep breath and whispering one final prayer, Sharif opened the car door and climbed out, feeling the blood leave his feet as his shoes rested on the pavement. He shut the door and made his way up the walkway to Karim's door.

Sharif sensed that after a single knock, his life from then on would never be the same.

Part III

Seventeen

On Tawheed: A Life It Touched
By Umm Sumayyah

When I think of Tawheed and what it has done for me, I have difficulty finding the words. Shall I speak of how it closed my lips and opened my ears? Or how it closed doors to falsehood and opened my heart to truth? Or shall I speak of how it dried my anger and wet my eyes with tears? Or how it made me abandon my bed in love of my Creator and stand at night hoping for His Mercy? Or shall I speak of how it removed my confidence and filled me with humility, and engulfed me with fear? Or how it lessened my focus on what others are doing and forced me to focus on myself?

Or perhaps I can speak of how I feel like a prisoner in this world where so many are entrapped by Shaytaan, too busy with their desires to efficiently tend to their needs.

Or perhaps I can speak of my feelings when I pass a grave, how I reflect on what its dweller must be thinking, must be feeling, and how awful his regret, his pain. Or how much he would give just to be *me* at this moment, because I have in my grip what he will never have again.

And that is a chance.

A chance to say, *O Allah, forgive me!* or *Glory be to You!* Or a chance to fall down in prostration, promising to never sin again.

Or perhaps when I think of Tawheed in my life, I should not overlook how it has filled me with love of *emaan* and hatred of disbelief. And perhaps I should mention too that it makes me say to my brothers and sisters, "I love you for the sake of Allah."

Shall I mention that it has put me on edge? Because I do not know what tomorrow brings. For what guarantee do I have that the warm bed from which I woke this morning will be there tonight for my sleep? And what guarantee do I have that after being angry with my sister I will live to say *I'm sorry*? And what promise do I have that, though I made amends with my father yesterday, he will return today so I can do the same? And what promise from Allah do I have if I did not pray my *Salaah* this morning that I can do it this afternoon?

And what guarantees me that simply because my mother woke me yesterday that tomorrow it won't be the Angel of Death?

Tawheed was changing my life before I was aware. It came to me unexpectedly, although I never knew it was missing. For I was born into Islam, reared upon the faith and grew up as a Muslim. My days were filled with Qur'an and exchanging the salaams. But as I reflect upon how Tawheed has shaped me, I cannot help wondering where I would be had its knowledge not penetrated my heart, and permeated my soul.

Yes I was Muslim. But I knew little of Allah. My lips said *I believe* but I cannot say that I actually did. I did not know the phenomenal power of *du'aa*, its power to change, its power to heal. And I didn't know of the Fire's frightening torment, or that its taunting flames could scald *my* skin. And I didn't think of Paradise except as a fairy tale, a mere dream. And little did I strive for it.

I had no reason to.

For I knew nothing of emaan,
How it rose or how it fell,
And I knew nothing of kufr,
And that it could engulf you before you could tell.
I did not even know there was anything special about being Muslim
As it pertained to my soul.
For I'd viewed other faiths as one of many,
Merely offering different paths to a single Goal.

So how has Tawheed changed me?
Should I say...
That it moved me to embrace Islam,
Although I was a Muslim the previous day?

Some say, You're so lucky, when they hear how I was raised,
To have a Muslim family, Muslim friends,
They shower the praise.
But I force a smile,
Because they have no way to know.
That I struggle, like they, wherever I go.
Even if amongst those raised Muslim,

Like me.
The scorn, the misconceptions, the finding fault,
With Islam, with the Sunnah
With me.

But when I think of Tawheed touching my life,
I'm shy to say what it has done for me.
For my road is just beginning,
And I've much before me.
My bags are still in my hands,
And my palms are still moist with sweat.
And I don't know if I'll benefit from my travel,
Because I haven't died yet.

For when Tawheed touches one's life
It doesn't matter the changes it renders today
Because the fruits of pure belief
Cannot be tasted until
The much awaited, but fateful
Judgment Day

Speechless, Sharif stood in his room holding the draft of the newsletter's Shawwal edition, engulfed by the words of a young woman embarking on the tender age of fifteen, yet speaking in the voice of one with decades of experience on life's path.

And in the voice of Sharif himself.

Spent, Sharif sat down in his desk chair to gather his thoughts.

It was the last Wednesday in Ramadan, and it had been more than a week since Sharif had met with Brother Karim to share the recurrent dream.

But Sharif hadn't received even a phone call from Iman's father after that, nor had he seen their family since. This past Friday Sharif had a meeting scheduled with Asma and Iman, but only Asma sat with him after the prayer. Sharif had asked Asma if she had seen Brother Karim or Iman, but Asma said she hadn't. She also said she had been unable to reach her friend for the last few days. "Whenever I call," Asma had said, "Sister Mona says Iman can't come to the phone."

The news weighed heavily on Sharif, and he began to doubt the wisdom of his decision to divulge the dream to Brother Karim.

But you didn't propose, Sharif told himself. *You just shared what you had seen and asked what he thought.*

Was that wrong? Had he made a grave mistake?

But Sharif had prayed *Istikhaarah* and sought the advice of a trusted Islamic studies professor. Was there more he should have done?

At that moment, the guidance of the Prophet for those who had prayed *Istikhaarah* returned to Sharif, reminding him that no harm could come to a believer who placed his trust in his Lord.

One who seeks guidance from his Creator and consults his fellow believers and then remains firm in his resolve does not regret, for Allah has said: "…and consult them in the affair. Then when you have taken a decision, put your trust in Allah…"

Eighteen

"Each of us has his own little private conviction of rightness and almost by definition, the Utopian condition of which we all dream is that in which all people finally see the error of their ways and agree with us."
—S. I. Hayakawa

"*This* is sick." Arms crossed, Mona sat with her back supported by a pillow propped against the bedpost Wednesday night, and her husband sat next to her, an exhausted expression on his face. "I would have never expected something like this from him."

"I know…" Karim drew in a deep breath and shook his head. "But maybe it means—"

"Karim, come on." Mona glared at him. "Please tell me you don't buy his little dream story. I certainly don't."

Karim chuckled and looked at his wife, amusement in his eyes. "You think he's lying?"

"Why not? It wouldn't be the first time people used the unseen world for their own benefit. Look at what our so-called Sheikh claimed to dream about." She grunted. "Nothing. That's what his vision for Islam was, and what did we do? We bought into it like a bunch of fools."

"This is different though…"

"No, it's not. Think about it, can you prove *any*thing he's saying?"

Karim grew quiet and looked away, and Mona could tell something was on his mind that he wasn't revealing.

"What?"

He shook his head. "Nothing."

"What?" Her voice rose, insisting.

Karim met his wife's gaze. "But does it matter whether we can verify it? He's a good brother, so we should at least—"

"Iman is a *child*," she cut him off. "There is no way I'm going to sit here and approve of something like this."

Karim laughed. "Sweetheart, do you think I'm crazy enough to marry my baby daughter to a grown man?" He shook his head. "That's not what I'm saying. I'm talking about giving him the benefit of the doubt. Maybe he really did see the dream, and it means something we don't understand."

"Like what?" She blinked, waiting.

"I don't know." He chuckled. "I'm just saying..."

Mona groaned. "I can't believe I let her meet with him privately. I *trusted* him."

"Sweetheart, it wasn't private. Asma was there, too."

"But how do you know that? What if that was just a cover?"

Bewildered, Karim creased his forehead as he regarded his wife. "A cover for what?"

She shrugged. "Ask Iman. I can't get anything out of her."

Karim did not respond for some time, and his eyes grew distant in thought. In the silence, Mona became painfully aware of the unfounded nature of her speculations. Perhaps she should have kept her thoughts to herself, but the possibility of there being deceit behind this had troubled her all week. She was already struggling to handle Hasna's surreptitious motives to "go out with friends" when she was really meeting Vernon. And this conclusion was not based on suspicion, this Mona was certain about.

Having felt unsettled one night after Hasna had "to go out with friends," Mona had, on a hunch, driven to the law offices where Hasna worked. Two cars were parked in the otherwise vacant lot, and one of them was Hasna's. There was a light on in one of the offices, but from where Mona was parked, very little was visible behind the trees. Feeling horrible for having come, Mona had started to pull off and return home when she saw movement behind the glass window. She quickly steered the car to a far end of the parking lot where she would not be easily noticed.

Minutes later, Hasna had emerged from the building holding the hand of an attractive, well-built man, who was saying something as Hasna laughed. After embracing Hasna for longer than Mona could stomach, the man who Mona assumed to be Vernon opened the passenger side door of the car that was parked next to Hasna's. Face aglow with laughter and flattery, Hasna climbed inside, and the man leaned in the door to whisper something, a grin still on his face seconds later as he walked around to the driver's side.

May Allah give you children just like you.

The shadowy claws of Mona's past wrapped their cold fingers about her neck, the curse of her father haranguing in the night. As if one exiled, Mona sat dejected, her hands weakly gripping the steering wheel of her car, feeling helpless in her inability to steer even the direction of her own daughter's life. Only yards away was her firstborn, conceived in sin, even as she and Karim had imagined they were married at the time.

Hasna's laughter was a distant mockery of the insobriety Mona had so carefully hidden from her daughter. The scene beyond the glass windshield made Mona shudder, its uncanny parallels piercing the barrier between mother and child.

Vernon's car disappeared out of the parking lot, and Mona felt her heart being ripped open as Hasna disappeared from her life. Vernon's fading engine created an immeasurable distance between mother and daughter, as they were now cruelly joined in a bond Mona yearned to break.

In the silence of the night, Mona had cried, her head bowed in submission, feeling as if her heart would burst. In that moment, she hated herself, her family, and Karim himself for merely existing and having played part in her degenerate life. She vowed right then that this moment would remain secret, between Hasna and her, although Mona imagined her husband already knew.

The realization that Hasna's life was merely a repeat of her own had paralyzed Mona in agony and fear. Was Iman too destined to tread the dark path of a grandfather's curse? No, Mona would not accept it, she thought in bitter resentment of her parents' spite. Mona would not allow both of her daughters to tread the path of destruction. She too was a parent, and her supplications of those born from her womb were answered too.

In concentrated stoicism, Mona had calmly steered the car from the parking that night and headed to a local store, where she picked up a few items she didn't really need. Upon returning home, she presented the items like an offering to her husband, a fulfillment of his expectations after having given her permission to shop.

Yet her mind had been far removed from the paltry items that would line the cabinet shelves gathering dust. Mona was saturated with thoughts of Hasna's sudden elation after having spent more than a month sulking pitifully in her room.

And now Mona knew that the answer lay not in Hasna's having turned sincerely to Allah seeking repentance for sins past, but in Hasna's renewed entanglement in the clutches of corporeal vice, with the very one Hasna had resented for weeks.

Meanwhile, in the pathetic naïveté that plagued so many parents gone voluntarily blind, Mona had missed the sign, having believed that Hasna had merely slipped momentarily from the rarely-trodden golden path. Yet all the signs had been before Mona that her daughter was going terribly astray, and she had idiotically missed each one. She had, instead, shut her eyes in preference for the script of the cozy fairy tale she had written for Hasna, and herself, in her mind.

Now Mona wondered if she was blinded from a similar sign with Iman. Perhaps Iman's sudden religiosity had been inspired not by spiritual inclinations but by a desire to impress Sharif. Had Iman known all along that he didn't plan to go through with his marriage to Hasna? How long then had Iman and Sharif been in contact?

The question nagged Mona until the veil over her eyes lifted to reveal the tiniest signs that something was askew. She had assumed that her youngest daughter's spiritual growth was due to the same source hers had been: being exposed to Islam through Imam Rashad's wife Irum.

But now Mona realized that there was a more nocuous explanation.

In retrospect, Mona had thought it odd that Iman had chosen the all-black, Saudi-style hijab that covered even the face, as opposed to the simple shoulder *abaya* and *khimaar* that Irum favored. Mona recalled that even Irum had been taken aback by Iman's preference to cover so fully. Iman had claimed to have been inspired by hearing Sister Irum explain the conditions of the Islamic hijab during Islamic studies class. But even though Irum had discussed the scholarly disagreement concerning the obligation to cover the face, it was unlikely that such an extreme form of covering could be drawn from that. Covering the face was one thing, but wearing the style of dress specific to a particular country was another, especially when that country happened to be where Sharif was residing at the time of Iman's decision.

Forehead creased, Mona glanced at her husband as she thought of something. "Do you remember that poem?"

He squinted his eyes as he met her gaze. "What poem?"

"The one Sharif read during his first *Jumu'ah*?"

Karim tried to recall, and recollection slowly came to him. "Oh yeah, the one about a war and some girl reading a magazine?"

"Yes, that one."

"What about it?"

"Do you know who wrote it?"

Karim lifted a shoulder in a shrug. "I can't say I've heard it before."

"Iman."

For a second, Karim just looked at his wife, obviously not understanding what she was saying. "Iman?"

"Yes, Iman. Our daughter. She wrote that poem."

Karim gathered his eyebrows, obviously impressed. "*Iman*?"

"Yes. She's using the name Umm Sumayyah in this little newsletter of hers."

He shook his head. "What newsletter?"

"Remember the one she and Asma were doing for the masjid?"

Karim was silent as he tried to recall. He shook his head. "I remember seeing her at the computer a lot. I just assumed she was writing like she always is."

"Well, her latest writing project is a masjid newsletter."

"But what does that have to do with the poem?"

"Remember the newsletter they gave out after *Jumu'ah* a couple of weeks ago?"

Karim nodded. "I do remember them passing out something."

"Iman did that."

Taken aback, Karim creased his forehead, and Mona could tell he was proud of his daughter. "Really?"

"Karim, don't you get it? Sharif was reading Iman's poem during his first *Jumu'ah*."

He was silent as he considered this. "Okay…" he said, shrugging, his nonchalance shocking his wife. "You said it was from the masjid newsletter. Why wouldn't he read from it?"

Mona's eyes widened. She couldn't believe her husband didn't see the connection. "That means they've been in contact without our knowing."

Karim narrowed his eyes, doubt reflecting in his expression. "I don't know about that."

"Then why would Iman deny knowing how he got the poem?"

He furrowed his brows. "She did?"

"Yes. Not only that, she said he didn't even know it was hers."

Karim shrugged. "Maybe he didn't."

"How could he *not* know?"

"Mona, I don't know." Karim sounded exhausted. "This is a lot to consider right now. It's Ramadan." He sighed and looked away from his wife, apparently uncomfortable with Mona's conclusions. "Let's just pray on it and leave it to Allah."

At the reminder of the holy month, Mona felt slightly ashamed. It was in the last ten nights of Ramadan. She should be engaged in worship, not in giving voice to her suspicions about Iman and Sharif.

But even her worship had been disrupted by Sharif, Mona thought bitterly. Mona, like her husband, had stopped going to the masjid. Karim had found one closer to work where he could pray *Tarawih*, but Mona's options were slimmer. She hadn't prayed the night prayer in the masjid since Karim had told her about his meeting with Sharif.

"I'll pray for patience," Mona said finally, exhaling with the words. "That's what I need. I think the issue of marriage is already clear. There's no way we can even consider it."

Karim nodded, placing his hand on his wife's leg to comfort her. "I agree. We'll both need patience." He sighed as the reality of what was before them weighed on him. "And guidance on how to tell Iman we can't allow her to contact Asma anymore."

Iman sat cross-legged on her bed quietly reading from the Qur'an as the small lamp on her night stand glowed next to her, illuminating the pages of the large book on her lap. She hadn't been feeling well earlier, so she was behind in reading today's thirtieth of the Qur'an. She was also behind in her schoolwork that her mother had asked her to complete.

Iman had begun the month of Ramadan by remaining at least one section ahead of the daily allocation of one thirtieth she had assigned herself, but now she was struggling to keep up with a single day's reading. Fortunately, the schedule Iman and her mother kept for her homeschooling was year-round and allowed for more flexibility.

But Iman's mother wanted Iman to apply to community college next month, which was why it was important for her to stay on task even though she had only two subjects left to complete high school. Iman herself hoped to be in college when she turned fifteen in January. It was a competition between her and Asma, who had turned fifteen earlier this month. So far Iman was ahead of her friend, who wouldn't be able to enroll in college for another six months. With Asma studying alone at home instead of with Iman and her mother, Iman imagined it might take even longer for her friend. Asma had said Sharif was helping her, but he was too busy to do anything other than answer a question whenever Asma had one.

But Iman's energy to study had waned this week. She had forgotten to take her iron supplements for the past few days, and she couldn't even think about schoolwork. She had nursed a headache most of the day today, and it hadn't subsided until an hour before. She mentally reminded herself to keep the small jar of iron tablets with her during breakfast the following morning.

A soft knock at the door interrupted Iman's reading and she glanced at the clock. It was three minutes after eleven o'clock. She had assumed everyone else was sleeping.

"Come in," she said a second before the door opened and her mother appeared in the doorway, her father steps behind.

Upon seeing her mother's expression, Iman creased her forehead in concern. "Is everything okay?"

Iman's immediate thought was that something had happened to Hasna. Iman had no idea if Hasna had even come back home that night, but Iman had grown so accustomed to her sister's erratic comings and goings that she no longer kept count.

But Iman was suffering greatly from the sudden halting in her own comings and goings, which had only amounted to going back and forth to the masjid. She really wished she could have prayed in the masjid during these last nights of Ramadan. Even though she hadn't been feeling well, being in the company of so many Muslims and hearing the recitation of Qur'an always soothed her, even if she sometimes used a chair for parts of the long prayer.

Up until about a week ago, Iman had prayed in the masjid every night, except for the first two nights, when her cycle prevented her. Asma's family would pick Iman up if Karim wasn't able to pray at their community's masjid on a given night. However, a week ago, Iman's mother had said they would "pray at home for a few days."

But more than a few days had passed, and Iman was still praying at home.

Currently, Mona's expression was difficult for Iman to read, and Iman had a sinking feeling that her mother was upset with her for something. But she had no idea what it could be.

"Iman," Mona said as she took a seat on the edge of Iman's bed, the bed sinking slightly as it received her weight. Iman's father lingered in the doorway with his arms folded, an expression of awkward discomfort on his face. "We need to talk."

Iman creased her forehead, the Qur'an still open in front of her. "What happened?"

Mona drew in a deep breath. "That's what we need you to tell us."

Iman grew perplexed. She glanced at her father for any indication as to what was going on, but he was looking at something on the carpet.

"About what?" Iman said.

"What's going on." Mona's head was turned to face her daughter, and her lips formed a line, disappointment written there.

Iman didn't know what to say, unsure how to form the question in her mind. Her heart began to pound, fearing that something wrong had happened that they assumed she was responsible for.

"You can start with the story of your poem and how Sharif got a hold of it," her mother said, accusation in her tone.

Confounded, Iman stared at her mother. Days before, Iman had told her mother what Asma had told her, that Sharif just happened to find it on a pile of recyclables in the kitchen and had no idea it was hers.

But why did it matter? That's what Iman could not understand.

"He just found it." Iman spoke with her eyes narrowed in confusion, searching in her mother's expression for some reason for the sudden interrogation.

"So you didn't give it to him?"

"No…"

Mona sighed, glancing at her husband before turning her attention back to Iman. "Iman, we need you to be completely honest with us." She held her daughter's gaze for a moment. "Are you and Sharif in contact with each other?"

Iman blinked. *What?* Iman felt the illicit insinuation of the inquiry, and she was shocked. Was her mother serious?

Or perhaps Iman misunderstood.

Iman's mother already knew about the weekly meetings for the newsletter. Mona had even cancelled the last meeting, saying they would have to reschedule it for another time, and that she herself would convey the message to Sister Nadirah's family. When Iman had asked if she could call Asma to tell her some things to share at the meeting, Mona had said she was suspending all rights for anyone to use the phone for the rest of Ramadan. The sudden rule had taken Iman aback, but she had figured it was her mother's idea of utilizing the last ten days of the month solely for worship. But when Iman had asked if she could e-mail Asma the information, Mona had said that the Internet too was off-limits for the rest of the month.

Iman tried to make sense of everything, and there was a lingering sensation that this was all connected somehow.

"…We talk at the meetings we have for the newslet—"

"Iman," Mona cut her off. "I'm talking about outside of that. Have you every spoken to him on the phone or through e-mail?"

Iman blinked. What in the world was her mother getting at, and why was she so upset? Had something happened to Sharif that made it risky for her to communicate with him? Perhaps he was in legal trouble like Jafar had been...

Iman shook her head. "No. Except when I ask to speak to Asma when he answers."

"Sweetheart." Iman's father was looking at his wife. "Let's just go to bed."

Karim's uncomfortable expression was still on his face, and his last words suggested that this conversation was an investigation of some sort. But Iman had no idea what she was being accused of.

"Karim," Mona said turning to her husband, her impatience thinly veiled in that single word. It was as if the utterance of his name was a code between them, a reminder of something left undone, something Mona wanted to continue.

Karim started to say something, but he shook his head instead, his gaze returning to the carpet. Iman sensed that he didn't want to be there but was reluctantly fulfilling a duty.

Mona turned back to Iman, a disturbed expression still traceable on her face. "Well, to cut off anything," Mona said as if calling Iman's bluff, "we can't have you talking to him for any reason."

"But what about the newsletter?" Iman's voice was a whine. "Me and Asma are the only ones working on it."

"Well, Asma will just have to find someone else."

"But why?" Iman felt herself growing upset. She could not understand why her parents were being so unreasonable.

"Because we said so."

Her mother's use of the pronoun "we" prompted Iman to look in the direction of her father. But his mind seemed to be elsewhere as he stood with his arms folded. He lifted his head as Iman started to protest.

"Iman," he said, apology in his voice. "I know this is difficult to understand right now. But it's for your own safety."

Iman stared at her father, disbelieving. "What is dangerous about writing a newsletter?"

"It's not the newsletter we're concerned about."

Iman was silent momentarily as she considered something. "Did something happen to Sharif too?"

Mona's expression changed to curious concern. "Who else is involved in this?"

"I'm talking about what happened to Jafar."

Mona's face relaxed somewhat. "No, it's nothing like that."

"Then why can't I work on the newsletter?" Iman was on the verge of protest. She didn't want to complain, but she was confounded, and hurt. She and Asma had spent months gathering articles and writing poetry and articles of their own. The formatting alone had taken several days because Iman was unaccustomed to using publishing software. But her eagerness to complete the project had motivated her to learn. She and Asma spoke daily, often several times a day, about the ideas they had for the publication, and they were elated when they saw their first newsletter in print after *Jumu'ah* two weeks ago.

"You can work on it alone then." Mona's tone was firm. "But not with Sharif or Asma."

Iman's mouth fell open. She couldn't believe what she was hearing. "I can't work with Asma either?"

"No, Iman. I'm sorry, but you cannot." Mona's eyes showed empathy, and she patted Iman on the leg from where she sat on the edge of the bed, apologizing in that gesture. But Iman was unmoved. She felt that this was unnecessary and unjust.

"But Mom, she's my best friend." Iman's voice cracked at the last word, realizing how devastating this would be. Asma was not only her best friend, she was her only friend.

"Honey, I know that, but your safety is more important."

Iman drew her eyebrows together, searching in her mother's expression for some answers, some trace of mercy or even uncertainty. Her mother had to know how much Asma meant to her. Asma and Iman had grown up together. They were like sisters. It was inconceivable to not even be able to speak to her.

"Why do you keep saying that?" Iman said. "What did they *do*?"

"I think you know." Mona held Iman's gaze until Iman shook her head at a loss.

"About what?" Iman was exasperated.

"That's what we need you to tell us. And until you do, these are the rules."

"But how —"

"But nothing," Mona interjected. "Until you are more forthcoming about your communication with Sharif, you're not allowed to speak to anyone in that family."

"But, Mom," Iman whined, "I already told you..."

"No, you did not." Mona's voice was raised. "And until you let me know exactly how he felt comfortable talking to your father like he did, you aren't allowed to speak to him or Asma for any reason, especially regarding that silly newsletter."

Deeply offended by her mother's last words, Iman dropped her gaze. Iman's eyes burned and her chest ached as she realized the two things closest to her heart were being snatched from her, her writing and her best friend.

How could her mother call the newsletter *silly*? All that hard work, all that effort — all that heart. Iman's writing was a part of her, something that helped her breathe. It was like a dagger being driven into her chest to hear it rebuffed so flippantly, and dismissed in a simple word. This newsletter was Iman's first opportunity to see herself published, and that meant the world to her. Why couldn't her mother understand that?

"Do you understand?"

In the suffocating confusion that clouded her mind, Iman heard her mother's voice as if coming from a distant world. She didn't even realize her mother was speaking to her.

"Iman?"

Iman gazed distantly at the yellowed pages of the Qur'an before her, hearing her mother just then.

"Do you understand?"

"Yes," Iman lied in a begrudging mumble, folding her arms across her chest, her heart still aching for her writing — for her friend. "I do."

"Good."

Mona turned to her husband and nodded, and Iman felt her bed lighten as her mother stood. But she could not look at her parents as they left the room. She was trying to calm the frustration that was threatening to surface, and she was afraid that she would glare at her mother and father if she offered even a simple glance. Iman had promised to work on her attitude and ungratefulness this Ramadan, and she didn't want to ruin it now.

When the door closed, the quiet of the room settled around Iman, and she stared at words on the page before her. She still had about five pages to read, but she couldn't think of that right then. It was a shame, she reflected, that a simple talk with her parents had driven all the spiritual energy out of her until she didn't have the desire to read a single word from Allah's Book.

Iman hated herself for her weakness, but she could not reignite the determination to complete the day's reading that night. She didn't want to resent her parents, but the flame of frustration was burning within, inciting a storm of emotional protests in her mind. Her parents were being unfair. And cruel.

Until you are more forthcoming about your communication with Sharif, you're not allowed to speak to anyone in that family.

The words returned to Iman, settling upon her like a puzzle to be unscrambled, although each word was already in its proper place.

But what did her mother mean? And what role had Iman played in this puzzle, even if unwittingly?

And until you let me know exactly how he felt comfortable talking to your father like he did, you aren't allowed to speak to him or Asma for any reason…

Did the answer lay with Asma? Perhaps, her friend knew what Sharif had said to Iman's father to make Iman's parents so angry with her. If Asma knew, then why had she told Iman nothing, nothing at all?

At the thought, Iman grew aggravated with her friend. Why wasn't Asma being open with her? Wasn't openness and honesty central to a friendship bond?

Sighing, Iman shut the Qur'an, the frustration releasing itself right then. She needed to pray. It was the only way to clear her mind.

Iman lifted the heavy book and placed it on her nightstand before shifting herself until her feet rested on the soft carpet of her floor. As she slipped on her house shoes, a realization came to Iman.

If she wasn't allowed to speak to Asma or Sharif, then she wouldn't be allowed to attend the masjid either.

Iman's heart dropped, the possibility overwhelming her. Was it possible that her parents would go *that* far?

Iman recalled her mother's expression when she had insisted that she have no contact at all with Asma, and the somber reality set in.

No, Iman wouldn't be allowed to go to the masjid.

She had lost the blessing of Sister Irum's classes when Imam Rashad's family returned to Pakistan.

And now she was being robbed of the blessing of Sharif's classes that she had begun to eagerly anticipate all week.

And that hurt most.

Nineteen

"If one whose religion and character pleases you proposes to you [to marry your daughter], you should marry him [to her]. If you do not, there will be tribulations in the land and widespread corruption."
—Prophet Muhammad (peace be upon him)
(At-Tirmidhi and Ibn Majah)

Eyes still moist from the extended supplication he had recited during *Tarawih*, Sharif greeted the last of the brothers who had come to pray behind him. It was Thursday night and droves of people had come from various parts of the D.C. metropolitan area.

As the crowd gradually drifted from the *musallaa*, Sharif found it hard to believe that they all had been praying behind him. Tonight a resounding *"Ameen"* had filled the prayer area after each *du'aa* Sharif uttered into the microphone, reminding him of the days he himself stood in the rows of believers in Riyadh with his hands raised as he begged Allah for forgiveness, mercy, and guidance.

Tonight had been particularly emotional for Sharif because he had included a special supplication for the preservation of Muslims suffering around the world, and for those incarcerated. Sharif had thought of Jafar as he recited the heartfelt prayers, and he knew that almost everyone standing behind him had in their hearts someone who was suffering right then.

Sharif too was moved during the supplications as he reflected on his own sins that haunted him still, particularly the transgressions against his father before he died. Sharif had earnestly prayed for forgiveness and mercy for the believers, himself amongst them, and he yearned to be united with his father in Paradise. The regret Sharif felt for being ungrateful to his parents in youth was so immense that it was painful. He could only hope to be granted the forgiveness he knew he didn't deserve.

Sharif thought too of his mother and was weighed down by regret as he realized he should be more sensitive and compassionate to her. She had given most of her adult life to raising Sharif and his siblings. The least he could do was be patient throughout the inevitable disagreements he would have with her in life. No two people agreed on everything. A person himself disagreed with his own prior convictions as he gained experience and wisdom in life.

Sharif should not allow the least bit of frustration to enter his heart when speaking to his mother, even when she expressed views contrary to his. How could he become frustrated when it was she, like his father, to whom Sharif was deeply indebted for being Muslim in the first place? And she too was the reason he had even studied in Riyadh. Thus, anything he knew about his faith was because of the mercy Allah had granted Sharif through placing his mother and father in his life.

Thoughts of Iman had also hovered while Sharif recited the long supplication, although she hadn't been in the forefront of his mind. But now, as Sharif stood in the prayer area of the masjid, his heart grew heavy with anxiety.

It was difficult to not feel uneasy as Sharif recalled how natural it had been for him to be honest with Brother Karim about the recurrent dream, and about his inclination to believe it meant something in reality.

During the first few minutes of the meeting, Sharif had found it difficult to form the right words to broach the topic. But thereafter, there was no discomfort, and Brother Karim himself seemed genuinely intrigued by the dream. Sharif had left Karim's house with a good feeling, as the meeting itself was lighthearted and warm. If anything, he felt closer to Karim afterwards.

But in the past few days Sharif played the details of the meeting over in his mind, combing every detail in search of what had gone wrong. But he could find nothing out of the ordinary.

The sudden silence between him and Karim was so perplexing that it was uncanny. It made no sense. Sharif himself had called Karim twice since that night, and each time Mona had answered and given the same response that Asma had said she herself received when she asked to speak to Iman. "He can't come to the phone right now."

The lack of emotion or apology in Mona's voice was the most unsettling to Sharif, and he almost didn't call back a second time. But, having chalked up his perception to paranoia, he had called again, only to receive the same chilly response.

"A simple no would have sufficed," an American classmate had told Sharif many years ago in Riyadh after sharing with Sharif the story of how his life had been threatened by the family of a young woman in America after the brother had approached the father to propose marriage to her.

"When I first became Muslim," the brother had said, a distant sadness in his eyes, "I would never have imagined that people from Muslim countries could act like that." He shook his head, and Sharif could tell the memory still haunted and pained him. "It felt like a movie. I still can't believe it was real."

But Brother Karim was not like this, Sharif reflected. Iman's father was not part of a culture of pathological self-worship, a worship that incited vicious indignity at the mere idea that a man "beneath them" would even look in the direction of their women. This was a sickness Karim himself abhorred due to his own brushes with those suffering from this disease. It was inconceivable that he would embrace this destructive ideology for himself.

Or was Sharif merely being naïve?

Perhaps it was not a foreign land that inspired such pathology, Sharif considered, but a sick heart residing in the breasts of those of every land. How many Muslims held within their breasts ailing hearts attached obsessively to the world? And how many Muslims were willing to viciously destroy the closest bonds of Islamic brotherhood, and even sully their own souls, when they perceived any obstruction to eating from the fruits of this transient existence? From this bloodthirsty greed, crimes as heinous as honor killings and vicious slander were born, and the lives of the innocent were senselessly taken or destroyed irreparably for the trivial crimes of thought, temptation, and unrequited desire.

Was Brother Karim suffering from the clutches of a culture that viewed adulthood, and thus eligibility for marriage, as attached to a numerical number decided by a group of men who had not even considered the guidance of the Creator? Did Karim then, like they, view even the idea of early marriage as a crime?

Where then was the Islam Karim claimed? Where then was the Sunnah?

Karim was certainly under no obligation to marry Iman to Sharif, even as she was eligible according to the religion they both claimed.

A simple no would have sufficed.

Why the coldness? Why the sudden abandonment of even cordiality amongst brothers in Islam?

Was this what Muslims had come to? This man had known Sharif since childhood, so how could he judge him harshly, and for what? For merely respecting him enough to put before him a matter Sharif could not decipher alone?

Sharif shook the thoughts from his head, seeking refuge in Allah as he exited the *musallaa* alongside the last trickles of people who had prayed in The Masjid Center that night. As he reached down to pick up his shoes, Sharif mentally scolded himself for harboring suspicions about his brother in Islam. Sharif silently asked Allah to forgive him. It was unjust to assume the worst when there were so many other explanations for what Sharif was perceiving.

Maybe Karim wasn't abandoning him or treating him coldly. Perhaps, the brother really couldn't come to the phone. Simple as that. Sharif himself was not always available to talk to everyone who called for him, and he certainly wasn't enthusiastic to have a phone to his ear every hour of the day. That would explain Mona's voice tone. Maybe Sharif had simply called at a bad time.

But in the past, Sister Mona had at least been cordial…

Sharif stopped himself. He pulled his shoes on his feet, deciding then to put the matter to rest until Allah himself made it clear what was going on. Sharif reminded himself of the Qur'anic injunction, *"Avoid [much] suspicion. Indeed, some suspicion is a sin."*

Allah's words made Sharif immediately ashamed. The verse made Sharif realize the destructive path he was treading—the very one he was criticizing in his mind. Was not the pathology of cultural self-worship born of suspicion and assumption, in denigrating others and in worshipping the self?

Sharif shuddered to think of the negative results he was inciting by speculating about something he had no knowledge of.

Sharif should not harbor resentment or ill feelings toward his brother in Islam, or toward the brother's family, especially as Sharif hoped for Allah's pardon and forgiveness during these last few days of the month of Ramadan. The gates of Paradise were open and the gates of Hell were closed. Why then was Sharif standing at the gates of the latter, shaking its chains and vying for entry?

The corruption of the human soul was vast and caustic, Sharif reflected, bewildered by his egregious transgression only minutes after praying the long night prayer. His legs and arms were still sore and his eyes barely dry from his extensive begging of Allah's mercy that night, his hands having been raised as he stood almost an hour leading the congregation in the emotional supplication. And Sharif hadn't even left the lobby of the masjid. Yet, already, his ailing heart was hungering for the torment from which he had just begged to be saved.

No, Sharif decided in self-reproach. He refused to be a slave to the corroding darkness of a tainted heart. He refused to further distract himself with that which could result only in cultivating animosity where Islamic brotherhood should be.

Even if Karim was intentionally abandoning Sharif, could he be blamed? Sharif himself before studying hadn't even considered the five daily prayers to be integral to Islam, even as their establishment determined the very belief or disbelief of a person. Everyone was a product of his environment, Sharif reminded himself, and that could not be helped.

Harsh judgment harbored in silence was the cultivation for that spoken aloud. Even Sharif himself had harbored doubts, so what of him? And wasn't it only natural that doubts marred normal cordiality, friendships, and speech? Sharif should be thankful he had to speculate about Karim in the first place, for this itself was a sign. Whatever doubts Karim may have about Sharif, he was upstanding enough to keep them to himself, leaving Sharif unharmed.

Sharif decided that, after Eid, which was projected to be on Saturday, he would focus on the further establishment of the masjid. He would leave these personal distractions, and destructions, alone.

Besides, right then, that's where Sharif's heart lay, in the masjid. How many brothers were blessed to spend their entire day in a house dedicated to the worship of Allah? Yet Sharif had this immense blessing. Sharif spent most of his day in the masjid and left only to pick up his mother from work or to take his sister home if she grew tired of studying her schoolwork there.

Sharif savored the tranquility of praying all his prayers in the House of Allah and conducting classes to draw others closer to Him. Many times he had forgotten completely about his personal troubles, until he would meet with Asma and Iman regarding the newsletter.

Admittedly, Sharif had been disappointed when Asma had said that Iman couldn't come to the meeting. But now, as he raised his hand to get the attention of Asma and Wali who were waiting for him in the lobby, Sharif thought of it as something positive. Allah was protecting him from himself. Sharif and Asma had actually accomplished a lot during the meeting, and he hadn't been distracted at all. That was a blessing.

The affair of the believer is always good, Sharif reminded himself of the famous teaching of the Prophet. *In times of ease, he is grateful. In times of hardship, he is patient.*

As Asma and Wali joined him and he opened the main door, the cool night air drifted toward him in that motion. Sharif smiled into the darkness of the parking lot ahead of him, his heart finding rest in the simple reminder. He would have to keep this prophetic guidance in mind.

"Sharif." Nadirah's expression was grave and her eyes red as she met her son in the living room after he and his sister and brother returned from praying in the masjid. Asma and Wali glanced back at their mother, concern and confusion in their eyes. Sharif could tell that they sensed that something terrible was about to unfold, and they slowly treated to their rooms, wanting no part.

Sharif's mother was hugging herself and rubbing her arms as if she were cold, exhaustion in her face and eyes. "We need to talk. *Now*."

Brother Karim. The thought came to Sharif immediately, and he felt sick with dread.

Without waiting for a response, Nadirah turned and headed to her room, and Sharif followed, his head bowed slightly, as if walking toward the dismal fate of one sentenced to death.

Knots of pain tightened at his temples and Sharif's heart pounded as he closed the door to his mother's room. With narrowed eyes and arms crossed, Nadirah turned to face her son, a look of disgust distorting her face as she stood feet from him.

"What the *hell* is going on with you?" Nadirah spoke through gritted teeth.

Sharif winced, having not expected his mother's anger to be so fierce. Inadvertently, he gathered his eyebrows and started to ask what had happened, but his mother put a hand up and shook her head.

"Please, Sharif. Spare me. I don't have time for games. You know exactly what I'm talking about."

But he didn't know. He had only an idea. And in case he was wrong—and he was hoping that he was—he didn't want to use this moment to reveal what he had discussed with Brother Karim.

Sharif still wore a puzzled expression as he looked at his mother, hating himself for causing this much stress.

"Speak." Her nose flared. "I want to hear every word of this."

"Of… what?" Sharif heard the breaks in his voice, his feigned innocence betraying him in the awkward tone of his inquiry.

"Are you involved in that much *crap* that you can't even keep track?" She regarded him, her disgust even more pronounced.

"I'll give you one hint," she said, and Sharif could almost taste her fury in the taunt. "You had a little meeting with *Hasna's* father, but about *Iman*." She contorted her face as she said the name, as if its mere utterance was repulsive to her.

The pain in his temples pulsated, and Sharif averted his gaze. The moment felt surreal. He didn't want to believe it was his mother standing before him livid and furious with him. In that moment, Sharif saw just how abhorrent his actions had been, and how grossly naïve.

What had he been thinking? Was he insane? How could he have imagined that things would transpire any differently?

"Do you think that marriage is some *game?* Where you can just hop from one daughter to the next?" She was motioning with her hands, as if stiffly conducting a band. "If you can't have this one, you can have that one." She shook her head, spent.

"Is *that* what you learned over there?" Her eyes were narrowed into slits.

Sharif's face grew hot until his eyes blurred. He felt so ashamed of himself he could barely look his mother in the eye. His head pounded until he felt the aching in his throat.

"And based on what? Some, some…" Her face contorted more as she searched for the word, her hands moving as if urging the question itself, her shoulders lifting with each movement. "…*dream* of all things."

She regarded him, as if more perplexed than repulsed. "Are you *sick?*"

Perhaps he was, Sharif considered, his mind clouding in self-reproach. Maybe he was suffering from a destructive imagination. Maybe the dream itself hadn't been the least bit blessed. It could have come from his subconscious, or from the devil himself.

Sharif should have known better. He should have been more vigilant, more aware of the corruption lurking in his breast. Given the enormity of his crime, Sharif could think of no words to defend his tremendous transgression, of the mind or the self. No words existed that could accomplish such a feat, even though his heart fervently wished there were.

"And now your whole family has to suffer. And I don't blame them for one second. If I were in their place, I'd forbid my children from having anything to do with you, too." She regarded him in disgust. "Or your family."

Nadirah was silent as she tried to calm herself, shaking her head in disbelief, now walking away from her son. She sank onto the edge of her bed and covered her face with her hands, her elbows resting on her knees. For some time she remained in this position until Sharif saw her shoulders quiver, a sharp pain stabbing his heart as he witnessed the distress he was causing.

"O Allah, help my son," she murmured, her voice cracking with the utterance. "O Allah, help him. And guide him. And heal him for whatever disease this is."

Sharif's eyes burned in helplessness as he witnessed the frailty of his mother. The love he felt for her was tormenting, and all the more so because he could do nothing to take away her pain. Since he himself had incited it.

It was at this moment that Sharif realized that Nadirah's prayer was a cry of desperation, a cry of agony. A cry of suffering from the immense weight of life's obligation, a task she now carried alone. She was charged not only with carrying her children, but with carrying herself. And she could no longer hold up under the weight.

Right then, Sharif felt so completely the absence of his father. Sharif felt the utter emptiness that his death had left in their lives, an emptiness that permeated every corner of the room. Opposite Sharif was not his mother but a fragile widow, a mere shadow of the woman who had raised him and given him strength.

And now she needed the strength of a man to carry her through.

She had lost almost everything when she had lost her husband so suddenly that unforgettable night.

What had been the last words whispered between Nadirah and Dawud? Had they fought? Or had they held each other that fateful night and relished in the warmness they thought would last forever, never expecting that the ink of fate had granted them not a moment more.

How had Nadirah found her husband the following morning? Was his body cold and heavy next to her? Had she screamed? Or had she calmly shook him, hoping against hope that this was some perverted trick of the mind? Were his eyes shut peacefully when he lay there motionless? Or were they wide open, staring into nothingness, the signs of their having followed the seizing of his soul in alarm?

How many days had this image haunted Nadirah? And how many days did the ghost lurk beneath her smile and tired eyes? How many nights did she lay restless in bed or wake to reach for someone who was no longer there? How many tears had she shed or wiped away before calmly making breakfast for the loved ones who remained with her still?

Sharif couldn't even conceive of the depths of loss his mother was grieving right then. There was so much that he could not measure of the grief sustained by losing a husband to untimely death.

And now she was losing a son to dementia.

If only Sharif could somehow calm the anguish. If only he could lessen the grief.

If only he could erase the part he played in her distress.

Saying "I'm sorry" seemed too trite, too insulting and disingenuous to utter right then. But he could think of nothing else he could offer in the way of words.

There were some transgressions that spoken apologies could only worsen, and make more grating, more painfully felt.

And this was one of them.

Instead, as if mute, Sharif stood guilty as accused, unable to utter a single word or offer a single gesture that could make it better for her. Or him.

So Sharif merely stood, unable to tear his eyes, or heart, from the woman who had raised him, the woman who loved him, the woman who stood by him even when no one else would.

And the woman who had lost the only person who could have made it better for her right then.

On that dreadful night, Nadirah had lost the man who had loved Sharif until it hurt. And Sharif's scathing carelessness had then, like now, torn the very life from someone who offered him only the deepest depths of love.

Twenty

"Behold, you received it on your tongues, and said out of your mouths things of which you had no knowledge, and you thought it to be a light matter, while it was most serious in the sight of Allah. And why did you not, when you heard it, say, 'It is not right for us to speak of this. Glory to You [O Allah!] this is a most serious slander'?"
—Qur'an, *Al-Noor* (24:15-16)

Pedophile. This was the scarlet letter branded on Sharif's chest. And although it did not aptly describe his crime, pedophilia was the ailment that his mother had bemoaned befalling her eldest son. The branding, viciously unjust in its summation of what had truly occurred, somehow found place on the tongues of those scorning the perversity of Sharif's transgression.

So Sharif was condemned to wear it on his breast as he drove in the quiet darkness of dawn Friday morning as he made his way to the masjid to pray the first prayer of the rest of his life. The haunting sentence followed him in every motion of prayer, in every word he recited, and in his very breathing that afternoon. He turned to face the small congregation of believers who had abandoned work and school to pray behind him and listen to the sermon of one who did not deserve to even speak.

After *Jumu'ah* Sharif shook the hands of his brothers in faith as if giving them a final farewell. His days were numbered as part of this Muslim community, Sharif could feel it in the very veins of his arms. When someone addressed him as "Imam," Sharif felt unsettled, as if preparing himself for losing even that title, even as he had always felt that the title was undeserved.

Sharif felt the noose around his neck in the stillness of his home when he returned from the masjid that night, having announced that the Eid prayer would be held at 7:30 the following morning.

Sharif felt the tattered rope against his throat in the quiet hurt and confusion of Asma as she sulked next to her oldest brother as she rode next to Sharif that night, having no idea that the culprit for the crime for which she was suffering was her brother himself.

"But why?" Asma had complained to her mother early that morning after Nadirah had told Asma that she was no longer allowed to talk to Iman.

But Nadirah had merely glanced at Sharif, in that single gaze tormenting him more than she could have with words. "Don't worry about why," Nadirah had said, frowning as she turned away from Sharif. "You're just not allowed to talk to her. And that's that."

It was in this climate of distress that Sharif decided he would visit Jafar again after the Eid prayer Saturday morning. He felt that Jafar was the only person to whom he could talk to feel a sense of normalcy, however ironic that was. Of course Sharif wouldn't share with his friend the details of his crime, but he imagined that visiting his friend would be a consolation that he was not alone in being punished for crimes of intentions—intentions that neither Sharif nor Jafar had been aware of themselves.

"I'd marry you to my daughter," Jafar told Sharif Saturday afternoon after Sharif found himself divulging bits and pieces of what was disturbing him, even as the judging eyes of the officers cut him in a glance.

Nervous laughter erupted from Sharif as he held the receiver on his side of the glass.

"I'm not joking," Jafar said, and upon recovering from laughter, Sharif met the eyes of his friend and saw sincerity there. "My father used to always say, 'That's a good young man.'" Jafar chuckled at his impersonation of his father.

"I appreciate it, man." A smile lingered on one side of Sharif's mouth.

"I'm for real. My father was dead serious." Jafar smiled, a reminiscent glow in his eyes. "I used to get sick of how much he talked about you. To be honest I was a little jealous."

Sharif creased his forehead, a grin on his face. "Are you serious?"

"Yeah, man, why you think I always slapped your weak jump shot? It was payback."

They both laughed.

"You never mentioned it before," Sharif said, his voice playfully accusing in its tone.

Jafar shook his head, grinning. "Why would I mention something like that? I think your head was already big enough after being chosen as the imam."

Sharif was quiet, having never considered that Jafar himself might have wanted the role.

"He even said he wished he could marry you to Humaira."

Sharif gathered his eyebrows, taken aback. Humaira was Jafar's younger sister, who couldn't be more than twenty right then. Sharif didn't know what to say.

Jafar shrugged. "But with Hasna in the picture, he didn't feel he had a right."

Sharif recalled talking to Brother Rashad as they stood next to the pool in the yard of his old home, and Sharif missed him right then.

Sharif started to say something to this effect but was interrupted by the voice of an officer saying they'd better wrap it up because they were almost out of time.

"*InshaaAllah*, I'll come by Monday," Sharif said, sadness filling him as he realized how much Jafar must have lost with his family so far away.

Jafar averted his gaze and dusted something from the panel in front of him. "Don't make any promises, man. Just come when you can."

"Monday's good for me."

"Like I said," Jafar said, his voice stiff as he continued avoiding Sharif's gaze. "Just come when you can."

It was then that Sharif understood. An incarcerated person could not risk broken appointments, especially from those who were close to him. Some inmates felt it was better not to have scheduled visits at all. That way, every visit was unexpected and pleasant. The word *hope* had left their vocabulary when the iron bars had closed on them, and it was a destructive term if relied on regarding anything other than from their Lord on Judgment Day.

"Okay man," Sharif said quietly, averting his gaze himself. "I hope to see you soon."

"Yeah, me too."

With a nod and mumbled greetings, Jafar was re-shackled and guided away by the officers. He glanced back only once, distressing Sharif in that one look. Sharif couldn't fathom the routine that awaited Jafar when he disappeared from view. Sharif wondered at the depths of sadness Jafar veiled within.

He would return on Monday, Sharif was determined, and he made a silent prayer to Allah that he would never abandon his brother, especially when he needed him most.

And by Allah's will, Sharif did return on Monday as he had promised.

But he was turned away.

"He's no longer an inmate here," Sharif was told at the desk.

Taken aback, Sharif stared at the man who hadn't even as much as looked up at him. "But I just saw him Saturday."

"Like I said, he's no longer an inmate here."

"Where is he then?"

"We can't release that information."

Sharif shook his head, in that moment recalling how Jafar had averted his gaze. *Don't make any promises, man.*

Did Jafar know? Or was this sudden transfer a standing threat that had hovered every day of his life here?

Sharif had driven home, perplexed, his heart torn. He banged the steering wheel in frustration with the injustice of it all. These were the days of Eid, the most joyous and festive occasion for Muslims around the world. And yet Sharif couldn't muster a single emotion except that of melancholy and regret.

Where was Jafar now? Would Sharif ever know?

He thought of the imam who had helped him get on the visitation list, and when he approached the exit for home, he passed it, deciding to stop by the imam's masjid instead.

"Are you serious?" Hasna contorted her face from where she sat in the lobby of the convention center where her family had gone for Eid. Next to her was an old friend she hadn't seen in years.

"That's what I heard." Jabirah pulled at the cotton candy she held and placed the soft pink cotton in her mouth, letting it melt on her tongue before speaking again. "So it's a good thing you cut it off with him."

Hasna didn't know what to say. The news was too bizarre to comprehend. Was it possible that Sharif had actually asked to marry her little sister? Hasna's stomach churned, suddenly losing her appetite for the wax-paper wrapped gyro that warmed her hand.

"How do you know though?"

"My friend's sister is friends with a sister whose mother knows your mom."

"My *mother* said this?"

Jabirah shrugged, pulling again at the fluffy pink and putting it in her mouth. "That's what my friend said."

Some children ran past, apparently engaged in a friendly game of tag, a sign that today's festivities were just beginning. But Hasna wanted to go home. She doubted she would last another minute in this noisy, annoying place where she could hardly hear herself think. But she hadn't brought her own car, instead having ridden in the back seat of her father's, Adam in his bulky child seat between her and Iman.

Hasna felt a headache coming on. The information was too disturbing to be correct. Maybe there had been some misunderstanding. That was normal with hearsay.

But there was a nagging that told Hasna that it was somehow true.

"Look, look, there she is," a voice said quickly, and Iman had the sudden feeling that someone was staring at her. She halted her steps, gripping Adam's hand more firmly, but her little brother protested, tugging her forward.

Iman already felt out of place walking around in all-black with her face covered, only her eyes exposed. The pointing fingers, and from fellow Muslims, made it all the more difficult to relax on this festive day.

"That's the one that new imam's trying to marry," the voice whispered, and Iman stiffened. Annoyed, Adam tugged at her hand and pointed to a moon bounce in the distance.

"I wanna jump!" he whined.

"Are you serious?" another voice said from behind her. "The one looking like she some Arab?"

"Yeah, I know."

"How can you even tell who she is?"

"Because my friend knows who her brother is."

"That little boy's her brother?"

"Yeah. Plus I thought it was her because…"

Their voices faded, and Iman felt as if pins were pricking her all over. Adam tugged on her hand again, and this time she let herself be guided by him, her mind befuddled from what she had just heard.

That's the one that new imam's trying to marry.

The words settled in her mind, struggling to find place, and sense, there.

Certainly they couldn't have been talking about Iman…or Sharif. That was impossible.

Until you are more forthcoming about your communication with Sharif, you're not allowed to speak to anyone in that family.

The words stunned her until she halted her steps again, Adam now stomping his foot in frustration. "I wanna *juuuuump*," he whined, on the verge of tears.

Was this the missing link? The final piece to the puzzle that had perplexed her all week?

Slowly, she walked on Adam's urging, her mind a storm of thoughts.

But how could such a rumor emerge? It was preposterous to think that she and Sharif were talking for marriage when she could barely relax in the masjid office across from him.

And until you let me know exactly how he felt comfortable talking to your father like he did…

Iman brought a hand to her mouth, her eyes wide in disbelief. Her heart raced as everything suddenly made sense. The accusation. The punishment. The sudden halting of the newsletter.

The meeting with her father and Sharif.

Iman's heart pounded wildly and she could barely gather her thoughts as the noise level rose almost unbearably in the presence of screaming children, overexcited to jump in the inflated house. Adam wriggled impatiently as she stood in line with him, but Iman's mind was far from her little brother's display even as her hand gripped his firmly.

"Iman?"

At the sound of her name, Iman turned and found herself staring into the face of the very person she was forbidden to talk to.

Asma glanced over her shoulder, as if making sure no one saw her greeting her friend. *"As-salaamu'alaikum,"* she said, forcing a smile.

Iman glanced over her own shoulder, conscious that her parents could be near. She forced a smile from behind her veil as she replied in kind, her eyes drifting to Adam struggling to free himself so he could run and play.

Iman's heart was pounding. She was still recovering from the sudden realization of what was likely going on. She wanted to ask Asma about it, but she withheld. Iman doubted that even Asma knew about the meeting her brother had had.

For a few seconds the friends said nothing, but Iman fought the urge to ask Asma to remain with her. Asma's face glowed a golden brown next to the lavender cloth that framed her features, reminding Iman of the day that they both decided to wear hijab.

"Is your family here?" Asma asked, waving to Adam playfully as he stomped his feet in agitation. But Adam turned away from her, now trying to pry Iman's hand from his.

"Yes. We all came together."

Asma nodded, her gaze still lingering on Adam.

"What about you?" Iman asked.

Asma shook her head. "It's only me and Wali. Mom was too tired after the prayer and Sharif had some appointment he had to go to."

At the mention of Sharif, Iman averted her gaze. The man in charge of the moon bounce waved the waiting children inside. The other children who had had their turn were now putting on their shoes. Relieved to end the wrestling with Adam, Iman released her grip, and Adam shot to the air-filled house. The man yelled at him to take off his shoes, and Iman hurried to catch her brother. When she caught him, she had to peel him away from the entrance and kneel to force his shoes off him. When she finished, she found Asma standing next to her, a smile on her face as she watched Adam shoot back toward the bounce and begin jumping.

They were quiet momentarily.

"I guess I better go..." Asma dropped her gaze. "You know, since you're family's here."

Iman nodded absently, the questions filling her mind but getting stuck in her throat. She didn't know what she should say to her friend.

"Did you hear what happened?"

Iman's forehead creased and she shook her head, anticipating the confirmation of what she already suspected. "No. What?"

"Mom says I can't talk to you anymore."

Iman nodded. "Yeah, I know."

Asma shook her head, a confused expression on her face. "Do you know why?"

Iman drew in a deep breath, her eyes resting on Adam bouncing up and down in front of her. "No," she lied. "Do you?"

Asma shrugged. "My mom wouldn't tell me."

Iman was quiet momentarily. "That's strange."

"I know." Asma sighed.

A second later, Iman felt Asma regarding her, and she glanced in the direction of her friend. "Did my mom tell you not to call?"

Iman shook her head. "No. My mom just told me I'm not allowed to talk to you."

Asma twisted her face in confusion. "This is so stupid. Nobody's even saying what's going on."

"I know," Iman said quietly, feeling slightly guilty for having an idea, and for inadvertently playing a part in the transgression.

"Maybe our parents had a fight." Asma's expression was still distorted, confusion written there.

"I don't think so."

"What else could it be?"

Iman sighed. "Allah knows."

At the reminder, Asma's face relaxed. She nodded, her eyes distant.

"I better go," she said finally, looking again in the direction of Adam, sadness in her eyes.

Iman nodded. "Okay, *inshaaAllah.*" She had started to say she'll talk to her later, but she stopped herself. Maybe she wouldn't.

"*As-salaamu'alaikum,*" Asma said, lifting a hand in a reluctant wave.

"*Wa'alaiku-mus-salaam,*" Iman replied, forcing a smile although Asma could not see her face. But they had grown so close as friends that Iman sensed that Asma understood that parting was hard for them both.

For a second, Iman watched the back of her friend's head as she walked away from her, and her heart fell. How long could she last like this? Would her parents ever relent?

Iman thought of how angry her mother had been when she suspected that Iman had merely communicated with Sharif.

No, Iman realized. Her parents were not going to change their minds.

But she hoped that Allah would change their hearts.

Twenty-one

"Toward the end of time, hardly any dream will be untrue.
That will be because Prophethood and its effects will be so far away
in time, so the believers will be given some compensation in the form of
dreams which will bring them some good news or will help them to be
patient and steadfast in their faith."
— Prophet Muhammad (peace be upon him)
(Bukhari and Muslim)

December 17, 2004. Prince George's County, Maryland. Wednesday a 26-year-old local Islamic cleric was asked by area Muslims to relinquish his post after evidence of an illicit relationship was uncovered between him and a girl that sources report to have been as young as twelve years old. It is unclear the extent of their relationship, but area authorities are investigating the life and ideals of the young charismatic leader who subscribes to a radical interpretation of Islam. The cleric is reported to have used his post to endorse conjugal relations between adult men and young girls, whom he believes the Koran sanctions in marriage. Sources say he defended his relationship based on the marriage of Muhammad, whom Muslims believe to be a prophet, to a young girl of nine when he was more than fifty years old. Area Muslims are enraged at the cleric's defense and contend that his teachings do not represent true Islam, which they say is "moderate" and does not permit the marriage of children below the age of eighteen under any circumstances…

Sharif sat at the desk of his room, the newspaper spread before him, the lamp glowing above it in the otherwise darkened room. Sharif had read the article at least three times before, and he should have trashed it six weeks ago, when it was first published. But he found himself drawn to it, as if his re-reading it would uncover the mystery behind the harrowing experience in which he was nearly imprisoned for his alleged involvement with Iman. The investigation ceased only after Iman had been forced to undergo a physical examination that revealed that she had never been involved in intimate relations of any kind, and after she herself insisted that she had only spoken to Sharif during their weekly meetings regarding The Masjid Center newsletter.

Sharif folded the paper and pushed it to the side of his desk, next to where his stamped passport now lay. His work visa had been approved, and he had picked up his passport from the Saudi embassy a few days before, his heart now looking forward to returning to Riyadh. Sharif felt indebted to his former professor Sheikh Abdullah for assisting him in finding a post teaching English and Islamic Studies at an international school in the city. It had been Sharif's dream to return to the company of Muslims, but he hadn't imagined that it would be under these circumstances.

He should have been relieved to finally be free from the title of imam, but the slander that continued to surround his name left the loss of the imam title less an unfettering for him than the further shackling in a web of lies and suspicions that would forever haunt his name. Legally, he had been exonerated of all charges, but the publication stating this fact had been only three lines long and insinuated that something uncouth had transpired between him and the "young child" although the article remained elusive as to exactly what that might be.

Sharif's mother had used the unfortunate experience as evidence of the numerous harms that came from interpreting the religion literally and thinking that the stories of the Prophet and his wives held any relevance to modern times.

"They lived according to their culture," Nadirah had said to Sharif, waving her hand dismissively, when he defended himself against the charge of pedophilia by saying Ayesha was young when she married the Prophet, so it was un-Islamic to levy such an outrageous claim.

Sharif didn't mention that there hadn't been any marriage proposal in the first place, so the charge was premature even if she and others imagined it to be just. But Sharif had remained quiet after his reference to the life of the Prophet, as it was clear that even the Messenger held no authority in the minds of many Muslims today.

Sharif had not expected to return to Riyadh, but the tension between him and his mother had reached a point that remaining in the house was becoming almost unbearable for him, and perhaps for Nadirah herself. Nadirah had once, amidst the public allegations against Sharif, said that she wished he would move far away from her and the children.

That was when Sharif realized he was helping no one by remaining where he was. He was no longer the imam, and he no longer had even the inclination to marry Hasna or Iman. So there was nothing keeping him in the city except his having imagined that he was somehow needed at home. But his mother made it clear that even that assumption was mistaken. His presence was more a hindrance than a help, and though that realization cut deeper than Sharif could comprehend, he knew too that through it Allah was facilitating his return to where his heart found peace.

But having disappointed and distressed his mother hurt more than the slanderous charges. He could have withstood the accusing glances and indignant glares and parents' snatching their children close to them and even the dwindling of his class to only three students if he had the support of the woman who meant more to him than his life itself. It had been out of love and obligation to his mother alone that he had agreed to travel and study in the first place. And now it was due to having fallen miserably short of even maintaining the natural affection of a mother that he felt condemned and exiled from his childhood home.

"May Allah remove you far from me!" she had cried when she read what had reached the local papers.

Amidst all of it, Sharif had remained stoic in front of the people, and even in front of his mother herself, although inside he was groping for some relief.

Do men think that they'll be left alone on saying, "We believe" and that they will not be tested? We did test those before them, and Allah will certain make known those who are truthful from those who are lying.

These were the verses that Sharif read over and over late into the night, tears moistening his cheeks as he stood alone in his room praying *Qiyaam*. As he stood before his Creator in the last third of the night, Sharif reminded himself that anyone who recited the proclamation of *Tawheed* would be tested regarding that claim, and Sharif asked Allah to keep him firm upon His Religion.

His forehead resting against the soft carpet of his room, Sharif implored Allah each night, *O You who turns hearts! Make my heart firm upon Your Religion.*

During the terrifying investigation in which the threat of imprisonment was very real, Sharif's dreams had increased, and through them his heart found peace. But he did not see the recurrent dream during this time, having made him wonder if it had been a true dream in the first place.

But he had seen it again last night, and although he told himself it was merely his subconscious bothering him, there was a lingering feeling that there was some meaning to the dream that he had yet to uncover. The experience during the past two months assured him that the literal interpretation had been mistaken, but he wondered what its figurative meaning could be.

Perhaps it merely meant that he and Iman were joined in their struggle to remain firm upon the Right Path while so many others were going astray, hence his feeling that she was his "wife" when she was merely his partner in faith. It was possible that the recitation of the last verses of the Qur'anic chapter *Al-Fajr* was Allah's manner of giving them the good news of reward in the Hereafter should they remain unwavering upon their faith, particularly while facing the severe trials that would befall anyone seeking to avoid the innumerable paths that led one astray.

O reassured soul, Return to your Lord, well-pleased and pleasing [to Him]. And enter among My servants, enter My Paradise.

O Allah, Sharif prayed, *make me of the inhabitants of Your Paradise!*

When Karim was a sophomore in high school and Islam hadn't yet graced his life, his mother was diagnosed with ovarian cancer. But the disease had been so advanced by the time the doctors discovered it that there was nothing they could do. They had given her three months to live, but she had died in less than two weeks.

The night that the doctors gave Karim's father the three-month life sentence for his wife, Karim met Sharif for the first time. Karim had lain awake most of the night bitter, confounded that God would do this to their family. He had been too angry to shed tears, and he refused to grieve. Grieving would be merely submitting to what the doctors had said when they didn't know anything at all.

"Brother Karim, give this to her," the young man said to Karim. Karim was so taken aback by the strange name that the boy was using to refer to him that he barely registered what he was being told. His name was Corey, not Karim, and why was the boy calling him "Brother." Was the boy Catholic?

Corey regarded the boy who appeared to be about his own age at the time, and Corey noticed a spiritual glow on the boy's smooth brown face, an illumination that penetrated Corey's heart.

"Who are you?" Corey asked.

"I am your son."

Corey stared at the boy, perplexed by the impossibility of it. "But..."

"You don't have a lot of time," Corey's son told him, urging Corey to take something from his hands. "Make her drink from this."

It was then that Corey noticed the large bowl of water in the boy's hands. The water sparkled and winked in the light coming from the boy's face and the bowl seemed to be made of silver but it was somehow transparent too. Corey stared at the vessel, overcome by its splendor. He had never seen the likes of it before.

"What is it?"

"It is water."

"But from where?"

"From your Lord."

The boy passed the bowl to Corey, and Corey took it. Corey opened his mouth to speak but was interrupted by the shaking of the sky above him. Startled, he almost spilled the water, but the vessel remained in his hands. Strange melodious words came from the heavens, but Corey could not understand what they meant, nor could he determine who was reciting the beautiful words that permeated his heart and made him yearn to listen to them forever.

"Who is —"

At that sound, the boy looked up to the heavens where a bright cloud opened above him. "I must go now."

"But wait..."

"You don't have a lot of time."

"But what is your name?"

"It is your name you must know."   The strange recitation *reverberated louder in the heavens above them. "Brother Karim, you don't have a lot of time."*

"Who is this for?"

"It is for you."

"But I thought…"

"Pray for your forgiveness, Brother," the boy said, his eyes holding a distant sadness that tore at Corey's heart. Corey felt the urge to cry, in that moment realizing the enormity of his sin even as the nature of it eluded him.

In an instant the boy was gone and Corey stood alone in his bedroom holding the vessel that was no longer transparent, its silver now merely shiny stainless steel. But the water within retained its sparkle.

"Corey," a weak voice said, and he lifted his gaze to see his ailing mother in front of him. "I'm thirsty. Can you bring me some water?"

Karim woke, his heart heavy in guilt and his stomach sick from the enormity of his sin. He had pushed the dream to the far corners of his mind years before, and he hadn't expected to see it again. But it had lingered in his heart for more than two decades, and it was this vision that had returned to him when he first met Dawud, whom Karim taught about Islam. Karim was drawn to David because he saw in his features those similar to that of the boy in the dream he had seen as a teen. But he never mentioned the dream to his friend. He hadn't even mentioned it to his wife.

But years later when David's oldest son was a teen, Karim knew with certainty that it wasn't Dawud he had seen in the dream but Sharif, his son. Even Sharif's voice was like the boy's had been in the dream. This perplexed Karim, and he wondered what the dream could mean. It wasn't until Sharif had shared his own dream that Karim began to realize, more than twenty-five years after his own dream, that the vision could mean something greater than he understood right then. Even the verses that Sharif had heard in his dream were the same ones Karim had heard in his. This was too farfetched to dismiss as coincidence.

There was some meaning in this, Karim had thought as he listened in genuine interest to Sharif recount the dream. But it was only this week that Karim was forced to face the fact that he had avoided on the night Sharif had sat down in his living room and shared his dream.

When Sharif had spoken to him that night, Karim was intrigued although for some reason he wasn't surprised. Oddly, he had expected the meeting although he didn't know the details of what would be discussed. And he had no idea that they would involve his youngest daughter. He had expected some closure to Sharif and Hasna's relationship, not the suggestion of kindling one with Iman.

That information had been difficult for Karim to digest.

But he had been immediately reminded of the dream he had seen the night he learned of his mother's cancer diagnosis.

And now he had dreamt it again.

Karim lay awake in the stillness of his room. The darkness of predawn was shadows behind the drawn curtains of his room. He couldn't hope to sleep, and he sensed that Mona too lay awake, restless, although her back was to him.

How could they sleep on such a night when, less than twelve hours before, the doctors had informed them of the results of Iman's biopsy?

The growth in her ovaries was malignant.

Twenty-two

"At this point, all we can offer is chemotherapy," the oncologist explained, her expression empathetic, but her words gave little hope. The doctor looked like she was about Hasna's age, and her brown eyes and pale olive skin reminded Mona of her sister. The doctor's short dark hair was pulled away from her face, accenting the distant concern written there.

"During the cytoreductive surgery, we removed as much of the cancer as we could," the doctor said, slipping her hands into the pockets of her white coat. "But it's highly recommended to combine the surgery with chemotherapy, especially for stage three patients."

Mona sat next to Karim listening to the medical jargon as if deciphering a foreign language although she understood every word. What made the words so foreign was that they were referring to her daughter, and this Mona found difficulty comprehending.

It was the last week of February, and only four weeks before, Mona and her family had celebrated Eid Al-Adha by taking a quiet road trip to Virginia. The weather had been cold and the mood sober, and shared guilt cast a shadow on every word spoken and tainted even the quiet moments between them. Iman and Hasna did not speak to each other for the entire trip, their mutual frustration revealed through Hasna's irritable outbursts when Adam annoyed her and through Iman's clenched jaw as she stared out the window next to her, her face veiled flipped up and, like a curtain, shielding her peripheral view of her older sister.

When the rumors about Iman and Sharif had begun to spread in late November, Mona noticed darkness in Iman's eyes and agony that was thinly veiled by Iman's grave silence as she went about her house chores. Mona could tell even then that Iman was not well, but Iman did not complain or sulk. When addressed, Iman was cordial, almost to a fault, but Mona could see that her daughter was struggling to keep her composure under the immense strain required to sustain the vicious talk.

Once Mona had heard sobbing coming from Iman's room late one night in early December, and concerned, Mona quietly turned the door handle expecting to find her daughter crouched with bedcovers pulled over her head. Tears had gathered in Mona's own eyes as she stood outside the door, feeling the urge to join Iman on her bed and embrace her daughter warmly until the tears dried from both of their eyes.

But Mona found her daughter sitting on the desk chair that had been positioned toward a corner of the room and a prayer mat lying on the carpet in front of the chair. Iman was wearing a white floral prayer garment, revealing folded hands across her chest, and her face was bowed as tears streamed down her cheeks.

The scene had penetrated Mona's heart, and she quickly closed the door hoping to keep her own composure. But she was fighting her own sobs and she covered her face with her hands as she made her way downstairs to her own room.

At the sight of Iman praying in such a weak state, Mona had been stricken with guilt. She felt ashamed for her central role in Sharif's name being maligned and his honor mercilessly disgraced, and Iman's too. Mona could not have fathomed the deadly harm that would be caused when she had vented to a friend of hers about Sharif's interest in Iman.

"I find it disgusting," Mona had said on the phone to her friend. The cordless was held to her ear with one hand, and the other was folded under her chest as she walked the length of her room and back again. Karim had not yet returned from work, and Mona felt the need to talk to someone.

It hadn't occurred to her that, other than her husband, her only confidant should have been her Lord.

"I mean," she had said, wrinkling her nose into the receiver, "where does he get his ideas? Is this what he calls *Islam*?"

Mona's friend had been equally repulsed, if not more so than Mona, because Mona's friend did not know Sharif personally, although before then her friend had known only good of him.

"Mona, this is serious." Her friend's tone was etched in worry.

"I know. I just don't know what to do."

"You can't allow him around her."

"Karim and I already took care of that. They're not allowed to talk."

"But you need to monitor her phone calls and Internet. People who prey on children know how to manipulate people."

The comment had taken Mona aback momentarily. She hadn't been thinking of Sharif as a predator. She had only feared that Sharif's contact with the family would put ideas of marriage into her daughter's head. But, admittedly, Mona had suspected that there had been some phone conversations exchanged between Iman and Sharif without her knowledge.

"I don't think he'd try to manipulate her," Mona had said, doubtful. "But still..."

"No, Mona," her friend said, her voice grave in concern. "You don't know what these people are like."

At that moment, doubts gripped Mona's heart. Was it possible that Sharif was fighting some darkness within himself? The possibility terrified her.

Everyone was human, and was thus struggling with some disease of the heart. Could this be Sharif's?

As Mona considered it, she realized that it was possible. Sharif had always struck her as too perfect...the ideal profile for these types of people. As she thought of how he tried to present himself as Islamic, she was annoyed. She hated when people painted holy pictures of themselves and expected everyone to put them on a pedestal. Did he think that his role as imam absolved him of accountability, that Mona was just to assume he had only the best intentions for Iman?

She told her friend about the dream.

"Are you serious?" Her friend's voice was a whisper, shocked disquiet in every word. "Maybe he has some psychological problem."

Mona shuddered. How had she missed the sign? She had already imagined he was embellishing the story of the dream, but what if he actually believed that he had seen the dream? Karim himself had suggested that…

The possibility was frightening. Spent, Mona sank her weight into the bed, her legs having weakened at the thought. Sharif had always seemed a bit different from boys his age. Was it possible that he had a chemical imbalance of some sort?

"I don't know…." Mona was hesitant to speak her thoughts aloud. They seemed too premature.

"Think about it," her friend said convincingly, "this is an imam we're talking about, Mona."

Her friend was right. This was more serious than Mona had imagined. She had called her friend hoping to merely have a sympathetic ear. Mona hadn't expected to discover the possibility of Sharif needing sympathies of another kind.

Mona thought of Nadirah and how distressed she had been when Mona had called to tell her what had transpired. Mona's heart sank at the thought. She should have been more sensitive. How was Nadirah handling this? Mona thought of how difficult it must be for Nadirah to shoulder this burden without her husband's support. Mona felt sickened by her insensitivity. Maybe she should call to see if Nadirah needed a sympathetic ear herself.

Currently, Mona lifted her eyes to the medical posters on the doctor's wall, the events of the past months gnawing at her heart, shame seeping into the gash there.

"Even if he had no right to marry me," Iman had said one afternoon in late December, her eyes brimmed with tears as her gaze met that of her mother's. There was a plea in Iman's eyes as she held the December 17th newspaper in her hands. Iman stood in the doorway of her mother's room, feet from where Mona stood silent, unsure what she could possibly say in response to her daughter. She herself was at a loss after reading the article. "What was so wrong with just saying *no*?"

One of the most tormenting ordeals for Mona was having her daughter subjected to physical examinations, and Mona was not even allowed to accompany her in the room. Mona could scarcely talk to Iman about menses. How then was she to explain what the authorities were looking for during the physical?

As it turned out, there was no need to talk to Iman about it, as Iman had emerged from the ordeal as if mute, and only Iman's eyes reflected the torment stirring within.

"But it's recommended that you start treatment in the next six weeks," the doctor said, disrupting Mona's thoughts. A phone rang suddenly from one of the doctor's pockets, and the oncologist quickly retrieved it, glancing at the number before pressing a button and slipping it back inside the white coat.

What was so wrong with just saying no?

The words echoed in Mona's mind as she rode quietly next to Karim after leaving the doctor's office, the authentic simplicity of Iman's inquiry inciting a migraine. Mona leaned her head against the glass of the passenger side door, her ailing heart making her head heavy.

Stage three.

Chemotherapy.

Malignant.

Surgery.

Six weeks.

Would Iman *die*?

Mona felt a hand on her lap and glanced in the direction of her husband, whose emotionless expression was difficult to read. His lips were pressed together in a line, a sign that he was hurting more than he let on.

Mona looked away.

No, they wouldn't subject Iman to the torture of chemotherapy. They could beat this through the love for her that swelled in their hearts and flowed through their veins. This was not a job too big for Allah. He could say simply "Be" if He wished to decree anything, and the matter would be settled at once.

But would He decree Iman's recovery for them?

Did they even deserve such a decree?

Or would Allah take Iman, leaving them in tormented agony for the rest of their lives?

Mona's eyes clouded as the throbbing in her head blurred her vision. She shut her eyes, too weak to keep them open. There was painful tightness in her stomach and the sudden sensation that she would faint.

It was then that she realized she hadn't eaten in more than twenty-four hours. She had completely forgotten about food. She needed nourishment for her body if she were to function enough to tend to Iman.

And she needed nourishment for her soul if she were to function enough to tend to herself.

Her back against a pillow on her bedpost, Iman sat with her knees bent in front of her supporting the notebook in which she wrote. Soreness from the incision in her abdomen distracted her only slightly from revising her poem.

With the red pen that she held, Iman put a line through the word *emanating* and replaced it with *illuminating*. *The hearts illuminating Islam's beauty...* she recited the words in her mind.

No, it's too many syllables, she decided. She scratched out *illuminating* and re-penned *emanating* in the margin.

The hearts we lost/Where do they wander?/The hearts emanating
Islam's beauty/Are they gone? I ponder.

Iman frowned. There was something wrong with the last line. It didn't seem to fit. And the rhyming of *ponder* with *wander* seemed forced. Was there another way to say this?

The hearts emanating Islam's beauty/falling in submission, split asunder.

That was better...

But was it right to equate submitting with something being split open?

She considered it, the bottom tip of the pen on her mouth, her eyes intently on the page.

That's the one that new imam's trying to marry.

The reminder came to her, and her incision became inflamed suddenly. Iman drew in a deep breath, the familiar distress building in her chest as she recalled the article in the local paper, and Sharif's humble agreement to step down as imam.

"I am innocent of what I've been accused of," Sharif had said that day, Iman and her parents one of the few families who had come to the community meeting in mid-December when he announced his official resignation.

Her parents had insisted on coming, and on Iman coming with them, as if their presence would somehow right the irrevocable damage they had caused to his life, and Iman's. But Iman had no desire to attend the meeting and had asked if she could please stay home. There was no doubt in Iman's mind that her family owed Sharif at least moral support during this time, but their presence at his resignation could be taken to mean the opposite, Iman felt. Iman knew too that she and her family would be stared at and pitied, as if Sharif's offer of marriage was a moral crime that robbed Iman and her family of some irreplaceable peace.

But more than harboring selfish concerns that night, Iman didn't want to be present to witness the painful ordeal. Iman's family, like most members of the center, already knew about the large number of area Muslims insisting that Sharif step down, mostly amongst those who rarely attended The Masjid Center. So Iman's family had had a fairly good idea what the emergency community meeting would address.

But it was one thing to have an idea, and another entirely to witness it unfolding.

"But I cannot say that I disagree with your conclusion that I do not deserve to hold this post as imam," Sharif said to the crowd of about fifty men and women before him, his eyes glistening. "There are many others, possibly even present before me today, who are more worthy of holding this title."

It was difficult for Iman to listen to him, so she tried to think of other things.

For several minutes Iman's mind wandered, and she thought about the poem "The Hearts We Lost" that she was writing. The title made her sad as she heard Sharif's voice in the microphone as he continued his resignation speech, but she had chosen the title for a reason wholly disconnected to what was happening...

"...So I ask you all to forgive me for any wrongs that I have done, and I praise Allah for even the smallest amount of benefit that I may have offered in my short time as imam."

From where she sat in the back of the *musallaa*, Iman dropped her head, recalling his classes on Islam that she had looked forward to, and his spending his own money to print and

308

distribute her and Asma's first and only published newsletter. It was heart-wrenching to hear the calm in his voice and to see the sad sincerity in his eyes. She couldn't look at him any longer. She couldn't sit there any longer.

But she had no choice.

As he continued speaking, Iman listened to his final words, her head bowed, ashamed for Sharif, ashamed for herself.

"And to those who are responsible for what I can only describe as a tragedy to me and my family, and to the believers of this city," he said, taking a deep breath, his eyes glistening more and his voice wavering, inspiring Iman's own eyes to fill with tears, "I say that I am very pained and troubled, and..." He glanced at the paper on the podium to gather his composure, his voice having left him momentarily. He breathed, in that sound revealing the heaviness in his heart. "...I say, I forgive you, and May Allah forgive you. I love you for the sake of Allah. *As-salaamu'alaikum wa rahmatullaahi wa barakaatuh.*"

Presently, Iman's eyes filled with tears, her heart as if splitting open, her eyes cast down from where she sat on her bed. She cried silently, her incision aching with each sniffle.

Her vision blurred, and she saw the poem as if before her, the last lines she had drafted coming into focus. It was then that she realized that submission was in fact related to the heart being split open.

Sometimes they were the very same thing.

Twenty-three

"O son of Adam, so long as you call upon Me and ask of Me, I shall forgive you for what you have done, and I shall not mind. O son of Adam, were your sins to reach the clouds of the sky and were you then to ask forgiveness of Me, I would forgive you. O son of Adam, were you to come to Me with sins nearly as great as the earth and were you then to face Me, ascribing no partner to Me, I would bring you forgiveness nearly as great as it."
— Qudsi Hadith
(At-Tirmidhi and Ahmad, authenticated by Al-Albani)

Wednesday afternoon Hasna pulled her car into an empty parking space in back of the clinic Vernon had referred her to two weeks before. She had made the appointment a week ago, and she had left work early today to make it to the doctor's office on time. She turned off the car and picked up her purse, pulling the straps over her shoulder as she opened the door. Instinctively, she checked her appearance in the rearview mirror, running a hand over her hair that had now grown to the length of her ears. Black eyeliner lined the hazel eyes that stared back at Hasna, sadness and confusion written there. She looked away and climbed out of the car and shut the door, the horn beeping as she pressed the button twice to lock the car.

"There's no way, Tweetie," Vernon had told her a few weeks ago. "I can't. That's too much to ask."

"But I want to keep it," Hasna had said, having hoped he would be excited at the news. But Hasna knew she was lying to herself. Even she had been stricken with anxiety when the plastic wand revealed two fading pink lines after she had sat on the edge of the toilet seat. Fully dressed for work, she waited the required two minutes for the results of the home urine test to appear.

"Tweetie," Vernon had said, aggravated. He talked in a loud whisper from where he sat on the corner of her office desk. "This was not part of the plan."

"But you said I could have what I wanted in this relationship."

"And you can. But this…" He took a deep breath, shaking his head. "…I can't do. I have Kenya to think about."

At the mention of his fiancée, Hasna's offense was fierce. "What about *us*?"

"Tweetie, I already told you, nothing will change."

"Even after May?" Arms folded, Hasna regarded Vernon from where she sat in her office chair, eyes watery in anger.

He exhaled, his eyes growing distant. "I hope so."

"If Kenya doesn't suspect anything," Hasna mocked him in a whine. She rolled her eyes.

His expression showed agitation, but he did not to respond.

"And what if I keep it anyway?" Hasna said, her tone a dare.

Vernon's eyes slowly met hers, his gaze grave. "I don't think that's a good idea."

"What if I disagree?"

Anger flashed in his eyes, and he contorted his face. "You don't have that option."

Hasna raised her eyebrows. "I think I do."

For a second, he looked desperate, as if he were going to beg her, and his helplessness emboldened Hasna and she enjoyed the power she held over him right then. A smirk formed on her face, but his expression relaxed finally.

"Then I'll just deny having anything to do with you."

Her mouth fell open. She didn't know what to say.

"Yes, Tweetie," he said, fuming as he held her gaze. "You're not the only one who knows how to play games."

She was stunned. She would never have expected this from him.

"Don't play with fire, Tweetie. You'll get hurt."

She somehow found her voice, but when she spoke her voice was tight with indignity. "I'm not playing. To me, this isn't a game. We made this together, so we should—"

"No we did *not*."

His words derailed her, and she momentarily lost her train of thought.

What the—

"You said I didn't have to worry about anything like this." Vernon's eyes were narrowed in accusation. "You said things were taken care of."

Oh. She had said that. But...

Perhaps she had missed taking the pills once or twice. She couldn't remember...

"I thought they were," she said innocently, defensiveness in her tone.

"Well, apparently something went wrong."

At his last words, she thought of Kenya and became enraged. She clenched her jaw. "Would you say the same thing if this happened with Kenya?"

"Now, Tweetie, that's not fair."

"It *is* fair."

"Kenya will be my *wife*," he said, his face regarding Hasna in contempt.

In that moment, Hasna felt her smallness, how completely worthless she was. She had imagined that if she loved Vernon enough he would forget about Kenya. Hasna was more intelligent and more beautiful than Kenya. And Hasna had never even had relations with anyone before Vernon. How could he still prefer someone so worthless, so *beneath* her? Didn't he see what he was getting with Hasna?

Couldn't their having a child together make him change his plans and marry her instead? It would be better for him, for them both.

Hasna felt cheated, and deceived. He had misled her all this time...

"I thought you cared," she said, her eyes filling with tears and her voice cracking.

"Tweetie, I do," he said, his voice softening just then. He sighed. "But you know this is too much to ask."

Hasna grated her teeth and stared off into the distance. She made no effort to wipe away the tears that escaped, hesitantly rounding her cheeks.

"You have to understand, Tweetie. This is my life you're asking me to give up. I can't do that."

She heard his voice as if from far away, and she felt her utter stupidity right then. She had sacrificed her chastity, her fiancé, and even the trust of her own parents, hoping against hope that she would win Vernon's heart and turn it away from Kenya.

She had sacrificed her *soul*.

"I know a clinic you can go to," Vernon spoke softly, his tone conveying the deep concern he felt for her. "The doctor's a good friend of mine. I can get you the number tomorrow."

Hasna had heard the sound of Vernon's voice but barely registered his words. Her thoughts drifted to Sharif, whom she had, in vicious envy, rallied to publicly malign amidst the heinous allegations against him.

She felt the bile in her stomach rise to her throat.

Even if her former fiancé had been guilty of what the media claimed—and Hasna knew he was not—being in the good graces of even Sharif right then would have been better for her than having given herself to someone as disgraceful as Vernon.

There was something to say for Sharif's summation of Vernon he had written in an e-mail so many years ago. Hasna had just told Sharif, in excitement, that her new friend Vernon used to be Muslim and really respected Islam.

"If he respected Islam," Sharif had written, *"he would be Muslim."*

At the time, Hasna had been insulted, and she imagined that, again, Sharif was being fanatical. *"And if you respect yourself,"* Sharif had added, *"you would leave him alone."*

"Yes," Hasna had told a reporter who had called her cell phone in early December to ask about Sharif's religious ideology, "I would agree that his ideas are extreme. But he doesn't represent the Muslims."

"O-kay," the woman had said, making notes as Hasna spoke.

In the background, Hasna could hear the woman pecking on a keyboard. The reporter's voice was unable to contain the excitement she felt at securing this quote, even as she retained the obligatory tone of professional objectivity.

"And one last question, ma'am, if you don't mind."

"It's no problem," Hasna said, feeling important as she sat behind her desk, proudly glancing at her law degree hanging on the wall.

"Is it true that his relationship with your twelve-year-old sister was the reason you broke off your engagement with him?"

Startled, Hasna creased her forehead. She hadn't intended to discuss Iman. The reporter had said she was calling regarding the "young, handsome, charismatic leader" who was growing in popularity in the region, and that some Muslims felt his religious ideas were radical. Hasna had had no idea that the woman knew the rumors about Iman, or of Hasna's prior engagement to him.

"My *sister*?" Hasna said, confounded.

"Isn't your sister the young girl he wanted to marry?"

"Yes…"

"Is his relationship with the twelve-year-old what caused the break up?"

Hasna contorted her face, realizing that the stereotype about journalists having no heart was not unfounded at all. They were *worse* than lawyers. Attorneys' most glaring flaw was lack of integrity. Even when lawyers openly cast doubt on something that they knew to be true, at least it was in the presence of the accused and his or her attorney — giving *some* opportunity for counterarguments. But journalists gave no opportunity for refutation, nor any forewarning of their true intentions.

Hasna was disgusted with this vindictive woman.

"She's almost *fifteen*," Hasna had said, hoping her raised voice underscored the absurdity of the charge.

"I'm sorry," the woman said too sweetly. "I'll note that correction. Thank you for your time."

Hasna shut her cell phone, her face distorted as she glared at it, as if looking at the reporter herself. Hasna was disgusted with herself for even giving the woman her time. She was glad that she caught on to the woman's bait when she did.

A second later, Hasna's heart fell, her eyes widening as a thought suddenly occurred to her.

Is his relationship with the twelve-year-old what caused the break up?
She's almost fifteen.

Oh. My. God.

By correcting the age, Hasna had confirmed the relationship.

Right then, Hasna had to fight the urge to call the woman back and give her a piece of her mind.

But even as the idea came to her, Hasna knew it would do no good. Words meant something only to those with ears to hear, and hearts to receive what they heard.

And a journalist has neither ears nor heart, she thought angrily.

In the law office that afternoon as Vernon promised his financial and emotional support for the termination of the life budding in Hasna's womb, Hasna realized that she wasn't too different from the journalist.

Except that Hasna did have ears and heart.

She had just chosen not to use them.

"If a person is willing to sacrifice their own soul," Sharif had said once. *"What do you think they'll do with you?"*

Currently, the words returned to Hasna as she made her way up the steps leading to the doctor's suite, resenting Vernon for pushing her to this point.

It was at this moment that Hasna realized that Sharif's question could relate to Vernon, and how he was treating Hasna right then.

If he's willing to sacrifice his own soul, Hasna, what do you think he'll do with you?

Jolted, Hasna halted her steps as she stood in front of the polished wooden door of the doctor's office, her hand on the cold handle right then.

"Obstetrics and Gynecology," the door plate read. "Drs. Wanda Kramer and Samuel Fares."

Wanda. Hasna pressed her lips together, envy flaring in her chest. She wondered what sort of "friendship" the doctor and Vernon had.

Hasna pushed the door open and immediately the cozy atmosphere distracted her. Soft music played in the small waiting area whose two walls were aligned with leather couches, a glass-top table with magazines scattered atop at arm's reach.

"Good afternoon," a kind-faced woman who appeared to be of Chinese descent greeted Hasna in a small voice. "Do you have an appointment?"

...What do you think he'll do with you?

Hasna nodded, distracted, her heart racing. "Yes, at 2:30."

Instinctively, the woman glanced at the clock on the wall, as did Hasna. It was 2:23.

"Your name?"

Self-conscious, Hasna glanced to her left, noticing a woman thumbing through a magazine as she sat on the leather couch, a bright pink maternity blouse revealing her swollen belly. At the woman's feet, a boy who shared the woman's reddish blond hair and appeared to be the age of Adam played with some blocks, the only toys available since the office was not pediatric.

For a second Hasna just stared at him, the four-year-old content with entertaining himself with toddler toys.

"Ma'am?"

Hasna turned back to the receptionist. "Hasna Christian."

The name had always sounded awkward to her. She had once asked her father why he didn't change his last name to a Muslim one.

"You mean to an *Arabic* one?" he asked.

"Well… yeah," Hasna had said.

He had regarded Hasna momentarily before saying, "It's not my name. It's my father's."

Oh.

"Besides," he added, "I can't think of any name more Islamic than that showing kinship to Allah's Prophet Jesus."

But now as she stood in front of the receptionist's desk, Hasna felt that she was being deceptive, hiding her Islamic identity in the affirmation of her family name. She felt also that she was betraying her family by having any written record of what she was about to do.

What would her parents say if they knew?

The lady glanced at the chart and then back at Hasna, showing no sign that she was aware of what the appointment was for. Perhaps, it wasn't noted next to her name. Perhaps it was…

"Take a seat," the lady said politely, professional cordiality in her one. "We'll call you in a few minutes."

Hasna sat near the pregnant woman and absently reached for a magazine, setting it on her lap before opening it. But Hasna couldn't keep from staring at the woman. The pregnant woman periodically laid an open palm on the cloth of her protruding shirt, rubbing her swollen belly beneath.

Hasna should have gone to an abortion clinic, the thought came to her just then, her eyes dancing from the woman to the magazine on Hasna's lap. Hasna had had no idea that the same doctors who were responsible for sustaining and nurturing the life of an unborn child were also engaged in snuffing out that life.

How would they do it? Hasna wondered, her fingers trembling as she turned the pages of the magazine, her mind registering none of its printed pages. Hasna had once read that if the pregnancy wasn't too advanced, methotrexate could be used, which was the least invasive. It was like taking a contraceptive shot, except after the fact.

Hasna could stomach that. One needle pricking her skin, a cotton ball pressed lightly on the puncture, a small bandage in its place, and she was done. She wouldn't have to think about it anymore.

Except that methotrexate was the same drug that was used in chemotherapy.

The thought made Hasna's head ache as she thought of Iman.

Iman was deciding whether or not to use the drug to save her life, and Hasna was contemplating using the drug to take an innocent child's.

Hasna's stomach churned at the thought, and her temples throbbed.

A back door opened and Hasna looked up, her heart pounding wildly in anticipation of her appointment with Wanda. A second later, a nurse holding a clipboard appeared.

"Anna Wiener," the woman called.

Hasna's eyes halted on the nurse at the same moment she realized that it was not her name being called. For a brief moment Hasna and the nurse looked at each other, and Hasna sensed that the woman thought she was Anna, most likely due to Hasna's nervous expression.

"Come on, Ronnie," Anna said, pushing herself up belly first, holding onto the armrest.

"But I'm building a house." Her son frowned and pouted dramatically.

Anna reached out a hand. "Ronnie." Her voice was soft but stern, apparently not wanting everyone to hear.

"I don't wanna go with you," the boy whined.

"It's okay," the receptionist called out kindly, an affable smile on her face. "He can play here."

Anna looked doubtful, her gaze shifting to Hasna.

317

"Ronnie," she raised her voice, threatening.

He stood, his arms still folded, and he stomped away, following his waddling mother behind the nurse and out the waiting area.

It took a second for Hasna to recover, and she shut her eyes trying to relax in the soft sound of music. She didn't know what was more unsettling, to hear the door open and anticipate her turn, or to have seen the unmistakable sign of Islam in the room. The nurse's small white *khimaar* had been tucked neatly about her head, a silver brooch perched on one side.

Hasna was immediately reminded of her soul.

If a person is willing to sacrifice their own soul, what do you think they'll do with you?

The question stung as she realized that it wasn't Hasna who should ask this question of Vernon—

But Hasna's unborn child of Hasna herself.

If she's willing to sacrifice her own soul, darling, what do you think she'll do with you?

Inadvertently, Hasna's hand went to the cloth of her shirt at her abdomen, and she rubbed it absently, as she had seen Anna Wiener do earlier.

"Hello," the soft voice of Lionel Richie wafted from a speaker welded to the ceiling. *"Is it me you're looking for?"*

Distracted by the words, Hasna thought of the touching video she had seen of the song—a blind woman the singer loved making out the features of Lionel by touching the contours of his face with her hand, and sculpting the finest details of the countenance of her beloved better than an artist with sight could have done.

As a teen, Hasna had never tired of seeing the video, moved by how it was the heart of the woman who had seen Lionel's gentle face, not her eyes.

It was not physical sight that had inspired the vision, but the sight inspired by affection.

Like that between a mother and her unborn fetus.

What will you do with me, Mommy? a hesitant infant's voice asked in Hasna's mind. Right then, Hasna saw the child's pale skin wrinkled from months in the womb, a touch of brown rounding the ear, prickly hair matted to its head, curling fingers soft to the touch...

No, a syringe filled with a lethal drug would not protect Hasna from tracing the contours of the life within her, or from seeing him, or her, in every detail that a mother's heart could sculpt. She could not shut her eyes at the prick of the needle and open them a second later, expecting a cotton ball dabbed with alcohol to wipe away the memories like it had the germs on her skin. And the cotton gauze and medical tape that she would pull off minutes later could not hold in its bloodstained cloth all that needed to be tossed when Hasna disposed of the used bandage in the trash.

And what of the disposal of the fetus weeks later, in clots of blood?

Could Hasna flush the red-tainted water and never look back, charting in her mind the future wanted pregnancies with the husband she imagined she'd have one day?

"...You're all I've ever wanted. My arms are open wide..."

Would she live the rest of her life scheduling the death and life of a child like she did food choices on a restaurant menu? *I don't want this now, but I may want it later.* This one shall die, this one shall live.

At that moment, Hasna shut her eyes, the magazine loosening in her grip as she closed it absently. Her heart ached, and the image of the child's large eyes and innocent gurgle sculpted itself in her mind, chubby arms open wide, a toothless smile forming at the sight of its mother, a soft fist moving in excitement...

"... Are you somewhere feeling lonely? Or is someone loving you?"

Hasna thought of Iman, who would never be able to have children, even if she survived the horrific chemotherapy treatments. Could she look her little sister in the eye after today?

Could she look herself in the eye?

Hasna opened her eyes, and her gaze fell on the closed magazine lying in her lap. It was then that she noticed its title for the first time.

Motherhood.

But how could she take care of the child? Where would she even begin? She herself barely felt worthy of being Muslim, or even alive right then. How then could she give to a child?

"Tell me how to win your heart, for I haven't got a clue..."

Hasna's eyes filled as the words touched her heart, a private tune from mother to child.

"...But let me start by saying, I love you."

Twenty-four

"Every soul shall taste death.
And We test you with evil and with good as a trial.
And to Us you will be returned."
— Qur'an, *Al-Anbiyaa'* (21:35)

"Anyone for whom Allah intends good, He makes him suffer
some affliction."
— Prophet Muhammad (peace be upon him)
(Bukhari)

Imam Bilal had laughed self-consciously, his pale, freckled skin forming creases next to his blue eyes as he patted Sharif on the shoulder from where he walked next to Sharif the Monday that Sharif had been told that Jafar was transferred to another prison.

Bilal's graying blond hair brushed the collar of his white *thobe*, and his light beard framed his face, accenting the spirituality that emanated from there. Minutes before, the imam had informed Sharif that he knew only that Jafar was now in a high security prison in another state where Jafar wasn't allowed visits. Hurt by the news, Sharif had changed the subject to something less grating.

"Now, I'm no Ibn Sireen," the imam had said in good humor, referring to the famous scholar of dream interpretation who had died centuries ago, "but my guess would be that it means the person in the dream is going to die, and Allah is telling us the good news of their place in Paradise."

Sharif had shared the dream with the imam but told him that it was the recurrent dream of a close friend who was seeking clarification on its meaning. The part involving the recitation of the last verses of *Al-Fajr* had intrigued the imam most. The imam's perspective was enlightening to Sharif. Sharif had never considered the approach of death as relating to the dream at all. He had been thinking about marriage.

Considering this new perspective, Sharif replayed the dream in his mind, the interpretation making sense.

But who is getting the tidings of a good death? he had wondered. Sharif himself or Iman?

"Is the brother religious?" the imam asked.

Sharif grew quiet, his hands nestled in the pockets of his jacket, his gaze on the bare branches of the trees lining the parking lot of the masjid where Bilal was imam. "Allah knows best," Sharif said. "But he appears to be."

Bilal nodded. "Does he have a good reputation amongst the believers?"

Sharif had grown quiet again, thinking of the words of his mother after she discovered his meeting with Karim regarding Iman. "For the most part," Sharif responded, having no idea that in a matter of weeks even that fact would change.

"Then *inshaaAllah*, it means good. Tell your friend not to worry."

Saturday morning in early March, two weeks before his scheduled flight to Riyadh, the memory of the conversation with Imam Bilal came back to Sharif as he sat at the breakfast table next to Asma and across from Wali, their mother at the head. Asma's head was bowed, her eyes brimmed with tears, and Wali sat slouched in his chair, his face twisted and gaze distant as he toyed with a piece of food left on his plate. Nadirah's eyes were red and exhaustion was visible in her pained expression, the graying hair at her temples underscoring her melancholy.

"...so keep Iman and her family in your prayers," Nadirah said, having just shared with her family the stage three cancer diagnosis. "They opted not to do chemotherapy."

"Then what are they going to do?" Asma's eyes gleamed with tears as she lifted her gaze to her mother.

Nadirah drew in a deep breath. "They're looking at natural alternatives now."

"But..."

"Asma," Nadirah said, her voice rising slightly, making it clear that she did not want to discuss any more than she had to. "Right now, she just needs your prayers."

As Nadirah spoke, Sharif's thoughts had drifted to what the imam had said of the dream months before.

"Can we visit?"

The table grew quiet at Asma's question, and Sharif averted his gaze. It had been a question he was wondering himself, although he felt the urge to be near Karim more than he did Iman. He couldn't imagine what the brother must be going through.

Nadirah's eyes reflected sadness as she met her daughter's gaze, her expression softening in empathy. "I don't know," she said quietly, apology in her tone. "I don't know."

Hasna hesitated outside Iman's door Saturday morning, her hand raised in preparation to knock. Mona and Karim were asleep, but Hasna had been unable to rest since dawn, when she had heard her father leading prayer downstairs. The sound of his recitation had stirred something inside Hasna, but barely. Islam still seemed foreign to her, and she doubted her place in it. She had come to accept that the religion required much more than mere affirmation in the heart, but that's where her problems lay. She wondered if she had the wherewithal required to fulfill even the minimal requirements. Being consistent in her prayers was her biggest struggle.

Ironically, Hasna no longer wrestled with the concept of covering in Islamic garb. Wearing loose-fitting garments and a cloth on her head seemed a trivial concern in light of the tremendous burden that was now upon her with the life now budding in her womb. The simplicity of the act of covering was actually a mercy, Hasna realized. There was so much reward in something that was quite simple.

And there was so much distress in leaving this simple act.

Hasna wasn't so naïve as to imagine that wearing hijab would guarantee her spiritual health, but she was no longer under the assumption that she could obtain proper spirituality without it.

Obeying Allah, she realized, was to the soul as food was to the body. Eating one's daily food did not guarantee perfect health, but not having it at all certainly guaranteed the body's malnourishment — and ultimate degeneration.

It was like the concepts of life and death. Obedience ensured spiritual life. Disobedience ensured spiritual death.

Yet the health of spiritual life depended on the purity of the heart.

And Hasna's spiritual life was in dire need of nourishment and purification.

Hasna wanted to start over, to taste the sweetness of faith that she had heard righteous Muslims speak so fondly of, a sweetness that she herself nearly tasted before her heart was turned, eager for the affection of Vernon over the pleasure of Allah.

Currently, Hasna put an ear to her sister's door. She didn't want to wake Iman if she was sleeping. But Hasna heard the soft murmurs that she had minutes before. Lightly, she tapped the back of her knuckles on the door and waited. Iman didn't respond. Hasna knocked again, but there was still no response. Concerned, Hasna let herself in and found Iman sitting on the floor covered in white Islamic garb, her knees folded beneath her, and she was turning her head to the right then to the left, signifying the completion of prayer.

Iman turned to look over her shoulder, and she met Hasna's gaze.

"What prayer is that?" Hasna said, her brows furrowed. She glanced at the time. The clock read 8:36. She didn't know there was a morning prayer after *Fajr*.

"*Duhaa*," Iman said, placing a palm on the chair behind her to help her stand. Hasna resisted the urge to assist her sister. She knew Iman did not like to be treated like she was disabled.

When Iman stood fully, Hasna noticed how the prayer garment fell over Iman's frame. Iman had lost weight. Where she had once been slightly overweight, she was now slim though Iman did not appear malnourished. She was actually rather attractive, especially with her countenance glowing with spirituality.

"I thought *Dhuhr* didn't come in until afternoon," Hasna said.

"It doesn't. This was *Duhaa*, not *Dhuhr*."

Hasna grew quiet, her forehead creasing, slightly embarrassed at her ignorance. She had never heard of this prayer.

"*Duhaa* is a voluntary prayer." Iman pulled off the prayer garment, revealing the long, faded pink T-shirt that hung to her calves and frizzy hair that was pulled back by an elastic band into a bun. She hung the garment on the back of her desk chair that was facing the corner of the room toward which she had prayed.

"Is everything okay?" Iman asked as she walked to her bed. She lifted the bedcovers and shook them and fluffed the pillow against the sheets before sitting on the edge of her bed facing Hasna, a curious expression on her face.

Hasna remembered that she had entered Iman's room unexpectedly. "Yes, I just wanted to check on you."

Iman grinned, and Hasna sensed a tease would come. "Now *this* is new."

Hasna grinned herself, averting her gaze. "Yeah I know. I just…"

"I know," Iman said with a sigh, a smile lingering on her face as she waved her hand dismissively. "It's okay. I'm getting used to it. Everyone thinks if I'm left alone for too long I'll fall off the bed or something."

Hasna chuckled self-consciously. "Yeah, I guess you're right."

"I'm fine. Don't worry." Iman stood briefly to pull the covers back before climbing into bed. She pulled the comforter over her after she lay down.

"I'm just tired a lot," Iman said, settling her head on the pillow, facing her sister.

Hasna glanced at the open curtains, the morning sunlight spilling into the room making half of Iman's face glow. "You want me to close the curtains?"

"No," Iman said. "I like resting in the light."

"You can sleep like that?"

"Not really. But I'm not trying to sleep. I just want to rest."

Hasna nodded as an awkward silence followed. She didn't know what to say.

Iman shut her eyes, a smile on her face.

"What?" Hasna asked, smiling herself.

Iman opened her eyes partly, her smile widening. "You. You're still here. And I'm trying to rest."

Hasna laughed self-consciously. "Oh yeah. I'm sorry."

"It's okay," Iman said, still smiling. "I just find it funny."

"Why?"

"Because you usually don't like coming in here."

"Yeah, well…"

"It's okay. I'm enjoying the attention. I'll just have to think of all the things I want you to do if you're going to stand in attention at by bedside."

Hasna laughed. "I'm sorry. I'll go."

Iman's eyes closed again, her smile fading slightly.

Hasna studied her sister for a second, wanting to say something more, but she withheld. She had no idea how to put into words everything she wanted to say. But mostly, she wanted to say she was sorry and that she loved her. But that sounded too…mushy. She and Iman never spoke like that to each other.

Hasna headed to the door, her steps hesitant. She had no idea how much longer she had with Iman. She didn't want to procrastinate sharing what was on her heart. She had so much to apologize for, and she needed to make amends. She thought of what had happened with Sharif…

"Hasna?" Iman's voice sounded tired.

Hasna turned to look at her little sister, whose eyes were still closed. "Yes?"

"Don't worry about it."

Taken aback, Hasna gathered her eyebrows. "About what?"

"Everything."

Hasna bowed her head slightly in the beginning of a nod.

"I haven't been the best sister myself," Iman said. "So I hope you forgive me too."

Iman opened her eyes a bit, squinting in the sunlight, and she smiled. "But don't let it go to your head."

Humored, Hasna smiled. "Don't worry. It won't."

Pleased, Hasna turned to go.

"And Hasna?"

"Yes?" She turned to Iman, whose expression was now more serious, her eyes opened more fully now, though the sunlight made her blink.

"It's not as hard as you think."

Hasna lowered her gaze. She had been wondering how Iman was withstanding all the pain. She imagined that it was unbearable, and she wanted to ask if it hurt too much. But she didn't know how to form the words.

"Just ask Allah to forgive you," Iman said. "And He will."

It took a moment before Hasna realized that Iman hadn't been talking about her pain in enduring the illness, but Hasna's in enduring her sins.

"I really don't want them here during this time," Mona said that afternoon, where she sat on the edge of the bed, Karim standing opposite her with his hands in the pockets of his dress pants, his eyes distant in thought, the white T-shirt an awkward complement to the black pants he usually wore to work.

"It's hard enough as it is." Mona drew in a deep breath and exhaled. She was wearing a peach cotton *shawar kameez*. "I can barely function myself. I can't deal with company right now, and certainly not if Sharif is going to be with them."

Karim bit his lower lip, remaining quiet momentarily.

"I know, sweetheart," he said, exhaustion in his voice. "No one wants to be reminded of what happened, especially now. But we can't keep avoiding them forever."

"Karim, I know that. And I don't intend to. It's just that now..." She sighed. "...it's just too much to think about."

He lifted his gaze to look at his wife, his forehead creased. "But what about Iman? Don't you think she wants to see her friend?"

At that, Mona grew quiet, her eyes on the cloth of her pants. She hadn't thought of that. She was so focused on saving her daughter's life that she hadn't imagined that Iman needed company during this time.

"If Iman wants it..." she said, her voice hesitant, "then only Asma." She looked at her husband, her voice a plea. "But no one else, Karim, please."

"Why don't we ask Iman?"

Mona creased her forehead, offended. "For what? Isn't Asma the only person she needs to see?"

Karim shook his head. "I don't mean that. I'm saying in general. Maybe there are some things she wants to do, more than just seeing her friend."

"You're talking like she's already leaving us. I think it's best to just keep things as they are. Normalcy is most important. If we start asking her final wishes, then we've already given up."

"But that's my point, Mona." His eyes were concerned. "Where is her normalcy in the first place? She doesn't even have it. I don't think any of us do."

"What are you trying to say?"

"I'm saying we took that from her months ago."

Mona sighed, guilt weighing on her. "Then we should just let her talk to Asma."

"That's not good enough, Mona. We need normalcy ourselves."

She folded her arms and exhaled through her nose. "How are we going to get that, with all that's going on?"

"By at least trying to be a family again. We should let Nadirah visit, and we should visit her. You should continue homeschooling, and we should see if we can find a way for Iman to do that newsletter with—"

"No," Mona said. "That's out of the question."

"But why? She doesn't have to work with Sharif on it. She can just—"

"It'll bring back too many memories, Karim. I don't think she can handle that."

"Is it Iman that can't handle the memories, Mona, or you?"

Mona grew quiet, unsure how to respond. It was true that Mona didn't want to be reminded of all that had happened, and she certainly didn't want Iman to be subjected to the ordeal again, even if in recollection. But was it realistic to imagine that as possible?

"We should ask what she wants," Karim said. "Not because she may not be with us, but because she is right now."

"I'll have to think about it."

"Well," Karim said, his voice exhausted, "you think about it. In the meantime, I'm going to talk to her myself."

Mona stared at him, hurt. "That's not fair."

"Mona, look." Karim's voice was on the verge of frustration. "I'm not going to stop everything for you. If you have some things you need to work through, work through them. But I'm not going to let everyone else suffer because of it."

"That's not fair, Karim. I'm not causing any suffering."

He gathered his eyebrows. "But how do you know that?"

She started to speak but found she didn't know what to say. She fumbled for some defense. "Who am I causing to suffer?"

Karim sighed, meeting his wife's gaze before responding. "For one, yourself," he said.

He paused, apparently unsure if he should say what was on his mind. "And maybe Iman, too."

That evening, Iman sat sideways on the couch in the living room, her back supported by a pillow leaning against the armrest, her notebook perched on her bent knees as she scribbled her thoughts on the page.

"What are you doing?"

Iman glanced up to see her father standing several feet from her, his hands in his pockets, a distant smile on his face.

"Writing."

"Writing what?" He came closer.

Iman grew self-conscious, hoping he didn't want to see. She didn't like people reading her work before she had a chance to revise it.

"A poem." She set the pen on the page and shut the notebook.

Karim chuckled. "I guess it's not ready for reviewers, huh?"

She grinned, lifting the notebook close to her, the pen peeking out at the top. "Not yet."

"What's it about?"

"A lesson."

"Really? At school?"

"Yes, but..." Iman smiled, trying to find the words to describe what the girl in the poem was learning. "...it's not a normal lesson."

"Hmm," Karim nodded. "Sounds interesting. Is it okay if I read it once it's done?"

Iman nodded, hesitant. She wasn't sure she wanted to share the poem. It was too personal. "But I have to change some things first."

"It's okay," Karim said, smiling. "I understand."

He paused, his expression thoughtful. "You mind if I sit down?"

Iman immediately shook her head and started to turn her body so that she would be sitting normally on the couch.

"No, no," Karim said good-naturedly. "Don't move. I can just sit here."

He sat down a comfortable distance from where her bare feet lay flat on the couch, and Iman pulled her knees closer to herself so that her feet would not touch her father.

Iman grew concerned as her father's expression changed to one of reflection.

"Iman," Karim said, as if exhaling her name, his forehead creased, eyes distant. He placed his left hand on her foot as he spoke. "I wanted to ask you something."

She creased her forehead. "Okay."

Her father seemed uncertain how to express what was on his mind. Or perhaps he was just uncomfortable.

Iman dropped her gaze. She hated to see her father like this. It seemed that her cancer diagnosis made everyone so formal and guarded around her, as if a single slip of the tongue would hurt her in some irreversible way. But the truth was, it was more hurtful to see how hard everyone was trying to be polite. At times, these strained conversations were more difficult than the illness itself.

"I was thinking..." Karim said, glancing at her, a hint of a smile on his face. "...that maybe I should invite Asma to come over."

Iman immediately looked up as her eyes widened. She was unable to restrain the smile forming on her face. "Really?"

He nodded. "If you want."

"What time?" Iman glanced at the clock.

Karim laughed. "I'm not sure if she can come today."

"Can I call to see?"

Karim shrugged. "If you want."

Iman started to get up to reach for the phone.

"Just a second," he said, chuckling. "I wanted to ask something else too."

Iman sat back, her feet now resting on the carpeted floor, the notebook close to her chest as she was looking at her father. But her mind was on calling Asma. She missed her friend a great deal.

"Iman, is there...anything you want?"

She gathered her eyebrows. "You mean from the store?"

Karim shook his head. "No...well, if you want. But I was thinking in general. Like seeing Asma more often or....something like that."

Iman sensed what her father was getting at, but she glanced away, unsure how to respond. The question embarrassed her, much like the sudden formality, but she understood the relevance of the inquiry, and even its necessity. And there were in fact things she wanted, this she could not deny, even if she couldn't articulate them to her father. But most of them no human could offer even if she could find words to share them. And the most important had already been taken from her when the doctors removed her ovaries.

Yet the desire had only grown with the cementing of impossibility.

So much had changed in the past few months that Iman tried to keep from thinking of the dreams nestling in her mind, and heart. She had no idea what her life would be like from then on...or if she had much life left at all.

With her waning health, Iman's desires of the heart had waned as well, at least as they pertained to the transient world. It was tormenting to allow herself to want much of anything these days, and she tried to focus on the Hereafter. Perhaps, all she needed right then was spiritual preparation for death.

But that was her despondence speaking. Iman was human, and there were some things that simply would not leave her heart, no matter how short she imagined her life would be. It was true that Asma's friendship was one of them, and her writing too. But that was not all.

She still wanted children, and that hurt most.

And she wanted someone to love her like only a husband could.

On Eid day, when Iman had heard the rumor about Sharif wanting to marry her, after the initial shock, she could not quiet the flattery in her chest. She found it difficult to believe, and difficult to resist wanting to believe. She had even imagined, if it were true, then certainly her parents would at least consider the proposition and ask what she thought. After all, why wouldn't they?

But now she understood. Or at least she now understood that she would never understand.

And that was something she wasn't prepared to discuss with anyone, much less her parents. They were the ones who had obstructed the path before there was any chance for her to traverse it.

Throughout the ordeal, one thing had become clear to Iman. Worldly pursuits took precedence over marriage, which was half the religion. She learned too that, in her family, it was a sin punishable by immeasurable proportions to even *imagine* otherwise, let alone vocalize it, especially for a man.

Iman was young, but she wasn't so naïve as to imagine that a woman's education and career held no relevance in the discussion of marriage. But relevance was one matter, and making the two mutually exclusive was another entirely.

Couldn't her parents have suggested that Sharif come back in a few years? Or that they could marry on the condition that she finished school? Iman had heard of similar contracts. Why couldn't her parents have considered that?

It was hurtful that they hadn't even asked her feelings, even as Iman accepted that the final decision rested in their hands. But what was even more hurtful was having witnessed how Sharif himself was chastised for doing nothing other than what the religion instructed him to do: talk to the father. Even if his proposal were in fact practically or culturaly impossible, or repulsive even, couldn't her parents have simply said *no*?

It broke Iman's heart when she heard her mother rant about how "disgusting" it was for Sharif to ask to marry a "child." The words were so offensive that during these moments, Iman had to keep herself from resenting her mother. Was this a religious woman speaking? The same one who had taught Iman that Allah came first...in *everything*?

Even if her parents imagined that they were under no religious obligation to accept the proposal of a righteous Muslim man, did they imagine that they too were absolved of the responsibility to respect his honor? Or was his "disgusting" proposal license to tear into his flesh, ripping it from his very bones, and invite the whole city, Muslims and non-Muslims, to eat their brother's flesh?

And had they gotten what they wanted? Were they happy now? Sharif was no longer the imam, and the masjid was now locked, the parking lot ghostly vacant, and even *Jumu'ah* services were no longer held there.

Iman couldn't imagine the multitude of sins that would be upon her parents on the Day of Judgment. She feared that the magnitude of their transgressions against Sharif and the community would follow them even into the grave, as the closing of a masjid alone hurt not only the Muslims present in the community, but their progeny too.

For the first time in her life, Iman had felt ashamed to be part of her family. And she agonized daily over her family's souls. This stress inspired her to offer voluntary prayers, even in poor health. The cancer alone could not have given her the determination to pray as much as she had since she'd become weighed down by the sins of her parents. Daily, Iman prayed for the guidance of her mother and father, beseeching Allah for their forgiveness—

Especially after she overheard the mention of the recurrent dream Sharif had seen.

It was chilling, the realization that had gripped Iman at that moment, the details of the dream she'd just heard recounted playing over in her mind...

It wasn't that her parents imagined that Sharif's marriage to her was not sanctioned by Allah. *But they feared that it actually was.*

And they were doing everything in their power to frustrate something that they feared was already decreed.

"Mostly I want to see Asma," Iman said finally, her gaze averted. She hoped she wasn't being completely dishonest. "That's all I want for now."

Iman's father glanced at her. He looked like he wanted to say something more, doubt in his expression. But a second later, he smiled at her, a hand patting her foot.

"Okay then," he said. "Let's call Asma."

Twenty-five

The Lesson
By Umm Sumayyah

In the dark, she felt the moisture
As it slid down her brown cheeks
She tasted its salt brush her tongue
And at that moment, she felt...weak
It was a word she still hadn't grasped
But somehow it fit
At six, she didn't know much
But she had learned quite a bit

But there were words, words she liked
But didn't quite comprehend
Like hope, like dream, success and love,
The words she knew were...sin
She knew, 'cause when she said 'em
Momma grew real mad
And she could never say 'em again
But she'd wonder, why were they so bad?

But today she knew, she understood
For she'd said the words, eager, believing
But then a classmate stared and laughed
Then she quieted, understanding...retreating

For the rest of the week, Karim was restless in his concern for Iman, her health and her spirit. Although he and Mona had found a homeopathic doctor with a history of successfully treating cancer patients, the doctor had said that his treatments were most effective in cases of early diagnosis and that he had little experience treating ovarian cancer. He suggested that Karim and his wife reconsider chemotherapy for Iman and that thereafter he was willing to work with them in revitalizing Iman's body after treatment.

Mona had told the doctor that they wished for him to treat Iman anyway, even if the chances of successful treatment were slim. But the doctor declined although he expressed his deepest sympathies to them. However, he told them they were free to purchase his products and take some treatment manuals for free.

Karim and Mona had come home from the office with two bags full of herbs and natural tablets and a stack of books. Mona abandoned her homeschooling schedule to read every line. Periodically, she boiled the dried leaves and twigs and sweetened the darkened liquid with honey before serving it to Iman. Mona also had Iman taking the tablets regularly, and she would stress if Iman fell asleep before taking her dose.

After returning home from work, Karim watched the often tense exchanges between his wife and daughter as if from a distance. His heart hurt to see his wife in agony and his daughter in frustration, and he felt powerless to help either of them. He wanted to believe that Iman would recover and stay with them for many years to come, but the memory of his mother haunted him, leaving him with little hope. He knew the power of prayer, and he prayed daily for Iman's recovery. But a shred of doubt sat in the back of his mind, and he could not remove it. He knew it was incorrect to pray while harboring doubt, but he felt powerless to overcome it. He feared that his own sins were blocking the acceptance of his supplications.

There too was that dejected resignation that he saw in Iman's eyes. It was as if she did not want to be healed, and merely sat reflecting on when and how it would come upon her. Her eyes lit up only when Asma visited or when she and Asma spoke on the phone, and part of Karim felt jealous of Iman's friend. Why couldn't he or Mona inspire the same elation, or at least something similar?

There was something weighing heavily on his daughter, Karim could tell, and he found it difficult to shake the feeling that it had something to do with what had transpired at the end of the previous year. So much had been left unsaid at the time, and he wondered if it was a topic he should revisit. But how could he broach the subject? In what context could he bring it up? It was out of the question to mention anything in his wife's presence, but there was rarely a moment that he and Iman were home alone.

Or perhaps this was just the excuse he was giving himself. Perhaps he didn't want to face the issues at all, as part of him already knew what was tugging at his daughter's heart.

Because it was tugging at his too.

But Karim couldn't imagine mentioning his own dream, especially in the presence Sharif, whom Karim had dismissed for having one himself. Besides, under the circumstances, what could he possibly say to Sharif?

It would be cliché for Karim to say he would give anything to make things better for Iman, but it was true. He really would. But that was the irony. Why was he willing only now to offer what his daughter wanted, when she couldn't fully benefit from it?

In November, Karim and Mona had been making frivolous plans for Iman's future, for homeschooling, for the college she'd attend, for the life they wanted for her... They had never imagined that she did not have much of a future left.

Yet, even if she had possessed what they imagined to be a "normal future" ahead of her, what had they been so afraid of?

This was the question that confounded Karim.

Were they terrified that she wouldn't finish school "on time"? That she wouldn't go to college? That she would have children while young?

But none of these concerns were directly related to marrying Sharif himself.

Then there was another issue grating at Karim's conscience. Sharif had not even proposed, nor had Karim given him opportunity to. The prospect itself had been unimaginable.

But why?

That's what Karim could not answer fully. Was it the American cultural taboo attached to a girl marrying young? Or was it pride that made Karim and his wife react so indignantly? And for what? What had they gained from the ordeal?

Except a tremendous burden to carry with them throughout life — and on the Day of Judgment.

And a daughter dying of heartache more than she was from cancer.

Early Thursday afternoon, Hasna shivered from where she sat on the cold bathroom floor, her head bowed in front of the open toilet seat. Her hands, like claws, grasped the edges of the commode the tips of her fingers growing pale in the grip as her knees pressed uncomfortably against the tiled floor. Her abdomen heaved again and she lifted her body, beads of sweat forming on her forehead as the bile released itself from her stomach, its bitter taste grating her tongue before spilling into the already sullied water from her vomiting of moments before.

The growling that escaped from her throat was pitiful, and, powerless, Hasna could not quiet the feral outburst. Dropping back to her knees, her heart raced and her teeth chattered. Eyes watering, she coughed as remains of the bitter, warm liquid stuck to the back of her tongue.

Hasna struggled to catch her breath. There was a painful soreness in her stomach muscles as her chest heaved, Hasna's heart rate slowing to normal. She lifted her chin to spit into the toilet before weakly reaching to pull down the metal handle. The sudden rush of water in the bowl created a whirlpool of stench before sucking the soiled water down the drain. The foul smell of vomit lingered in the bathroom as Hasna sank back to the floor, relieved and drained at once.

She rolled herself against the toilet, her back against the ceramic glass and her head hung as if in submission as she fought the tears stinging her eyes. Hasna's bare legs were crossed in front of her, the night tee that she still wore bunched up at her thighs. Hasna wiped her forehead with the back of her hand, her head growing heavy with the motion.

Overcome with the unbearable sickness of pregnancy that lasted day and night, Hasna had been unable to report to work the entire week. Vernon had called her cell phone several times each day, but she did not pick up. It wasn't that Hasna was intentionally avoiding him, but she simply had no energy to speak. She had lain in bed hearing the ringing as if from a distant place, wishing only that the annoying sound would cease. On the third day, Hasna shut off her phone, unable to stand the sound. Each shrill of her mobile incited a ringing in her head that throttled into a migraine. Head pounding, Hasna would throw an arm over her head and shut her eyes, imagining that her boss was wondering where she was, but her depraved state made her only vaguely concerned.

Hasna had read books that discussed the morning sickness of gestating women, but she had imagined the sickness as a brief nausea that passed with the rising of the sun. She had been completely unprepared for the continuous cramping of her abdomen that seemed to stretch and pull throughout the day. And the nausea *never* left. She was throwing up at least three times each day. The slightest smell made her stomach churn, even if the scent of perfume or scented lotion or food. The mere thought of eating distressed her, and she had not the slightest inclination to bring even a cracker to her mouth, although pale tasteless crackers were all she could keep down.

Gradually, Hasna's strength returned as she sat on the bathroom floor. But she couldn't muster the energy to stand and return to her room, her limbs still recovering. She could hear movement in the hall and the pattering of feet as Adam ran throughout the house. But the life beyond the wooden door did not belong to her. And she had no desire to bridge the distance.

Hasna had told no one of the pregnancy, and she did not plan to. Time itself would reveal her sin as her belly began to protrude, but until then Hasna would do all she could to hold onto the little dignity she had left. Given all that was upon her parents right then, she imagined that it would be cruelly unjust to reveal what she was carrying in her womb. Her family simply could not shoulder this burden.

Hasna exhaled, her eyes resting on the house slippers that sat perched on the floor in front of the sink, a familiar sign that she associated with home. *Was it better to leave?* Should she announce, of a sudden, a desire to travel somewhere, and then find shelter until she could gather her bearings and deliver the child in solitude?

How then could she return home with a life in her arms?

Or should she give up the child for adoption, entrusting the newborn to faceless parents willing and able to care for the child?

But was it ethical to leave her family when Iman's life was withering with each passing day?

Was it *fair*?

Hasna's leaving would be sure to create bewilderment. Yet her staying would be an added stress.

Either way, she would be exacerbating an already burdensome reality in her home.

But what of her own burden that she carried in her womb?

And what of the even weightier one that she carried in her soul? Could leaving possibly remove that burden from her breast?

"Spiritual toxins," Earl had replied to Sharif, an amused expression on his face as he lay on his back in the Makkah hotel suite he was sharing with Sharif and Professor Mashal. Earl's hands were clasped behind his head, and Sharif could make out the features of his classmate's freckled face and the red color of his hair in the dim light of the lamp that glowed on the night stand between the beds.

Sharif was sitting on the edge of his disheveled bed, stuffing his belongings into his carry-on in preparation for their return to Riyadh late that night. Mashal was out meeting with an old friend of his in the city while Sharif and Earl tidied the room, where Mashal had favored a floor mat for sleeping because there were only two beds. Both first year students at the Islamic university, Sharif and Earl had traveled with Mashal to 'Umrah then traveled to Madinah by car and returned to Makkah hours before.

Curious and wishing to pass time as he packed, Sharif had asked Earl what had first sparked his interest in Islam.

Sharif paused his packing and looked at his classmate, brows furrowed. "What?"

Earl chuckled, and he turned his face toward Sharif, a grin still on his face. "I'm serious. That's what made me study Islam."

Sharif retained his confused expression. He didn't know how to form the question in his mind.

"You never heard of spiritual toxins, man?"

"I've heard of *toxins*..." Sharif said.

"But physical ones, right?"

Sharif moved his head forward in a nod. "Yes..."

Earl swung his feet to the carpeted floor, sitting up to face Sharif. A grin still lingered on Earl's face as his expression grew more serious. "I was always sick as a kid, you know? And my parents had no idea what was wrong. At school I was always in special ed classes." He chuckled, but Sharif could tell it was due more to embarrassment than humor. "But it wasn't because I was stupid or anything. My teachers just didn't know how to deal with me."

Sharif listened, perplexed, the question still in his mind. He had no idea why Earl was telling him all of this. But he sensed that he shouldn't interrupt. It was apparent that Earl saw this information as relevant to his acceptance of Islam as a teen. Or that Earl simply wanted to talk.

"I had this problem, you know..." Earl's eyes grew distant as he thought of something, growing quiet momentarily.

Finally, he shrugged, apparently deciding against saying too much more. "Well, they finally diagnosed me with Tourette Syndrome."

Sharif creased his forehead more. He had never heard of the disease.

"You heard of it?"

"No, I don't think so."

"Well..." Earl said, the embarrassed grin returning, trying to find the best way to explain. "It makes you do things..."

Sharif was quiet momentarily. "Like what?"

"It's different for different people, but for me it was head jerking and screaming. I'd also curse a lot."

Sharif smiled, humored. "Man, I don't think cursing a lot is a disease."

Earl coughed laughter. "No, I mean I did it without intending to."

He shrugged. "And sometimes I'd even hit myself over and over."

Sharif didn't know what to say. "They say this is caused by spiritual toxins?"

Earl shook his head. "No, but that's what I found out it was."

"But how?"

"When I was in middle school, it got so bad that my parents were going to put me into an asylum."

"Are you serious?"

"Yeah, man, it was crazy." Earl shook his head. "But I wasn't doing it on purpose. I just couldn't stop."

"Did it make you sick too?"

"No, I don't think so... But I always had really bad skin rashes and headaches. I'm not sure if that had anything to do with Tourette though."

Sharif regarded Earl momentarily, as if seeing him for the first time. "This...Tourette Syndrome, you don't have it anymore?"

Earl shook his head. "It turns out I didn't have it in the first place."

Before Sharif could ask, Earl explained. "A Muslim psychiatrist— Well, we didn't know he was Muslim at the time, but he was the doctor my parents were referred to. Anyway, he was known for using diet regiments, exercise programs, and sound therapy to treat patients, and he had a pretty good reputation amongst doctors."

"He's the one who told you about spiritual toxins."

"Yes." Earl laughed. "And that saved my life."

He shook his head. "It turns out that I just needed to cleanse my system. Physically and spiritually."

"But how?"

"A strict diet and sound therapy."

"But... how?"

"Black seed, Zam Zam water, and Qur'an."

Taken aback, Sharif's eyes widened as a smile formed on one side of his mouth. "Are you serious?"

"Yeah, man. Can you believe it? All that time, and all I needed was *ruqyah*."

At Earl's last word, Sharif drew his eyebrows together. "All you needed was what?"

"*Ruqyah*," Earl repeated, looking at Sharif with his eyes squinted in confusion. He was apparently surprised that Sharif hadn't heard of the natural treatment method.

"You never heard of *ruqyah*?" Earl asked.

Sharif shook his head. "I can't say I have."

"It's Qur'anic medicine."

He just looked at Earl, blinking.

"Using the Qur'an as medicine. It's used for healing."

Oh. This was the first time Sharif ever heard of such a thing.

"But how do you do that?"

Earl shrugged. "I'm not sure all the ways it's done, but the psychiatrist recited Qur'an over me and had me drink Zam Zam and water he recited over."

Sharif was stunned. *"Psychiatrists* do that?"

Earl shook his head. "No, not normally, but he did."

"In *America*?"

Earl laughed. "I know. It shocked me too. But it turns out that diet changes, de-stressing programs, and sound therapy are typical methods used by doctors treating depression or psychological problems."

"Yeah, I know," Sharif said. "But I never knew they used Qur'an too."

"Like I said, most don't. Most just use music therapy or something like that."

"Music therapy?"

Earl chuckled. "That's what I thought when I first heard of it. But music and natural sounds like the ocean are actually used to heal psychiatric patients." He shrugged. "They use drugs too most times. But my doctor didn't."

Sharif didn't know what to say, and silence filled the space between them for several minutes.

"Qur'anic medicine," Sharif said aloud, shaking his head.

"You should ask Dr. Mashal about it," Earl suggested. "They use it a lot in Muslim countries."

"You think they use it here?"

"In Saudi Arabia? Yeah, why not? That's where my doctor learned it."

"He's Arab?"

"No, he's American. But his parents worked in Jeddah when he was growing up."

Earl squinted his eyes as he thought of something. "It's really sad how many diseases are not even medical problems, or even psychiatric ones." There was sadness in his eyes. "And so many patients just die or get locked up in psych wards because the doctors can't do anything for them."

They were quiet for some time.

"You don't think Tourette Syndrome is a real psychological problem?"

Earl shrugged. "It could be. But in my case it wasn't. Just like a lot of people with so-called medical problems just need *ruqyah*."

"Like what?"

"Cancer for one."

Sharif's eyebrows rose in surprise. "You don't think cancer is a medical problem?"

"Of course it is," Earl said. "But a lot of cancer patients just need natural treatments like *ruqyah*."

"You think it would work for something like cancer?"

"Sure I do."

Earl added, "It's the Qur'an. It heals anything."

In the quiet of his room Saturday afternoon, days before his scheduled flight to Riyadh, Sharif thought of his conversation with Earl, his thoughts on Iman's failed natural treatments. He wondered if *ruqyah* might work for her.

Sharif rolled the last of his clothes into the luggage bag and patted down the contents before pulling the zipper closed. Because he had not fully unpacked after returning to America in August, packing had not taken long, and he hadn't acquired much since he arrived.

And he hadn't accomplished much either.

Except for the strained relationship between him and his mother and the crumbling of a Muslim community founded more than twenty years before, Sharif had little to show for the seven months he had been home. Six years of study abroad and a strained then broken engagement to a childhood friend. Senseless sacrifices, they seemed right then.

Sharif wished things could be different. But he had no power to shift the irrevocable movements in the world in which he lived, even those set in motion by his own hands.

Fortunately, his mother's fury had mellowed, but it had quieted only to give way to a solemn silence that inspired only obligatory cordiality between them. Sharif saw the disappointment on her countenance each time she saw him, and it was as if his mother aged years in a matter of months.

As had been the case more than six years ago, it was for his mother's sake that Sharif was leaving America again. But years ago, Nadirah had been reluctant to see her oldest son go. Now Sharif imagined that she was counting the days until she could regain some semblance of peace without ghosts of the months before reminding her of all she had lost in a son.

Sharif glanced at the clock. It was two forty-five. In fifteen minutes he was to meet Karim.

Late Friday morning, as Sharif was getting dressed in preparation to take the Metrorail to *Jumu'ah* more than forty minutes away from his home, Karim had called asking if they could talk.

Hearing the brother's voice alone incited anxiety for Sharif. Sharif had so many mixed feelings surrounding his now strained relationship with Karim that he was unsure how to respond to the request. Of course, Sharif could not refuse; it was not an option. Karim had been like a father to him, and the time of refusing a father's request was part of a distant past life.

When the doorbell rang at two fifty-eight Saturday afternoon, Sharif was already in the living room wearing his jacket in preparation to go. He had been waiting on the couch, his thoughts straying to his mother who had been in her room most of the day. There was so much Sharif wanted to say to her, but he could not find the proper moment or words. He wanted more than anything to just embrace her, or have her embrace him. He wished she would tease him for ruining her hardwood floors with his cars. He wished she would laugh about his putting shaving cream on her dessert. He wished she would become frustrated with him, anything. But the cold silence he couldn't bear. It hurt too much.

"*As-salaamu'alaikum*," Karim greeted when Sharif opened the door. Karim's countenance revealed a deep affection for Sharif that hadn't been altered with time or circumstance. The familiar creases next to his dark eyes reminded Sharif of a world in which

345

he had once been part, and how much he had taken for granted in years past.

It was funny how a single moment could destroy decades of bonds, even those cultivated before one was born. What had Sharif been thinking when he imagined he could share in reality what had transpired in his sleep? Did he think Karim could look at the vision objectively, even though it was his daughter being discussed, and implied?

Sharif returned the greeting as he stepped outside, the early March air cool as a breeze massaged his face.

"You mind if we take a walk?" Karim asked.

Sharif shook his head. "That's fine."

They walked in silence for several minutes before Karim spoke. "How is everything?"

Sharif was quiet momentarily. He was unsure how to respond, in that moment reminded of Jafar's terse remark to Sharif's asking, *"How are you, man? I mean, really?"*

"*Alhamdulillaah,*" Sharif said finally, his tone suggesting a contentment that did not exist in his heart.

"How is your family?"

Sharif nodded cordially. The questions were more for Karim's peace of mind than to ascertain Sharif's. But that didn't bother him. It was to be expected. "They're good, *alhamdulillaah.*"

There was a brief pause and Sharif realized that it was proper etiquette to ask the same of Karim. "How is your family?"

Karim sighed, revealing anxiety in just that sound. "Just pray for us, Sharif. We need the prayers."

Sharif didn't know what to say. He lightly kicked a rock from the sidewalk, pushing his hands into the pockets of his jacket in the motion. "I do," he said honestly. "Every day."

"I appreciate that." Karim's voice was sincere but distant, and Sharif wondered what was on his mind.

Karim drew in a deep breath and exhaled, and Sharif sensed that Karim was trying to find the words to say something to Sharif.

"You know," Karim said, his voice thoughtful. "I've been thinking a lot about all that's happened since November."

Sharif listened, unable to temper the dread knotting in his stomach. He lifted his gaze to some children playing with a dog yards away, shouting commands in Spanish.

"And I know it can't change what's happened. But I wanted you to know that I'm deeply sorry for all you went through."

"*Deja de hacer eso!*" Sharif heard someone shout playfully as he and Karim neared.

"We never expected…" Karim sighed, and Sharif sensed this conversation would be difficult for them both. "I just…"

The dog barked as Karim and Sharif approached the sidewalk in front of the yard, but it was quickly distracted when a girl threw a stick and called out something.

"We're sorry, Sharif. We really are."

Sharif drew in a deep breath himself. He wanted to say something, but the words would not come. Besides, he had no idea what he should say, or could say even. It would be dishonest to say *It's all right* because it wasn't. It wasn't all right. Nothing seemed right right then.

They walked in silence for several minutes as Karim seemed lost in thought, Sharif distracted by his.

"I am too," Sharif said finally, his gaze lifting to the sky momentarily as he exhaled the words.

Next to him, Karim shook his head. "You have no reason to be sorry."

"I shouldn't have sh—"

"No," Karim interjected. "You did the right thing. My wife and I are the ones who were wrong."

A thoughtful silence followed. A car passed, its music pounding disruptively.

"It wasn't fair to you," Karim said, his tone regretful. "Or Iman."

At the mention of Karim's daughter, Sharif lowered his gaze. He felt ashamed for having imagined the dream could mean what he had thought. He wished he had talked to Imam Bilal before he spoke to Karim. Then things would have turned out differently.

But Sharif had prayed *Istikhaarah*. He shouldn't regret what he had done.

Everything that's supposed to happen will happen, Sharif remembered his father saying once, *even if things don't happen the way they're supposed to.*

Sharif had been perplexed at his father's words. But now the words returned to him, and they seemed apt right then.

Perhaps, everything would ultimately turn out for the better, Sharif considered, although he couldn't fathom how this could be.

"I'm worried about Iman." Karim spoke as if confiding in a friend.

Sharif felt awkward.

"How is she?" he asked, unsure if he had place to express concern.

Karim sighed. "She's managing. *Alhamdulillaah.*"

"What about the natural treatments?" Sharif asked, wondering if *ruqyah* would have been a better option. "Are they helping?"

"We don't know yet. Right now, we're just doing all we can."

Sharif nodded, recalling just then a day that he and Hasna were babysitting Wali, Asma, and Iman. Iman had come to them running, tears glistening in her eyes. *"Mommy made me a boy!"* Seeing her shaved head, Sharif had laughed, sending Hasna into hysterics too.

"Let us know if there's anything we can do," Sharif said sincerely. "We'd love to help."

Karim had grown quiet at Sharif's words, and Sharif sensed he had said something inappropriate.

"Sharif," Karim said seconds later, his mind clearly on something else, his tone serious. He glanced at Sharif. "There is something that could help."

Sharif met Karim's gaze, his forehead creased.

Karim looked away. "But it may be too much to ask…"

"We'll do whatever we can. You're like family to us."

Karim's gaze grew thoughtful. "This is something only you can do."

Taken aback, Sharif gathered eyebrows. *"Me?"*

"Yes, but you don't have to tell me now. I know you have a lot on your mind…" Karim's voice trailed. "…given all that's happened."

Sharif listened, a question on his face.

"I've been thinking a lot about that dream you had." Karim's eyes narrowed in deep thought, and Sharif could tell something was on Karim's mind that he was not saying. "And I just want to retract what we said to you."

Confusion lingered on Sharif's face. "What do you mean?"

"I mean it's up to you."

Sharif started to speak. It took him a moment to comprehend.

"I know now," Karim said, exhaling the words, "things are different. But I know it would mean a lot to Iman if—"

Sharif looked away, his heart pounding.

"—she could have this opportunity before…" Karim's voice trailed, and Sharif's heart ached as he heard the pain in a father's voice.

"…as she's going through this," he corrected himself.

Sharif couldn't look at Karim. It was so unexpected. Sharif struggled to gather his thoughts, and there was a strained silence between them. He didn't know how to feel about this…offer.

"We don't ask for anything except your company," Karim continued, the plea in his voice tearing at Sharif's heart. "That's all she would need."

The reality of the proposition created a vast space between them. But it somehow bonded them more than years before. The compassion Sharif felt for Karim right then made him weak, sadness burning the back of his throat.

"But I'm leaving."

It was the only intelligible response that Sharif could think of. But it sounded befuddled, distressed even, and Sharif hated himself for that.

Karim looked shocked. He turned to Sharif, his eyebrows drawn together. "Where are you going?"

Sharif met his gaze. "You don't know?"

Karim just stared at him, oblivious.

How would Karim know? Sharif realized just then. Even though Nadirah was back in touch with Mona, it was unlikely that Sharif would be mentioned. It would be too painful for them both.

"I'm leaving for Riyadh in a few days."

The creases in Karim's forehead became more defined. "*Riyadh?*"

"Yes," Sharif said, his heart sinking in sadness, realizing how tormenting this news would be for Karim. "On Tuesday."

"*This* Tuesday?"

Sharif nodded, looking away from Karim just then. "Yes, *inshaaAllah*."

"For what?" Karim seemed genuinely confounded, and troubled.

"My mother—" Sharif stopped himself. He shouldn't share too much.

"I have a job there and…." Sharif drew in a deep breath as he searched for the right words.

How could he explain this all to Karim? He had had no idea what was on Karim's heart. Had he known, then perhaps things could have turned out differently…

Sharif exhaled, unsure how to complete his thought, the realization of its necessity hurting more than the revelation itself.

"…I'm getting married."

The air seemed to shift, and for a moment even the neighborhood grew quiet, halting at the news. Sharif felt anxiety burning in his chest, and he could not look at Karim, even as his peripheral vision registered more than he wanted to see.

Karim's expression was pained, his eyes shifting in confusion. He shook his head slightly in astonishment, finding great difficulty digesting this information.

"But…" the sound escaped Karim's throat, and its irrationality made Sharif self-conscious at being a witness to Karim's utter desperation.

Sharif wanted to speak, to say something to make up for the news he had just shared. But he could think of nothing, nothing to lighten the blow. Karim had reached out to him, sacrificing his dignity and pride. Sharif saw in Karim's eyes the distressed father of a dying child, his love for his daughter inspiring the frantic fulfillment of a final wish.

Sharif wanted more than anything to make some concession, some compromise. But, rationally, he could not. He was to marry Hisham's daughter the Friday after he arrived in Riyadh. And knowledge of this impending marriage had been the only thing that brought peace to Sharif's heart in the last month.

But even if Iman hadn't fallen sick, Sharif's desire to marry her (if it could be called *desire* at all) had dissipated when the rumors had spread about an illicit relationship. Marrying Iman had been only an idea, a possibility that had traced the contours of his mind, but it hadn't had time or opportunity to find place in his heart. The idea itself had been incited merely by an enigmatic vision that had been repeated in his sleep.

The compassion he felt for Iman was like that toward a baby sister, and as such was ineffaceable. Iman had been a part of his life since she was a child, and for that, she would always hold a place in his heart. But it was Hasna whom Sharif had grown to love, despite their having grown irreparably apart.

Yet the thought of Iman suffering from a cancer literally eating away at her young body tormented Sharif day and night.

Now the idea that she was suffering from another pain, one that was heartfelt, was even more unbearable to him. The news of this final wish was so agonizing to Sharif that his legs weakened, and he felt the need to sit.

"I..." Karim stammered "...had no idea. I'm sorry."

"It's okay," Sharif said, his calmness betraying the anguish erupting in his breast.

"Well," Karim said, forcing a chuckle, a tinge of regret and jealousy in that sound, "congratulations."

He regarded Sharif, his smiling eyes thinly veiling his tormented expression. "Who's the lucky girl?"

"A daughter of a friend," Sharif said quietly, conscious of the uncanny parallels to what Iman and Karim had been to him. "She lives in Riyadh."

"She's Arab?"

Sharif nodded, unable to look Karim in the eye, his mind wandering to a suffering Iman. "Yes."

Karim grasped Sharif's shoulder, a tight smile forming a line on his face. "Good for you," he said. "You deserve that."

The sincerity of Karim's words cut Sharif deep, and he wished they hadn't walked far from his home. He wanted the solitude of his room.

Good for you. You deserve that.

Because Sharif knew that Karim was really talking to himself, not to Sharif, right then.

Twenty-six

The Hearts We Lost
By Umm Sumayyah

The hearts we lost
Where do they wander?
The hearts emanating Islam's beauty.
Falling in submission
Split asunder

Sometimes I search for them,
But often I give in

For where is the love that filled the hearts
Of Abu Bakr, of 'Umar,
And 'Uthmaan?
Where is the love that filled the hearts
Of the people of Tawheed
The people of emaan?

Who, when Allah revealed a verse,
Tore from their very clothes
And broke the vessels
In their hands

Their faith was not a feeling in the breast
It was the blood in their veins,
The muscles in their limbs
The hearts in their chests

The hearts we lost, O Allah!
Where do they wander?
Sometimes I search for them,
But often I give in

Yet they must be there,
O Allah, I implore You, they must be!
Perhaps it is my eyes that are blind
When I look within

O Allah! Lift the veil from my vision
The stains from my heart
The doubt from my breast
And tell me, O Allah

Will I pass this test?

O Allah! Why does my heart wander,
Why do I stray?

Why does my Islam not move me
To bow down
To submit?

Have we lost our emaan,
Is that it?

O ever-changing soul!
Submit with grace
For you shall gain the Pleasure of Allah,
And see His Face

O restless heart!
The Rope is before you
So take hold!
And take heed,
O lost one
And
Behold!

Before He takes your soul

"This woman..." Nadirah said, and Sharif knew his mother was speaking of Yasmin.

It was early Tuesday morning and the darkness of night had not yet retreated fully for dawn. The taxi that would take Sharif to the airport sat idling outside, its engine a soft hum through the closed screen door, a divider between the front door and the cool night air. Sharif stood with his hand on the handle of the front door he had opened seconds before, the lights of the hired car glowing in the quiet darkness of morning, a loud whisper in the driveway of their home.

Sharif had said his goodbyes to Wali and Asma the night before, but before retreating to his room, he couldn't muster the nerve to lift his hand to knock upon his mother's bedroom door. Perhaps it was better this way, he had thought. He could disappear from her life, and it would be as if he were never there.

But minutes before, the sound of heavy bags being shuffled out the house as Sharif took two trips to load the taxi had awakened his mother. He heard the sound of her door opening as he lifted his carry-on, his final piece of luggage in the house, to place the strap over his shoulder. He could have slipped away right then, but it was hope that halted his exit even as he had already pulled the door open in preparation to leave.

Seconds later Nadirah appeared, pulling closed the faded floral silk robe she wore, blinking sleepy eyes at her son. The braids of her hair were disheveled from a night's rest and her expression registered confusion as if she had no idea where Sharif was going this time of night.

But Sharif knew that she knew where he was going, and that she knew that they both knew.

For Nadirah had, three months before, insisted that he leave.

May Allah remove you far from me, she had prayed.

And now Nadirah had come from her room to see him off.

But hers was a goodbye spoken in code, her words *"This woman..."* a truce, an expression of love, of concern. Though disapproval was written in her eyes.

"...the one you plan to marry."

His mother's eyes lingered on him long enough for Sharif to see the exhaustion there, and the apology. "Do you love her?"

Sharif looked away. He was unable to conceal his heart from the woman who had carried him in her womb, and had watched him crawl. She had seen him stumble and fall until he could walk like a man, even when his breast concealed only a boy's heart.

He wondered if she were trying to hold his hand right then, to keep him from faltering, to keep him steady, so he could walk upright, her hand grasped to his, a mother's support.

No. He did not love Hisham's daughter. He could not lie.

Love had never entered his mind.

Ashamed, Sharif did not speak these truths aloud. But his mother read them in his averted gaze. He looked toward the taxi waiting outside.

"Go." His mother's voice was soft as she gave her blessing, though it was tempered by a sadness Sharif felt in his chest.

He could not lift his eyes to his mother. He couldn't face the disappointment he would find there.

But he knew that part of her discontent was because she blamed herself. Yet that didn't ease the pain Sharif felt in his breast right then. It only made it more pronounced.

"May Allah be with you," she said.

Sharif had to resist the urge to go to her right then, to embrace her. He wanted the comfort of his mother's arms.

"But son," she said, her voice quiet yet rising in an authority that reached Sharif's heart. "Don't think that you can just use some woman to repair your life—" She issued her warning in as even a tone as she could muster, her displeasure with his decision potent right then. "—and it's not going to matter to her."

Outside the driver's side door of the taxi opened and a dark-haired man stood, an impatient look on his face as he saw Sharif standing behind the screen. But Sharif's mind was on his mother's words.

"Women don't take this issue of love lightly," she said, her tone as if portending a disaster that awaited him.

I'm not using her though, Sharif said to himself. But he caught the insincerity in his tone, even as the words did not pass his lips. But he had never thought of his motives in that way.

"Especially an Arab girl marrying an American man. When an American chooses to marry them, they think it's because he actually cares for them a great deal."

Sharif looked at his mother then, regret and sadness in that glance, his expression reflecting the emotions in his mother's sober eyes.

"Not because he lost all hope in marrying his own."

The Hearts

"Whoever possesses three qualities will have the sweetness of faith:
Allah and His Messenger are dearer to him than anything else; he
loves a person and loves him only for Allah's sake; and he hates to revert
to disbelief as he hates to be thrown into the fire."
—Prophet Muhammad, peace be upon him (Bukhari)

Twenty-seven

*"Verily the creation of each one of you is brought together in his
mother's womb for forty days in the form of a seed, then he is a clot of
blood for a like period, then a morsel of flesh for a like period. Then there
is sent to him the angel who blows the breath of life into him and who is
commanded about four matters: to write down his means of livelihood,
his life span, his actions, and whether happy or unhappy.*

*By Allah, other than Whom there is no god, verily one of you behaves
like the people of Paradise until there is but an arm's length between him
and it, and that which has been written over takes him and so he behaves
like the people of Hell-fire and thus he enters it; and one of you behaves
like the people of Hell-fire until there is but an arm's length between him
and it, and that which has been written over takes him and so he behaves
like the people of Paradise and thus he enters it."*
—Prophet Muhammad (peace be upon him)
(Bukhari and Muslim)

Hasna stood in Wal-Mart in front of a rack of maternity wear
early Tuesday afternoon in late July, her swollen belly of nearly
six months protruding beneath the long-sleeve T-shirt she wore
with an elastic waist floral skirt. A small, thin white scarf was
wrapped neatly about her head, and a blue scarf pin held the scarf
in place at the side of her head.

Iman had helped Hasna wrap the *khimaar* before she left, and
today was Hasna's first day to venture outside while wearing the
Islamic headdress. The experience was awkward for Hasna
because she felt so self-conscious and imagined that everyone was
staring at her. But when she glanced about her in nervousness,
she found that no one was even looking in her direction.

When Hasna had first pulled into the sparsely filled parking lot
and turned her car into a space close to the doors, she felt the urge
to put the car in reverse and return home. She was terrified for
anyone to see her in the Islamic dress. What if someone thought

she was a terrorist? What if someone scorned her when she passed?

Would they even serve her at the checkout?

In her rearview mirror, Hasna had seen a woman dressed in an Indian sari pushing a baby stroller toward the Wal-Mart entrance. Hasna had turned in her seat to see the woman, amazed that the woman strode toward the store as if her presence were the most natural thing in the world.

The sight shocked and emboldened Hasna, and she relaxed somewhat, telling herself that she was just being paranoid. Suburban Maryland was a multi-ethnic region. No one was likely to even notice her.

At that moment, Hasna had felt remarkable admiration for her little sister. A year before, Hasna had regarded Iman's decision to cover so fully as exceedingly stupid and extreme. Now, as she sat in her car with a pounding heart slowing to a normal pace, she believed Iman's choice to be remarkably brave and commendable.

When Iman had first decided to wear the all-black *jilbaab*, Hasna was disgusted, and she refused to be seen in public with her sister. But now she wondered how Iman did it at all when Hasna couldn't even muster enough courage to open the door of her car and walk into a discount store. And she was wearing nothing as off-putting as Iman's preferred dress would appear to people.

Hasna had made the decision to wear hijab in mid-May after resigning from her job a week after Iman's doctors officially stopped the chemotherapy treatment to which her parents had finally consented. The doctors' decision was due to repeated complications with Iman's health. However, Hasna's decision to cover properly had not culminated into reality until today, when Iman suggested that Hasna simply go to Wal-Mart to test the waters of her comfort in Islamic garb.

The topic had come up when Hasna had mentioned casually that she needed new clothes, as her other ones no longer fit. It was no longer a secret that she was expecting, as her parents had discovered the pregnancy almost a month before, when her small shirts began to cling to her swelling abdomen. But neither Hasna's mother nor her father showed any marked reaction at the time, although Karim would frown whenever he saw her, and Mona initially refused to speak to her.

Their silence hurt, but Hasna understood that there were no words to describe what her parents must have been feeling right then. And Hasna was grateful that there weren't because she was suffering enough.

After officially resigning, Hasna had spoken to Vernon briefly when she had come to clear her desk. But his initial compassion turned cold after she told him she did not follow through with the abortion.

"I hope you don't have any big plans for yourself." He spoke sarcastically as she carried a lightweight box out the office, her back to him.

"I do," she said, raising her voice so he could hear her.

"Tweetie, you're being unreasonable," he said falling in step next to her, his voice lowering to a whisper as they passed through the hallway.

"Maybe I am," she said, not bothering to lower her voice.

"I hope you don't expect to show up next week and ruin my —"

"Vernon," Hasna snapped, turning to face him in front of the door leading outside, her face hot with anger. She spoke through gritted teeth. "I have no desire to be anywhere *near* your stupid wedding."

Embarrassed, he glanced over his shoulder to see if anyone was passing before he reached past Hasna and opened the door, not wanting to speak in front of anyone.

"And no," she said, raising her voice, not budging from her place, "I don't expect one red cent from you to pay for *our* child."

Vernon glanced over his shoulder again, shell-shocked when he saw Attorney Wynmore approaching them, a confused expression on his face.

"I don't want child support, and I don't want you."

"Tweetie," Vernon said, his eyes widening, hoping to quiet her.

"And don't worry," she said, glaring at him, fully aware that their boss was hanging on to every word, "my *big* plans don't include you. I'm perfectly fine with raising this child *alone*."

Presently, as Hasna stood before the clothes rack in Wal-Mart, a long-sleeve purple tunic of thin material caught her eye. She lifted the hanger of the shirt, examining the blouse closely, liking it a great deal.

Instinctively, she checked the price tag.   It was $49.99. Disappointed, Hasna put the shirt back and wheeled her cart in the direction of the clearance rack. If she couldn't find maternity clothes there, she hoped to at least find some decent shirts well above her size.

The marriage of Sharif and Yasmin had simply been the signing of a contract in the presence of Hisham and two witnesses, Sheikh Abdullah one of them. Afterwards, the sheikh had driven Sharif back to the quiet of Sharif's Riyadh apartment that was a ten-minute walk to the international school where Sharif would start work in August. It would be another twelve months before he and Yasmin would celebrate their *waleemah*, the wedding feast announcing the marriage. Thereafter, Sharif and Yasmin would move into a small villa on Hisham's family compound.

Sharif had seen Yasmin only twice prior to the signing, once several years before when Hisham first presented the idea of marriage to Sharif and again a day after Sharif arrived in Riyadh. During the second meeting, several family members had been present, and Sharif felt awkward sitting opposite her in the large room, as it was apparent that it was Sharif who was being judged. It had been impossible to find out more about her during the meeting because he himself was answering questions of concerned and curious family members.   It felt like an interrogation.

But Sharif was pleased to discover that Yasmin had memorized Qur'an and was now working toward an *ijaaza*, an esteemed certification that one's method of recitation traced back the Prophet himself. Sharif also learned that she preferred to speak *Fus-ha*, although she was fluent in at least three colloquial Arabic dialects, as well as in the English language itself. Her reason for the preference of *Fus-ha* was simply that it was the language of the Qur'an and hadith, and she wished to speak nothing else unless the circumstance dictated. She also wished for her children to grow up with proper Arabic as their native language and the colloquial dialects as subsequent ones.

After the signing of the contract, Sharif visited Yasmin's family compound several days each week and they spent extended time together on the weekends although they rarely left her parents' villa unless Yasmin needed to pick up something from the neighborhood store and he walked with her.

It was part of Arab custom for the woman to remain in her family's home until after the *waleemah*, which sometimes was held years after the initial marriage contract. During the time between the legal marriage and the wedding party, local custom permitted only minimal contact between the bride and groom. It was for this reason that Sharif and Yasmin's current relationship resembled more a courting period than it did marriage.

But Sharif did not mind, as the time he and Yasmin spent together allowed them to get acquainted with each other and build a friendship before they lived as a couple. It also gave Sharif opportunity to get to know Yasmin's family, which was extremely large on both her father's and mother's side though much of Javeria's family still lived in Pakistan.

Often when Sharif was with Yasmin, he reflected on the immense blessing he had in a wife and he found it difficult to believe that he had turned down Hisham's initial offer in favor of Hasna. It was true that Sharif did not love Yasmin, as his mother had surmised, but Sharif was learning that you could learn to love someone. He hadn't known Yasmin long enough to imagine that he loved her, but he and she were getting along well and he was becoming fond of her.

"Ana ghayoorah." *I'm jealous,* Yasmin had teased Sharif one evening as they sat on chairs in the gated terrace of her parents' home. Like most of the homes in the region, Yasmin's was surrounded by a stone gate more than ten feet high, allowing residents to relax outside in privacy, the night sky a canopy above them.

Sharif grinned, unable to keep from looking at her. Her blue eyes were an awkward contrast the honey brown of her skin, and the tight curls of her black hair were gathered at the back of her head in a ponytail, some tufts having escaped the elastic band and framed her face at the temples. She wore a sleeveless white summer dress that stopped inches above her bare ankles, and white sandals were on her feet. Sharif wore the traditional white *thobe* and brown leather sandals.

Self-conscious, Sharif wiped beads of sweat from on his forehead and he saw Yasmin do the same. The July heat was oppressive although it was late evening. Sharif had prayed *Maghrib* in the masjid across the street thirty minutes before.

"Li maathaa?" Why are you jealous?

Yasmin turned from him, a shy grin on her face. *Because you refused me for her.*

Sharif laughed. *No, I refused her for you.*

Yasmin kept her gaze lowered as she toyed with the cloth of her dress, unable to keep from smiling.

Why didn't you get married all this time? Sharif teased. In her family, a woman marrying at twenty-four was considered late.

I was waiting for you.

Sharif smiled.

Why didn't you *get married all this time?* she asked, teasing, her eyes meeting his.

Because I was waiting for you.

Iman had begun the chemotherapy in early April and supplemented the modern treatment with the herbs and teas prescribed by the homeopathic physician. Every Monday morning, Iman had sat in a hospital room, the immaculate counter orderly scattered with individually wrapped alcohol wipes, trays of empty glass test tubes, boxes of medical gloves, and plastic covered cups used for urine samples. The sight was always the same, and it was always depressing. Iman had wondered why, with all the modern technology in hospitals, the more basic human sensitivity had occurred to no one.

The routine was the same. A nurse with the obligatory cordiality of health care professionals would come in with a sterile needle and a smile as Iman lay her bare arm on the armrest. A wide, pale rubber band would be tied on her arm as Iman's heavy black cloth hung on a hanger at the back of the door.

Then the first stage of torment began, locating a vein in Iman's already weak arm, sore from the pricking of a week before. Once the vein was located, a plastic tip remained in her arm or hand, where the intravenous poison would be released into her bloodstream. The feeling at the tip was like that of liquid fire slipping into her arms and hands, although the rage of the fire calmed to a blaze after the first few minutes, making the ordeal tolerable though painful nonetheless.

While the drug was being released into her system, Iman would lean her head back, turning away from the IV and squinting towards the colorless open blinds that covered the window, imagining the life of normalcy beyond.

Periodically, Iman would recite Qur'an to herself or whisper supplications to Allah, but mostly she wondered what it would be like in the grave. She wondered if the squeezing of the ribs that was experienced by all who had died would hurt more than the chemotherapy did right then. She wondered too how it would be to sit opposite Munkar and Nakir, the two angels assigned to ask the deceased questions in the grave.

Who is your Lord? What is your religion? Who is your prophet?

How would Iman respond?

Iman also thought about the nature of her future should she would win her life back at the end of this suffering. Or if she wanted it back at all.

Many nights Iman settled under her covers, her limbs sore and her body enflamed in pain, and tears would fill her eyes after she recited *Ayatul-Kursi* and the last three chapters of Qur'an in a murmur, and she'd hope that she would not wake to see morning. She would feel a tinge of guilt at the thought and then utter in the stillness of night the supplication for one on the verge of wishing for death. *O Allah, let me live if life is better for me, and let me die if death is better for me.*

And each day she would wake, the red numbers on her clock glowing in the darkness of her room, reminding her that she had only thirty or forty minutes remaining if she wished to pray *Qiyaam* before dawn. Although she whispered the prayer for waking that began with the words *Alhamdulillaah*, praising Allah for having given her life, her heart often wished that He had taken it from her in her sleep. Exhausted, Iman would then weakly pull herself out of bed and make her way down the hall to the bathroom. Sometimes she held on to the walls of the hall to steady herself as she walked. Thirty minutes later, having used the bathroom and completed *wudhoo*, Iman would begin prayer, slowly taking a seat on the chair that faced a corner of her room, as her weak state had left her with no choice but to pray sitting down.

After the weekly treatment, Iman spent most of her time in bed, her body exhausted and degenerating. It would take almost an entire week for her to regain even a semblance of strength.

Then the cycle would begin again.

Seeing Asma everyday was the only highlight of the relentlessly painful routine. But Iman could tell that the ordeal was extremely confusing and hurtful to her friend. Nevertheless, Iman was grateful that Asma did not speak of her misgivings and instead distracted Iman from her depraved state through conversation of things that would keep them talking for over an hour. After some time Iman would drift to sleep, but her eyes would flutter open an hour later, her body exhausted from want of sleep. She often would find Asma still sitting in the desk chair next to her bed, her gaze distant as she looked beyond the window.

Asma's job was a difficult one, Iman knew, so Iman could not blame her for striking up a conversation one day, four weeks into Iman's treatment, that hurt Iman more than the routine itself.

"Mom says Sharif is married now." There was sadness in Asma's tone, and a regretful smile creased one corner of her mouth. "I guess he won't be coming back for a while."

The news had jolted Iman from her straying thoughts, and she met her friend's gaze from where she lay on her side. "Your brother's married now?"

Asma nodded, her gaze lowered as she rubbed the back of a hand. She apparently missed her brother terribly. "I wish he married you," she said, lifting her eyes to her friend, having no idea her words touched on something sensitive to Iman's heart.

Iman averted her gaze, an embarrassed grin forming on her face. "Yeah right. I don't think he'd marry someone as ugly as me."

"You're not ugly."

"I am now."

At that Asma grew quiet.

"Iman, why do you say that?" Asma's tone was sincere and pained.

Iman's grin faded and her thoughts drifted to her weak body and her hair that she imagined would begin falling out in a matter of weeks, if not days.

"I don't know," Iman said quietly, her response honest. "I guess I just don't think anyone would want to marry someone like me."

"But he proposed to your father, didn't he?"

"That was before I was sick."

"And I don't think he would change his mind now."

Iman didn't know what to say. Perhaps Asma was right. It was true that his proposal had been withdrawn not because of her illness but because her parents had refused to even consider it.

At the reminder, Iman felt the warmth of anger in her chest, and it was difficult to keep from resenting her parents for ruining her life. She could endure this current torment much more easily if she had someone to hold her hand through it all. And make her feel beautiful even as her body fell apart.

"*Allahua'lam,*" Iman muttered more to herself than her friend. Yes, only Allah knew where Sharif's heart now lay.

But Iman found it difficult to imagine he would reconsider even if he had the chance, given all that had happened since he first spoke to her father. And her cancer diagnosis was only one strike against her in light of all he had suffered as a result of her parents' actions against him.

"How is your family now?"

Asma shrugged. "Better, I guess."

Iman didn't ask, *Better than when?* She already knew. She gritted her teeth as a sharp pain shot through her leg and abdominal area.

"How was...your brother before he left?" Iman asked, her voice tired and emotionally distant.

Asma shrugged. "He pretty much kept to himself. Mom was really mad when she found out what happened."

Iman slowly closed her eyes, another sharp pain shooting through her, but remaining and flaring for some time.

"Iman? Are you okay?"

Behind closed eyelids, Iman heard Asma's concerned voice, but the pain was so intense she couldn't speak. She wanted to ask Allah for mercy, but her jaw was clenched and she was unable to relax the muscles enough to speak. She felt her head trembling in an effort to withstand the pain, and she tried to remain patient under duress. But Iman could not fathom from whence she could gain such forbearance. She could not wrap her mind around this pain, amazed that the human body could withstand such torment.

"Iman?"

Gradually, the flaring subsided, and Iman let out a moan seconds before she opened her eyes. The image of Asma was slightly blurred but she could see that Asma was partly out of her seat, as if in preparation to leave the room and ask for help.

"I'm okay," Iman said weakly. "It was just a cramp or something."

Asma was still frozen in place, halfway out of the seat, an uncertain expression on her face. Slowly she sat down. "Should I get your mom?"

"No, no," Iman said, lifting her hand in a gesture motioning Asma to sit down. "Just sit with me. I'm fine."

It took a few minutes, but Asma calmed down yet regarded Iman more cautiously than she had minutes before.

"Are you sure you're okay?" Asma asked when Iman gritted her teeth again.

"Yes," Iman said in a hoarse whisper.

But she wasn't sure herself, and she could find nothing to ease her pain.

Because now it was also coming from her heart.

An image flashed in Iman's mind. *Sharif sitting and laughing. A healthy, beautiful woman with large, dark eyes and raven black hair next to him, laughing herself.*

A woman who would bear him many children.

Iman moaned, pain clutching her again.

This time she didn't protest when Asma said she would get Iman's mother.

Twenty-eight

"The whole world is a provision, and the best benefit of this world is the pious woman."
—Prophet Muhammad (peace be upon him)
(Muslim)

"SubhaanAllaah," Yasmin said, averting her gaze from Sharif.

They had decided, a half-hour before, to escape the July heat in favor of the cool indoors. They now sat next to each other on the Arab-style floor couch that lined the walls of the sitting room. The coolness of the air-conditioner drifted toward them and the wall-mounted machine hummed as they sipped the guava juice that Yasmin's family maid had just served.

Yasmin set her glass on the table in front of her. She was at a loss for words.

"Ana…" *I'm sorry to hear that,* she said finally. Her eyes were cast down as she spoke. Yasmin wondered about the well-being of the younger sister of the woman whom Sharif had been engaged to marry.

Yasmin looked at Sharif again but darted her eyes, afraid he would see the guilt written there. *I can say nothing of a surety, habeebati,* her Qur'an teacher had told her. *But…in many cases like these, people resort to sihr.*

Had Sommer's friends in America targeted Iman, thinking her to be Hasna? It was possible, Yasmin considered. Yasmin herself hadn't known Hasna's name at the time she had solicited Sommer's help in contacting Sharif. All she had known was small details about the family. From what she had shared, it was very likely that Sommer's companions would not know who the fiancée was. It was only tonight that Yasmin learned that Sharif's fiancée had a sister.

"Mataa…" *When did this happen?* Yasmin asked.

"December, taqreeban..." Around December, I believe. I'm not sure. *But I found out in March.*

December. Yasmin shuddered. She had spoken to Sommer in August. It was possible then that this could have resulted from the hands of her friend.

Sharif chuckled uncomfortably, and Yasmin could tell something else was bothering him. Her heart thumped in her chest. Did he find out about her past? Would he judge her for it?

Did Sharif suspect that Yasmin had a hand in what had happened to Iman?

"Ya'nee, maa 'adree..." I mean, I don't know what can be done, but... Sharif's voice trailed as he became lost in doubt.

"Laakin," Sharif continued, a confounded expression on his face, *"qabla rihlatee..."* But before my trip here, her father spoke to me about...

As Sharif explained to Yasmin the conversation he had had with Karim, Yasmin stiffened, dreading what he would say to her right then.

So he might abandon her after all...

Yasmin felt panicked at the thought. A part of her felt guilty for not being more compassionate toward the sick girl, but she didn't want to lose Sharif. She simply couldn't lose him, not now. It would mean her utter crumbling in her family's eyes, in her own eyes even. How could she ever hold her head up again?

No, she could not let him go a second time. She simply could not.

"Wa maa 'araftu..." And I didn't know what to say to him, Sharif was saying.

Yasmin's heart nearly skipped a beat as an idea came to her suddenly, an idea that could preserve her and Sharif's marriage as well as help the sick girl.

But my guess would be that it means the person in the dream is going to die, and Allah is telling us the good news of their place in Paradise.

Imam Bilal's interpretation of the recurrent dream returned to Sharif as he spoke to Yasmin about his conversation with Karim. He had no idea why he was sharing the conversation with his new wife. But he couldn't get it out of his mind. Even though his heart was not inclined to marry Iman, Sharif felt terrible that he hadn't been able to fulfill this simple wish of a terminally ill girl.

Was there *something* he could do to help? Maybe he could perform *ruqyah* for her?

But why had the dream been given to Sharif?

What was he supposed to take from it? Was Allah telling him to fulfill one last request, to offer kindness to his sister in Islam?

But he was already married. He couldn't possibly…

"Sharif?" Yasmin's voice interrupted his thoughts. Her sudden use of English distracted him momentarily. But the language shift was something they both did, often without forethought. "Are you okay?"

Sharif nodded, taking a sip from his glass of juice, his thoughts on Karim and Iman. "I'm just thinking about my friend's family."

Yasmin frowned, reaching for her glass on the table. "I'm sorry you can't be there with them."

Sharif thought of Iman. "I am too."

"Do you think they would like it here?"

He recalled Iman's "O Mujahid" poem and the article "The Death of Islam," and he nodded. "I think so."

"Then why not bring them?"

Sharif's brows furrowed and he met his wife's gaze. "How?"

"They can get an 'Umrah visa, *inshaaAllah*."

Could that be Sharif's compromise, pay for their trip here? Sharif considered it though he had little funds himself. He had no idea how practical the sudden trip would be for them, but Sharif imagined that Iman, as well as Karim, could benefit greatly from Makkah, where they could perform 'Umrah and drink from the well of Zam Zam, the blessed water that contained in it the effect of whatever the person wished. There were many documented stories of the water's miraculous effects, even on those who had been upon the throes of death.

And Sharif had heard many accounts of it healing cancer.

Why hadn't he thought of it before?

Was there enough time to bring Iman and her father here for 'Umrah?

"Can't he just bring the water *here?*" Mona asked Karim, a concerned expression on her face as she leaned against the counter in front of the sink of their kitchen Friday evening in mid-August. Two weeks before, the doctors had told them that the cancer had reached Iman's bloodstream and there was nothing they could do to save her. "I don't think her body can withstand the trip."

Karim nodded, his gaze distant. "I could ask, but..."

"But what?" Mona's forehead was creased.

"But he's married now. I'm not sure if he can just leave like that."

Mona folded her arms under her chest. "Can't he just ship it then?"

Karim shook his head. "I mentioned that, but there are some regulations that restrict the shipment of fluids via airmail."

Mona sighed. "Then ask him to bring it. He can bring his wife if he wants."

She shook her head. "As long as we don't have to make that trip. Iman can't handle it."

At that moment, Karim thought of the dream he had had.

"You don't have a lot of time," Sharif had told him so many years before. Karim wondered if the dream he had seen while a teen held its relevance only now.

"Okay," Karim said, feeling the urgency of the situation just then, "I'll ask him *inshaaAllah.*"

"Make a wish." Asma grinned from where she sat cross-legged on the carpeted floor of Iman's room next to Hasna, who too sat on the floor, one hand on the T-shirt covering her large abdomen. They both were facing Iman who sat on her bed with her back supported by pillows, small braids that Asma had plaited for her covering her head, exposing some of her scalp where her hair had thinned. An IV pole and machine stood next to her, monitored by a nurse that visited twice daily.

Hasna laughed. "Make a *wish*?"

"Yes," Asma said. "Why not?"

"This sounds like some shooting star game or something."

Asma shook her head. "No, it's not that type of wish. This is a game me and Iman play all the time."

Hasna's eyes widened playfully as she looked at her sister. "Really?"

Iman smiled weakly. "Yes."

"I want to hear more about this," Hasna said, grinning.

"It's not anything bad," Iman said, the strength of her voice coming. "This isn't *shirk*."

"We're making a wish about what we hope from Allah," Asma said, beaming.

"Isn't that called a *prayer*?" Hasna asked.

"In the game it's not," Asma said, sitting up straighter in preparation for the game.

"Now who's first?" Asma asked.

"But what's the object of the game?"

"To make the best wish."

"But how do you know who wins?"

"You just know."

Hasna looked confused.

"It's a game of the heart," Iman said from her bed, shaking her head in amusement at her sister. "Cheating's not possible, Hasna, so don't try anything."

"O-kay," Hasna said, doubtful, a confused smile on her face. "I'm last because I have no idea what we're doing here."

"You're first then," Iman said, looking at Asma.

"Okay," Asma said, her eyes narrowing as she thought. Her face relaxed a moment later as a thought came to her. "I wish Iman was my sister."

Iman laughed, but it sounded like a soft cough. "You lost already."

Asma rolled her eyes playfully. "Your turn," she said to Iman.

"Okay…" Iman's expression became thoughtful, and Asma and Hasna waited. Iman looked ashamed for a second, her gaze skipping over her sister self-consciously. She lowered her eyes, her voice a whisper. "I wish I could have a wedding."

The room grew quiet suddenly, and Asma's gaze dropped, as did Hasna's. They didn't know what to say.

"Hasna," Iman said seconds later, a gentle smile forming on her face.

Hasna looked up expectantly, sadness in her eyes as she met the gaze of her sister.

"It's your turn."

"Oh. I'm, uh…"

"Just make a wish," Asma said, the joy gone from her voice, quiet sadness now there.

Hasna shook her head at a loss. "I can't think of anything…"

"Anything," Asma told her.

"Okay… I wish—" Hasna drew in a deep breath and exhaled, not wanting to mention Iman's recovery but wanting to be honest at the same time. "—the masjid was unlocked and Sharif was the imam again."

For a few seconds, no one spoke.

"Hasna wins," Iman said quietly, a reflective smile creasing one corner of her mouth.

Asma nodded, smiling herself. "I think so."

"I like Iman's better," Hasna said, a shy grin on her face as she leaned back on the palms of her hands.

Iman shook her head. "No, because mine is only for me," she said, her voice growing slightly weak, and she breathed audibly. "But yours, everyone could benefit from."

The earliest flight that Sharif could reserve was for late September, even when he inquired about first class. The news was distressing to him, as he couldn't imagine Iman waiting more than a month for the water.

Sharif also wanted to be back in Riyadh for Ramadan, which was scheduled to begin during the first few days of October. He had been looking forward to performing 'Umrah during the holy month, as well as spending most of his time in the masjid.

He had no idea how long he would need to remain in the States, but he had projected that he should stay at least three weeks, especially if he were to follow his wife's advice to offer not only the Zam Zam water but to also perform *ruqyah* for Iman.

"*Laa tahzan...*" Yasmin had told him. *Don't stress. Allah is in control of all things.*

Twenty-nine

"The believers in their affection, compassion, and love for one another are like a single body. If a part of it suffers from pain, the whole body aches in restlessness and fever."
— Prophet Muhammad (peace be upon him)
(Muslim)

On Thursday morning, the twenty-second of September, Sharif rode in the back of a taxi, his body exhausted from the long flight. He had prayed *Istikhaarah* three times before taking the trip, once for the trip itself, and twice for discussing with Karim the proposition to marry Iman.

We don't ask for anything except your company.

"Is that all they wanted?" Yasmin had asked, tears shining in her eyes.

"Yes."

"And you said no because of *me*?"

Ashamed, Sharif hadn't known what to say to his wife. He hadn't mentioned to Yasmin that it was marriage he was thinking of more than keeping Iman company. He had told Yasmin he would return to America to perform *ruqyah* for Iman and to "keep her company" during her final moments.

"But, Sharif, she is *dying*. How could you say *no*?"

As Sharif leaned his head against the back of the seat in the taxi and his eyes stared at the passing trees, the question tugged at his heart, and his body ached in regret.

He would marry Iman. It was the only way he could perform *ruqyah* without difficulty. If he did not marry her, he wouldn't be able to be alone with her, and his touching her, though necessity was involved, would be limited to some extent. Sharif wouldn't feel comfortable crossing any bounds, and marriage was the only way to remove them.

But should he have made this plan clear to Yasmin?

In his mind, Sharif saw Iman standing in the masjid lobby opposite his sister holding the hand of Adam. He saw her hair caked in sauce and her face smeared with tomato pulp after the spaghetti fight between her and Asma. He thought of Iman giggling after Asma whispered something to her. He recalled too standing in the kitchen of his home, his heart moved by the poem "O Mujahid" even as he had no idea it was Iman who had penned the words. He thought of Iman's parents, Karim and Mona, and how they had helped Sharif's family, financially and emotionally, after Sharif's father died.

In the quiet of the taxi, Sharif felt Karim's firm hand pat his shoulder and draw him close at the funeral, and Mona's warm embrace of his mother.

How could he abandon them now?

"How soon can you come?" Karim shut the door to his office, his voice lowering as he spoke into the mobile phone. Sharif had called him to say he had arrived.

"Whatever is best for you."

Karim glanced at the clock on the wall above his desk. It was a few minutes after ten o'clock. "Can you meet me at my house at twelve?"

"Yes, inshaaAllah."

"Okay, then, I'll see you in a couple of hours, inshaaAllah."

Karim closed his cell phone and exhaled, his heart relaxing. He had been awake most of the night hoping and praying that Sharif would arrive safely, the urgency of the situation making him restless.

A week ago the doctors had projected that Iman had only three months to live, but Karim knew that this was only human estimation. Iman could expire sooner, as her grandmother had, or she could live for decades more.

No one knew. It was all in the hands of Allah.

Karim was determined to think the best. There was no need to prepare for the worst.

Yet, in so many ways, he already had. There was always that haranguing trepidation that something so close to his heart would be taken from him in a matter of seconds.

Iman herself seemed to have accepted the worst of fate. She no longer spoke much to anyone, not even to Asma or Hasna, who had drawn close to her in the last month. Daily, Asma sat at Iman's bedside reading aloud from the Qur'an or reading a book quietly to herself, hoping that her company alone would be soothing for her friend. Hasna slept on Iman's floor every night, having moved her mattress and bedding into the room. She barely left Iman's side except to use the bathroom. She even took her meals next to her sister.

Occasionally, Karim would wake at night to check on Iman and find Hasna's mattress empty, the blankets tousled. Concerned, he would go to Hasna's room and put his ear to the door when he heard murmurs and sobs. Once, Karim invited himself in and found Hasna on her knees, her hair and body wrapped in bed sheets, her hands raised in supplication. She was moaning so desperately that she hadn't heard the door open.

Karim also discovered that Hasna was carrying Iman's Islamic books with her, reading even as she walked down the hallway and falling asleep with a book next to her at night. One late night he heard Iman's voice, and, concerned, he put his ear to his daughter's door. What he heard both stunned and pleased him. Iman was explaining to Hasna the proper pronunciation of *Al-Faatihah*, the opening chapter of the Qur'an recited in every unit of prayer.

"If it's a girl," Karim heard Hasna saying to someone on the phone one day, "I'm naming it Iman for sure. If it's a boy, well…" She laughed "…I have no idea what I'll call him."

Karim was pacing the living room when he heard the sound of a car turning into the driveway of his home. He peered through the sheer white curtains and saw a taxi slowing to a halt, the right-side passenger door opening seconds later.

Quickly Karim went to the front door and opened it. When he saw Sharif walking around to the back of the taxi, Karim put on his shoes and went outside to join him.

"*As-salaamu'alaikum*," Karim said, smiling and raising a hand to greet Sharif.

Sharif looked up from where he was removing something from the trunk. Upon seeing Karim a smile spread on Sharif's face, the kind expression warming Karim's heart. Karim missed Sharif dearly, Karim realized at that moment. His presence had given heart to the community. Without him, so much seemed to have become lifeless.

At the car, they embraced.

"How was your trip?"

Sharif chuckled, lifting a large plastic jug of water from the trunk. The container appeared to be holding about three gallons. "*Alhamdulillaah*, I made it in one piece."

"Let me give you a hand," Karim said, reaching into the trunk to remove the other two.

Sharif slipped a hand into a back pocket of his dress pants and retrieved his wallet as he walked over to the driver's side window of the taxi.

"No, no," Karim said, setting the water containers on the ground before raising a hand. "Let me."

"It's okay, I—"

"No, please." Karim cut in front of Sharif and asked the taxi driver how much. He then reached into a pocket and removed a fifty-dollar bill that he handed to the driver.

Karim walked over to where Sharif stood next to the water jugs.

"Let's get these inside," Karim said, lifting two, one jug in each hand, their weight making him wobble slightly as he walked.

Sharif lifted one himself and followed Karim, the taxi pulling out of the driveway as they made their way to the front door.

"Should we start now?" Karim asked, turning to Sharif after setting the containers on the kitchen table.

Sharif looked uncertain. "We could, but…"

"But what?" Karim grew concerned.

"But I'll need to explain some things first."

"About what?"

"The *ruqyah*."

Karim's forehead creased. "The what?"

"*Ruqyah*. It's the treatment I'm going to do for her."

"I thought we were just giving her the water."

"We are," Sharif said. "But with her condition, I think she'll need more than that."

Karim grew silent, thoughtful. "But what more can we do?"

Sharif started to speak but was interrupted by someone calling from upstairs.

"Karim? Is that you?"

"One second," Karim said, leaving the kitchen. "Let me let my wife know you're here."

Sharif stood in the quiet of Karim's kitchen, the familiar sight evoking memories of years past. He remembered sitting next to Hasna waiting for the timer to sound and the food to simmer. He recalled the crippling self-awareness that had made it impossible to relax around her. He remembered too Iman as a toddler, her diaper sagging between her chubby brown legs, her hair a wild mass of tight curls her mother could not tame.

"I want mato," Iman had said to Sharif once, patting his leg.

"What?" Sharif had stared at the child, her large eyes looking into his innocently as she pointed to the refrigerator.

"I want mato," she said again.

"A mato?" he repeated, perplexed.

She nodded, pointing to the refrigerator again. He had walked over to the refrigerator and opened it, deciding it was better to let the child point out exactly what she wanted.

He stepped to the side so Iman could see inside. "Now, what do you want?"

Her small hand reached for a bag of vegetables.

Sharif grinned. "*To*-mato," he corrected, leaning down to her. "You want a *to*-mato."

"No," she said, shaking her head, pouting. "I don't want two mato. I want *one* mato."

It had taken a second for Sharif to register her complaint, and when he did, he burst out laughing. He repeated the story to Hasna minutes later when she returned, setting off a fit of laughter from her.

"And make sure you pick up some flour," Sharif heard Mona's voice. "But make sure we have enough eggs."

He heard footfalls drawing closer, and he moved away from the doorway and turned his back, unsure if Mona would be covered when she passed.

Seconds later, the footsteps halted, and he had the strange sensation that he was not alone in the kitchen.

"*Sharif?*"

The familiar voice prompted him to turn around. When he did, Sharif found himself looking into the face of a woman of pale olive complexion, her round face framed attractively by the white of a *khimaar*, her hazel eyes holding a distant familiarity. The lavender maternity blouse did little to conceal the swollen belly of the woman who appeared to be well into her last trimester of pregnancy.

Embarrassed, he looked away, having thought he was looking at Mona until he heard Mona call out again.

"And Hasna?"

The woman was distracted momentarily and turned toward the sound of her mother's voice, a ring of keys dangling from one hand. "Yes?"

"And see if we have any milk. Adam spilled some this morning."

"Okay."

Sharif's heart raced in discomfort, and he quickly left the kitchen as Hasna entered. He stood in the living room, his mind trying to process what he had just seen. He hadn't recognized Hasna immediately because of both the Islamic garb and the weight gain of pregnancy.

Was Hasna married now? The question disturbed him and he felt a pang of jealousy at the thought.

"I'm sorry."

Sharif turned to see Karim walking toward him. A moment later, Hasna emerged from the kitchen, passing them. She offered a cordial smile as she lifted her hand slightly in a wave, but he didn't know how to respond.

"Drive carefully, sweetheart," Karim said as Hasna opened the door.

For a second Sharif just stared toward the closed door, unsure how to form the question in his mind.

Karim chuckled. "Hard to recognize, huh?"

Sharif looked at him. "When did she get married?"

Karim's expression faded to reveal deep sadness, and he shook his head. "She's not married."

Sharif started to ask something but stopped himself as he slowly registered the information. Memories of Hasna talking about her friend Vernon returned to him, and Sharif felt sick. He recalled how fondly Hasna had spoken of the man who claimed to respect Islam and care for Hasna a great deal.

Sharif felt himself growing furious in upset. Where was Vernon *now*?

"What is it that you have in mind for Iman?"

Karim's question distracted Sharif from his straying thoughts. He met Karim's gaze, reminded of the weighty task before them.

"Is there somewhere we can talk privately?" Sharif asked, the sound of Hasna's car fading as it pulled out of the driveway.

"Here is fine," Karim said. "My wife and son are upstairs, and Mona knows we're talking."

Karim gestured a hand toward the couch, and Sharif sat down, Karim following suit.

Sharif was quiet as he gathered his thoughts. He had no idea how to convey all that was on his mind, and heart.

He decided it was wisest to start with the most difficult.

"Brother, I'm sorry about what happened before I left."

Karim creased his forehead. "What do you mean?"

Sharif drew in a deep breath and exhaled. "When we discussed all that had happened and…" How could he put this into words? "…and you asked if I could keep Iman company."

Karim's face relaxed and his gaze dropped to his clasped hands, sadness in his eyes at the reminder. "It's okay, Sharif. You have your own life now. I'm sorry I didn't know that."

"I don't think my mother wanted everyone to know…"

"You didn't do anything wrong, Sharif. And it was selfish to ask. You're an attractive, healthy young man. I can't expect you to give up your life for someone who is as ill as Iman."

Sharif shook his head. "I didn't refuse because she's not well. Honestly, I was wishing you had told me before I agreed to return to Riyadh."

A reflective smile creased a corner of Karim's mouth. "That's thoughtful of you, Sharif. It really is." He sighed. "But Allah's plan is best, so we place our trust in Him."

A thoughtful silence followed.

"But what if this *is* His plan?" Sharif asked, the nervousness leaving him as he thought of the dream and of Iman's weak state. "What if Allah wanted everything to happen as we thought it should?"

Karim gathered his eyebrows and looked at Sharif, a question on his face. "What do you mean?"

"I think it's still possible," Sharif said. "If you think Iman won't mind."

Karim studied Sharif for a moment, as if trying to determine his meaning.

"Brother Karim," Sharif said finally. "I'm asking permission to marry your daughter."

For a second Karim did not speak, and Sharif feared his words had been offensive to Karim in some way. Karim's lips formed a line and when Sharif met his gaze Sharif saw that the brother's eyes were glistening.

"There's no one I would be more honored to give her to," Karim said.

Iman blinked as her eyes fluttered open in the dimly lit room, the light of morning peeking through the closed curtains next to her bed. Her body was slightly reclined on the adjustable hospital bed that the nurse and her parents had set up in her bedroom two weeks before, pillows behind her neck and back. Soreness seemed to pierce through her very bones, making it difficult to move, but once she wrapped her mind around the pain she could maneuver herself relatively well by reciting *dhikr* with each movement of her limbs.

Instinctively, she glanced at the bedding on the floor next to her and saw that Hasna was no longer there. Sighing, she turned her head, the silent loneliness of the room awkwardly soothing right then. She knew it was only a matter of minutes before someone knocked on the door, interrupting her solitude. She was never left alone more than thirty minutes, and even that was rare.

Iman wanted to open the windows. The darkness was depressing. But she could not risk moving that much, at least not without someone assisting her.

She sighed, glancing at the time. She still had a couple of hours before she had to pray *Dhuhr* and *Asr*, and the preparation for the combined prayers would take nearly half an hour.

Although her sickness gave her the option to remain in bed and pray, Iman preferred to get out of bed and pray sitting in her desk chair if the pain was not unbearable. She had the morphine pump, but she did not use it as often as the nurse suggested because it made her too drowsy to communicate, and Iman hated that feeling, especially during prayers. But the pain of the advanced cancer was indescribable, so she sometimes regretted not using the pump as often as she could.

A soft knock at her door interrupted her thoughts, and she sighed, having expected the company sooner or later. At least now she could have her curtains opened. She didn't bother calling out to say come in. No one expected her to anyway. The knocking was more out of politeness than necessity. Besides, Iman was in no position to have the privacy she had taken for granted for so many years. Even the simple act of going to the bathroom required the assistance of her mother, sister, or Asma, if not all of them, though there was the despised bed pan she could use.

"Are you awake, sweetheart?"

"Daddy?" Iman had thought her father was at work.

"Yes, it's me."

"What day is it?"

Karim chuckled. "It's Thursday. I came home early today."

Iman smiled, flattered, her spirits lifting at the thought of her father leaving work to see her. "That's nice."

"Yes, I know." He walked over to her and brushed her forehead with a kiss. "I'd like to take the credit," he said jokingly, "but it's really someone else who's here to see you."

"Asma?" Iman had thought her friend couldn't come until the afternoon because of an exam Asma had to take at the community college she now attended.

Karim shook his head, a grin forming on his face. "It's someone else. But I wanted to ask you first."

She creased her forehead. "Ask me what?"

He sighed, shutting the door behind him as he walked over to the desk chair where Asma usually sat next to her bed. "If he has permission to keep you company."

Iman stared at her father, a question on her face. She sensed that he was teasing her, but she couldn't be sure. "Who?"

Karim's grin spread. "Sharif."

Iman's heart sank and she sighed at the reminder. She dropped her head, her gaze on the blankets pulled around her thin body. "Daddy, that's not funny."

He patted her hand softly. "I know, sweetheart."

She stared distantly at the lint gathering on her blanket and thought of Sharif living in a Muslim land with a beautiful Arab wife.

And to think it could have been Iman herself...

"That's why I wouldn't joke with you. He really is here asking about you."

Iman smiled dryly. "Asma already told me he went back to Saudi Arabia."

"He did. But he came back to ask if he could marry you."

Iman lifted her gaze to her father, too weak and exhausted to laugh at his humor, but an amused grin formed like a shadow on her face. "And she told me he's already married."

Karim frowned slightly, apparently disappointed that Iman knew too much to play along. "Does that bother you?"

Iman didn't know what to say to her father. Did he realize how much this very conversation tore at her? Of course it bothered her. But she couldn't say that aloud. It hurt enough to carry the burden of knowledge in her heart.

"Let me do this," Karim said. "I'll talk to your mother, and once she straightens up in here a bit and makes you presentable, I'll let Sharif come in and tell you himself."

He smiled. "In the meantime, I'll be calling some brothers as witnesses, so if you object, let me know within the next hour."

Despite her sour mood, Iman couldn't suppress the giggle that escaped with his words. "*Daddy*," she whined, a playful frown finding its way into a smile.

He patted her hand again, standing with the motion. "But as far as I'm concerned, you're as good as married."

She laughed again. "Thanks, Daddy."

He winked at her then walked toward the door and opened it.

A second later the door closed and a sad smile lingered on Iman's face as she thought of her father. She chuckled to herself and shook her head. *Okay*, she thought to herself, it wasn't the funniest joke in the world, but it *did* make her smile, even if for only a moment. And that was all her father had wanted.

Sighing, Iman wished she had remembered to ask her father to open the curtains. She could use the sunlight, especially as thoughts of Sharif now swam in her mind. She slowly shut her eyes, a small smile on her face, as she allowed herself to imagine, even if for only a second, what it would be like if Sharif had really returned to ask to marry her.

"But before I start the *ruqyah*," Sharif said from where he sat next to Karim on the couch, Hasna having returned from the store minutes before and was now upstairs in Iman's room, "I have to say I'm completely inexperienced in this form of treatment."

Karim creased his forehead, turning to Sharif, intrigued. "So this is an actual form of *medicine*?"

"I wouldn't say medicine...." Sharif searched for the proper way to describe Qur'anic healing. "It's more like a mixed method of medical and spiritual treatment."

"And it works?"

The question was a bit offensive to Sharif, and he frowned slightly. But he couldn't blame Karim. It was the same question that Sharif himself had asked of his classmate Earl. The spiritual healing method had seemed far-fetched to Sharif at the time, and it had taken detailed study of its foundation in the teachings of the Prophet, in addition to talking to those experienced in the field, as well as witnessing the treatment himself, before Sharif's mind was able to completely separate *ruqyah* from the realms of superstition and black magic that it had initially resembled.

It had been more difficult, though, for Sharif to overcome the cultural arrogance that had plagued him, even after living years abroad. "Western Expat Syndrome" was what Earl had called it.

"Even as we are fed and housed by them and even learn from them," he had said, *"we still assume we know better."*

Sharif hadn't thought about it like that before, but it was true. Even amongst the most traveled and studied Americans, ancient spiritual medicine conjured up images of "witch doctors" reciting unintelligible incantations, their faces and chests painted monstrously as leaves dangled over their groins, hoping through the incantation to heal a sick person lying in burlap tied to trees in the woods.

Superstition, Sharif remembered an elder saying once, *that's all that is.*

Yet for healing methods that involved *shirk* — the invoking of "spirits" and the use of charms and the like — the method, if not superstitious, was certainly unblessed in Islam. But could these pagan methods be compared to the use of Allah's Words in healing someone?

If so, Sharif imagined, then it was equally "superstitious" to expect a small pill or drug to effectively treat an illness. It was as if the specimen contained some hidden magic power known only to the "magician" who had concocted the potion. These were America's modern day medicine men and witch doctors who donned mysterious white coats and preferred the titles "physician" and "scientist."

It was only through understanding the sometimes microscopic world of Allah's creation that one's mind could embrace the minute details of science involved in the fulfillment of what the Prophet had referred to when he said that Allah sent down the disease and He sent down the cure. Even doctors themselves, daily, were mesmerized by the phenomenal intricacies of the human body and its various reactions to certain treatments.

If a single human body contained in it mysteries so vast that they were still being uncovered today by the most learned among scientists and doctors — after centuries of inquisition and research — what then of the miraculous intricacies involved in the world that lay outside that single creation?

It was far more unfathomable, then, in Sharif's view, that one should trust a fallible human being concocting some drug in a laboratory — a process in itself that non-scientists had neither time nor inclination to comprehend — than it was to trust the One who had taught that very doctor or researcher about the human body in the first place.

Two people do not learn, the Prophet had taught. *The shy person and the arrogant person.*

It was no wonder then that, even amongst Muslims, so many Westerners literally suffered from ignorance in their shunning of anything not socially or officially accepted amongst "their own."

"Yes," Sharif said. "It works very well, actually."

Karim exhaled, and Sharif sensed Karim's doubts.

"Just make *du'aa,*" Sharif said. "That's all we can do."

"But what if something goes wrong?" Karim asked, troubled. "Shouldn't we talk to her doctor about this?"

Sharif creased his forehead. "If you want to…"

Sharif had to resist becoming frustrated. Of course, modern medicine and Qur'anic healing were not mutually exclusive, as both were from Allah, but the doctors had already given up on Iman. What options could the doctors possibly offer at this stage?

It agitated Sharif that, in the modern world, doctors had replaced God himself in the hearts of most people. Doctors could make a million mistakes, as they did daily, but they enjoyed people's full trust and faith. And Allah made no mistakes—even if He decreed not to heal someone—yet it was His treatment that was trusted the least.

"It's up to you and Sister Mona," Sharif said. "If it's not something you feel comfortable with, she can just drink the Zam Zam."

Karim was thoughtful. "We're willing to do whatever we can at this point." He was quiet momentarily. "And if the treatment you suggest is not questionable in Islam, then I don't have a problem with it."

"Any *ruqyah* that doesn't involve *shirk* is allowed," Sharif said. "This is what we were taught by the Prophet, *sallallaahu 'alayhi wa sallam*. But using Qur'anic treatment in particular was done by the Prophet himself."

There was a brief pause.

"But since this is a spiritual treatment," Sharif added, "it's important that Iman wants to be healed and believes it will work for her."

Thirty

Mona stood on one side of the living room, her hands in the pockets of her *abaya* as she watched with a sense of detachment the commotion in front of her. Two brothers sat next to each other on the couch reading through a document as the imam stood feet from them talking about something in a low voice to her husband and Sharif. She had never seen the imam before although she vaguely recognized the two witnesses. Earlier, Karim had told her that Sharif mentioned a trustworthy imam who might be willing to perform the ceremony at a moment's notice.

For a moment, Mona studied the imam from where she stood. His pale skin was blotched with freckles, but his blue eyes held a soft kindness and deep spirituality that seemed worlds apart from Mona's dejected state right then. This was not how she imagined her daughter's wedding day would be. But, then again, she could barely recall if she had imagined the day at all. So much had transpired in the last year that she just felt numb. When the doctors had said that there was no more hope for Iman, Mona had not even stirred at the news. She had merely listened with her head slightly bowed, as if being justly punished. Mona thereafter spent her time in quiet reflection, a distant observer of her life then and past.

Part of Mona imagined this tragedy to be the culmination of her father's curses against her, but she knew intuitively that she was merely deflecting blame from where it rightly belonged.

Or perhaps there was no one to blame at all. Did there have to be?

The imam walked over to the couch and reviewed the paper that the two brothers had been reading moments before. He then reached into the pocket of his *thobe* and pulled out an ink pen and scribbled onto the page what Mona imagined to be his signature. He then passed the paper to Sharif and then to Karim, who both took the pen in turns and scribbled something at the bottom.

The imam then recited something in Arabic and read the document aloud. "...hereby pronounce the marriage of Sharif Benjamin to Iman Christian in accordance with the laws of Islam."

At these words, Mona felt a lump in her throat, and her eyes stung with tears. She turned her head away from the men as her shoulders trembled. Then she quietly made her way downstairs to her room.

Iman was barely conscious when she felt someone gently shaking her awake. As her thoughts slowly registered her surroundings, Iman noticed the light spilling in from the open curtains. Upon seeing the rays of sun, her spirits lifted, but only momentarily, as a second later she felt the sharp pain tearing through every part of her. She wanted to cry out but she clenched her teeth instead and shut her eyes waiting for the pain to pass, if it would pass at all.

"Iman?"

The voice was that of her father, and the sound of his caring tone was soothing but she could not move her lips in reply.

"Iman, sweetheart."

Slowly, the pain crawled from her, leaving a soreness as it moved through her bones and limbs. In her grogginess, Iman recalled her mother administering the morphine pump an hour before while she said something to Iman about needing to tidy up the room and for Iman to change clothes.

"Are you ready?"

The words slowly took meaning, but only vaguely, as Iman remembered her mother bathing her, changing her clothes and styling her hair some time before.

Iman nodded weakly, but she couldn't recall if her mother had told her why she needed to bathe and change clothes.

Iman heard the door open and she heard the clanking of something. Curiosity inspired her to open her eyes. She saw her mother approaching carrying a large hand-held mirror and a makeup case. Mona's eyes were reddened and swollen, as if she had been crying. Steps behind her was Hasna carrying a small gift bag, her expression difficult to read.

"Is everything okay?" Iman's small voice was strained in concern.

"Congratulations," Hasna said handing the bag to Iman. "You got your wish."

For a moment, Iman just looked at her sister. Hasna appeared uncertain as she glanced at her parents, who said nothing to clarify for Iman what was going on. Shrugging, Hasna reached into the bag and pulled out a pair of gold earrings from a small jewelry case.

"Can I put them on you?" Hasna asked.

Iman did not respond, still trying to comprehend what was happening, even as Hasna carefully inserted the dangling gold into her ears.

"What is....?"

But Hasna had already turned her back to turn on a CD player, the soft sound of Iman's favorite nasheeds playing in the room just then.

A moment later Mona was kneeling in front of Iman, quickly applying makeup, her eyes brimming with tears. Iman's father stood feet behind his wife, his arms folded as he watched the ordeal with a tight smile on his face, his eyes reflecting a distant pride.

It was then that Iman recalled her father joking with her earlier about Sharif. Her heart raced as she realized what might be happening.

What if...? No...

But—

How?

The sound of a phone ringing interrupted Iman's thoughts and Karim quickly reached into his pocket and retrieved it, stepping into the hall as he answered, his voice a hushed whisper.

As he finished his call, Iman's mother packed her makeup bag quickly and Hasna quickly lifted the empty gift bag from the floor.

"He's ready," Karim said quietly to his wife.

"But I want her to see herself," Mona said, her hand on the mirror.

Karim shook his head. "Let him show her. It's better."

Iman's heart continued to race but it was difficult to think clearly, as she was still groggy from the morphine.

Karim quickly brushed her forehead with a kiss then followed his wife and Hasna out of the room, leaving the room door wide open.

Iman felt hopeful, stressed, and confused.

Was it possible that her father hadn't been joking? But Asma had told her that Sharif was gone...

"As-salaamu'alaikum." The sound of a deep voice prompted Iman to look in the direction of the door.

For a second she just stared, her heart seeming to have stopped as she beheld the tall, handsome young man standing in the doorway, the sweet scent of cologne light in the air.

"Sharif?" Her voice was slightly weak as she said his name, but she imagined the weakness was more from shock than sickness.

Immediately, she grew self-conscious, realizing at that moment that she was uncovered. She glanced about her for something to cover herself, but he approached her, his expression shy and his hand raised slightly.

"It's okay," he said, his voice making Iman's heart flutter. "Your father wasn't joking," he said with a slight grin. "We really did just marry you off."

It took a second for Iman to comprehend his words, and when she did, she felt self-conscious all over again. "But..."

"Don't worry," Sharif said. "I can explain later. But right now, I just want to know how you're feeling."

Smiling, he sat down in the seat next to Iman and reached for her hand, cradling her thin fingers as he waited for her to speak.

The softness of his hand over hers made her cheeks go warm, and she turned away from him shyly, still having difficulty comprehending all that was happening. Everything felt surreal. The soft Islamic songs playing in the background created the aura of a life ahead, a life for which Iman could only dream.

Sharif himself felt self-conscious as he sat opposite Iman holding her hand. He hadn't known what to expect. Mentally, he had prepared himself for the worst, as he had no idea what physical state he would find Iman in. Whatever her state, he had told himself, he would overlook it and be by her side. Sharif could tell that Iman too was uncomfortable with him seeing her in this weak state, but he hoped his comfort and presence would be enough for her.

Iman was noticeably thin, but she did not appear as sickly as Sharif had imagined she would. She actually looked quite well, considering the circumstances. Beneath the light makeup, Iman's face was soft though subdued, and was framed attractively by soft plaits in her thinning hair. The makeup concealed her true countenance, but Sharif found her attractive nonetheless, as her beauty was beyond what he could touch or see.

Her eyes were cast down, and Sharif sensed that she was uncomfortable and perhaps a bit ashamed, and overwhelmed.

He wished things had been different. But, as Karim had said, Allah's plan was best, even as Sharif didn't understand it.

"I'm...not a poet." Sharif stammered, his heart pounding in his chest. His voice was awkward even to his ears. "But I wrote something for you."

There was an awkward pause as he looked at her. "Is it okay if I read it aloud?"

Hesitantly, she nodded, still unable to look at him.

Still holding Iman's hand, Sharif reached into the breast pocket of his *thobe* with his left hand and pulled out a folded piece of paper.

He gently let go of her hand to unfold the paper. He chuckled self-consciously as his eyes grazed what he held.

"But don't laugh," he teased her, glancing up. "I know you're the writer, *maashaAllah*."

Sharif detected the hint of a smile on her face as she glanced at him then averted her gaze.

"It's okay," she said quietly.

"I was inspired by you," he said. He smiled, waiting for her to meet his gaze. When she did, he added, "Truly."

There was an extended pause as they held each other's gaze before Iman looked away, a sadness there that Sharif could not interpret.

He cleared his throat, now looking at the creased white paper in his hands. *"Bismillaah....*

> *O Mujahidah, shall I tell you of my life,*
> *Of its ups and its downs*
> *Or of its hardship and its ease*
> *And how Allah turned my heart?*

> *In moments of loneliness*
> *I'd go to sleep,*
> *my life breaking at the seams*
> *And when I closed my eyes*
> *Allah gave me peace,*
> *O Mujahidah*
> *by showing me you*
> *In a dream*

> *O Mujahidah, each time I saw you,*
> *Allah would soothe my heart*
> *And I'd wake with a sense of tranquility*
> *Inspired to please Allah and do my part*
> *O Mujahidah, I knew when I saw you*
> *That you were to be my wife*
> *But I had no idea how, or when,*
> *Or even if in this life*

> *I heard the words of Ar-Rahmaan*
> *Recited from the sky above me*
> *And I heard the laughter of a woman*
> *Who stood in front of me*
> *Enraptured by the Divine words*
> *And by the woman covered modestly*
> *I stepped toward you to see your beauty*

> *"O reassured soul, Return to your Lord,*
> *Well-pleased and pleasing to Him.*
> *And enter among My servants,*
> *Enter My Paradise."*
> *These were Words from Him*

O Mujahidah, shall I tell you
How much this moment
This very moment
Means to me?
To have a dream fulfilled
And you before me

How many days I dreamt of this moment
How many nights I felt certainty
That it would be
Only a matter of time
Before our lives would cross
You and me

In moments of loneliness
I'd go to sleep,
my life breaking at the seams
And when I closed my eyes
Allah gave me peace,
O Mujahidah
by showing me you
In a dream

O Mujahidah, shall I tell you of my life,
Of its ups and its downs
Or of its hardship and its ease
And how Allah turned my heart?

Or shall I tell you,
O Mujahidah,
How your words touched my heart
As I only hope mine too
have touched yours

Even if only in part

For I am your husband,
Abu Sumayyah
And I want to keep you company
For now and forever

Iman's cheeks were streamed with tears as she met Sharif's gaze, a hesitant smile on her face. For a moment, the soft sound of nasheeds filled the silence between them.

Now it was Sharif's turn to look away, self conscious. Unsure what to say in the awkward quiet, Sharif folded the paper and tucked it back into his breast pocket.

"You wrote that?" Her voice was soft, almost a whisper. Her eyes glistened in an admiration that Sharif felt he didn't deserve.

Sharif chuckled and nodded, still unable to look her fully in the eye. "Yes."

"*MaashaAllah*," she said, her voice a reflective whisper.

A thoughtful silence followed.

"That dream...," she said tentatively, glancing down momentarily. "Was it really me you saw?"

Sharif met her gaze and reached for her hand again. "Yes, it was," he said, gently squeezing her palm. "It was really you."

Thirty-one

*"We send down [stage by stage] in the Qur'an
that which is a healing and a mercy to those who believe."*
—Qur'an, *Israa* (17:82)

*"Whenever the Messenger of Allah (peace be upon him) was
suffering from an ailment, he would recite Mu'awwidhatayn (Surah Al-
Falaq and Surah An-Naas) over himself and blow [over himself]. Then if
his pain became severe, [his wife] Ayesha said that she would recite the
Mu'awwidhatayn over him and take his hand and wipe it over him
seeking the blessing of those Surahs."*
—Recorded from Ayesha by Imam Malik
(Bukhari, Abu Dawud, An-Nasaa'i, and Ibn Majah)

Before beginning the *ruqyah* for Iman, Sharif brought to her
room the containers of Zam Zam, which he had recited Qur'an
over. He poured a glass for Iman and instructed her to supplicate
to Allah for her healing. After her supplication, Sharif held the
glass to her lips, and she sipped as much of the liquid as she
could. He then told Iman to relax.

Seconds later, he began reciting *Al-Faatihah, Al-Ikhlaas,* and
Mu'awwidhatayn over her, placing his hand lightly on her head
and periodically blowing over her.

As Sharif recited, Iman's head lay on her pillow, her gaze
distant and reflective as she listened to the soft sound of Allah's
Words, the melodic words permeating every part of her. Her
heart raced and her body trembled with the recitation, and her
eyes brimmed with tears until soft streams trickled down her
cheeks.

Iman drifted to sleep listening to the beautiful recitation.

When she woke, she found Sharif still reciting and blowing
over her. She had no idea how much time had passed, imagining

396

it had been over an hour. Iman vaguely recalled Sharif talking to her while she was asleep, but she couldn't be sure.

A soft knock at the door interrupted Sharif, and Mona stood in the doorway a second later. Her eyes were slightly red, a worried expression on her face, but Sharif sensed it was unrelated to what she had come for.

"Sharif…"

He finished reciting the verse and turned to Mona. "Yes?"

"Can we take a bathroom break?" Mona smiled.

Iman exhaled in relief, having felt the urge to go to the bathroom but she was too shy to interrupt Sharif. She looked at her mother, grimacing momentarily in discomfort.

"Yes, sure, I'm sorry."

There was a brief pause while Mona walked over to Iman to help her stand.

"Can I…help?"

"It's okay," Mona told him. "I'm fine."

He watched as Iman steadied herself next to her mother. When they began walking toward the door, he spoke again.

"I was thinking…since she's already up, maybe she can take a Qur'an bath."

Mona creased her forehead and glanced back at him, Iman's thin arm around her neck and shoulder. "A what?"

He pointed to the Zam Zam containers. "It's a part of the *ruqyah*. If you can put some of the water into a container and pour it over her, that would help."

Mona appeared doubtful. "Okay."

A second later she continued out the door, slowly guiding Iman into the hall.

Thursday night after Sharif had completed another lengthy session with Iman, he met with Karim as Mona was busy helping Iman take another Qur'an bath. Sharif had asked Karim if it were possible for Iman to have a second IV line attached where the Qur'an water could be administered directly into her bloodstream.

It was something about which Sharif had spent many hours in prayer, feeling in his heart that this measure was necessary since the cancer had already reached the blood. He knew that they would need legal approval to do something as medically unorthodox as putting "holy water" into an IV bag. But Sharif prayed that, due to Iman's condition, permission wouldn't involve too much red tape or unnecessary time.

Fortunately, on Friday afternoon, Karim came with good news. Because Iman was considered terminally ill and incurable, the process was not as tedious as it normally would have been. It was simply a matter of Karim and Mona signing paperwork Friday morning, taking full responsibility for the repercussions of this decision should any complications arise. The nurse would then attach the second line and give them instructions on how to use the IV machine appropriately.

For this stage of treatment, Sharif decided to use the additional *ruqyah* of writing verses of the Qur'an in saffron then leaving the saffron papers to soak in Zam Zam overnight, removing the papers once the saffron had dissolved into the water. This water, in addition to the Zam Zam he had recited over, would be put into the IV bag for Iman.

Beyond that, Sharif could only pray.

"Hasna's water broke."

Mona's eyes were red from exhaustion as she stood in her night robe next to the side of the bed where her husband was sleeping early Saturday morning shortly before dawn.

Karim sat up on an elbow, rubbing his eyes from sleep. "You're going in?"

Mona drew in a deep breath before exhaling audibly. "We have to."

"But what about Adam? How is he?"

She sighed. "Not well. He's still running a fever, and I can't keep it down."

"Don't worry," Karim said, sitting up. "I'll look after him."

Mona grew quiet, the stress of her life overwhelming her just then. Iman. Hasna. Now Adam. *O Allah! Help us.*

"When did you give him his last dose?"

"An hour ago."

"You checked his temperature?"

"Yes. It's one-oh-two."

"*What?*"

"I know..." Mona's voiced trailed. "I was thinking to take him in, but then I heard Hasna cry out and..."

"It's okay." Karim turned and brought his feet to the floor. "I'll monitor him for another hour. If he's still not well, I'll bring him in."

"And Iman?"

Karim creased his forehead. "Isn't Sharif here?"

"Yes, but..."

"She'll be fine, Mona. *InshaaAllah,*" he added.

"But then there'll be no car here."

Mona could tell from her husband's expression that he hadn't thought of that. They had taken Hasna's car to the repair shop earlier that day.

"Okay..." Karim thought aloud. "Then let's take them both."

"Iman and *Sharif?*" Mona drew her eyebrows together.

"No." Karim shook his head. "Hasna and Adam. We'll all ride together."

"Do we *both* have to leave then?"

"No, but..." He looked at his wife, confused. "If you're with Hasna, who will be with Adam?"

Mona hesitated before speaking. "I was thinking to stay with Adam, and..."

"And leave Hasna *alone?*"

She looked at Karim then. "Karim, she'll be fine. The labor and delivery nurses are —"

"No," Karim interjected, standing. "We'll both go. I'll leave my car keys with Sharif, and we'll take your car."

"But —"

"*Mona.*" Karim glared at his wife. "There's no way I'm going to leave either of them alone."

"But I want to be with Adam. He's really sick, Karim..."

Karim walked over to the closet and opened it, pulling some dress pants from a hanger. "Then I'll stay with Hasna."

"But she'll be...in *labor*."

"It's not the most comfortable thing for me," he said, shrugging. "But if you won't be there, I will."

Mona grew quiet, distracted. She started to say something but decided against it, starting for their door instead.

"I'll get Adam ready," she said before disappearing into the hall.

"Sharif. Sharif. *Sharif.*"

Sharif felt a hand on his shoulder as he blinked into the darkness. Remembering where he was, he sat up quickly, his heart thumping.

"Are you okay?" Sharif asked, his eyes darting to Iman's bed. But he found his wife sleeping peacefully, the blue glow of a night light outlining her thin form as her soft breathing mirrored the slight rising and falling of her covers.

"No, it's me. Karim."

Sharif glanced to his other side and found Karim kneeling at Sharif's floor mat.

Relieved, Sharif's heart slowed to a normal pace. "I'm sorry. I thought..."

"It's okay. I'm sorry to have frightened you."

Karim glanced at Iman, his mind clearly elsewhere. "Are you two okay here?"

Sharif nodded. "We're fine, *alhamdulillaah*." He too glanced at Iman. "She seems to be improving. But it's too early to tell..."

"Good, *alhamdulillaah*. Because my wife and I have to step out for a bit."

Instinctively, Sharif glanced toward the clock, but Karim's frame was blocking his view. "What time is it?"

"It's almost *Fajr*."

Sharif realized he had slept longer than he had intended. Perhaps he was still jet-lagged. He had wanted to pray *Qiyaam*.

A thought occurred to Sharif. "You're going out now?"

"Hasna's in labor, and Adam is running a high fever." Karim drew in a deep breath then exhaled. "So we're taking them in."

At the reminder of Hasna's pregnancy, Sharif's heart grew heavy in disappointment. He didn't know what to say.

"May Allah make it a purification for you and Sister Mona," Sharif said finally, referring more to Adam's sickness than to Hasna's labor. But Sharif realized the prayer could apply to both.

"Thanks, son."

Sharif nodded. He heard the jingling of keys in the dimly lit room, and a second later, Karim held out a key ring to him.

"I'm leaving my car," Karim said as Sharif hesitantly accepted the key ring. "In case...you need it."

"Okay."

How much pain can a heart hold before bursting under its weight?

This was the question that Mona couldn't answer as she sat next to her son, his small body lying on the hospital bed in the emergency room. Adam's eyes blinked wide in uncertainty and fear, and his face twisted in agony. The fever. That accursed fever. Why wouldn't it go down?

Already Adam was hooked up to an IV so that he could receive fluids intravenously. He had become dehydrated from being unable to hold anything down. His constant diarrhea and vomiting had only complicated matters.

At home, Mona had sat with him the whole day, her heart tearing in two as his fever went up, then dipped only slightly, only to shoot up again. His small body would convulse in horrible vomiting until he fell against her breast breathing heavily. Then he was on the toilet every few minutes it seemed, his forehead cold and sticky.

She could not leave his side now, even though she'd told Karim that she would sit with Adam only until she was sure he was fine. Then she'd go to Hasna.

They were admitting Adam though. They had already admitted Hasna.

Mona grated her teeth. *Where was Karim?* Shouldn't he be with his wife and son right now? Hasna would be fine. She'd have to be. She had no business going off and getting pregnant in the first place. What a disgrace —

May Allah give you children just like you.

To hell with her father's curse, Mona thought angrily. She could reverse this vicious cycle.

Next to her Adam moaned. Mona's heart moaned with him, and her eyes burned. She wanted to cry, but she had no tears left.

"It's okay, love," she consoled her son, patting his hand then rubbing his moist head. "Just make *du'aa.*"

At the sound of shuffling feet, Mona lifted her head from the hospital bed, realizing just then that she had drifted to sleep. Instinctively, she looked toward Adam and found him asleep, too.

"We have a room ready for your son, Ms. Christian, but —"

"Ms. Khan, please."

The nurse shrugged. "Ms. Khan. But we'll need you to sign some release papers before taking him up."

The woman handed Mona the clipboard and pointed to the places she needed to sign. They already had a copy of Adam's insurance card.

Dutifully, Mona signed the papers, her heart aching.

The nurse disappeared into the hall then reappeared seconds later pushing a wheelchair. "If you can just help me put him in here, then we can take him upstairs."

Mona nodded absently, lifting her son's emaciated body into the large chair, careful not to disturb his slumber or disrupt the IV line.

She then pushed the wheelchair herself along the corridors as she followed the nurse to the elevator.

Mona cringed at the sight of the obdurate halls and busy nurses. She hated hospitals. She really did. Right then she could not fathom what had made her in youth imagine that she would become a doctor. She could barely tolerate the place as a visitor.

It was late Saturday morning, hours after Mona had prayed *Fajr* in a quiet corner of her son's hospital room, having used a simple bath towel as a prayer mat, when she finally called Karim's cell phone. They could trade places, she told him, and she would sit with Hasna for some time. But she would get them both something to eat first.

Adam's fever had gone down to one hundred degrees, and although that wasn't at all an indication of recovery, it was an improvement over yesterday. At receiving this news, Mona's heart had begrudgingly agreed to leave her son's side.

After Karim arrived to Adam's room in the pediatric ward, Mona made her way to the elevators, remembering having seen a small pharmacy store on the first floor. Mona took her time in the store, dreading the task before her. She really didn't want to go to the maternity ward, her heart twisting in anxiety at the thought.

Mona walked the small aisles picking up crackers, chocolate, and drinks, taking time to study each brand amongst the modest selection.

Would Karim want cheese crackers or Wheat Thins?

Sighing, Mona decided on both. Minutes later she carried an armful of snacks to the checkout counter and deposited them there before opening her purse.

The plastic bag handles pulled heavily on her palm as she left the store and started for the elevator, glancing at the morning sun spilling through the glass of the front doors. She halted her steps at the sight.

In that moment, she suddenly changed direction and made her way for the door, deciding to take a short walk outside. She needed the fresh air. She needed to clear her mind. If she were going to sit with her daughter, all of her needed to be there for Hasna. She didn't think it wise to harbor resentment to her own flesh and blood.

The automatic doors swished open as Mona reached into the plastic pharmacy bag and withdrew a chocolate bar. The hustle of visitors and hospital staff moving about outside was strangely relaxing as she tore the foil from the chocolate. On the walkway, she took a bite of the dark sweetness, shutting her eyes slowly to enjoy it melting on her tongue.

There was something to the myths of chocolate being an immense joy and stress relief. She felt better already.

The shrill of her cell phone made Mona's heart stop, and she froze, her heart stricken at the sound. Nearly dropping the chocolate bar, she fumbled in her purse for the phone, knowing, even as it still rang, that it would be Karim. And he would tell her something had gone wrong, terribly wrong.

She withdrew the phone, hand trembling.

But before she could silence the incessant shrilling by accepting the call, she felt the confirmation of her fears in the very pit of her stomach.

Adam.

When she saw her husband's name on the caller ID, her heart dropped, and she had to hold on to a nearby wall to steady herself.

O Allah! Please...

"What?" she spoke as if catching her breath.

"Mona," he said, his voice tight. "You need to come now."

Thirty-two

"Your little ones are da'aamees of Paradise. They will meet their parents and grab them by their garments or their hands to no end other than that Allah will enter them into Paradise."

"By the One in Whose hands is my soul, the miscarried fetus will drag his mother to Paradise by his [umbilical] cord if she was patient [with the miscarriage], hoping to be rewarded."
—Prophet Muhammad (peace be upon him)
(Muslim)

Sunday night, Karim stood in front of the locked masjid fumbling through keys until he located the one that opened the main door. Sharif stood feet behind him, his mind befuddled and sad as he waited, Karim inserting a single key into the lock. Sharif's thoughts were of Yasmin and his new job, even as he had fulfilled his teaching role for only four weeks before rushing to America to be with Iman. Window blinds rattled against the glass door leading to the lobby as Karim pushed the door open, Sharif's mind drifting to Iman just then. *How was she?* he wondered.

The masjid was eerily dark as they stepped inside, and it took a few minutes for them to find the light switch in the hall.

"We'll just need to clean up a bit before the *ja—* people come," Karim said, correcting himself. The fluorescent ceiling light buzzed and flickered on, the thin layer of dust covering the lobby illuminated right then. "There's a vacuum in a back room. We can use it for the prayer area. But for this area..." Karim glanced about him. "...we'll just need some rags and a broom. It shouldn't take long."

"Did he have a name?"

Karim turned to Sharif, as if startled, his forehead creased. "What?"

Sharif immediately regretted the question. But it had been tugging at him. He felt it insensitive to lead a *janaazah* for a child without even knowing its name. "The boy. What was his name?"

Karim's expression grew sad and he cast his eyes down. "Hasan." His voice was quiet. "She named him Hasan."

Sharif nodded absently, pain tugging at his heart as he thought of Hasna.

Would she come tonight? he wondered. But he couldn't ask Karim this.

"May Allah join them in *Jannah*," Sharif said, his voice barely above a whisper.

"Ameen," Karim muttered.

People trickled into the lobby of the masjid in preparation for the funeral prayer, and Sharif stood, arms folded, in the doorway of the imam's office surveying the empty shelves and dusty desk. He had to resist the urge to take a seat in the large leather chair. His heart ached in regret, and a tinge of grief struck him. He didn't want to return to Riyadh, he felt suddenly. He belonged here, with Brother Karim and Sister Mona, with Hasna and Iman, with his mother, Wali, and Asma.

"You're welcome to stay with us, Sharif," Karim had told him earlier. *"We'd be happy to have you back."*

But there was too much to overcome, Sharif thought sadly. Far too much. Besides, he had Yasmin to think of. He was a married man now; he had been married even before he married Iman.

Maybe it was Iman he had wanted all along, Sharif considered. He didn't wish only to keep her company. He wanted her to keep him company too.

"Is it true?" a soft voice asked him tentatively, prompting him to turn in the direction of the sound.

Standing feet from him in the lobby was an attractive woman whose eyes were reddened from crying, her smooth round face framed with a white *khimaar*. Her sad eyes were looking at him, a question in them, hope. It took a moment for Sharif to realize it was Hasna standing opposite him. He cast his eyes down.

"That... he will wait for me?" Her eyes were now cast down.

Sharif nodded, feeling awkward all of a sudden. "Yes, I believe so, *inshaaAllah.*"

"But..."

He glanced up to see the question in her face, but her eyes were looking to her side, a distance reflected there.

Hasna shook her head, deciding against the inquiry. Sharif sensed her hesitation was due to the sin she regretted in conceiving the child. He was grateful that she didn't mention it.

"I named him Hasan," she said, tears welling in her eyes as she looked at him again.

"Yes, I know," he said quietly, growing more uncomfortable.

"I knew you'd do a good job raising him."

Stunned, Sharif met her gaze with his brow furrowed. He opened his mouth to form words, but he found no way to ask what he wanted.

"I was going to give him to Iman." Hasna sniffed, lifting a tissue to her nose. "I thought she'd be better....you know."

Slowly, Sharif understood.

"I thought he might..." Tears dripped from her chin, and her words slurred slightly as grief choked her. "...learn Qur'an over there." She lowered her gaze.

"Hasna?"

Sharif lifted his gaze toward the lobby as Hasna turned at the sound of her name.

It was Mona, and Iman, in a wheelchair, was being pushed by her mother. Adam was asleep on Iman's lap, his head nestled against her chest. Iman was wearing her favored black *jilbaab,* Sharif noticed, her veil as he remembered it during newsletter meetings, revealing her attractive eyes. A gloved hand held her brother's small body close, the other lightly resting on a handle of the wheelchair.

As Iman's and Sharif's gazes met, Iman smiled beneath the veil, her eyes revealing this gesture, sadness there. She lifted her free hand in a wave, and Sharif, embarrassed, responded in kind.

"Yes?"

"Are you coming inside?"

There was an awkward pause.

"I can't," Hasna finally said, her voice a hushed whisper. Apparently, she was embarrassed for Sharif to overhear.

"I can't pray," she said after an extended pause, her voice quieter than before.

Oh. Mona's face registered realization just as Sharif himself understood.

"Well..." Mona looked uncertainly from Sharif to Hasna. "We'll be in the *musallaa* if you need us."

Hasna nodded, as did Sharif, his gaze following Iman.

"I'm sorry," Hasna said after they entered the prayer area.

Sharif started to say *It's okay*, but Hasna spoke before he could.

"Can you pray for me?"

He glanced at Hasna, confused.

"For me and Hasan."

He moved his head in the beginning of a nod. "Yes, *inshaaAllah*." He smiled slightly. "I will."

Tweetie,

I was sorry to hear what happened. You can't imagine how hurt I was when I found out. I know I haven't been much of a support throughout all of this, but trust me, my thoughts are with you, as they always have been.

We don't have to give up on each other.

I love you. Let's talk. Give me a call.

My deepest love and condolences,
Vernon

Hasna set the letter on the grass next to her, and she drew her legs to her, wrapping her arms around her shins. Tears gathered in her eyes as she lowered her head to her knees, her thoughts confused as she looked beyond the fence of her family's small backyard. The afternoon sun warmed her face and hands as the cool mid-November breeze gently rippled through her navy blue *abaya* and matching floral *khimaar* that was wrapped around her head, the fabric tucked securely under her chin.

Ramadan had come and gone, as did Sharif, who had returned to Riyadh during the last week of the blessed month, in late October. He had stood in as imam for nearly four weeks, his first official post being the imam of Hasan's *janaazah* prayer. Thereafter Sharif had led the small Muslim community in *Tarawih* prayers during Ramadan. His captivating recitation had moved Hasna to come to the masjid lobby and listen, even as she had been unable to pray for the duration of the month following her childbirth.

Hasna's eyes grazed the letter next to her, its ends moving slightly in the afternoon air, and she felt that familiar tugging in her heart. She shut her eyes, her chest aching in longing, and she could almost hear Vernon's voice right then...

Tweetie, I'm so sorry...my thoughts are with you...I love you...Give me a call.

Tears escaped her eyes as she remembered the soft skin of their child, his curled fingers, his eyes nearly shut...

Hello, is it me you're looking for?

The song's words came to her right then, the same ones she had heard played in the doctor's office the day she decided to give life to her child, to give her very heart.

You're all I've ever wanted. My arms are open wide...

The lyrics gripped her and Hasna's buried her head in her arms, overcome with emotion as the melody stirred her. She traced the contours of Hasan's face with her heart, with her affection, imagining him waiting for her, alone, delaying his own entry into Paradise.

Are you somewhere feeling lonely? Or is someone loving you?

Hasna sobbed, thinking of her son alone, without her. She wanted to hold him right then, nurse him, to rub her nose in his soft hair. She wanted to put her finger in his small fist and have him hold it tightly, for now and forever.

Tell me how to win your heart, for I haven't got a clue.

Hasna wished Allah had taken her too, so she could hold Hasan right then. She had no idea how she would go on without her child, or if she would ever join him in the Hereafter.

But let me start by saying, I love you.

Minutes later, Hasna recovered, her heart heavy, eyes still moist. For a moment her eyes lingered on the letter next to her. Tears filled her eyes again as she looked at the blurring lines, the careful, deliberate ink strokes of Vernon's words.

Hesitantly, she lifted the letter that had arrived in her family's mailbox two weeks before. The scent of Vernon's cologne rose from the paper, and she slowly brought it to her nose, closing her eyes as she inhaled the sweetness of many nights past.

My thoughts are with you, she heard Vernon's deep voice say. Her heart fluttered and her legs weakened. She lowered the paper and gazed at it, imagining Vernon's strong build and handsome form, his firm embrace.

Tweetie, I was so sorry to hear…

"*Can I at least nurse him before you take him away?*" A stabbing pain came to Hasna as she recalled holding Hasan's still body as she sat in the reclined hospital bed. Tears streamed from her eyes as she begged the hospital staff for a moment longer with her child. Her parents were paralyzed in shock and disbelief as Hasna kept telling the doctor that her boy was hungry, that he needed nurse. He hasn't eaten at all, she'd said.

Then I'll just deny having anything to do with you.

Hasna's chest tightened at the memory, and her hand stiffened, in that moment the creased paper feeling rough between her thumb and forefinger. Her hands trembled as she faltered for just a moment before she lifted the letter and ripped it in half. Her heart began to pound as the familiar fury returned to her, and she ripped it again, and again, then again.

This was not part of the plan.

Hasna pushed herself up with one hand, and with her other, she crumpled the torn letter into a ball.

She walked over to the large rubber garbage pail in the corner of her yard and lifted the lid and let the wad fall into the empty pail with a thud.

And Allah gives only to those who ask.

Hasna returned the lid to its place and turned her back, leaving the crumpled words behind her as she walked back to her house. At the patio door that led to the kitchen, she held its edge to open it, the sliding glass a soft rumbling as she slipped back inside, the sound of Qur'an being recited coming from a stereo somewhere upstairs.

Sliding the heavy glass closed behind her, Hasna noticed the time on the clock near the kitchen table. It was time for *Asr*. She walked swiftly to the stairs that led to the hallway of her room. She hoped to pray the afternoon prayer in the solitude of her room before the approach of sun set.

Thirty-three

It was a Saturday morning in mid-December, and Nadirah sat on her couch an arm's length from Mona, her eyes brimmed with tears. A large gift bag sat on the floor between them, the modest form of gratitude Mona wished to show Nadirah for all her family had done.

Nadirah nodded as she listened to the tearful *Thank you* Mona kept repeating as she dabbed at her eyes with a tissue.

"Are you sure?" Nadirah asked.

Mona nodded, sniffling. "Yes, the doctors have been running tests for two weeks."

"*SubhaanAllaah.*" Nadirah would have never imagined it possible.

Her mind drifted to her son, and her heart knotted in regret as she thought of how Sharif had embraced her before he left for Riyadh at the end of Ramadan.

"*I'm sorry, Mom,*" he'd said. "*For everything. I…*" The words got caught in his throat, and he shook his head at a loss for words.

"*I love you,*" he said finally, embracing her, his voice slightly muffled by the embrace. "*Please forgive me. I know Dad would have expected better of me. I'm sorry I couldn't live up to that.*"

Presently, Nadirah's throat closed, and she found it difficult to speak herself.

"The cancer's gone, Nadirah," Mona had told her moments before, her eyes shining with tears as she looked at her. "Can you believe it?"

And it was Sharif who had administered Iman's treatment. *SubhaanAllaah.*

"Thank you so much, Nadirah," Mona said. "Sharif is such a blessing, may Allah bless him and increase him in good. I'm so grateful that Iman has a husband like him."

Nadirah nodded absently, cringing inwardly as she recalled the filthy word she'd flung at him when she discovered his conversation with Karim.

"When will Iman join him?" Nadirah asked, her heart yearning for her son. She wished Sharif could be near her right then. She wanted to apologize to him, and ask his forgiveness.

Mona shook her head. "Not for a while. She wants to finish school."

"But..." Nadirah didn't know how to ask the next question. After all, it was likely Mona could ask it from her. "What about his family in Saudi Arabia?"

Mona nodded, distracted momentarily by the inquiry. "Iman said they talked about that..."

"And what did he say?"

"That he would talk to the young woman there and see what she wanted."

Nadirah hesitated. "And if she doesn't like this...arrangement?"

Mona shrugged. "Then he'll return to America and resume his post as imam."

Inside, Nadirah exhaled, having not realized she was holding her breath. She hoped that he would return. She missed him dearly.

The sound of laughter carried from upstairs through the vents. Nadirah smiled inwardly.

Asma and Iman. She was pleased that Iman had been well enough to join Mona on the visit.

"Iman is also seeing a homeopathic doctor who's helping her regain her strength," Mona said, "and cleanse her system."

"So then it'll be some time before she travels there to live?"

Mona smiled as she nodded, and Nadirah felt a tinge of jealousy as she saw that her friend was grateful to still have time with her daughter before she left to live overseas. "At least another four years."

"That's a long time…"

Mona shook her head. "Not for Iman." She beamed. "She said she wants to be totally healthy and beautiful again before she joins him."

Nadirah couldn't keep from smiling herself. She understood this comment also meant that Iman had overcome her insecurities about her appearance. Apparently, the sickness had clarified for her that physical beauty was reflected in good health, not in skin complexion and body size. Nadirah was pleased, deeply. She had always been concerned for Iman. She was happy her son had had a hand in this new burst of self-esteem.

"And Hasna plans to go with her."

Nadirah's eyes widened. "*Hasna?*"

Mona nodded, chuckling. "She wants to live in Makkah or Madinah."

A smile formed on Nadirah's face as she shook her head. "I must say I'm surprised at that one."

"I know. I was too." Mona paused, her eyes squinting in deep thought momentarily.

"But I'm happy for her, Nadirah," she said quietly, sincerely. "I really am."

Nadirah nodded. "I am too." She sighed, recalling the somber *janaazah*. "I am too."

Mona stood. "I better go."

"But you just arrived," Nadirah said, standing too.

"Karim has some errands to run, and I told him I'd watch Adam today."

Nadirah nodded, understanding, but she was sad to see her friend go. "I was just hoping Iman and Asma could spend some more time together."

"Oh," Mona said, laughing, bringing a hand to her mouth. "I'm sorry. I should've told you I'm leaving Iman here for the day."

Nadirah laughed too. "That's fine. We're happy to have her."

Mona walked over to the door and removed her coat from the cast iron jacket tree that stood in the foyer.

"Thanks for having me today."

"Thanks for stopping by. It was good to see you again."

Mona nodded her head in the direction of the gift bag. "I hope you like the gift."

Nadirah smiled. "I'm sure I will."

"It's not much, but I thought you'd like it…"

"Thanks, Mona. It wasn't necessary though."

Mona slipped her arms into her coat and buttoned it. "What time should I pick up Iman?"

"Whenever you like."

She nodded, her expression growing serious again. "I don't know what we can do to repay you for all you've done." She shook her head. "I just—"

Nadirah waved her hand. "Don't mention it. Besides, it's Sharif who deserves the credit, not me."

Mona shook her head, sadness in her eyes as her gaze fell on the buttons she was closing. "No, it's you, Nadirah." She sighed, distracted by a memory. "You and Dawud. You were always better parents than me and Karim."

It took a moment for Nadirah to register her friend's words. She creased her forehead in disapproval. She shook her head and started to say something, but Mona interrupted her.

"No, Nadirah. It's okay." Mona drew in a deep breath. "You don't have to agree with me, but Allah knows I'm saying the truth." She paused. "And Allah knows best."

Nadirah didn't know what to say, but she felt uncomfortable at her friend's words.

"I was jealous of you," Mona said quietly, pulling her purse strap over the shoulder of her coat. "I just couldn't accept that Sharif was better than Hasna, so I—"

"Mona." Nadirah raised a hand, her voice a higher tone than she intended. "Please," she said, lowering her voice a bit. "Don't speak like that."

Tears welled in Mona's eyes again as she shook her head. "But it's true. I just wish—"

"Please, Mona. It's okay, really. We all have thoughts and feelings we don't understand."

"But—"

"I forgive you," Nadirah interjected, "if that's what you're worried about."

There was an awkward pause as Mona looked up at her friend, her eyes shiny with tears. "You do?" She looked uncertain and spoke barely above a whisper.

"Of course." There was a brief pause.

"We're family now, Mona."

Mona nodded hesitantly, a smile forming on her face at the realization until she met Nadirah's gaze.

"We are family, aren't we?"

"Yes, we are," Nadirah said, reaching out and squeezing her friend's hand. "Yes, we are." She smiled, "And I'm very happy that you'll be a second mother to Sharif."

Yasmin prostrated in gratefulness after Sharif shared the news of Iman. Her forehead rested on the prayer mat in her room for several minutes, tears stinging her eyes as she cried to Allah in relief. The month of Ramadan had clarified for her the magnitude of her sins in likely playing a hand in harming her sister in Islam, and irreversibly. She had only hoped that the girl's life wouldn't be lost too.

Yasmin had shared with no one but her Qur'an teacher all that had transpired between her and Sommer, and she had no plans on telling anyone — not even her family, and certainly not Sharif. But she was unable to let go of the guilt that gripped her every time she thought of an innocent Muslim girl literally dying from cancer, her ovaries having been removed upon diagnosis months before.

And that dream...

O Allah! That dream. It kept coming to her, night after night, until Yasmin herself fought sleep, terrified that she would see it again.

Those thin, treacherous black wings. The girl in her bed, fighting and fighting. The girl slapping at her skin...

Then Yasmin would wake, certain that this was no vision of the subconscious or even of the devil.

This was a sign from Allah.

But she'll never be able to have children, Sharif had told her sadly.

It was a horrible thought, a terribly selfish feeling, even if felt for only a moment. But Yasmin had been pleased that the girl would be unable to offer Sharif that joy.

Right then, Yasmin felt sickened at that thought. Had she, then, *hoped* that Sommer's actions—if *sihr* was in fact involved—had been successful in destroying this girl's role as a full wife?

Tears lingered in her eyes as Yasmin sat up, her heart racing, a storm of emotions in her chest.

Sharif had called from his apartment minutes before to tell her the good news.

Thank God, thank God, Yasmin had thought. *Thank God!*

Iman's cancer was gone. Completely.

Now Yasmin needed only to continue to implore Allah for forgiveness.

So that her guilt, too, would be gone.

Completely.

That evening, Nadirah took a walk outside, the December air chilling as light snow flurries disappeared into the soggy grass. She had spoken to Sharif an hour before and expressed her apologies although he was unconvinced she had done anything wrong.

"I'm the one who was wrong, Mom," he had said, and the sincerity of his voice made her eyes fill.

Presently, Nadirah reflected on her life, lifting her gaze to the bluish black horizon outlined by homes, the moon a crescent glowing in the sky. A smile lingered on her face as she thought of Dawud, and how he had come into their room the night she had last seen him alive.

He had chuckled, shaking his head as he closed the door behind him. "Do you know that boy just talked back to me?" His expression was of bemusement.

Nadirah had rolled her eyes, drawing her husband into an embrace as a knowing grin passed her face. "What'd I tell you? If you spoil the child, you'll ruin him."

Dawud shook his head, his eyes deep in reflection. "No, I don't think I've ruined him."

Nadirah huffed jokingly. "Yeah right."

"But I saw something in him that I never saw before."

Nadirah drew back from her husband and studied his eyes as Dawud's expression grew serious. "What's that?"

He shook his head. "I don't know. He just seemed... grown up."

She laughed. "He talks back to you, and you think he's *maturing*?"

"No, I don't mean like that. I felt like..." He frowned momentarily. "...like we were growing apart, but—"

"And you think that's *good*?"

Dawud was silent momentarily, and Nadirah could tell that it was difficult for her husband to articulate what he meant.

"No, but... I had this feeling, babe."

She regarded him. "Really? About what?"

He put his arms around her waist and drew her closer. "That he would grow up to be someone..." He searched for the word. "...different."

There was an awkward pause.

"What do you mean?"

He exhaled, unsure how to explain. "Allah knows best, but I sensed that he would disappoint us, Nadirah."

Her chest tightened, terrified by what he would say.

"But..." He drew in a deep breath, shaking his head, letting Nadirah know she was misunderstanding. "...he would be the one who's right."

At his words, Nadirah had looked up at him, perplexed.

"What?" She whispered the question.

"Remember when he was born and you said, 'This ain't no ordinary child'?"

Nadirah chuckled. "I was joking, Dawud."

"Well," he said, seriously, "he's not an ordinary child."

He paused, drawing in a deep breath before speaking the last words he would say to her about their son. "And I think we'll live to learn from him."

A stranger.

This was the word that came to mind as the December evening thrust a draft of cool air on Nadirah's face.

That was her son, a stranger in the world.

And she...

Nadirah stood immobile, paralyzed momentarily by the sudden realization.

She had thought her country God, and its citizens His kinsmen.

In that brief moment, she knew her sin, the transgression that had divided her and her firstborn. All of her images of right and wrong, even in religion, had been shaped by the piece of land couched between the Atlantic and the Pacific, the place she happened to be born. And anything learned beyond was suspect, was called into question, not because it held no roots in truth — but because it held no roots in the land she called home.

Yet her own ancestors had come from the distant lands of Africa and Europe...

In the chilly winter night, Nadirah bowed her head, understanding for the first time the simplicity of the universality of Islam. A religion, a way of life, it was. Islam was not bound by culture, time period, or location.

It was the religion of Allah, for all people, for all lands, until the end of time. The earth was His servants' home, and they could move about it as they liked, in search of beneficial knowledge and spiritual tranquility, to draw them closer to Him.

An epiphany.

That's what this was. A sudden realization of what she had intuitively known all along.

"I don't live here because I don't trust my own people," Sharif had told her in their conversation earlier. "I live here because you and Dad always taught us that all humans are brothers and sisters, children of Adam and Eve. And that the greatest obstacle to universal brotherhood is self worship, being unable to see beyond a stranger's skin color or culture, or even beyond their faults, and appreciate the great blessing Allah has placed there."

He paused before adding, "It's what made you accept Islam."

She had listened only distantly, but the conversation returned now with clarity. She was humbled. Sharif was right. He was, in her husband's words, living the spirit of Islam, the essence of faith. His heart was unshackled by cultural rituals and fetters of imagined self-sufficiency.

And I think we'll live to learn from him.

And Nadirah had.

She had.

She wished only that her husband was there to share in the blessing.

Epilogue

Nearly a year after I returned to Riyadh, which would be my home for years to come, I saw my wife for the final in a dream. Naturally, I didn't know that this moment (which was years before she joined me overseas) would be last time I would see Iman in my sleep. But aside from its odd timing—it was the night Yasmin and I had our *waleemah*—I couldn't have registered the significance it would hold in my life.

In the dream, Iman was dressed a beautiful white garment. Her eyes were larger and even more beautiful than I remembered, and her brown skin glowed luminescent, light seeming to emanate all around her. She stood in a lush green pasture, with rivers flowing on either side of her.

Next to her was a little boy, Hasan, who was pulling on the garment of a beautiful woman I could not see.

When the woman lifted her gaze, I saw that it was Hasna, who was draped in a beautiful white hijab and flowing gown.

I then saw my father walking in the distance, Jafar behind him. And I saw others too, some I recognized, others I did not.

Then I saw myself.

We all began walking to our large homes, which were set on lush greenery, rivers flowing beneath. Vessels of transparent silver twinkled in our hands.

My heart filled with such pleasure and longing that I didn't want to wake up. Above us, the blue sky trembled as the last verses of *Al-Fajr* were recited, the beautiful recitation coming from a source we could not see.

"*We are strangers in this world,*" a voice that sounded like Jafar's spoke. But when I looked, I saw no one speaking. At that moment, I recalled the words of the Prophet, *sallallaahu 'alayhi wa sallam*. "…So give glad tidings to the strangers."

"*And as believers, we all shall receive the glad tidings of Allah's Paradise,*" the voice said. "*As long as we, in the brief life of this world, remain firm on our religion, patient with what befalls us, and seek solace in prayer. Then, and only then, will we taste the sweetness of faith."*

About the Author

Umm Zakiyyah was born in 1975 in Long Island, New York, to parents who converted from Christianity to Islam after they married. She graduated in 1997 with a Bachelor of Arts degree in Elementary Education from Emory University, and she currently teaches English grammar and writing to high school students. Umm Zakiyyah is the recipient of the 2008 Muslim Girls Unity Conference Distinguished Authors Award.

To contact her, write to ummzakiyyah@yahoo.com. For her latest books and updates join her Facebook page or visit ummzakiyyah.com or uzauthor.com.

23243754R00267

Made in the USA
Middletown, DE
19 August 2015